WHAT WOULD ROSE DO?

Also by Melissa Hintz

On Chagrin Boulevard—
A Collection of Fluff, Fables, Fabrications,
Flapdoodle, Free Verse, and Flash Fiction

WHAT WOULD ROSE DO?

A Novel

MELISSA HINTZ

What Would Rose Do?

ISBN: 978-1-66789-549-9 (print)
ISBN: 978-1-66789-550-5 (eBook)

Dedication

To Mary Rynes

A woman of grace, wit, grit, humor, and talent

I loved your writing from the first time I read it and even more when I heard your words in your slightly Southern silver voice.

I was thrilled when you generously invited me to become part of your writing group.

I joined a writing group and found a family.

Acknowledgements

It takes a tribe to create a novel. At least that has been my experience. And I have been so fortunate to have so many amazing people in my writing tribe.

My writing groups have been essential to the creation of this novel, in offering encouragement and honest, insightful but kind feedback. I have been blessed with not one but two writing groups that have been part of my life and the life of this novel for many years. So take a bow:

Lliterary Llamas (Lisa Ferranti, Angela Watts, and Mary Rynes)

and

WOW (Donna Lewis Fox, Diane Millett, Susan Rakow, and Susan Rzepka)

You women rock!

While my writing groups were essential for my novel getting launched into the world, the beginning of my journey as a novelist started with an amazing nine-month writing workshop run by Tania Casselle and Sean Murphy called *Write to the Finish*. That workshop connected writers on three continents, sharing energy, inspiration, and the joy of writing. I learned so much from Sean and Tania and also from my fellow novelists and nonfiction authors.

To my last-eyes line editor, Paige Lawson—thanks for your insights.

While input from other writers is invaluable, Beta readers who are not writers offer a whole new perspective. So, sending gratitude for their insights and honest feedback to my always-first Beta reader Debyn Knight and to my first book club readers, the Hotties (hosted by Barbara Belovich).

It's-not-what-you-know-but-who-you-know thanks go to Don Krosin and Linda Betzer for sharing their legal expertise by reviewing critical chapters involving the legal issues my protagonist faces and making sure (I hope) that there are no (major) legal faux pas. So much better to get their vetting than to go to law school.

Special thanks to Mary Rynes for my author photo. You are a woman of so many talents.

To my last-set-of-eyes editor/proofreader extraordinaire, Donna Lewis Fox, sending hugs and thanks.

Finally, thanks and hugs to my friends and family—especially my husband Jim—for your support, encouragement, and time.

Sewickley, PA high school yearbook, senior year, 1968

Goal Agnes wrote:

Accountant

Goal her twin sister Rose wrote (as a haiku):
swim naked, find love
see the world, never be fat
make people happy

(The yearbook editors were not amused and changed Rose's goal to Airline Hostess)

Chapter 1

February 14, 2009

you are my lighthouse
my raft is battered, sinking
will you guide me home?

Rose's Haiku Diary
Cleveland
Age 59

When you're a twin, you grow up with a best friend and often wonder why other people have to find one. That's why when my twin sister Rose showed up on my doorstep at ten at night on Valentine's Day, saying, Turkle, I need a big favor from you—a huge one—the biggest favor ever, I knew she was in trouble. Big trouble.

"What's wrong," I asked, searching her face for clues.

"Okay if we go inside?" Rose said. "It's so cold and I'm so hungry. Later, okay?"

I nodded, squeezed her shoulders and took hold of her trembling hand.

She stumbled as she stepped into my vestibule and braced herself on the door jamb for a moment. Then she shook her head, smiled, and walked into my kitchen.

Rose's exotic and erratic life had left her on the brink of one disaster or another ever since she was old enough to soup up her roller-skates so she could beat Jimmy West down the hill she called Vertigo Valley. As the older sister, if only by twenty-two minutes, it had been my job for over five decades to bail her out. Broken hearts, broken cars, and once, even a broken jaw. Mostly I was gratified, perhaps even a bit proud, to know there was no problem I couldn't fix. Money solved most dilemmas, since money for Rose was a fickle friend—it always left town when she needed it most. Love, talk, hugs, and sisterly advice, either long distance or in person, had always fixed the rest.

I put my arm around her shoulder and hugged her, wanting to know what the problem was, yet somehow terrified that I might not be able to fix it this time.

I poured each of us a glass of Chardonnay, toasted two thick slices of sourdough bread and reheated some of the leftover seafood tomato chowder I'd had for dinner. All the while the question of the biggest favor ever skulked in the shadows, like some Edgar Allan Poe character. Rose ate in silence, which almost never happened, especially when we first reunited. I watched her, thinking of dozens of questions, sensing she was too fragile to answer any of them just yet. I smiled when she made slurping sounds when the bowl was almost empty, as the soup seemed to rejuvenate her. Her color, her whole demeanor changed. "Not enough garlic," she said. "But then again, it is Valentine's Day. Good choice."

I breathed a sigh of relief.

I carried her suitcases upstairs so she could unpack enough for tonight and returned to do the dishes. When the kitchen was again spotless, I headed upstairs, hoping that Rose would be awake and I wouldn't have to wait until morning to learn about the problem I needed to solve.

When I reached my bedroom, Rose was already in a pair of my flannel pajamas, under the covers but sitting propped up with pillows behind her on my queen-size bed.

"Nightcap?" she said as she pantomimed taking a stocking cap off her head, then lifting a glass and drinking.

Liquid courage, I thought. It must be bad.

"Cognac?" I said.

Rose gave a thumbs up. I went to the nightstand drawer for the special bottle of Courvoisier XO Imperial I'd bought four years ago when Rose came to help clean out Mom's house and get her resettled at Shady Oaks.

"You haven't finished that yet?" Rose asked.

"I saved it for us to share."

She tilted her head and smiled, making her look more like twelve than almost sixty. At least to my eyes.

I slipped into my attached bathroom and rinsed and dried the two snifters before changing into my pajamas. Then, I splashed half an inch in each glass and joined Rose. We sat on the bed, pillows at our backs, as if we had both been transported back to being sixteen again, solving the problems of the universe or at least of the snotty girls and arrogant jocks of Sewickley High. I lit the vanilla-scented candle Rose had brought when she arrived, with a note saying *Cupid hasn't given up—stay tuned*. The candle bathed my bedroom in a soft glow that almost masked the fatigue that seemed to radiate from Rose like a noxious perfume. So unlike the joyous cloud she normally created.

I waited a moment, until I was sure my voice would be steady.

"What's wrong, Sapphire?" I asked, using the nickname I had given her when we were ten and she bestowed Turkle on me, a name I'd hated for years but eventually accepted and grew to love. At the time, she'd said they'd be our secret names, like if you're ever kidnapped and want me to know it's really you.

"I can't," she said.

"Take your time. Whenever you're ready." I took her hand in mine.

"It's not fair."

"We always figure it out."

"Not this time. You'll hate it. I just can't ask you."

Rose bit the thumb of the hand I wasn't holding. She always did that when she was nervous or scared. Then she started to rock back and forth, ever so slightly, like a wind chime in a soft breeze. She let go of my hand, scooted around so she faced me and took my hands in hers.

"You can," I said.

Rose took a deep breath, then another, and finally said, "My heart's busted."

I struggled not to have the fear I felt show on my face as she squeezed my hands harder.

"I have mitral regurgitation," she said and laughed nervously. "Sounds like something you should have to say excuse me for after you heart-burp, doesn't it?"

"What? How? Mitral regurgitation?" Words stumbled around in my brain. Rose sick? Rose couldn't be sick. She was broke, screwy, and impetuous, but she was never sick. Not really sick. A cold. Maybe the flu. But never really sick.

"I was tired. Tired all the time. I thought it was just depression about the divorce and that weasel leaving me with almost nothing. My clothes, my car." She snorted.

"Your heart," I prompted, not wanting to get sidetracked into the treachery and betrayal of her marriage to Luis.

"I don't know. I was always short of breath—sometimes I felt like I was suffocating, like a panic attack that went on for days. It seemed like a sign to get as far away from him and New Mexico as possible. Find some place where I could breathe."

Rose's voice trailed off and hundreds of questions swarmed in my brain, all trying to get to the head of the line. After Rose left New Mexico two years ago, she still called every Wednesday and Sunday, a ritual that went back to when we first separated to go to different colleges and one that had only been interrupted during that long year she spent in Nepal in the Peace Corps. After she left New Mexico, her good morning and good night emails soothed my worries that she and her '99 Isuzu Gemini had made it another day and not broken down in the middle of nowhere. She meandered through Arizona, California and Nevada before heading north. The only time I hadn't worried was the ten days she spent with Uncle Roger and Uncle Gus at their rustic Arizona cabin. She settled in Sturgis, South Dakota, when her money ran out. I begged her to come stay with me, but she said she needed time alone to figure out what to do next.

"That's what you said about Sturgis," I said, nudging her back to her story. "I remember you told me you could finally breathe there." Why hadn't it occurred to me you meant literally?

She nodded. "I loved it there. Sort of reminded me of Bandipur. A simpler place. Just what I needed." She rubbed her forehead. "Then, one day at work, the left side of my body went numb—just for a few seconds. I almost spilled coffee all over one of my regulars, Bronco Bob. It scared the Hell out of me."

My heart slammed in my ears. Why hadn't she called me?

"So that's when you saw a doctor?" I said.

She shook her head. "No money. No insurance. And it went away, so I thought I was okay. Two days later I passed out at work and my boss took me to the ER."

Tears were running down both of our faces. The steel band across my chest kept getting tighter.

"I guess if you're unconscious, they have to take care of you," she said. She bit her lower lip and then her thumb and wiped away tears. I started to reach out to hug her, but she shook her head.

"Oh, Sapphire..."

"I need to finish." She closed her eyes, as if preparing to recite a memorized poem. "That's why I borrowed that money a month ago—to pay for the tests. Weird it costs so much just to find out what's wrong, huh? Anyway, the EKG and chest x-ray showed I have two really screwed-up heart valves. The doc called it Myxomatous degeneration."

"What do..."

"They have to be replaced. Soon. Doc said I shouldn't wait."

"What causes that? I mean why..."

"Too many broken hearts, I guess." She forced a laugh. "Don't worry. It's not hereditary. I checked."

"I wasn't thinking that. I wasn't," I said. Here she was worrying about my heart when hers was damaged. That was my crazy, infuriating, wonderful sister.

Rose picked up a pillow and hugged it to her chest.

"I know." She sighed. "Remember on my trip back to the US after the Peace Corps when I got so sick in India? They think that the strep infection might have turned into rheumatic fever and screwed up my heart."

"Oh, Sapphire," I said. "Why didn't you call before? I could have been researching doctors and hospitals."

She sighed. "Guess I thought I should be a grown-up for a change." She shrugged. "Thing is, I've looked into it. Looked into it fourteen ways backward and forward and sideways." She paused and bit her lip. "Remember when Grandpa Luke got his cancer diagnosis? How you'd call me in tears because you couldn't get answers?"

"I remember. But what's that got to do..."

"Everybody kept telling you to call someone else. You'd call and get transferred and transferred, trying to get the insurance company to talk to the doctors and hospital. You called it enough red tape to wrap around the world."

I nodded.

"Well, multiply that by a hundred," Rose said, "and that's how hard it is if you don't have insurance."

"Couldn't we get you medical insurance now? I know it'd be expensive, but..."

"Pre-existing condition. Not covered." She sighed and closed her eyes again.

My mind flopped like a fish on a dock, but instead of desperately requiring oxygen, it was a solution I needed. There had to be a solution. I'd fought battles with insurance companies for Grandpa Luke and then Mom with her Alzheimer's, but with them, pre-existing conditions had never been my nemesis. "What about Medicaid?"

She shook her head. "Not in one of the eligible groups. There's only one way I'm getting it," she said as the candlelight illuminated half of her face, the other half obscured in darkness. "That's my huge favor. You have to let me pretend to be you so I can use your medical insurance."

Chapter 2

sometimes the wrong path
can take you to the right place
story of my life

Rose's Haiku Diary
St. Augustine, FL
Age 37

I told Rose to get some rest, but we were both too keyed up to sleep. So we went back downstairs for what, in my former life as a senior forensic accountant, would have been called a financial deep dive. Hours later, the results—my assets and my budget, separated into the money for Mom's nursing home and my living expenses—were spread out on my kitchen table. It was after midnight and we had gone over them repeatedly, but the answer refused to change.

"I could sell my house," I said.

"No. You can't," Rose said. "I could never ask you to do that. Look at this place. I see you everywhere."

"They're just things..."

"No. Not just things. There." She pointed. "What about that tapestry you bought on our big fifty-five trip."

My eyes followed hers to the two-story piece I called Tree of Life that hung from the second floor to the first by my staircase. I'd bought it on our most recent Big-Fives birthday trip. It was made of thousands of hand-knotted yarns of hunter green, peach, chocolate-brown, silver and gold. How could Rose know I looked at it every day and thought of our adventures four years ago? How I always smiled as I ran my fingers across the threads—some rough as twine, some silky soft—remembering how Rose had haggled with the merchant for twenty minutes. Then, when he finally dropped his price by half, she told me, Pay him full price-it's worth it. It left me somewhere between confused and amazed.

"I'll put everything in storage."

"You're going to put your gazebo in storage? The porch swing that you love? How about all your bird feeders? You've got families of sparrows, wrens, and cardinals counting on you."

"I can find another place," I said, almost choking on the words since I knew it was a lie. I'd be broke and lucky to afford a cramped studio if I sold my cottage to pay for Rose's operation. I'd never have another sanctuary like this. A place where colors seemed more vibrant, where nature painted an ever-changing canvas, where even the stars were brighter. Maybe my life wasn't glamorous, but I was content. Even more important, I was in control. I'd devised a plan that gave me peace of mind, with enough money for my comfortable retirement, a big trip every five years to celebrate our birthdays, and Mom's Alzheimer's care at Shady Oaks.

I got up and stretched, stood behind Rose and then rubbed her shoulders, which felt like she was wearing armor.

"Maybe I should just..."

"Don't say that. There's got to be another way."

"I feel so damn stupid. And selfish. What right do I have to ask you..."

"Every right. If you hadn't come to me and something happened, I just couldn't have..."

"Oh, Turkle. Don't cry." She stood, turned and ran her finger over my wet cheeks. "Men—husbands, lovers, boyfriends—come and go, but twins are forever. You always have my back and I'll always have yours."

Rose closed her eyes, started to sway and grabbed the back of the chair.

"You okay?" I asked. "You look tired."

"I am dog-tired," Rose said, barely stifling a yawn. She looked at her watch. "Look at that, not even one AM and I'm bushed. Don't let that get out to my adoring public. It'll ruin my reputation."

"Go to sleep. We'll figure it out tomorrow."

"You sure?"

I nodded, we hugged, and I watched Rose shuffle to the staircase. She leaned on the railing as she climbed the stairs and stopped halfway up. When she caught her reflection in the mirror that used to hang in Grandpa Luke's house, she frowned and ran her fingers through her hair before taking a deep breath and continuing her climb.

I stayed behind and stared at the paper trail of my life. I paced. I rearranged the stacks of papers, checked the addition on my calculator, then strode to my picture window and stared at my beloved backyard. The lights were still on in Hank's kitchen and I wondered why he was up so late. Had he also come to his window and wondered why my lights were still on? I climbed the stairs to the landing and stared in Grandpa Luke's mirror at the woman looking back. Rose once said we should adopt Helen Mirren and become triplets, as all shared the same distinctive cheekbones, ivory skin, pale blue eyes and five-foot four slender frames, although I somehow couldn't imagine either Ms. Mirren or Rose with my straight gray hair.

As I stared at my reflection, I heard Rose's voice in my head with one of her signature lines: Could a face like this lie? Then she'd wink, laugh, and say, You bet. And get away with it.

As I trudged back down one last time to see if I could shake a different conclusion from the paperwork, I thought, Yes Rose, you can lie, but can I?

Around two in the morning, I finally accepted that my choices were grim. My head told me to go by the book. The way I always had. My heart told me to save my sister and my mother.

So, Agnes, a voice in my head said. Time to choose.

Door Number One. Let your sister die. Keep your organized life and your promise to keep your mother safe.

Door Number Two. Save your sister but lose your home and life savings and abandon your mother to the Russian-roulette nursing home system for those without funds.

Door Number Three. Save your sister and your mother but lose your integrity. Live a lie for a few months to let her get the life-saving operation she needs before you get your life back.

I swirled the last of my tea. The mug was, of course, the one Rose gave me on my 19th birthday, which I had lugged from place to place for the last forty years. It was decorated with a cartoon princess regarding a frog on a lily pad, her head tilted as if deciding what to do next.

I started to sip my tea, but spat it back, as the dregs were cold and bitter.

Chapter 3

my doorway to you
when I look in my mirror
I see you, not me

Rose's Haiku Diary
Bandipur, Nepal
Age 21

"Weird, isn't it," Rose said, "that it's so much easier for you to look like me than it is for me to look like you?" It had taken Rose twenty minutes to change my aluminum-guardrail-gray hair to her honey blonde color and an hour for the permanent to curl it. Straightening Rose's locks, stripping the color out, and turning them gray had been a four-hour process involving half-a-dozen bottles of various liquids that smelled like turpentine mixed with bleach. Rose had given me the list of what she needed and I'd driven to Ambridge and Aliquippa and stopped at a few different drugstores to make the purchases, already feeling like a criminal.

When I'd kidded her that she looked like a mad scientist with all the potions she mixed to accomplish our switch, she laughed and said, "See, Mom was wrong. My time at beauty school not only didn't ruin my life, but it may also have saved it."

Rose wouldn't let me see my new persona until she was satisfied with both her own hair and mine. She even insisted I don one of the prize T-shirts from her rock concert collection, a black one emblazoned EAGLES HOTEL CALIFORNIA TOUR 1977 CAPITAL CENTRE / WASHINGTON DC against a sepia background of a few palm trees and a building with a steeple. I was never sure if the building was the hotel or the mission. When she finished with my hair, she'd covered it with one of the extra-large shower caps she'd told me to buy and instructed me, "No peeking." When she finally stuck her head out of the bathroom wearing the matching cap and the first smile I'd seen since she'd arrived, she asked, "Ready for the moment of truth?"

I nodded and she motioned me to come join her. We stood by the sink looking at our reflections in the mirror and then Rose said, "Now," and we reached up together and pulled off the shower caps.

I stared at our reflections. It was remarkable. I turned to look at Rose and saw myself. I turned back to the mirror and saw her. I almost jumped when the blonde woman raised her hand to her face when I did.

"It's astonishing," I said. "You're amazing. You should have worked in Hollywood."

She shrugged the way she does, but I could tell by her smile that she was proud.

We turned to face each other and she opened her arms and we hugged. The first step, I thought. But it's just a few months. Just until Rose has recuperated. You can live a lie for a few months.

"Now to do your hands," Rose said.

"What's wrong with my hands?"

"Not a thing, for Agnes-hands. But if you're going to be me, you know I'd as soon go out stark naked as without fingernail polish. This one," she said, holding up a cobalt blue polish.

I shook my head and pointed to the creamy peach one. We butted heads, but in the end, I had to admit that I needed to get into Rose's skin to pull this off.

When she finished, I felt like a Martian, with my finger and toenails no color that occurred in nature, except perhaps for some exotic monkey or macaw.

We settled in my living room and Rose poured us both a glass of pinot grigio to sip as my nails dried. We were going over the plan for me to call my doctor the next day when the doorbell rang three times and then once.

"What a dope," I said. Rose cocked her head. "That's my neighbor. We have dinner together on Sundays."

"That old biddy Clara Clarke?" Rose asked as her eyes widened.

"No, not her," I said, although I had to laugh at Rose's reaction. Clara, the neighborhood gossip, busybody and purveyor of the oddball conspiracy theory du jour, was the last person I'd invite to share a meal. I didn't even like seeing her house across the cul-de-sac, knowing she was probably peeping out her window.

"Hank. My other neighbor."

Rose and I started to get up at the same time to answer the door.

"It's my house, remember," Rose said. "You've got the easier job. Just act a little wacky."

"We shouldn't do this yet," I said. "We're not ready."

"It'll look suspicious if we don't," she said as I sank back into my chair. "But you're right. Not ready." She grabbed her oversized purse and pulled out blush and eye shadow that she applied to my cheeks and eyelids before she trotted to the door and opened it. Hank smiled as he set down a shopping bag and Rose didn't miss a beat as he bent forward to kiss her cheek and hug her, our new ritual. She even held the hug a bit longer than I expected and he didn't seem to mind.

Rose turned and started to point at me, but Hank didn't notice as he reached into his shopping bag and pulled out a bouquet of pale and deep pink, red, and white Gerbera daisies.

"I thought you'd like these," he said.

I felt like a voyeur as Rose dropped her hand, then raised it to take the flowers. She beamed as she said, "How beautiful, thank you," before she kissed Hank quickly on the lips. He looked more pleased than startled, giving me a tweak of irrational jealousy. "I have exciting news. My sister Rose is visiting." She pointed at me and I stood as Hank strode toward me, took my hand in his and shook it.

This is it, I thought. He's going to know. We've been neighbors and friends for eight years. He called me his rock of strength during the two years his wife Jane battled breast cancer. We walk his dog Doodle together several times a week and have dinner almost every Sunday. He's going to look confused, look at Rose and then at me and ask why we're doing this masquerade. Instead, he said, "I've heard so many stories about you."

I laughed, not a full-blown Rose laugh, but one that still sounded too loud in my ears, closer to hers than mine. "Well, only half of them are true," I said. "The other half are much worse." It was one of the lines Rose used so often it emerged from my mouth without thinking.

"Rose must be tired from her trip," my sister said. "She'd normally give you a bear hug."

"You do already feel like family," Hank said, so we hugged briefly before he asked, "Is that your car out front?"

"That's Beulah," I said. Why was it Rose felt the need to name everything? "If I'd known she would last so long, I'd have given her a better name."

"Although Beulah did last longer than any of your marriages," Rose said, before realizing she was slipping back into being Rose.

"Stealing my punch line," I said in my best Rose voice. "Oh, where's..." Then I caught myself. "Doogle? Dudley? Your dog. Agnes said you bring him sometimes."

"Her. It's Doodle. I call her the Douglas fur," he said, and I remembered just in time to look confused.

"Sorry for the pun," Hank said. "Agnes and I love to play word games. My last name's Douglas." I chuckled and Rose did, too, even though as Agnes she'd heard the quip before. "Doodle is in the doghouse, so to speak. She was on the losing end of a close encounter with a skunk."

"Oh, poor Doodle," I said as I pictured Hank's Cairn Terrier-Shih Tzu mix slinking home after being skunked. His late wife Jane had been one wise woman when she'd insisted that they get a dog before she died. I think she did it, at least partly, so he'd have a reason to get up every morning when she was gone.

"Should I take this to the kitchen?" Rose asked as we crossed the living room to join her. "Something smells wonderful." Aromas of cardamom, cinnamon, ginger and garlic reached my nose as she said this and I knew Hank had brought my favorite—his Rogan Josh lamb curry.

"You'll never guess what it is," Hank said, looking into Rose's eyes and I wondered if we were about to fail our first test.

"It's either pizza or pancakes," Rose said. Hank shook his head, a bemused look on his face.

"It might be sushi," I added.

"Agnes always said you brought out the devil in her," Hank said, grinning at me.

"That's my sister," Rose and I said, almost in unison.

"Wait," Hank said. "It just occurred to me—maybe you just want some time to catch up. I can leave the curry..."

"Please stay," I said. "Agnes has told me a lot about you, too. I'll be here a week. We've got a lot of time to catch up." I tried to lift my voice at the end of my sentence, which Rose often did.

As we started toward the kitchen, Hank carrying the shopping bag, Rose lurched into an end table, knocking a lamp to the floor, before grabbing the back of one of my wing-backed chairs.

"Sapphire," I called as Hank simultaneously shouted, "Aggie." He dropped the shopping bag and grabbed Rose's waist to steady her. It felt a bit surreal, as if I was watching a movie, since Rose looked like me at that moment.

"I'm okay," Rose whispered, although her skin had a washed-out pallor. "Just got a little dizzy."

"Here, sit down," Hank said as he guided her to a chair.

We both watched as she sat, eyes closed, her hands folded in her lap.

Rose's breath was shallow. Should I call 911? Was this her heart failing? Where was my cellphone? Why couldn't I ever remember where I left it? I started toward the kitchen to use the landline.

"Where you going?" Rose asked.

"To call..."

"No," she said.

"Are you..."

"I'm okay," she said in a voice that sounded more like a little girl than an almost sixty-year old woman. "Just shouldn't have done that wine on an empty stomach."

I started to feel weak in the knees and sank into the wingback chair next to hers and turned to face her. Rose's skin was no longer gray and she forced a smile.

"You sure you're okay, Aggie?" Hank asked, putting his hand on her shoulder. The look of concern bordering on panic on his face wrenched my stomach.

"I'm sorry," I said. "I think my sister needs to take it easy. Maybe we can get together another time. I head back to..." My mind drew a blank. How could I not remember where she said her new apartment was?

"Cleveland," Rose filled in. "Imagine that, my sister living in our rival city?"

"A rain check, then," Hank said, his face still painted with worry. "You sure you're all right?" he asked her.

"I'm sure it's nothing," Rose said as she nodded. "I've had these odd symptoms. Like tonight. Just little spells. A little dizziness and… well I'm sure I'm fine."

"Get it checked out, please," Hank said.

"I will," Rose promised. "I was already planning to call my doctor tomorrow."

I started to speak, but Hank was focused on Rose, well me, but really Rose. His look of tender concern reminded so much of the many times I watched as he sat at his late wife Jane's bedside, just holding her hand and hoping.

Chapter 4

the gifts you give me
love, trust, hope—you are my rock
how can I repay?

Rose's Haiku Diary
Joplin, MO
Age 25

Rose and I sat on my loveseat and rehearsed the Monday morning phone call to my doctor half a dozen times. First, I played the role of receptionist and then she did. Even though we both agreed that I should make the call, I felt as if I'd had six cups of coffee too many when I dialed the number, as my heart jitterbugged.

"Dr. Finley's office," his receptionist said.

"Hi, Martha," I said. "This is Agnes Blumfield. I've been having some worrisome symptoms and was hoping the doctor could fit me in soon."

"What symptoms?" Her voice always managed to strike that special place between sincere concern and brisk efficiency, whether you were calling for a flu shot or you'd accidentally chopped your hand off.

I took a deep breath. I'm actually doing this, I thought. A pit the size of an apricot lodged in my stomach and my mouth became so dry I was sure the shredded wheat I'd had for breakfast was still in there. I inhaled. I told myself: This is easier than all those presentations you gave to CEOs and CFOs when you told them your product recall might bankrupt you or you need to cough up ten million more this year to fund your pension plan. "It started as shortness of breath and then fatigue. I thought I might be getting the flu. But I just couldn't shake it."

"How long?"

I looked at Rose. Weeks, she mouthed. "A few weeks. We've all heard something was going around. I was planning to call you today anyway, but this morning, my side went numb—just briefly—and I passed out."

"Oh, no," Martha said. "Did you fall? Did you hurt yourself?"

"No, I was in my easy chair. Fortunately. My sister and I were having coffee in the living room." Was I giving too many irrelevant details? It somehow sounded like it now. It wasn't like me. I always knew what I needed to say and said it. "I scared the daylights out of her. She said I was only out for a minute or two. She was all set to call 911 when I came to."

"Hold, please."

It couldn't have been more than a few minutes, but it felt like hours. I tried to calm myself by watching a dozen sparrows enjoying the black oil sunflower seeds I got to indulge them and one ambitious squirrel doing acrobatics trying to thwart my squirrel-proof feeder.

"Can you be here by 10:30?" Martha asked.

"Yes," I said, as relief surged through me. "See you then. Thank you for fitting me in."

I turned to Rose.

"You did it," she said.

"You ready to do this?" I asked.

She nodded. "Are you?"

"Let's get you better."

Ten minutes later, Rose dressed in my black slacks, white cable-knit sweater, and camel hair coat and me dressed in her jeans, Aerosmith sweatshirt, and leather bomber jacket headed out. She had grinned when I'd handed her the fuzzy red knit hat she'd given me a few years before.

We both look great in that hat, I thought.

"Watch your step," I said, as a dusting of snow from the previous night had coated the walkway from the mudroom to the garage. I looked up to see Rose not watching her step, but waving at Hank as he locked his side-door to take Doodle for a walk. So, I waved, too. I felt that odd little thrill that had happened every time I saw Hank wearing the L. L. Bean black Stetson wool hat I'd given him for Christmas. It always made me think he looked Indiana-Jones handsome. You need a rugged face to rock a Stetson in Sewickley, Pennsylvania.

"Morning," he called and started down his driveway. "Sunshine today and going to forty. Doesn't get much better than that for the ides of February." Doodle was pulling on the leash, anxious to come say hello.

"Can't talk now," I called. "Late for an appointment." I knew Rose-as-me should have said that, but I needed to move things along to avoid being late for our appointment and so Doodle didn't run to the wrong sister.

"You feeling all right?" he asked, looking at Rose. "You gave us a scare last night."

"Thanks. Doing better," Rose said. "Off to see the doctor just to be sure it's nothing."

I bit my lip as I'd been vague about the appointment intentionally so Hank wouldn't worry. Especially since I already knew the diagnosis wasn't nothing.

His smile disappeared and his look of concern gave my heart a flutter.

"Anything I can do?"

I hissed at Rose, "Open the garage door." She tilted her head and I motioned to the keypad with my eyes. She nodded, opened the box, and then looked at me quizzically for the code. "Your birthday," I mouthed.

So odd, I thought, as I had so often, we share so much, even our DNA, but Rose and I don't share the same birthday. Or Zodiac sign, as she would often point out, since I was born at ten to midnight on September 22nd, making me a Virgo whereas she was born twenty-two minutes later on September 23rd, making her a Libra.

"Shouldn't I drive?" Rose asked as I strode toward the driver's side of my dark blue Ford Taurus.

I paused. How had this gotten so complicated already? Did we really have to question every small action, even something as simple as who drives?

"No," I whispered so Hank couldn't hear. "We'll say it was a precaution since you were feeling unsteady. If anyone asks, which they won't. Other than Clara." I nodded in the direction of Clara Clarke's house where she was pretending to check for mail, even though we both knew it never arrived until after three.

"Can I moon her?" Rose asked, just to get a laugh, which it did. I pictured the look of horror on Clara's face as she raced inside, no doubt to grab the phone to spread word of the salacious deed.

Hank and Doodle had paused at the end of my driveway, on Rose's side of the car, and it seemed rude not to say hello, so I stopped the car. I expected Rose to roll down the window so we could exchange a few brief words, but instead she opened the car door and reached down to pet Doodle, who hopped in, tail flailing, still smelling slightly of skunk. Fortunately, Rose wrapped her arms around Doodle, since it was clear that the dog planned to greet me, phony blonde hair notwithstanding. Maybe you can fool some of the people all of the time, but you sure can't fool a dog.

Hank crouched by Rose's open door.

"Didn't want to hold you up," he said. "But please let me know how things go today. Have to look out for my two best girls." Even though I was rubbing her ears, Doodle was still struggling to reach me, but Hank didn't seem to notice. His eyes were looking into Rose's.

"You know I will," Rose said. She reached out her hand and Hank took it.

At least she didn't kiss him again, I thought. But then he leaned in and kissed her. Well, Agnes. Me. But her. The kind of friendship-bordering-on-something-else kiss we had been tentatively exchanging the last month. But now it was even more confusing than when we'd been trying to figure out if our friendship was changing into something else, because he was kissing Rose thinking she was me. I realized the crossroads that Hank and I had reached, where you wonder if risking losing one of your best friends if the romance doesn't work out, had to go on hold. I needed to tell Rose to politely put on the brakes while she was recovering.

As we drove off, Hank, holding Doodle in his arms, waved her paw. It's only for a few months, I told myself. Then you'll get your life back.

"Tunes?" Rose asked as I drove away and she reached for my car's radio.

"I guess I'd rather talk, "I said, knowing that her choice in music would probably grate my already frazzled nerves.

"Could do both," Rose said, although she returned her hand to her lap.

"Let's just go over it all again," I said. I guess that was the corporate America accountant part of my personality that remained, even though I'd retired. Always practice every meeting at least three times—think of every question the client might ask—and have an answer. I knew my part, concerned sister in the waiting room, was the easier one. We both agreed that I wouldn't have asked Rose to join me to see the doctor. I knew how to take care of myself and had been seeing doctors for decades alone.

Rose took a deep breath. "You always address your doctor as Dr. Finley and give him a firm handshake. There are two nurses: Joan is the blonde and Marigold has gray hair. Wouldn't you think it should be the opposite—that Marigold would be the blonde?"

"Maybe she was blonde as a baby. But back to the topic..."

"Your list of medications hasn't changed, just vitamins and some allergy drugs. You, I mean I, always look your doctor directly in the eyes when he's talking. You ask questions if they come to you, but take a breath first to make sure you ask well-reasoned ones."

We continued with me telling Rose everything I could think of from the sprained ankle I'd had six months ago to the need to get parking validated to where the ladies' room was.

We were about ten minutes away from my doctor's office when Rose said, "I'm good."

We stopped talking, although my heart pounded in my ears above the muffled sounds of traffic, punctuated only by the occasional horn.

"Tell me more about your cute neighbor," Rose finally said.

"Cute?" I said, thinking, is Hank cute? His athletic build, startling blue eyes and short-cropped salt-and-pepper hair made me think more rugged than cute.

"Hank Douglas?" I said, more to stall than anything else, since I knew Rose wasn't talking about Clara Clarke and had never met my other neighbors. I barely knew them other than to wave in a neighborly fashion. "He's about our age."

"Would have guessed that. How about the good stuff? What's his online profile say?"

I laughed. "I don't think he has one."

"What should it say?"

A bus stopped in front of us to pick up two bundled-up passengers. I drummed my fingers on the steering wheel, despite knowing we should make our appointment in plenty of time.

"Sixty-five-year-old..."

"You don't give age..."

"I give up," I said.

"Sorry," Rose said. "Guess I'm too proficient in the dating profile game. So, let's see. Mid-sixties dog-lover seeks hot, former accountant to hike, bike, go antiquing, visit bookstores, coffee shops, and farmer's markets, see the USA in his Chevrolet and sit by the fire with a good claret."

I was a little startled, as she'd captured a lot of what Hank and I loved to do together, until I figured out that she'd cheated, since they were all things I loved to do. Things Rose and I often did together, especially when we'd get together for our birthday celebrations.

"Pretty close," I said, feeling my face flush. Rose's profile of Hank, maybe it was just her saying it out loud, somehow made me see that our relationship had been subtly changing over the past couple of months. I think neither of us was sure where it was going. We both treasured our friendship and I think wondered if changing it was worth the possibility of losing it. I know I did.

"Favorite book?"

"Kerouac's *On the Road*. He's read it every year since he was seventeen. Once said his dream was to buy an RV and see the country."

"Hah," Rose said. "Look how close I was. Chevrolet, RV. Although you do know that Winnebago rhymes with lumbago. Road trip, oh yes, but in an RV? Seriously? How about a tandem bicycle? Maybe a motorcycle with a sidecar. You hang out in trailer parks and he'll have to buy a pair of striped suspenders."

"What?" My eyebrows must have gone up.

"They all wear them."

I tilted my head.

"At trailer parks. I've seen my share of them. You didn't really think Mountain Vista Estates was in the high rent district, did you?" She paused for just the right theatrical moment to let that sink in before continuing. "Job?"

"Retired. He was a civil engineer. Left his job to take care of his wife Jane when she got cancer. Their insurance didn't cover home health care and he refused to put her in a facility so they could get reimbursed. Went into debt taking care of her."

"Wow," she said and sat silent for a moment. I wondered if his selflessness had hit her harder because of her own illness. She turned to look out the window, but I saw her wipe a tear. "Bonus points for that. A nice guy. Not that many of them around. Figures he would be a civil engineer. Not much civility around anymore either. Went out of fashion with chivalry."

"You just have to know where to look," I said. Rose raised her eyebrows. "I'm not looking. We're just friends." Again, I wondered why I was telling Rose that, when I wasn't sure what we were.

"You should be looking. I saw how he looked at you, well me when he thought I was you. Here's your profile post: late 50's former accountant turned Renaissance woman seeks chivalrous engineer to build a love bridge."

I groaned, but smiled. It was good to see Rose at her wisecracking best. I was relieved that it took both of our minds off the ordeal we would soon face. "We're almost there," I said.

"Time to get to the deal-breakers. Bad habits? Drugs? Gambling? Smoker? Weird politics?"

"Nope times four."

"Any kids?"

"Two. A boy and a girl. Well, one now. A divorced daughter, Julie, somewhere near Cleveland with a teenage son. His son died in a car accident when he was seventeen."

"How sad."

"It happened long before I met him and Jane, but it still haunts him. Hank still has the last paper his son wrote for his Civics class. He let me read it ..." I slammed on my brakes as a Jeep darted in front of me from a side street. The near-miss derailed my train of thought, but the conversation would have had to have been postponed anyway, as we'd arrived at my doctor's medical building.

Chapter 5

fortune teller kiss
is my future in his arms
waking to his smile

Rose's Haiku Diary
Bandipur, Nepal
Age 22

Rose sat on the sofa with pillows propped behind her, listening to her iPod and tapping on her laptop as she updated her blog. I faced her, in my big rocking chair, Toni Morrison's *A Mercy* open in my lap. We were both exhausted from the whirlwind day.

A snow squall blocked the view of my garden, almost as if we'd closed the curtains to shut out the rest of the world.

The light from the flames danced off Rose's face, so it almost glowed. It made seeing her with gray hair—my gray hair—all the more surreal. Rose never looked older than thirty-nine to me, my Jack Benny sister. It wasn't her flawless peach skin—mine was too—no, it was more of the inner glow that she possessed that made men want to don a suit of armor, women confess their deepest secrets, and kids get into mischief. Even animals were not immune. When we were twelve, I saw her bewitch a snarling German Shepherd blocking our path. "You're a good dog," she told it over and over as I tried to decide if we should run or find a stick to defend ourselves. Then she crouched and held out her hand. I swear the dog looked confused for a moment before it stopped growling and its tail started to wag, ever so slowly. Moments later, the dog was licking her face. That glow started to fade the day she traded her honey blonde hair color for my gray. Or maybe it was because her damaged heart valves were taking their toll. But, in the light of the fire, her glow returned.

The aroma from the apple pie I'd made still lingered in the living room. I looked up from my book every few minutes to bask in the bliss on her face.

I thought of asking her what she was listening to, but didn't want to break the spell. Her cell phone rang and she picked it up. A flash of worry danced across her face and then disappeared as she stuffed the phone in her purse, where it continued to ring.

"Don't want to answer it?" I asked.

Rose closed her laptop and took out her earbuds.

"Nobody I want to talk to today other than you," she said

"I wish we could freeze this moment."

"Me, too."

"If you could go back to any time, what would you pick?"

Her cell phone buzzed from her purse, indicating a message. She pulled it out, turned it off, and stared dreamily into space as if watching a slideshow of her life.

"Mine would have to be a memory where you were there," she said. "I'm thinking of the day we hiked Devil's Lake."

"Why that day?" I asked, although the day was as crisp in my memory as if it was yesterday.

"I don't know. We were so young, so innocent."

"Maybe I was innocent," I said, making Rose smile.

"Not that way," she said. "I think it was almost the last day that I felt, that we both felt, like we could do anything. The world seemed so full of possibilities."

"It really did," I said. Where did they go, I wondered.

"That was the day I remember you as the happiest, the most relaxed, most confident I'd ever seen you," she said.

It had been a wondrous day, despite it being the Friday before the Monday Jack reported for induction, in all likelihood to become more cannon fodder shipped to Vietnam. I knew I should have spent the day with him, but I wanted to be with Rose.

Rose and I were juniors in college. I was at the University of Wisconsin and thought it unpatriotic to question our government's unpopular war. Rose was at Kent State and involved in every protest. She came to Madison for the weekend and we packed a picnic of sharp cheddar, rye bread, a can of smoked oysters, apples, and a bottle of Chianti.

"A loaf of bread, a jug of wine..." Rose said as she packed our picnic basket and held up the cheddar brick.

"I don't recall cheese being a requirement," I replied. "Just thou."

"I'd heard it was in Wisconsin."

I'd cut class that Friday in May, the first and last time. On the drive there, we sang every dirty song Rose knew, and she knew a lot. It was mid-forties when we left, but Rose assured me it would warm up and, of course, it did. We hiked to the top of the West Bluff Trail and stopped for our picnic. We didn't talk as we ate, just gazed at Devil's Lake, its sunlight-dappled water sparkling like a chandelier. After lunch, we decided to explore more, so we navigated the steep climb up Balance Rock trail.

"I'm so proud of you," she said as we shared our last apple and watched the sun start its descent. I wondered why she was proud. For my 3.8 grade point or for turning down Jack's marriage proposal? I didn't ask, not wanting to break the spell.

Sunday morning, Jack gave me a black onyx pendant.

"This should be an engagement ring," he said.

Jack asked me to marry him six months before, and I told him I needed more time. I was too young. Yes, I loved him, but I wasn't ready. We could get married after I graduated. After he got out of the Army. I couldn't tell him that I wasn't ready to repeat my mother's mistake of marrying too young and giving up her education.

"It would help me get a deferment," he'd said. "Especially if you get pregnant."

Chapter 6

picture I love best?
not Monet's Water Lilies
it's of you, smiling

Rose's Haiku Diary
Paris
Age 40

My mother, Louise Blumfield, didn't start to paint until she was admitted to the Alzheimer's ward at Shady Oaks. Her paintings had a haunting quality; images often seemed to be fading away or drifting off into space. Most included two figures. They might be girls or dogs, eagles or daisies, but one would draw the viewer's eye, with the second, almost identical one only noticed as an afterthought. One might be bathed in glowing light and the other obscured by clouds. Sometimes one would fill the canvas and I'd think she had gotten away from her duo theme, but on closer examination, I'd see it, gnat-sized in the background. I never had the courage to ask which one I was.

Since I started visiting her at Shady Oaks, Mom had only mistaken me for Rose once. It was before I took off the fluffy red knit hat Rose sent me for Christmas. Once Mom saw my gray hair, her face hardened as she said, "Agnes, you know I hate it when you try to fool me."

I had put off broaching the subject of visiting Mom until the tests and consultations were completed and Rose's surgery scheduled.

I still found the blonde, curly-haired woman staring back at me in my mirror startling. I wondered what Mom would make of us. Until we were six, she always knew which twin was which. Then around age ten, she started getting us mixed up. Maybe that was why she decided we no longer needed to dress alike.

Rose and I were in my breakfast nook, watching the sparrows and squirrels gorging themselves at my bird feeder. Crocuses flecked my garden with purple, yellow, and white. I poured coffee into two mugs—mine the one I used every day, the one with the frog and princess on it, hers the porcelain World mug with its images of continents bedecked with koala bears and pandas as well as the Taj Mahal and Golden Gate Bridge. She bought it from Tiffany's, telling me everyone should own something from Tiffany's. I took my coffee black and Rose always took at least two sugars and a dash of cream. That's what makes me so sweet, she always said. The remnants of the lox, bagels and cream cheese Rose insisted we buy were still on the table.

"I don't know, Turkle," she said. "Those places can be so depressing. That's not what I need right now."

"This one's nice," I said, not totally believing it. Nice, for what was a ward with nurses and supervised activities—activities that seemed more suited to summer camp for seven-year-olds than recreation for the elderly. It did have a cheery dining room, an airy atrium, and a big orange tabby named Melvin that swaggered around the premises. Nice, living in a single small room, like a cell that imprisoned Mom in the past, lost in the foggy memories of her once-sharp mind. Her wicked tongue quiet. Did she relish retreating to the past, choosing to live in the times she was happiest? I was never sure. Some days she was lucid and others she barely spoke a word.

"Last time I visited her, she really lit into me," Rose said. "You too good to visit the woman who raised you? The woman who spent twenty-two hours in labor to give you life?" A smile crinkled the edges of my lips. She'd perfected the rasp of Mom's voice. I knew what was coming next, the retort that always drove Mom crazy. "No, Mom. You did not spend twenty-two hours in labor for me—you spent them for Agnes. I only took twenty-two minutes."

Part of me didn't want to interrupt her soliloquy, but I needed to get the conversation back on track.

"She almost always recognizes me," I said. "She only thought I was you once. Though recently she gets confused about what year it is and how old we are."

Why had I added that? It would only make Rose more reluctant to visit Mom. Was I trying to get her to visit for Mom or for me? Or for Rose? Or was I worried about the prognosis the surgeon, Dr. Stein, delivered about the ninety-five percent survival rate for the operation Rose needed? Was I projecting on Rose what I would want, a chance to say goodbye if I was in the five percent? As an accountant, numbers always felt tangible to me. And ninety-five percent meant that one of twenty patients did not survive. But then, Rose always beat the odds.

Rose bit her pinkie finger. "I don't know," she said. Then her impish smile returned as she quoted from *Casablanca* in her best Ingrid Bergman imitation, "You have to think for both of us, for all of us."

I drummed my fingers on my cheek. "I think you should see her," I said. "It's been..."

"It's been since before she went to that place." She closed her eyes and her fingers moved as if she were counting them. "Four years ago."

"I was so happy you came back then," I said. "I really needed you." I'd been taking care of Mom for the six years before that, so long that I wasn't sure if my head was on straight. Even though I had the Medical Power of Attorney, I knew Mom didn't want to leave her house, to go to what she called "one of those places." I needed Rose to tell me that moving Mom into Shady Oaks was the right thing. And she did. Then we spent two weeks cleaning out Mom's house before Rose hugged me, told me she'd be back any time I needed her, and flew back to New Mexico.

Chapter 7

deal with the devil?
can't tempt me with money, fame
but pearl nail polish...

Rose's Haiku Diary
Sewickley PA
Age 17

"I told you what Mom calls this place, didn't I?" I said to Rose as I pulled into the parking lot of Shady Oaks.

She shook her head.

"Shaky Folks."

"She is so bad. But that is funny."

The normal half-hour drive took almost an hour, as the snow-covered roads were icy, feeding the caterpillars crawling around in my stomach.

We trudged through the slushy parking lot to the three-story, red-brick building, then navigated the maze of locked doors. Rose performed flawlessly, greeting each staff person by name, asking about their children, cats or that cold they were fighting off the last time I visited, almost three weeks before. She introduced me as her sister Rose. I took in her performance with awe at her impersonation skills mixed with the slightest tinge of annoyance that everyone accepted her as me and me as Rose. Was that all they saw—that gray-haired woman dressed in black or navy-blue who visited her mother twice a week?

I had called to explain that I was having medical problems, so they wouldn't wonder why my visits lapsed.

"How are you feeling?" Gustav, one of the orderlies asked. Rose let herself slip a little, I thought, when she took his arm and thanked him for asking, telling him she was having surgery on Friday, and wouldn't be able to visit until she recuperated. Although I had to admit that I might have been just as emotional at a seemingly mundane question if I was the one going under the knife.

"Your mother is in the art studio," Laarni, the young Filipino nurse told us. "That's usually a good thing. She tends to withdraw when she spends too much time in her room." Laarni turned to me, "You do know, Rose, that she may not recognize you or she may. Some days, she's here with us, but some days she doesn't even know what year it is."

Rose seemed to be swaying and I caught her arm. "You okay?" I asked.

"Just a little queasy," she said.

"Me too," I confessed. Laarni left us at the art studio, telling us to have the art therapist page her when we were ready to go.

"I'll be over there," the art therapist said and pointed to a table at the far end of the room where three women were cutting felt shapes using stencils and gluing them together.

We watched our mother paint like a woman possessed. Her back was to us, giving us an unrestricted view of her canvas. It showed a girl falling feet-first down a well. The bottom half of the canvas was the girl's face and her arm reaching up. Flowing snake-like tresses blocked most of the girl's face, but her pale blue eyes, the only color in the black and white painting, were visible and terrified. The walls of the well stretched up and up, until at the top there was the small face of another girl, her arms reaching down.

Rose clutched my arm, her bravado gone. "I don't think I want to know what that means," she said.

"Me, too," I said. "Better do this before we lose our nerve."

"Don't know about you, but I already have."

I put my arm around her shoulder, squeezed for a second, and then started walking toward Mom. "You're me, so you should speak first." Rose gave me one of those I'm-not-an-idiot looks that let me know she was starting to regain her confidence.

As we reached her easel, Mom turned and called to the art therapist, "Turn that infernal music down. How I am supposed to hear myself think?" Then her gaze fell on us.

"Hi, Mom. Rose is here to visit," Rose said as she pointed to me. Rose used to goad Mom by announcing herself as "your favorite daughter." I was glad that she left out the favorite-word—what Rose used to call the F-word—but somehow Mom heard it anyway.

"Favorite," Mom said, as if repeating it. "A mother is supposed to love each child equally. No favorites. But you can't. You try. You really do. I was special before he was born. I was their golden girl." Mom's eyes wandered around the room, finally returning to her painting. She picked up a small brush that looked like it belonged in a dollhouse, dipped it in red paint and began feathering the hair ribbon of the falling girl.

"They thought she was just tired," Mom said. Rose and I exchanged glances—we'd both heard this story dozens of times. "Tired from taking care of the baby. The house. Taking care of Daddy. He'd fallen off a ladder and broke his leg. They should have known she was sick. Was dying." She wiped the paint off with her fingers, then smeared it on her shirt, leaving a red streak. Rose and I waited for the diatribe that usually followed, about how Mom raised Uncle Roger after her mother died, taking on the roles of mother, housekeeper and cook. How she never got to do the things a teen-age girl should be doing. Having fun. Dancing. A boyfriend. "Mama never looked as happy as when she was holding Roger. Looking in his eyes. Singing to him. I was thirteen. I wanted to scream, I'm still here too. Look at me. I need you too. But I was supposed to be the big girl. When Daddy called our neighbor to take her to the hospital—we didn't have a car—he told me, take care of your brother. I was the big sister, but I was still little inside. I thought about making him go away, getting it back the way it was before, putting a pillow over his face." Rose gripped my hand. This part of the story was new. "I might have too, if he cried. But he looked up and smiled, and I couldn't do it."

We waited to see if Mom would say more, but she was examining her paintbrushes. She picked up one, then another, and rubbed the bristles against her face.

"Look who's here to visit," Rose said. She bent and gave Mom a quick kiss on the cheek, as I always did. Mom stared at us, first at Rose, then me, then Rose, then me again.

Her eyes came to rest on me. I felt them burrowing under my skin, like some x-ray of my soul. "So, my precious Rose has come to grace me with a visit," she said.

"Hi, Mom," I said. "Nice to see you."

"Where's that no-good husband of yours?"

I wasn't sure which husband she meant, but luckily, the answer was pretty much the same for both. "We're divorced—two years ago," I said, and then wondered if it was three. "I wrote you a letter."

"A letter," she said. "An envelope, a stamp, a piece of paper. That's all it's worth to you for the woman who raised you? The woman who spent twenty-two hours in labor to give you life?"

"No, Mom," I said. "You didn't spend twenty-two hours in labor for me—you spent them for Agnes." She shifted her gaze. Rose's hand was in front of her mouth and I wondered if she was stifling nervous laughter, until I saw the tears in her eyes. "I just took twenty-two minutes."

"Twenty-two minutes," she repeated. "Twenty-two minutes. I'd hoped you were going to be a boy." I stepped back, as if she slapped me. "Could have told you apart then. A son would visit more often."

"I'm here now, aren't I?" I said.

"She's come a long way," Rose added.

"You didn't come all this way to see me," Mom said. "Figure you'd only do that if I was on my deathbed." We both winced. Her head swiveled. "So why are you here?"

"Agnes..." I started to say, but Mom cut me off.

"You're not getting married again, are you?" she said, as she stared at Rose.

"Again?" Rose stammered, and her face flushed. "Mom, I'm Agnes. I've never been married and I'm not getting married. Rose isn't getting married either."

Mom frowned and looked from Rose to me and back to Rose. "Good," she said. "Men ruin your lives. Take what they want and leave you." Rose and I flinched. Dad disappeared from our lives when Rose and I were two, so we'd heard this rant for years, even before we were old enough to go to the playground alone. It was a miracle Rose and I ever wanted anything to do with men, although having Uncle Roger and Grandpa Luke as male role models helped counter her tirades.

"Mom," Rose as Agnes said. "I need an operation. Rose came to help me out while I recuperate."

"Figured she wouldn't just come to see me." She closed her eyes, and I wondered if she'd nodded off. Rose jerked her thumb toward the door and wiggled two fingers to signal walking.

The repeated beats of a gong-like sound filled the room. "Supper time," the art-therapist said. Mom opened her eyes. "Everyone put their supplies away. Time to go to dinner."

Mom looked at Rose and me. "You girls wash up for supper," she said. "It's a school night. No television until your homework is done."

Chapter 8

happy go lucky
that's what they say, what they see
they're only half right

Rose's Haiku Diary
Rio Rancho, NM
Age 58

"Friday, the thirteenth," Rose said. "What was I thinking when I agreed to have my surgery on Friday the thirteenth?" It was still pre-dawn on the day of her surgery and we were getting ready for the forty-minute drive to Oakvale Memorial General Hospital.

"It was the first available day," I reminded her.

"What do you think of this?" Rose asked as I brushed my teeth. She held up an outfit more appropriate to a cocktail party: a short black skirt, powder blue blouse and a black shawl. "With these." She pointed to a pair of sling-back high heels.

"Why don't you wear a pair of my sweats?" I suggested. "You'd be much more comfortable."

"No," she said. "You'd be more comfortable. That's what you'd wear." At these last words, she raised her hand and covered her mouth. "You're right. I forgot. I'm you."

She pressed me to wear her chic outfit, and I finally agreed to the blouse and shawl, but with black slacks and boots. At the last minute, I replaced the shawl with a jacket Rose gave me. She bought it when she was broke, but she bought it anyway. "I saw this," she said, "and knew I had to get it for you. It's perfect. Look at how the blue shows off your baby blue eyes." I hardly ever wore it, as it was more her style than mine. I called it my peacock jacket, as its raw silk fibers glistened in shades of peacock blue, turquoise, cobalt blue and silver. I always loved it. Loved that was how Rose saw me.

"Thanks for lending me this," I said, holding it up, and she laughed.

Halfway to the hospital, gritty snow started to pelt the car. I turned up the car radio to blot out the scratching sound. The pine trees that lined the road seemed as if they were melting into the hills.

"What's that smell?" I said as I glanced over and saw the source of the pungent fumes. Rose was painting her nails. "Are you sure that's okay?"

"It's called White Night. I figure it will go with whatever color hospital gown I get. How could it not be okay?"

"White Knight? Lancelot or Prince Charming?"

She laughed. "Not knight, silly. Night. Like the opposite of day. Like what it is right now."

"Looks gray to me," I said. I was sure the pre-op instructions said no makeup or nail polish, but it was too late.

Rose put her hand on my knee. "Quick," she said. "Do something Rose would do."

I paused, trying to think of something Rose-like while concentrating on the twists and turns of the roads. What would Rose do? A flash of inspiration leapt into my brain and I remembered a game we used to play. "Rose's heart's bad, violets are purple, I know the docs, will stop her heart urple."

She laughed harder than the quip merited, but long enough to get me laughing, too.

"My turn," she said. "Um. Rose is so glad, Turkle's her sister." She paused and I knew she was running through rhymes with sister. "She's my best friend, and I really missed her."

I smiled, turned off the radio and started to hum "My Wild Irish Rose." I glanced over. Rose's eyes were closed, but she was mouthing the lyrics. Rose knew every song with her name in it. She even told the band to play all of them at her first wedding.

Then the tires slid a bit as I negotiated one of those turns with the signs with the little rocks raining down on a car, pushing me halfway into the oncoming lane. Fortunately, there was no other traffic.

"Come on, Maggie," I said as I fought the steering wheel.

"Maggie," Rose said. "Aww. You kept the name I gave her."

"I only use it when I'm mad at her," I said, causing Rose to laugh again.

As we got closer to Pittsburgh, traffic got heavier and slower. At my insistence, we'd left by 6:00—a full half-hour more than we should have needed—so I wasn't worried about missing our 7:00 a.m. check-in time. Rose groused that it seemed uncivilized to get up at that hour and suggested staying up all night instead. "I always loved staying up to watch the sun rise." I pointed out that because of Daylight Savings Time, we'd be in the hospital before the sun started showing its face and that she needed sleep before the operation.

"What if my surgeon isn't a morning person?" she said as I slowed the car to take the hospital garage's parking ticket.

"Of course, he is." I said. "You know your luck."

"What if my luck doesn't recognize me? What if I get your luck?" She put her hand to her mouth. "Oh, Turkle, I'm so sorry. I didn't mean that."

"I know," I said, although that little doubt nagged me too.

The hospital seemed to be just waking up at ten to seven as we navigated corridor after corridor until we found Admissions.

"You'd think they'd put it closer to the parking garage," Rose said.

"You'd think," I agreed. As we waited for Jennifer, the admitting clerk, to finish the paperwork for the patient who arrived before us, my stomach seemed to be trying to crawl out of my body. Perhaps it was a protest at having no breakfast, only coffee, perhaps a message from my conscience. I glanced at Rose. She looked smaller, frailer than I could ever recall, especially in my gray sweat pants and sweatshirt. It jolted me when I thought, she looks like me. I glanced down at my own fancy outfit and felt a bit ridiculous. Who gets this dressed up to take her their sister to the hospital? Who? Well, Rose, of course.

Chapter 9

so many questions
how long, what if, how to pay
how can I ask her

Rose's Haiku Diary
Sturgis, SD
Age 59

After Rose removed her nail polish as required, we waited for the nurses to get her prepped. A red-headed nurse named Nadia stopped by at eight, then again forty minutes later, to inform us that her surgery was delayed. I paced like a caged animal. "Will you stop that," Rose demanded. "Come over here. Talk to me about something."

I pondered what to say, then decided to ask about something that always seemed to make Rose happy. "What's happening with your friend, Chris?" I asked. I had a love/hate relationship with her friend Chris, even though I'd never met her. Once or twice a year for the past ten years Rose regaled me with tales of Chris charging to the rescue of some poor soul or another. Rose seemed to almost revere her, although she admitted that Chris was something of a recluse, which was why she didn't even have a picture to show me.

"Chris is doing something amazing right now," she said. "Literally life-saving."

I arched my eyebrows. "Stomping out malaria?" I asked before I realized that I sounded a tad harsh.

"She's more of a saving-one-person-at-a-time type," Rose said. "Let's not talk about her."

"Okay, then what..."

"Oh my gosh," Rose interrupted me. "My blog. You need to update it while I'm in the hospital."

"What?"

"I've been writing about my sister getting an operation."

I looked around, panicked that someone might hear her, but no staff or other patients were nearby. Rose lowered her voice to a whisper. "My readers will want updates on my...Agnes' progress. They're worried about you, Turkle."

"But..."

"It's really easy. I can't remember more than one ID or password, so they're the same for all my accounts. Give me that notebook." I handed her the notebook where I wrote down everything any doctor or nurse said. She tore out a sheet and penned:

User ID -- Rose67fire

Password – turkle1025

Turkle, I thought. She thinks of me every time she types in her password.

"Fire?" I asked.

"Sapphire?" Of course.

"What about 67?"

"That was the year I...never mind." Rose laughed. When she caught her breath, she raised her arm, as if giving a command. "Now as they said on Mission Impossible, memorize and self-destruct that puppy." She pointed at the paper.

"I don't think I need to memorize our house number on Bowar Street," I said as I ran a pen over her password and tore the paper into bits.

Rose started humming the Mission Impossible theme and for a moment I expected the scraps of papers to disintegrate in a puff of smoke. When they didn't, I stuffed them in my jacket pocket, wondering why there were no trash baskets.

"You'll probably only need to post on my blog today," she said, "since I'm guessing I'll still be loopy from the anesthesia. Write whatever the doctors say. You know: all went well, blah, blah, blah, she needs her rest, should go home in however many days."

"But I don't know how to do a blog." I never felt comfortable poking around Rose's blog, seeing over five hundred strangers with their paws all over her words, gushing at her funny or sad or heartwarming stories. The IT guy at the library helped me figure out how to have her posts show up in my email box every day so I could feel like they were written just for me.

"If I can figure it out, you can. You only need to do the first one. I'll write the rest. It's not like I'm asking you to donate a kidney."

I smiled. "If you ever need one," I said, "I have a spare."

Rose held out her arms for a hug and I climbed onto the edge of the bed and wrapped my arms around her. "I know you do and you would. I would for you, too." We sat like that for several minutes, intertwined as we were in the womb. Then Rose started to gasp and I jumped off the bed.

"Should I get a nurse?" I asked.

Rose shook her head.

"I'm going to get a nurse."

"No. Please," Rose managed to get out between gasps. It was only seconds, but felt much longer. "Don't want to give them a reason to postpone the operation."

"You sure you're okay?"

She nodded and smiled, as she finally caught her breath. "Just a little panic attack, that's all."

"You want anything? Water?" Then I remembered she wasn't allowed anything to drink. "Music?" I held up my cell phone, but she shook her head again.

We sat in silence as I tried to think of something to lighten the mood. It was Rose who finally spoke first.

"We could play the Game," she said.

The Game was the twenty questions one she'd invented years ago to evaluate boyfriend material.

"Seriously?" I asked

"I'd love to know more about Hank."

It felt awkward to talk about him, since I was still trying to figure it all out myself.

"Fire away," I said, hoping this old ritual would take her mind off of the operation.

Hank got high scores for making the most incredible pancakes I ever tasted (lemon-blueberry), his college dream of hitchhiking across the country and his many interests that matched mine—classic movies, hiking, puttering in his garden, reading—but lost points for his stamp collection, playing the bagpipes (both traditional and jazz) and his dislike of coffee and orange food.

"Who doesn't like coffee?" Rose asked. She was going to dock him for his vintage Thunderbird car until I pointed out that it was not only a convertible but the same salmon color as the 1966 Dodge Polara her high school steady, Jimmy West, drove.

The game got a little embarrassing as Rose got more creative with her questions, but it kept her mind off the surgery, so who was I to rain on her picnic. When the nurses arrived to wheel her off, Hank had 84 points out of 90, with two more questions to go.

"Don't think you've heard the end of this," she said.

"Can't wait to hear your last questions," I said. She always did save the humdingers for the end. Never the same questions, either. She motioned me to put my ear by her lips. "I love you, Turkle," she whispered.

"Love you too, Sapphire," I whispered back as I squeezed her hand. "See you in a couple of hours." Then the nurses started to wheel her away.

The gurney was ten feet away when Rose sat up. "Wait," she said as she looked at the nurse and covered her hand. "I just need thirty seconds." I couldn't tell if the nurse was amused or annoyed, but Rose affected people that way. The nurse shrugged and I trotted to Rose's side. She whispered in my ear. "I almost forgot. I think we should get new secret names for our 60th birthdays. I'll pick a better one for you for the next fifty years."

She squeezed my hand again as the nurse tapped my shoulder to let me know it was time. I gave a little wave right before they turned the corner and she waved back. I took the notebook out and wrote:

Friday, 3/13

Left for surgery - 10:13 AM

Back from surgery -

Chapter 10

A boat sails in fog
past watercolor willows
weeping in silence

Rose's Haiku Diary
St. Augustine, FL
Age 35

The hospital waiting room was full of people, yet I felt totally alone. None of them were my people. I shared a common bond with them, as each of us waited for a loved one to come back, healed or fixed by the hands of strangers in blue scrubs, but each small tribe kept to itself, offered comfort only to one another.

I'd brought a book, but couldn't concentrate and read the same three pages over and over. The waiting room magazines provided scant entertainment, as I didn't care about what trysts the stars were having, the latest fad diets or how yoga saved the life of a twenty-something actress I didn't know. The television, on some all-day news channel, reminded me why I'd never bothered to get cable.

Rose had urged me to tell Hank about the operation and ask him to drive us to the hospital. I nixed the idea. Keeping up the deception while waiting would definitely be a burden, not a comfort. Now, though, a part of me wished he was here so I could put my head on his shoulder, hear his comforting words. I thought of calling him just to hear his voice. I started to dial before I remembered that he wouldn't pick up as he was one of three musicians playing his bagpipes at a military memorial service for an Iraq War veteran.

Not telling him had made sense at the time. Nobody but the staff at Shady Oaks knew Agnes was scheduled for surgery. We told them so they wouldn't wonder why the dutiful daughter stopped visiting. I did ask for phone updates on Mom and they called every few days, while Rose and I navigated the medical maze of tests and appointments interspersed with the infernal waiting.

I told everyone else, even Hank, I needed to spend with my sister. He'd seemed a little hurt, saying, "Only fair to share you with her. But I want..." I'd interrupted him, saying, "I knew you'd understand." Was I afraid he would say, but I want her to give you back?

We were told that the operation would take four to six hours. On all of those hospital television shows, some kindly nurse is always updating the worried relatives in the waiting room about how the surgery is going. I guess Oakvale Memorial General hadn't read that script.

"Go shopping while I'm in surgery. Go to a movie," Rose said. I looked at her with the yeah-right sister-look. "Okay, write me poem. I always loved your poems."

"I haven't written poetry since seventh grade."

I turned to the back of the notebook, and picked up my pen, but my brain felt as if it was wrapped in surgical gauze. I wrote:

For you, I am the earth, the wind, the water, the sun.

I exist so the rose can climb the trellis of life.

Where did that come from? I wondered. Pathetic. Even maudlin and a bit self-serving. Isn't our relationship symbiotic? Rose once told me that we were like a relief map of Devil's Lake State Park. "My life is the bluffs and boulders and canyons and caves. You're more like the beach and lake. We complement each other. I have more highs and lows, you're steady as she goes." Then she started to laugh at her inadvertent rhyme.

Maybe I could do a haiku. Rose kept a diary of only haikus which, at age fifteen, she vowed to write each and every day. Uncle Roger was in his coffee house/beatnik phase when we turned fifteen and he gave us both diaries for our birthdays and copies of a new publication, the 1963 and 1964 journal American Haiku. Somehow, for Rose, the two gifts melded, although I think Uncle Roger was as surprised as I was that she was the one fascinated with haikus.

"Who can't come up with a haiku?" she said. "Five syllables on the first line, seven on the second, then five again. Twenty-four hours to write just seventeen syllables. How hard could that be?"

I wondered if her journal was in her purse. I was tempted to read the most recent haiku, but couldn't betray her trust like that. I stopped writing in my diary three days before I turned sixteen, when she asked me, "Do you really like Dick Griffith?"

I tried to write again.

we are a puzzle

with interlocking pieces

two bodies, one brain.

Rose's cell phone buzzed and I jumped, since signs indicating they should be turned off were everywhere. I knew it wasn't mine since I used the old-fashioned phone ring, so I fumbled in the satchel Rose called her purse, found her cell and turned it off. As soon as I did, I kicked myself for not checking to see who it was. She always kidded me for never checking caller ID on the rare occasions when my cell phone rang, even though I explained that only half a dozen people had the number. Her phone was identical to mine, since it was cheaper to put her on my plan than bail her out periodically when she couldn't pay her cell bill. I actually smiled when I paid that bill, knowing that it kept Rose close to me in some way. After the first month of having her on my account, I knew we needed the unlimited plan.

I thought about calling Uncle Roger. Rose and I had argued whether to tell him before or after the operation.

"He'd want to know," Rose said.

"He'd want to come. And you know Uncle Gus just got out of rehab for his knee replacement."

She finally backed down. Rare for her.

Now I wished he were here. He could always make me smile. How many uncles do you know who insist on eating dessert first? "But don't tell your mother," he always said, "or Weezie will skin me alive." Rose and I loved that he called Mom "Weezie." Such a whimsical name for such a dour woman. He couldn't pronounce her name, Louise, as a little boy, so her nickname became Weezie. Maybe another reason she resented him.

I watched other groups of waiting people come and go, and saw the tension in their faces as they talked, read, played cards, or pretended to watch television. One lucky group had a five-or-six-year-old boy with them and their laughter periodically broke the mood when he made a face or told a joke. A few even napped. What a blessing that would be. I'd hardly slept the previous night and that nasty groggy feeling started to buzz my head. The waiting room population swelled as the hours trudged by. My head started to hurt by two o'clock, as it always did when I skipped lunch.

I repeated my mantra: soon it will get better. I'll stay in the hospital with Rose, play Hearts or 21. She'll get the good cards and win, unless she lets me win. We'll laugh, talk, and I'll get lost in her stories of exotic places and a cast of characters right out of *Star Wars* meets *Breakfast at Tiffany's*. I'll still be the big sister, caring for her as I always did. We'll talk about the upcoming five's-trip to celebrate our birthdays. Just the two of us. No Men or Dogs Allowed, as that sign in the Jersey City park we saw years ago read, the one that caused Rose to laugh so hard she had to grab the chain link fence for support.

Rose wanted to book our 60th birthday trip before the operation. "Buenos Aires or Paris," she said. Then she got a far-off look in her eyes, as if trying to make out a hawk on the horizon. "Or maybe Brisbane."

"Australia?" I asked. "Isn't that close to where Derek..."

She nodded. "I never forgot him. Course he's still thirty and wearing those tight cut-off jeans in my memory. I keep wondering...never mind. Just one of those silly ideas. You know, the ones I tell you and you say, you want to do what?"

"Let's decide when you're fully recovered," I said, wondering if she'd even know where to find him.

I must have finally dozed off, because the waiting room was empty when my brain registered a voice calling a familiar name, a voice that required a response from me.

"Mrs. Grimaldi," a nurse in blue scrubs called. As soon as my soggy mind translated the words, I bolted from asleep to alert.

I raised my hand, like a kid in school. "I'll be right there," I said. While I gathered up our coats, Rose's purse, the notebook, and my fanny pack, the nurse walked over to me. "How is she?" I asked. "When can I see her?"

"Come with me," she said. "The doctor will give you an update."

The nurse brought me to a room where white-coated surgeon Dr. Stein stood by a cozy little setting with two chairs and a couch. I wondered why a stethoscope hung around his neck. It was after 6:00 in the evening. Surely, he was done for the day. He didn't need the stethoscope to know my heart was racing. He motioned me to sit.

"I'm sorry to say there have been some complications," he said.

There can't be complications, I thought. This is Rose. Rose never has complications. Rose causes complications.

Part of my brain registered the next words he said, but they mostly bounced off and reverberated around the room. I tried to concentrate, but it didn't seem to help.

"Didn't go as well…bleeding…stroke…didn't expect…trouble weaning off… …intubate…clinically sedated and paralyzed…respirator…life support…like an induced coma…."

That word shook me out of my stupor. "Coma?" I repeated. "But you said the success rate was good, was ninety-five percent."

He nodded, no doubt thinking, somebody has to be part of the five percent. "The next twenty-four to forty-eight hours are critical. There's still a chance she'll pull out of it, but we have some concern …"

"A chance? How big of a chance?"

"If things don't improve in the next day, you may want to contact friends or relatives who would want to see her."

Chapter 11

man, I am dog-tired
want to sleep a hundred years
wake to Prince Charming

Rose's Haiku Diary
Bandipur, Nepal
Age 21

"If I talk to her, will she hear me?" I asked the nurse. I held Rose's hand, thinking how chagrinned she'd be to be here with gray hair and no makeup or fingernail polish.

The nurse gave me one of those smiles I think they must practice in the mirror.

"Each case is different. Some patients wake up and remember everything and some don't."

And some don't wake up, I thought.

"We always say to assume they can hear you."

If there was ever a time for secret names, this was it.

"Well, Sapphire," I said, "That's another fine mess you've gotten me into," trying my best to sound like her imitation of Ollie Hardy talking to Stan Laurel. It was supposed to be funny, but the words thudded. "I guess you know this is the part where I say, 'Wake up' and you do. Then you tell me about the fabulous dream you were having. Why is it you always remember your dreams when I don't? You're probably dreaming of being a secret agent in a slinky black dress playing Blackjack in Monaco with 007."

I fluffed her pillow a bit, and tried to tune out the rhythmic, mechanical rasps of the machine that kept her breathing.

"It's time to wake up. I don't care if you roll your eyes and scold me. Go ahead, ask me, 'Why couldn't you have waited five minutes—the double agent was about to confess.'

You'll have plenty of time for dreaming while you're recuperating. I'll even get premium cable and we'll watch whatever you want. The soaps, chic flicks, reality shows, those dancing shows. You pick.

You still owe me two questions, you know. Of course, you know that. And with all the time you've had to work on them, I can't wait to hear what you've cooked up. I'll never forget when you asked me if Danny Weatherspoon would water-ski naked."

I told her about the weather and the upcoming book sale at the library. I offered to read to her from the autobiography of Benjamin Franklin I'd brought and could almost hear her saying, "I don't like my men fat, bald, old and dead," like when I recommended a book about Khrushchev. I described my spring plantings, including a climbing rosebush I ordered last fall to plant in June called "Stairway to Heaven"—Rose and I both loved that song. I started to sing it to her but my throat closed and the words wouldn't come out, so I hummed instead.

My gaze returned to Rose. I wanted to comb her gray hair, but just brushed a stray strand from her eyes. I pondered finding the makeup kit from her purse.

"Would you like that, Sapphire?" I asked. Of course, besides being against hospital rules, it would have been almost impossible with that breathing apparatus in her mouth and those tubes and wires everywhere. Rose always claimed makeup possessed magical powers, especially eye shadow. If I applied some, would she open her eyes?

I searched for the words I would say when I called Uncle Roger. Isn't it strange that words take on a new level of meaning in a hospital? A positive test is bad and a negative one is good. And while the word malignant always has a nasty tone to it, benign is normally one of those boring words. Then there is the word "complications" meaning snags, glitches, hitches. Potholes in the road of life. But in a hospital, the word "complications" is a wrecking ball.

I gave my brain a mental shake. Why had I obsessed like that? To postpone my call to Uncle Roger?

Chapter 12

need happy endings
why can't life be like TV
white hats always win

Rose's Haiku Diary
Kent State, OH
Age 20

I begged for some crumb of hope, but got only rancid ashes that early Sunday afternoon when the doctor told me they saw no brain activity and no indication of a recovery being possible.

"It does happen," I said. "Right?"

"Almost never. The respirator is all that's keeping her alive."

"It's not impossible, though?"

"No, it's not impossible."

Even though this fear was my constant companion since the news of the complications on Friday, I'd ignored it, denied it. Now the same drenching nausea washed over me, punctuated by a knot in my stomach so hard it was as if I were being impaled on a spike.

"I said on Friday that we might reach the point where you should contact close relatives and friends. I'm afraid we're there. I don't expect any change in the next couple of days, although there has been some arrhythmia. You should go home, get some sleep, make those calls. Come back tomorrow morning. You know she signed a DNR when she was admitted, yes?"

Even though I signed an advanced directive and living will five years ago, this news jarred me. Why hadn't she told me?

I hadn't thought about my filling out those end-of-life forms for a long time. When I signed my name, it all seemed so hypothetical and so easy. Of course, I wouldn't want to live as a vegetable—none of that hooked to a machine, just existing, not living. Do Not Resuscitate. I even called Rose to tell her.

"I don't want to talk about this stuff," she said. "It's scary. Don't tempt fate."

"I'm not," I told her. "I'm being responsible. I'm giving you my Medical Power of Attorney. You need to know what I want."

"But how can you know what you want before it happens?"

I went on to tell her that I wanted to be cremated after any organs that could be used were taken.

"I'm with you there," she said. "If I'm not using my body, somebody else should." I heard her stifle a laugh. "I didn't mean that the way it sounded, no donations to necrophiliacs, please." I started to laugh.

I reluctantly took Dr. Stein's advice and agreed to drive home. The doctor promised to call me at home on Rose's cell if there were any changes. My plan was to shower, change clothes, call Uncle Roger and then sleep. My body longed for the comfort of its own bed as I had only slept fitfully at the hospital in that visitor's chair for the past two nights.

Uncle Roger is going to be mad, I thought. He's going to ask why I didn't tell him. How could I say, "Because I never thought anything could possibly go wrong? I thought I'd be calling you to tell you Agnes had an operation, but she's fine."

I worried if I'd have the strength to not confess that it was Rose in the coma and I worried that he'd somehow know, even if I didn't tell him. That he'd hear it in my voice.

Before starting my car, I turned on Rose's cell phone and put it on the seat next to me in case the doctor called. I'd parked on Level 4A and it seemed as if every fifth car wanted to back up and join the caravan. I let them all in, causing the SUV behind me to lean on his horn every time I slowed down after the first two. By the time I reached the exit, my fingers were choking the steering wheel.

I was second in line for the payment booth, when the Hummer in front of me started to back up. I jabbed the horn and slammed on my brakes so hard that Rose's cell phone clattered to the floor of the passenger seat.

"Why did I let you in?" I yelled. The behemoth did stop, then pulled up, paid and jackrabbited away. As I approached the booth, the cell phone rang. My heart raced—why was the doctor was calling so soon? Was something wrong?

The attendant gave me one of those annoyed, hurry-it-up looks. I handed her the ticket and a fifty-dollar bill with my left hand and leaned over to grab the phone, but my seatbelt wouldn't let me reach it. I sat up, took my change and receipt, unfastened my seatbelt, leaned over, groped the floor, grabbed the cell phone and flipped it open. I tried to wedge the phone between my shoulder and my ear, but it fell into my lap.

The driver behind honked repeatedly again.

I fumbled for the phone, eased off my brakes so I rolled forward, and put the phone to my ear.

I'd never heard the deep male voice on the other end before. "Did you hear me?" he said. "Stay out of my business, bitch."

"Who is this?" I shouted into the phone, but the caller had hung up.

Chapter 13

can't wait to get home
Dire Straits on the stereo
hot bath, glass of Zin

Rose's Haiku Diary
Searsport, ME
Age 33

How I made the half-hour drive home, I'll never know. My whole body started to shake after I pulled into my garage. As I sat there, I couldn't remember anything after leaving the parking garage. I clutched the steering wheel, then rested my forehead on it, waiting for the drumbeat of my heart to fade.

I sat there so long, the garage's interior light turned off, shaking me from my daze. I hit the button to close the door and pulled myself out of the car. My whole body ached from the tension of the past three days, as if I'd been run over by a bus. Could it have been only three days? It seemed like it was weeks ago Rose and I were heading to the hospital, full of hope. I traipsed from the garage to my mudroom, where I shed my boots and coat. A fog of exhaustion smothered me as I stumbled through the kitchen to the living room. Just twenty minutes, I told myself as I sprawled on the sofa, since the climb upstairs to my bed seemed more daunting than summiting Kilimanjaro. Come on, Rose, I thought just before I fell into a deep sleep. Come back to me.

When I woke, it was dark. The comforts of home—the feel of my sofa's plush fabric on my face, the lingering smell of wood smoke from Thursday night's fire, the ticking of my grandfather clock—disappeared when the words *stay out of my business, bitch* sprang back into my mind. My heart started to race again and I reached to turn on a light, the darkness no longer soothing. Had I locked the doors? I scurried to check them, and all were secure, although Rose's chiding about how unsafe it was to have glass panels in all my doors caused an involuntary shudder.

Who is this man, Rose? Why is he threatening you? Why won't you wake up?

An odd paralysis came over me. Me, the woman who always knew what to do next. I walked into the kitchen, but the same numb disdain for food that enveloped me in the hospital cafeteria reappeared. Then a thought clicked. A wrong number. It must have been a wrong number.

I gobbled down a bowl of bran cereal with almonds and dried cranberries, poured myself a glass of Riesling, then managed to fulfill my promise to post updates to Rose's blog and wrote:

There have been complications.

I couldn't even tell this group of now over 700 readers that 'Agnes' was in a coma. It would make it more tangible to write those words, hit the Post button and send them into cyberspace.

Wineglass in one hand, bottle in the other, I climbed the stairs. As I took off my peacock jacket, I noticed a bit of that odd clinical smell, Parfum de hospital, Rose called it. I sprayed the jacket with lavender before hanging it, then stripped off the rest of my clothes and dropped them on the floor—something I never do. I was about to climb into the shower, when the famous scene from *Psycho* decided to make an appearance—a remnant perhaps of the bizarre call that still rattled around in my brain. Realizing it was foolish, I wedged my reading chair against the bedroom door. Then I locked the bathroom door before indulging in a long, hot shower. I lathered up with the shampoo that smelled of raspberries that Rose had brought.

When I left the bathroom, wrapped in a fluffy, white terrycloth robe, I felt foolish for having barricaded my bedroom. No Norman Bates here, I told myself as I slid the chair back to its proper place.

I poured a second glass of wine and put the half-full bottle on the end table next to my favorite bedroom reading chair.

I searched for a single sentence to break the devastating news to the man who was always there for me, for Rose and me.

Uncle Roger was thirteen when Rose and I were born. He was a big brother to us when we were little and morphed into the glamorous uncle off in Greenwich village, digging the music at the Village Gate, playing his bongos in Washington Square Park, or penning poetry in the Bleecker Street coffee houses. Ever since I could remember, when Mom went to work at the beauty parlor weekends or the grocery store during the week, she dropped us off with her father, Grandpa Luke, who usually handed us off to Uncle Roger. Uncle Roger played Barbie dolls with Rose and Monopoly with me. He even taught us to play poker. Rose used to drive him crazy when she drew into an inside straight and seemed to always get just the card she needed. He chided us that we each had tells, things we did when we were bluffing, but he refused to share them with us.

Enough stalling, I told myself.

As Uncle Roger's phone rang, part of me hoped I'd get his voicemail, although that would only be postponing the inevitable. I was too polite to leave a message telling him his niece Agnes was in a coma and the prognosis was grim.

He must have seen it was my number, as he answered the phone, "Hi, Aggie-bear."

"Hi, Uncle Roger," I said, cursing myself for not using Rose's phone. I was already fighting back tears. "It's Rose. I'm calling from Agnes's phone." My voice started to crack.

"What? Is Agnes all right?"

"No," I choked on the words. "No, she's not. She's in a sort of induced coma, Uncle Roger." I heard him gasp and his partner Gus whisper in the background, asking what was wrong. I started to sob and he talked to me as he did when I was seven and broke my arm after riding my bicycle into traffic because I'd turned to tell Rose to be careful. His soothing voice brought me back from the brink. Eventually I relayed the details of the quick hospitalization and the complications that put Rose in a coma so severe that the chances of recovery were miniscule.

"Agnes thought it best to call you after the operation. She didn't want to worry you."

"Oh, Rose, Rose, Rose," he said, his voice unsteady. "What can I do to help?"

"Nothing," I said. "I'm fine. I'll call you when I know more."

"I'll be there as soon as I can," he said.

"No, you don't have to. The airfare's so expensive and Uncle Gus needs you." Even as I argued with him not to make the trip from their remote Arizona cabin, I knew he'd come. He always did.

"I'll be there as soon as I can, Rosie Posey. I'll call you when I get my flight information. I'll rent a car or take a taxi from the airport. It'll just be me. I don't think Gus is well enough to fly."

"I'm fine, Uncle Roger. Really, you don't need to."

"You know I do. Good night, punkin."

Chapter 14

staring at the phone
if I promise to be good
will you send good news

Rose's Haiku Diary
Rio Rancho, NM
Age 56

Rose would have liked the idea that getting an update on her condition required a password—very 007—and that I chose the word turkey, a variation on my secret name, something I was sure my muddled brain would remember.

I called for an update and Marianne, the night nurse, told me Rose's condition was unchanged. So, I laid out clothes for the morning—jeans, T-shirt, flannel shirt, underwear, warm socks—and packed a change of clothes, toiletries and my vitamins in a duffel bag, along with a couple bags of trail mix, some protein bars and a handful of books and magazines. Then I remembered that Uncle Roger was coming and I wasn't sure when, so I replaced my clothes, toiletries and books with Rose's. I re-corked the wine, astounded to find only an inch left, put it in the refrigerator and set my alarm for 7:00 AM.

March 15th. Beware the Ides of March. I'll be glad when this day is over.

I climbed under my flannel sheets and fell into the sleep of the dead. No dreams. No restlessness. As if I had joined Rose in her induced coma.

When a strident ringing penetrated my deep sleep, it took me a moment to recognize it as Rose's cell phone and not my alarm clock.

Answering it, I wasn't sure if I was more frightened that it would be the hospital or another call from the threatening male voice. Then I heard, "This is Marianne. We need you back at the hospital right away."

"What happened?"

"The doctor wants to talk to you in person." Oh, no, I thought. It's never good if they can't tell you on the phone.

"I can be there in thirty, maybe forty minutes." I donned the clothes I laid out, grabbed the duffel bag and was in my car in less than five minutes.

I was five minutes from Oakvale General when the wail of a siren hit my ears. I looked in my rear-view mirror, hit my brakes, and pulled to the curb, waiting for the police car to speed past me. Instead it pulled up behind me.

Son of a badger, I thought. Don't let me get hauled in on a DUI. I rolled down my window and did my best to look like a calm, rational, sober citizen—all things I was not feeling. Why had I poured that third glass of wine?

"Do you know how fast you were going, Ma'am?"

"I'm not sure. Thirty? I need to get to the hospital. My sister is..." I choked. I couldn't say the word dying.

"You were doing over forty," he said. "Driver's license please." I looked at the seat next to me and saw my fanny pack and overnight bag, but not Rose's purse. Rose's purse with her driver's license in it. Should I show him mine and hope I get off with a warning? But what if I get a ticket? A ticket as Agnes? Or worse, what if I flunk the sobriety test and get carted off to jail?

I rummaged through my purse and pulled out my cell phone. "Please, call the hospital. They're waiting for me. It's important. I'll dial the number."

"Have you consumed any alcohol or drugs tonight?" Should I lie? It seemed like so long ago. Those glasses of wine couldn't still be in my system, could they? Is it worse if you lie and they test you and find out you lied? Lies seem to breed like cockroaches. First there's one, pretty soon, you're infested.

"Officer, I'm sorry I was speeding. I know I look a mess. My sister is... my sister is in the hospital, in a coma." His eyes seemed to bore into my head.

He pointed at the printout I'd taped to the dashboard.

"Those the directions?"

I nodded. He held out his hand and I handed them to him. He studied them, then me. "I'm going to let you off with a warning, but you need to concentrate on your driving."

Relief flooded me. "I will, officer. Thank you."

"Driving under stress, driving distracted, can be as dangerous as driving drunk. Don't want you to join your sister in the hospital." He turned and walked back to his squad car.

I drove the last few miles going exactly twenty-five miles per hour. I reached the hulking parking garage and it gobbled me up. I found a parking spot on the second level, grabbed my fanny pack, and decided to leave the duffel bag in the car. It would only slow me down. I rushed down one corridor and up another, waited for the elevator for what seemed like days. As I raced past the nurse's station, toward Rose's room, an unfamiliar woman in one of those green patterned outfits nurses wear these days called, "No visiting now."

I stopped and turned. "I'm Agnes, I mean I'm here to see Agnes Blumfield. I'm her sister Rose Grimaldi." I started toward Rose's room again.

"Wait here," the nurse called. "She's not in her room. I'll call the doctor."

I stopped and returned to the desk. Because of the late hour, the normal din of clangs, dings and announcements did not assault my ears, which made the clicks and clanks, the sighs and muffled conversations louder. Almost like a Greek chorus. I squinted, as the light seemed brighter, harsher than in the daytime. My fingers started tingling, and I shook them to make the feeling disappear.

Why is it so hot, I wondered, as I struggled to take off my jacket. What is taking the doctor so long? Has that clock stopped? It can't be only three minutes.

Why don't I feel your presence, Rose? I always did, even when you were half a continent away. I always felt that I could go out and look at the stars and talk to you and you'd hear me. Why can't I hear you now?

The doctor finally appeared, looking as somber and tired as I felt, and we again went to one of those little rooms.

"Your sister went into cardiac arrest ten minutes ago. I'm sorry. I thought she'd have more time."

I did too.

Chapter 15

the howl of a wolf
how can it sound so lonely
if wolves mate for life?

Rose's Haiku Diary
Sturgis, SD
Age 59

It was like walking up to a mirror and finding your reflection no longer there. When I got home from the hospital, the pronouncement that Rose was gone was still something my brain had not accepted. I collapsed on the sofa. Rose gone? It couldn't be true. I felt her presence even when she was hundreds or thousands of miles away. But that feeling was gone now. She was gone. My brain felt like sludge. My body ached. I was exhausted, but wide awake.

I replayed the events of the past month over and over. What could I have done differently? Another surgeon? Hospital? What if I hadn't insisted we continue researching options, trying to find another answer, for those futile days?

Was it just stubborn self-delusion that I never contemplated the scenario I now faced? I always assumed we'd carry or bury the dirty little secret, each in our own way, when we traded back our lives. Probably never speak of it. Maybe even start to believe the false memory.

The next few days would change the path of my life, but even deciding if I had the strength to walk up the stairs to brush my teeth befuddled me.

I knew I needed to confess, but my throat constricted when I tried to imagine saying the words. I felt my soul melt as I tried to picture the consequences.

Financial ruin.

Reimburse the hospital, the insurance company, pay for lawyers, pay the fines. Where would I live? How would I live?

Public shame.

How could I ever face Hank, Luther, or my friends at the library again? I'd be front page of the Sewickley Herald. Clara Clarke would be in backbiting, gossipmonger heaven.

Private shame. The pain of telling Uncle Roger, of knowing the toll it would take on him and Uncle Gus. They'd try to help. They'd want to help. They had no money to help.

Jail.

Living in a dirty little box, with bad food, no sunshine, vermin, no privacy, tough women and rougher guards.

Mom.

No money to take care of her. No ability to be her advocate if I was in a jail cell. After all the years of caring for her, her last years would be tainted by betrayal and abandonment.

"Stay me," Rose said. "Stay me and all that goes away."

Chapter 16

too tired to think, walk
I forget, feet remember
the way to my cot

Rose's Haiku Diary
Bandipur, Nepal
Age 21

Rose would have been mad that she died the day before St. Patrick's Day. She always loved a good party. Had she been alive, she would have insisted we go out for green beer. "After all," she would have said, "we are half Irish."

And I would have answered, as I always did, "I think you got the Irish half." Then she would have thrown her head back and laughed. She could laugh so easily, tears running down her face—even at something as small as a bad pun or a shared memory that tickled her fancy.

How was it possible I'd never hear her laugh again? How will I get through life without that?

Uncle Roger used to tell us that if something seemed so overwhelming that we didn't know where to start, break it into pieces, then do a big piece and a little piece every day.

I called the funeral home, thinking that was the big piece, but of course it wasn't, as I'd already planned and paid for all the details of my exit from this earth. All we had to do was find a date that worked for them and me for the simple service. Uncle Roger hadn't been able to get a flight that didn't break the bank until Saturday, so I chose the following Tuesday, so he wouldn't think he had to change it to get here sooner.

My cremated remains would need no cemetery, as I asked Rose to take my ashes to the Fern Hollow Nature Center. There, where Hank and I had spent so many hours hiking the trails that we knew each of them like an old friend, they would drift back to nature among the maples and pines, the deer, sparrows, skunks, and raccoons. Let them nourish the earth after any useful organs were harvested.

Organ donation was one area where Rose and I were truly identical. The hospital dealt with the organ donor paperwork, but I asked the coordinator to tell me where each donation would go—not names but enough to hold on to. Rose gave her eyes for corneal transplants to a sixteen-year-old. Lucky girl, to see the world through Rose's eyes.

I was all set to cross call funeral home off my list, when the nameless woman there added, "Tuesday, the 24th, that's a good date—it will give the newspaper time to publish the death notice."

I had to write my own death notice? Of course, I did. Why had that thought not occurred to me? At first, it seemed like another small task, but I struggled with it and, in the end, could not bring myself to wax eloquent writing my own obituary. So, I went with the basics.

Agnes G. Blumfield, 59, survived by her mother Louise Blumfield (Sewickley, PA), sister Rose Grimaldi (Cleveland, OH), and uncle Roger Woodson (Snowflake, AZ). Memorial Service is Tuesday, March 24, 2:00 p.m. at Edgeworth Funeral Home, Sewickley. In lieu of flowers, the family requests donations be made to the Fern Hollow Nature Center.

I spent the rest of the day calling the nursing home, friends, former coworkers and volunteers at the library where I, where Agnes, spent weekday mornings, to tell them the sad news. It was an odd and surreal experience, even though I wasn't close to most of them. It just seemed that they needed to know.

I still hadn't told Mom and wondered if she should come to the service. Chances are she wouldn't know what was going on. But maybe that was for the best.

I dreaded my call to Luther, the blind man I read to on Thursday afternoons. We were still close even though, three years ago, his daughter moved him three hundred miles to live with her in Princeton. It was almost harder than my call to Uncle Roger. I heard the pain in his voice. It boomeranged back at me as it hit me that I'd never again pick up the phone and hear him ask: you feel like a blind date?

I knew I should tell Hank in person, but couldn't find the courage to look in his eyes and lie.

"Hi, Hank," I said when he answered. "It's Rose Grimaldi, Agnes's sister. I'm afraid I'm calling with some bad news." The lump in my throat went from acorn-size to walnut and I wondered if I could even get the next words out.

"What is it? Is she okay?"

I'd said the next words so many times today, they should not have lodged in my throat. It was a speech. I should have been able to repeat the words again. But I pictured his worried face and tears came to my eyes. Tears for myself? For the blossoming romance that Hank and I had just started to explore that was now doomed? Tears for Rose, my rock, my best friend? Tears for life, which as we all learned as children, is not fair?

"My sister's heart condition was more serious than we......"

"Her heart?"

"She needed an operation."

"Is she okay? Is she in the hospital?"

"She didn't make it."

"What? She's gone? I didn't even know she was sick. Why didn't she tell me?" His voice cracked and a sound like the cry of a wounded animal came from the phone. Part of me wanted to be there so badly, to put my arms around him. As I struggled to find words of comfort, I instinctively grabbed my house keys and started toward the door, to run to his house. I stopped and dropped my keys when he spoke again.

"Thank you for calling me," he said, his voice oddly formal, breathing jagged.

"Her memorial is at the Edgeworth Funeral Home. Tuesday at 2:00 PM."

"I'll see you there. If you need a ride, or anything, let me know. Any help, anything, let me know." Then he hung up without saying goodbye.

Again, I fought the urge to go to him. I stumbled to my kitchen and stared at his house. "I'm sorry," I said, tears gathering in my eyes.

I sank into my birdwatching chair, the day's events hitting me like a truck. I ached to collapse on my sofa and let the exhaustion of the day plunge me into sleep. But I couldn't let myself do that. Not yet. I had to do one last thing for the day. I needed to fulfill my promise to keep Rose's blog readers informed. I must have stared out the window for half an hour trying to find the right words, only to give up. My second blog post read: My sister did not make it. I am alone.

Chapter 17

his: Harvard hotshot
my lawyer's name was Bubba
what chance did I have

Rose's Haiku Diary
White Swan, OR
Age 43

Fortunately, I was in command of my faculties when I met with Lionel Bankerville to discuss my Will. His office was just as immaculate and impersonal as I remembered. I called him late in the day on Monday, the day after Rose died, the day I realized my only viable option was to take on my sister's life. I expected an appointment in weeks. Instead, his assistant told me to come in Wednesday.

As I started to sit, I thanked him for finding the time to see me so soon.

"Always important to get things moving quickly," he said, motioning for me to sit. "As you may know, since you knew to call me, your sister made me the executor of her estate."

Yes, I did do that. I thought it made sense at the time, four years ago. Rose was living in New Mexico, calling or emailing me four or five times a week. Mostly we talked about her living with Luis in his house with the pool, their dinners out, horseback riding, and hot air ballooning. She confided that she expected a marriage proposal soon.

"She felt it would be geographically difficult for you to be named."

What? I never said that. In fact, I think I said something like, "I love her, but she's a free spirit. And I need to ensure my mother—our mother—is taken care of."

"I'm not sure how much she told you about her Will," he continued, "but she left almost everything in Trust. The main purpose of the Trust is to pay the expenses at Shady Oaks, the facility where your mother resides."

"I understand," I said.

He let a smile slip across his lips. He must be used to giving out bad news—boy, what a lousy job that must be. "She did leave you $500 either in cash or toward items in her home, some jewelry and a jacket."

"I know the jacket," I said. "It has sentimental value."

He handed me a list of the jewelry: a string of pearls, a pendant and a man's watch.

"I should mention that our firm gets a modest fee as executor and for administering the Trust."

Modest fee. That hadn't bothered me at the time. Of course, that was four years ago.

"Her estate was modest. We'll sell the house..." Sell my house? "...and her belongings in an estate sale. The proceeds from that, her other investments and her residual annuity—she elected a form of payment that guarantees 120 monthly payments—will fund the Trust."

Boy, I'll never look at the word trust the same way again. Or modest.

"What if something doesn't sell?" I asked.

"We'll dispose of it or give it to charity."

My stuff. All my stuff. Sold, junked or given to charity. "Could I have it?"

He shook his head. "I'm afraid that would complicate the bookkeeping." He shuffled the papers. "She did leave you the family photos and any books you might want and said that if there was anything of a modest monetary value—something you might want for sentimental reasons—you should have it. We agreed to define that as items valued under $200, to a total of no more than $500. We have a bit of latitude, but not much."

"I see."

"She left this to deliver to you." He handed me a thin white envelope and looked at me expectantly, as if I should open it then and there.

I fingered it, trying to remember what I penned four years ago, then folded it and put it in my purse.

"Now this part is a bit awkward," he said as he rubbed the side of his face. "You mentioned that you were staying at your sister's house..."

"So, I could take care of her during her recuperation after the operation," I said.

"I'll need to have Miss Knight, my assistant, accompany you back to the house so you can collect your possessions and then she'll take the keys."

What? What did he say?

He folded his fingers together in a small tent. "You see," he continued, "the settlement of estates often brings out the mercenary side of people. Many people. Some people." He spoke these words as if he'd memorized them. "I would not be fulfilling my responsibility to your sister, to Agnes, if I assumed that you would respect her wishes and not remove anything from the house that she did not intend you to have. Yes, it is sad that we must take these precautions, but I am afraid we must."

"Oh, my," I said. I felt like tears should flow—not really sure if they would be for Rose or the death of my well-planned future—but they refused to come. Probably for the best, I didn't want to cry in front of this man in his steel gray suit with his dead fish eyes.

"There is a provision," he added, a little too cheerfully, I thought, "that if your mother dies and there are any residual funds left, they will be divided between you and the Fern Hollow Nature Center, eighty percent to you, twenty to it."

Well, that's kind of weird. Why did I do that? I do love its trails and wildflowers, and the sense of peace I get there. I guess I wanted to express my gratitude for all the wonderful hours. And Rose seemed in a good place financially when I signed this Will. I should have known Rose only visited good financial places, never took up permanent residence. If she won a ten-million-dollar lottery, she'd contact her friend Chris and find out who needed a helping hand and spend it all in a year. Except, unlike those broke, unhappy former lottery millionaires you always hear about, she'd have no regrets. She would splurge and travel and buy expensive clothes and gifts for anyone and everyone, but also hand out money to every man, woman or child—con artist or not—with a convincing hard luck story. Would she have listened to me and at least checked to see if they really needed the money? Not a chance. "Easy come, easy go," was her motto. "Something will always come up." And for her, something always did. Or more often, someone did. Usually a man. But only once the right man. And never for very long. Even the one time it should have lasted.

"She did stipulate that we provide you with quarterly statements. Is this Sagebrush Lane address current?"

"No, that was over two years ago. I, uh, just moved to Cleveland. I was in Sturgis before Cleveland and Arizona with my uncles and Las Vegas with friends for a while before that and then..." I tried to remember all the places Rose lived since leaving Rio Rancho after her divorce, when she started one of her nomadic phases. I looked up. Mr. Bankerville was checking his watch again and I realized he didn't really care.

Chapter 18

he called room service
croissants, champagne, strawberries
could learn to love this

Rose's Haiku Diary
Paris
Age 39

Miss Knight, who drove behind me back to my house, Agnes's house, appeared to be a female version of Mr. Bankerville. Even her thick black glasses looked like his. For a moment, I wondered if they were twins. Her sturdy frame, hair pulled back in a tight bun and pressed navy-blue suit gave the impression of a guard in a women's prison. But I guess you don't send a cocker spaniel to do a pit bull's job, like taking the house away from the twin sister of a woman who just died. She didn't make chit-chat as we walked to the parking lot, just verified my address and programmed it into her GPS. Rose would have made up a name for her. She would have assumed a German accent and said something like, "I am Frau Helga VonSauerbraten. You vill take me to zee house."

A marble-sized lump formed in my throat as our cars pulled into the driveway of my lovely little cottage surrounded by the redbud trees I planted after I bought it. Once inside, Frau Helga watched, arms crossed, as I packed the clothes Rose brought into her two suitcases. I went to my closet and retrieved the peacock jacket, then to my jewelry box for the pearls Rose gave me when I got my CPA, the pendant and man's watch. I emptied a cardboard box that previously held a bushel of fancy red grapefruit I ordered and put the family photo albums in it.

"I'd like to come back tomorrow," I told Frau Helga. She gave me a pained look, as if her Spanx was one size too small. "The Will said I could have keepsakes, and I'd like to spend a little time here, but I need to pull my thoughts together."

She sighed and then nodded, making me wonder if most people just whimpered and left. We agreed to meet again the next day at four in the afternoon. I would have two hours. I signed a receipt for the jacket and jewelry and she asked for the house keys. I handed them over, only to have her ask if this was the only set. I wondered what Rose would have done. Probably crushed this woman like a June bug. That gave me the strength to commit the lie of omission and not to tell the Frau about the extra set of keys hidden in the ceramic frog next to the garage. That's what Rose would have done.

"There's a nice Marriott near the airport off I376," the Frau said, surprising me by this tiny act of kindness.

I nodded. I knew where it was. I treated myself to brunch there once a month. Me, my Bloody Mary and the Sunday New York Times and Pittsburgh Post-Gazette, away from the prying small-town eyes of Sewickley.

"It's only about a fifteen-minute drive," she said as she shoved her boxy hand at me. I shook it and we said our good-byes. When her PT Cruiser was out of sight, I unlocked Rose's aging Isuzu Gemini and sat inside, my hands locked around the steering wheel. My head seemed packed in cotton batting. I thought about going back in my house and taking what I wanted, but my dread of being discovered there by Frau Helga overwhelmed me. "Aha!" she would say. "We were right. You can never trust the relatives." I thought of the $500 I'd hidden in the secret compartment under my workbench in the garage in the red plaid Thermos I'd inherited from Grandpa Luke. But the thought of retrieving it felt too risky. I was sure Clara was watching as she had a prime view of the side door to my garage and her radar was always on high alert for any vehicle she didn't recognize.

The drive to the Marriott took me past the liquor store I stopped at the first Tuesday of every month. Although I never considered myself a big drinker, this day seemed worthy of a stop. Inside, I recognized the clerk, Olive, a woman my age who I bantered with from time to time. We traded book titles, gardening tips, and hiking tales. I liked her right away, as the first time she looked at my MasterCard she said, "Agnes Blumfield, sounds like a sleuth."

Today, her eyes widened and I panicked. To have pulled off this charade, convinced the doctors and my lawyer, only to be exposed by Olive, the Stop 'n Sip Liquor Store clerk, seemed somehow unfair. My dyed and curled honey blonde hair felt like a clumsy disguise, as if I put on one of those pairs of black glasses with a nose and mustache attached.

"Miss Blumfield?" the clerk asked, her voice shaky. "I thought I read in this morning's paper, in the obituaries..."

I covered my face with my hands. Breathe, I told myself. Just breathe. In, out. In, out. Did she not see my blonde curls? I willed my hands down and rested them on the counter.

"I'm her sister," I said. "Her twin sister." The woman looked mortified and I felt oddly sorry for her, this almost-stranger who had read my scanty obituary. This stranger, this clerk, knew I died and some little part of her cared. That nice woman, she probably thought. We used to joke about the names of the wines she bought. She always liked Conundrum and Cardinal Zin.

"You couldn't have known," I said.

"I'm so sorry," she said. "I felt like I just saw a ghost." She winced. I could almost hear her thinking, what a stupid thing to say. And it was. But now every time I looked in the mirror, I saw that ghost, too.

I started toward the wine aisle, but stopped myself. "Bourbon?" I asked and Olive pointed toward the back. Rose was a Maker's Mark girl, sometimes with a splash of Grand Marnier. I picked up a fifth of bourbon, but decided to skip the Grand Marnier due to the price and my new economic circumstances. At the counter I couldn't bring myself to use one of Rose's credit cards—was I worried that Olive would learn Rose's name—and was grateful that Rose's wallet held almost $150.

Olive offered me her condolences. I thanked her, left the store, put my purchase in the trunk, got in the car and started to shake. After a few minutes, some primal need to find shelter took over and I managed to drive to the Marriott.

After I checked in and wheeled everything upstairs, I stood in the center of the room, my numb brain trying to figure out what to do next. It felt like being a dragonfly suspended in amber. After going on instinct for days, suddenly there was no logical next step. Then all my walled-off emotions punched me.

"No," I wailed. "No, no, no."

I staggered to the bed and let the sobs shake my body until there were no tears left. I pummeled the pillows like a child having a tantrum.

Then I poured two inches of bourbon into the hotel tumbler, not bothering to get ice and took a deep drink, waiting to swallow, hoping it would numb me. I overturned one of Rose's suitcases on the bed and stroked her clothes again and again. Some silky, some nubby, some soft as a kitten's cheek. She wore that pink flamingo sweater that smelled of vanilla at lunch the day she arrived. She insisted I wear that banana-yellow jacket the day we ran into Hank at Safran's. She wanted to wear that turquoise blouse to the hospital. Instead, I wore it.

I grabbed Rose's purse and retrieved the envelope Bankerville gave me containing my letter to Rose. Should I tear it into pieces? Or maybe light a match and watch the paper and words shrivel into ashes? Was it right to read something meant for Rose's eyes only, even if I wrote it? I took another swig of bourbon, pulled the letter from the envelope and started to read it.

Dear Rose, my Sapphire sister –

How weird to write you, the one person I love even more than breathing. It is strange to write this and hope you never read it. I hope I got to say goodbye and this is just another keepsake to remind you of my love.

You have to be strong now, be there for Mom, Uncle Roger and Uncle Gus. Especially Mom. Uncle Roger and Uncle Gus have each other, although you know what a softie Uncle Roger is, and losing one of his girls is going to hit him hard. Remember how he used to kid us and say, just do this one thing for me—live to one hundred and one and live well. And then he'd laugh and say, all right two things—that and eat dessert first.

Mom doesn't have anyone here, unless you count the ghosts that haunt her Alzheimer's world. Don't worry. I know caretaking is not your strong suit and I've found a good nursing home and an attorney to take care of the day-to-day decisions of her care. Please visit her. I know you haven't been on the best terms recently, but I think my visits help bring her back to the present.

This next part is hard, since I've always thought I'd be there when you needed me. I love being the big sister, your big sister, even though I'm only twenty-two minutes older. Being your twin is the best part of my life. I hope you'll forgive me for the times I seemed frustrated or angry when you were in trouble. I only wanted you to be happy. Maybe that's why I got so mad at the downturns of your life—the men who didn't treat you the way you deserved, the dead-end jobs you took, the friends who took advantage. I wanted everything to be perfect for you.

I guess I'm rambling now, maybe trying to avoid telling you that I had to leave most of my assets in Trust to take care of Mom. Her care is so expensive and her savings were gone after six months.

I wasn't sure if you'd want Dad's watch. (Isn't it weird he didn't take it with him?) I found it when I was helping Mom spring clean her house when her mind was just starting to free fall. It was in that penguin cookie jar we gave her for Mother's Day. What were we—maybe ten? She told me to throw the watch away. I told her I would but I kept it. I couldn't throw it away. I hope you'll feel the same about this little piece of him. There was a photo too – the only one I've ever seen of him – with the two of us. I'm guessing it was right before he left us – we look so little and he looks so happy. It's in my jewelry box next to the watch.

As I write this, you tell me your life is good. As you read this, I hope you're still in that good spot. Think of me when you wear the wonderful jacket you gave me, the one I call my peacock jacket. It will show off your blue eyes, too. I always thought we'd live together one day as little old ladies. As Uncle Roger says, it's up to you to eat dessert first. Have a wonderful life. I'm so sorry I'm not there to share it with you.

Love you always,

Turkle

Chapter 19

look what you have done
Pandora-let evils out
time to give us hope

Rose's Haiku Diary
St. Augustine, FL
Age 35

By the time I woke up in my room at the Marriott, it was almost lunchtime. I thought about ordering room service, but decided I needed to get out. I dressed in jeans and one of Rose's fuzzy sweaters—a pale orange one with hot pink cuffs and collar- something I never would have bought, but I found I loved its look and feel. Realizing I might run into someone I knew—with my recent luck, our entire high school class was probably having an early reunion in the lobby—I made up my face. I could almost hear Rose saying, good girl, dress for the role.

I picked up a club sandwich at a nearby Applebee's and drove to Fern Hollow, hoping I wouldn't see anyone I knew. If one more person told me how sorry they were for my loss, I was sure I'd break into a million pieces. I needed to restock my resolve before going back to my cottage for what might be the last time. I walked the Long Nature Loop, one of my favorite trails, even though it was muddy, due to an early spring thaw. I was almost late for my meeting with the Frau because I was mesmerized by a standoff between a hawk and a squirrel protecting its nest.

Once at my cottage, I walked around it as if seeing it for the first time. So much of Rose was there. Her housewarming gift of the framed watercolor painting of white birches in the fog. Definitely not Rose's taste, but something she knew I would love. The iridescent blue enamel vase, no bigger than my thumb she gave me on my 30th birthday. A wilted yellow crocus drooped in it now—the crocus she insisted we pick. Then there were the books. She never was much of a reader. "I'll wait for the movie," she used to say with that cat-that-ate-a-whole-flock-of-canaries grin of hers.

Yet she bought me dozens of books, because she knew they were my passion. Some were practical: the gardening, antiquing and travel books and the cookbooks. Once she discovered my on-again/off-again vegetarian diet, she sent me every Moosewood cookbook she could find, always with little inscriptions.

Hope you enjoy the recipes—just don't try them out on me

Or: Turnips of the world beware, Agnes has a cleaver with your name on it and it's not June.

Or: Sending you a bouquet of cauliflowers

Then she signed Rose/S in loopy letters and encircled her signature with a flower.

I felt a little pang of guilt at the gifts she sent that I never used. The iPod. The rollerblades. The sunglasses that sported little martini glasses in each corner. The CD's that I meant to listen to: *Great Women of Jazz*, *Torch Songs*, *The Best of Nat King Cole*, *Pink Martini*, and dozens more.

The Frau, dressed in a gray pinstripe suit today, followed me with a laptop as I selected the items for my allotted bequest. Her spreadsheet recorded each item I placed on the kitchen table and she periodically advised me of my progress toward that $500 threshold. I wasn't sure if I should have been relieved or insulted by the low prices she assigned some items. Was that a kindness or was she being lazy? I thought I almost caught her smile when I presented the cheap matching souvenirs Rose insisted we each get on every fives' birthday trip—the snow globe of the New York City skyline including the World Trade Center, the plastic Eiffel tower, the salt half of a pair of salt and pepper shakers shaped like palm trees we got in Maui. The Frau murmured something about those items fetching little more than spare change at an estate sale and charged me two dollars for the lot. I wondered if I'd find their mates among Rose's possessions.

Then I remembered the box of letters going back more than forty years that rested in my closet. After a quick peruse, the Frau told me to take them, as they had no value.

Sometimes the Frau caught me off guard with a price way above what I expected. She tagged the mirror that used to hang in Grandpa Luke's house and the watercolor Hank gave me after his wife died at $300 each, forcing me to leave them.

I also wanted to take the stained-glass panel that hung in my kitchen window, with its riot of yellow daffodils and tulips of every hue. Rose gave it to me for my 40th birthday. "So it's always spring in your kitchen," she said. But the Frau pronounced a price of $200 for it. I'm sure Rose paid more for it, more than she could afford at the time.

I tried to remember why I didn't specify in my will that Rose could take any of my clothes she wanted, then recalled my very logical reasoning—thank you Ms. Univac computer—that her taste and mine were so different she would probably not want my duds, but might feel obligated to take them if I left them to her.

I picked out a few things I wore all the time: my black wool pants suit, black pumps, my New Balance walking shoes and cushioned walking socks, my favorite jeans, all my underwear, the red flannel pajamas Rose gave me as a joke but that I wore all the time once the snow started to fly.

The Frau, a human cash register, recorded every item on her laptop spreadsheet. "We're exactly the same size," I told her. I felt my face flush and wondered if each out-of-character clothing choice screamed: Fraud, Fraud, Fraud.

I picked up my fanny pack—Agnes' fanny pack—and asked the Frau if I could have it, or at least the contents of it.

"I'd like her address book so I can contact her friends." The Frau nodded. "And I'll need to cancel her credit cards and driver's license," I said, as a bit more of my identity swirled down the drain.

"I'll take those," she said. "That's part of what your sister hired us to do." She held out her hand and I gave her the wallet. After extracting the credit cards, driver's license and cash, she returned it. She counted the cash—twenty-seven dollars—and made a note of it in her journal before putting the credit cards and cash in a plastic bag. Bagging the evidence from the scene of the crime, I thought.

Fingerprints. Oh my gosh. Fingerprints. My fingerprints. The credit cards had my fingerprints on them. The blood must have drained from my brain and a gauzy wooziness surrounded me.

The Frau raised her eyebrows. "Perhaps you should sit down," she said. I nodded, sat in the dining nook chair next to hers and put my head on the table. "It often happens," she said. "To me, they are just things. To you, they are your sister."

I wondered who this wise woman was and where the cold robot who sat there moments before went. When I raised my head, the Frau was looking at her watch. "Fifteen more minutes," she said.

I sat and waited for my gyroscope to realign. What made me panic about fingerprints? They don't fingerprint you after you die. I was sure of it. Besides, nobody had my fingerprints. Did anyone have Rose's?

Chapter 20

what do I miss most
hot showers, soft sheets, pizza
no, just you, you, you

Rose's Haiku Diary
Bandipur, Nepal
Age 22

It was almost seven in the evening when I finally loaded the bits and pieces of my life I'd just salvaged onto a Marriott luggage cart. Ever since last Friday, when I drove Rose to the hospital, I'd thought the same thing every day: this has to be the longest day of my life. This day, Friday, was no exception. Tomorrow Uncle Roger would arrive. Tuesday was the service and then...and then what? I didn't have the energy to think about it, since it took all I could muster just to face the next couple of days.

Finally, this day was almost over. I didn't even care about dinner. All I wanted was to unload my stuff and fall into bed.

I reached my room and slipped in the key card in the slot. The light blinked red. Son of a badger, now what? I tried it again. Go slower, I told myself. Okay, faster. I turned it over and tried again, even though the picture showed I was inserting it the right way before. I looked at the number on the door to make sure I wasn't trying to get into the wrong room.

I lugged the cart to the elevator and went to the front desk. Both clerks were busy. When I was moving, I was all right. But standing, with nothing to do but wait, my whole body ached and the first tendrils of a massive headache started to take root. I amended my plan. A long, hot shower. Then a nightcap. Then the pillow. Maybe a nightcap before the shower.

One clerk finished, but shook her head and pointed to the other one as she went in the back. I was starting to wonder if the couple the other clerk was talking to was booking their entire world tour, but they finally left.

"Hi, I'm Rose Grimaldi," I said. I was getting quite good at saying this, although all my practice being Rose as a kid when we switched identities was probably kicking in. "I'm in 402 and my key card isn't working."

"That happens. Sorry," she said and her fingers flew across her keyboard. As her eyes darted across the screen, her smile faded. She lowered her voice, even though nobody was near enough to hear. "We're having a problem with the credit card you gave us. Do you have another one?"

Good question. Did I? I fumbled in Rose's purse and found a MasterCard and a debit card. I handed her the MasterCard and held my breath as she swiped it.

I knew the answer before she told me. Her face said it all. "I'm so sorry." I held out the debit card. This time she handed me a keypad as she swiped it. "I just need your PIN."

"Just need my PIN," I repeated, trying to get my numb brain to focus. Then I remembered Rose telling me that she used the same login and password for everything, but the keypad showed only numbers. Her universal password was Turkle1025. I punched in 1025.

The clerk shook her head again.

I offered to write a check but she said they only took local checks. How stupid was that—if you were local, you wouldn't be staying at a hotel. Right?

"Could I just stay tonight?" I asked, trying to keep the desperation out of my voice. "You're probably not going to fill the room."

"I can ask my manager," she said. "I'm not allowed to authorize that."

"Please, would you?" For a moment I thought of adding the pity-play of telling her my sister just died and I was in town for the funeral, but I couldn't do it. She disappeared in the back, then reappeared with a man who had a face so bland it made Homer Simpson look like Clint Eastwood. He told me someone from security would escort me to my room to collect my belongings and that they would be mailing me a statement with the balance that couldn't be applied to my credit card.

The security guard helped me load my car and suggested an inexpensive hotel about ten miles away. That seed of a headache blossomed in my temples and my body went from feeling like I was hit by a bus to run over by a train.

At least there wasn't a No Vacancy sign when I finally found the dilapidated hotel and paid my $29 cash. Rose would have called it a Motel Three. There were no luggage carts, but I knew I couldn't leave all my stuff in the car based on the chain link fence and trash on the ground. I trudged up the stairs to 212 again and again until everything was safely inside. I wasn't sure if the two locks on the door made me feel more safe or less. I locked both of them, put the metal desk chair under the doorknob, took a lukewarm, low water pressure shower, set my alarm and crawled under the scratchy sheets.

Chapter 21

panhandled to eat
stuck out my thumb to get home
but I still have friends

Rose's Haiku Diary
St. Augustine, FL
Age 36

I woke at six the next morning, my back and shoulders aching from the cheap hotel's worn mattress coupled with yesterday's stress. Rose's wallet now contained $95. After I flattened the wrinkled and folded bills and sorted them by denomination, I pulled out her checkbook, which showed a balance of three hundred and seventy-four dollars—assuming she bothered to balance it. My sleuthing on her computer while I waited to head to the airport revealed that she maxed out her credit cards having almost $1800 on one and $2000 on the other. Of course, I inadvertently pushed them over the top with my charges at the Marriott. It never occurred to me to check the credit limit or balance, since I paid off my charge cards in full every month. How dumb. This was Rose.

I thought of all those soap operas where the rich uncle comes in to save the day, but I didn't have the starring role in any of those shows. Uncle Roger and Uncle Gus lived simply, sometimes joking that they wished they could afford the shoestring of a shoestring budget.

It was 9:30 by the time I finished crunching the numbers. Checkout was 11:00. I thought about Hank's offer to call if I needed any help. What choice did I have? Years ago, I would have dialed his number from memory, but cellphones now memorized phone numbers for us. I stared at Rose's phone, knowing it wasn't one of the numbers she would have programmed. I went to the Formica desk, but the only thing in the drawer was a Bible, not a phone book. Wait a minute, I thought and pulled the address book the Frau let me keep out and dialed his number on Rose's cell.

"Mr. Douglas," I said. "This is Rose, Agnes Blumfield's sister. Her attorney took her house keys and said I can't stay at her house and I wondered if that offer to help, that is I wonder if you have a guest room ..."

"Of course. Agnes was a dear friend. I can't believe her attorney kicked, er, took the keys to her house. I'm sure she would have wanted you to stay there."

"Could I..."

"Come over now," he said. "Or any time. I'll go put fresh sheets on the guest room bed."

"Thanks. I need to check out of here by 11:00 and get to the airport at 1:00 to pick up my uncle. Oh, my uncle. Gosh, this is kind of awkward, but I wonder if my uncle could stay with you too. It's just for a couple of days. He goes back to Arizona on Wednesday. I mean, if it's not too much trouble."

As I knew he would, Hank graciously offered to house us, and when I asked for yet one more favor, he didn't hesitate to tell me that I could store my stuff in his garage.

"You should have time to stop by before heading to the airport. I'll leave the key under the mat if I have to pop out."

Feeling like I not only inherited Rose's name and legacy, but her nomadic lifestyle, I again packed my car, thinking I'm too old to be lugging all these boxes around.

When I arrived at Hank's house, I listened for a moment outside his door as he played "Both Sides Now" on his bagpipes and wondered if he was trying to tell me something. I rang the bell and the ambrosial aroma of coffee brewing greeted me as he opened the door. How like him to brew a pot when he didn't even drink coffee.

Doodle, his little white dog, rushed to greet me.

"She remembers me," I said as I knelt to rub her back and she wiggled with delight.

"She can tell you're a good person. She loved your sister."

"You can never fool a dog; they're the best judges of character."

"Agnes used to say that, too."

I gave a little shrug.

Hank showed me to his guest room, where a bouquet of daffodils adorned the dresser. I walked over to smell them and then noticed the oil painting above the dresser of two fawns, illuminated in a shaft of sunlight. I held my breath, as if they were real and any noise I might make would cause them to bolt. Mom could have painted this, I thought, except that she would have placed one fawn in the meadow and the other on the horizon. And she wouldn't have included two eyes of the fawn's mother watching from the thicket. Then I wondered if the watchful eyes belonged to the doe or a predator.

"I've put you in here and your uncle in the sunroom—it used to be my wife's sewing room."

About six months after Jane died, Hank told me that he managed to give all her clothes to charity, except for the hunter green beret she wore the day they met. He sent her jewelry to her sister, except for her wedding ring. He confessed he wasn't sure what to do with the hippopotamuses she collected that still bedecked every table, nook and cranny of their house.

Before Jane went to hospice, she often fell asleep in a sunbeam on the sofa in her sewing room, ignoring the hospital style bed brought in to keep her more comfortable.

"But the hardest part," he told me, "is the sunroom. I even still slip sometimes and call it her sewing room. She loved that room. I just can't bring myself to change it."

Chapter 22

living in the past
time machine to happy days
would I, if I could?

Rose's Haiku Diary
Pittsburgh Airport
Age 55

When Hank offered me lunch, the smart part of my brain told me I should decline. He was the one person who knew me so well that I worried I could slip and expose my deception. But the need for a friendly face and a good meal won out.

"I went to Safran's after you called," he said. "I picked up tomato basil soup, turkey and corned beef. Rye bread or sourdough?"

I started to ask for turkey, but stopped, knowing that Rose would have chosen the corned beef. A little voice suggested that I was a bit paranoid to think that Hank would unmask me if I asked for turkey with mustard and mayo and cut my sandwich into six pieces. But wasn't one tiny inconsistency always leading the double-agent to his demise?

Over lunch, we made small talk about the weather, his dog, and his late wife's stuffed and ceramic hippo collection. Doodle begged.

"Is it okay to give her a bite?" I asked. As soon as I said it, I knew the answer, since his rule was to not feed her from the table.

"I should say no," he said, "but just between you and me, I sometimes do. So, go ahead."

I turned my head toward the window to cover up my surprise, as he had never confessed this to me. I guess we all have secrets, I thought.

As I got ready to leave to pick up Uncle Roger at the airport, Hank interrupted to give me two sets of keys to his house. Then he pressed a wad of twenty-dollar bills in my hand. The confusion on my face was genuine as he said, "Agnes loaned me $300. I'm just paying it back. I'm sure she'd want you to have it, not those lawyers." I stumbled out my thanks, but bewilderment must have painted my face. "She and I went to Antique Junction in Canonsburg. I forgot my checkbook, so she paid for the piece I wanted."

I remembered the day. It was about a week before Rose arrived and Hank and I did go antiquing. I found an antique shell cameo that looked so much like Rose, I wanted to buy it, but the $450 price was outside my budget. Then I spotted a white-gold pendant of a bouquet of tiny roses that was a perfect 60th birthday for Rose and borrowed $50 from Hank to buy it. But I already paid him back.

I pushed back tears, kissed him on the cheek, patted Doodle on the head and left, telling him we'd be back late, as we had to visit my mother.

Uncle Roger called me a couple of times every day since I first phoned him. Each time we talked, he apologized for not being able to get a flight sooner and each time I told him it was all right. I was coping. But he knew better. So did I.

I waited for him by the bottom of the escalator on the baggage claim level and almost didn't recognize him when he waved as he got off. He seemed so much older than the last time I visited him and Uncle Gus last year.

When our eyes connected, I rushed to him and hugged him as if he was the last life preserver on the Titanic. The tears I held back for days streamed down my face as I sobbed. He smoothed my hair, kissed me on the top of my head and waited for me to regain my composure, whispering, "It's going to be all right. We'll get through this. We always do."

As I pulled away, I saw that sweet smile that always made me feel safe and loved. He pulled out a handkerchief and wiped my face. "Your mascara was running. There, that's better." I felt twelve, but in a good way.

We walked to the luggage carousel, my arm around his waist, his arm around my shoulder more like a husband or lover than the big brother/uncle he was.

"Did you forget your line?" he asked.

"Excuse me?" I said, my brain whirling, wondering if this was a special Rose/Uncle Roger code.

"You're supposed to say, My mascara's running, quick help me catch it, like you did when you were thirteen." He sighed. "I guess today isn't a good day for humor."

His was the lone suitcase traveling around by the time we got there and he grabbed it.

During our walk to short-term parking, I told him about the funeral arrangements. Just a simple service, the next day at 11:30. I accepted Hank's offer to host any friends or relatives after the service at his house for coffee and cookies. It seemed easier than calling a restaurant.

On the familiar route to Shady Oaks, I wondered which figure would disappear from Mom's paintings after I told her Agnes was dead. I considered not telling her since, besides our recent visit before her surgery, Rose hadn't visited Mom in the four years she was at Shady Oaks. But the Victor/Victoria idea of me pretending to be Rose pretending to be Agnes was just too much for me. And, of course, Laarni or Gustav always announced my arrival, "Mrs. Blumfield, your daughter Agnes is here to visit." If they just said "your daughter," maybe I could have let Mom decide which twin I was.

When we arrived at Shady Oaks, Uncle Roger squeezed my hand, then left his wrapped around mine. "You sure you're ready to do this?"

"I called and spoke to the clinician. She said it's the family's decision whether to tell an Alzheimer's patient when a friend or family member dies. Some do, most don't, because they forget that their wife or sister or child died and have to experience the pain of learning it all over again. I don't know what to do, but I'm pretty sure she's too unstable to go to the service."

"I'll support whatever you decide."

"The clinician said that sometimes it makes them worse. Makes them retreat further back into the past."

"Oh, Rose. This shouldn't all be falling on your shoulders. I wish I could do more. Let's go in." The and-get-it-over-with part was left unsaid.

Once we wound our way past the series of locked doors, Laarni came to greet us. "I'm so sorry about your sister," she said, and I'd swear there were wisps of tears clouding her eyes. "She was a lovely person. So devoted. So kind."

"That was Agnes, all right," Uncle Roger said.

I was? I never thought of myself like that. I just did what anyone would do. I introduced Laarni to Uncle Roger. "He's her brother."

"Have you decided about telling her?" Laarni asked as we trailed her down the linoleum hallway to Mom's room. "I'm afraid today is not one of her good days. Although seeing her brother might help. Sometimes a visit can be a trigger."

When we arrived at Mom's room, she was sitting in a chair, staring out the window at the early spring day. Even though it was almost two in the afternoon, a mist still hugged the skirts of the lone pine tree like a lace petticoat.

"Hey, Mom." I said. "Look who's here."

"Hi, Weezie," Uncle Roger said, resting his hand on her shoulder like a butterfly on a petal.

She brushed it off. "Do I know you?" Her voice seemed both confused and frustrated. "Why are you here?"

"I'm your brother. Roger." He pulled up the other chair and sat facing her. "You know, that no-good kid you and Dad raised."

A little of the fog seemed to lift from her eyes. "Where is Father? Tell him I want to go home." Uncle Roger looked at me.

"This is your home now, Mom," I said.

She shifted in her chair and stared at me. "Will you take me home? I don't like it here." I shook my head, again fighting tears. "Where have you been?"

"I'm here now."

"We're both here now, Weezie," Uncle Roger said.

"Stop calling me that. My name is Louise. Louise Woodson. My beau, Richard Blumfield should be calling for me any time now. You look a lot like him. Are you his brother?"

"No," Uncle Roger said. "I'm not."

"Then go away. I'm tired. I need to rest up for Richard. We're going dancing." She closed her eyes and her head dipped forward. As Uncle Roger and I watched, her breathing turned into soft sighs. He mouthed a question about going and I nodded.

As we retraced our steps down the antiseptic hallways, Uncle Roger took my arm in that Fred Astaire way he has, and said, "Want to get ice cream?"

Chapter 23

how can I miss you
father I don't remember
your hugs, empty space

Rose's Haiku Diary
Sewickley, PA
Age 15

Of course, we went to the Sewickley Confectionery, a favorite haunt of Uncle Roger and Rose, although it was a Baskin Robbins back then. I rarely joined them, as I thought it silly to pay extra when the stuff in the freezer was cheaper and just as good.

We sat at the only table in the store, on the wrought iron chairs that looked like they belonged more in a Paris café. Uncle Roger and I perused the whiteboard menu of scoops and floats.

I looked up, all set to order a scoop of the green tea gelato, when I saw that sparkle in Uncle Roger's eyes. "Are you thinking what I'm thinking?" he asked.

"I am," I said, although I had no idea what he meant. Then it hit me. I'd witnessed the Rose/Uncle Roger ice cream duet often enough, sung to the tune of "Cockles and Mussels."

He started to sing. "In this ice cream parlor, Where girls are so pretty, 'Twas there I first ate..." His voice cracked. He took off his glasses and rubbed his eyes.

"My first banana split," I continued the song, just above a whisper, then hummed until I got to the next lyrics I remembered. "Topped with cherries, three cherries, to eat, slurp and burp."

The third cherry was for me. They always ordered a banana split and they always brought one cherry back in a paper napkin.

"Guess I'm still a lousy singer," I said and smiled as I squeezed Uncle Roger's hand.

"Nice to see that rosy smile," he said.

"It's good to have you here. But this will ruin my appetite for supper," I said, then wished I could take it back as it sounded very Agnes-like.

"You know I was saying life is too short, eat dessert first before anyone else."

"I know. You should have copyrighted it. Of course, lots of people say it now, but I think you're the only person I know who does it. Well, sometimes Uncle Gus. And us, when we're with you."

The clerk arrived and we ordered their traditional banana split, although we had to settle for vanilla since the Sewickley Confectionary didn't have coconut ice cream. I pulled out my wallet and started to retrieve a ten-dollar bill, but Uncle Roger put his hand over mine. "I always pay here."

The split looked huge when the pony-tailed server brought it to the table, but as I dug in, I realized I was ravenous. We ate in silence. When we were almost done, I set down my spoon.

"Uncle Roger, would you tell me about my dad?" I guess seeing Mom, back at Shady Oaks, waiting for Dad to arrive so they could go dancing, got me thinking about him.

His spoon stopped halfway to his mouth. Then he put it down. "What more do you want to know?"

"What more? Anything. I feel like there is this hole in my life."

He closed his eyes as if pondering what to say. "You know I promised Weezie I'd never talk about him to either of you girls," he said.

I nodded. I'd asked Uncle Roger dozens of times to tell me about my father, but he always refused.

"But I guess she's not the woman who exacted that promise anymore," he said. "And sometimes you need to break the rules. I kept hoping she'd change her mind and tell you herself."

"She didn't. Will you?"

"Well, he was handsome. Kind of Kirk Douglas handsome. Tall. Wavy dark hair."

I started to say something about the photo I found of him in Mom's stuff, but caught myself just in time, as Agnes had found that picture.

Uncle Roger looked out the window, as if searching for something. "He was a great guy."

"A great guy? How can you say he's a great guy? He deserted us."

Uncle Roger's head jerked up. "He didn't."

I felt the foundation of my emotional house shift. "He didn't?"

Uncle Roger shook his head. "I never thought it was fair, her telling you what she did. But I was fifteen when he died. I was a kid. She was the adult. She was supposed to know better. To know what was best." His voice faltered, as if reliving the experience was still painful almost sixty years later. "She couldn't cope with everyone telling her that her husband was a hero. I'm the hero, damn it, she told me. I'm the one who has to raise and support two kids. I guess she decided she could cope with being the gritty abandoned wife, but not the pitiful widow."

"He's dead?" For years I held this little hope that he'd walk back in my life someday. As a girl, I pretended he was abducted by aliens. Or went on a super-secret undercover mission.

"He died a hero."

"What happened?"

"Your dad was bringing me back from the train station. I was so excited to get out of Sewickley. It was my first train ride."

"Didn't we always live in Sewickley?"

Uncle Roger shook his head. "Your mother moved back in with us after your dad died. You were only two."

He was silent for so long, I wondered if he changed his mind about telling me what had happened.

"Moved from..."

"Weezie and Rich moved to Port Royal in central Pennsylvania after they tied the knot."

He sighed.

I waited.

"I remember the road we were on twisted so much—one hairpin-turn after another—I said it was like being on the Blue Streak. You know the one—at Conneaut Lake Park. Then this black Lincoln roared up behind us. Your dad started cursing and yelling as the Lincoln passed us on a curve."

I waited, again.

Uncle Roger's hand started to quiver and he put down his spoon and rested his hands in his lap. "That car hit a station wagon head-on. We heard the crash before we saw anything. It was a horrible sound. I'll never forget it. Like the world had exploded. He managed to stop our car on the side of the road. Stay in the car, he yelled at me. There was smoke everywhere and both cars were on fire. He pulled a woman and her four-year old son from the station wagon. He was trying to get the driver of the Lincoln out when it exploded."

Tears were in both of our eyes as we stared at the bowl the banana split had been in, empty except for one cherry.

Chapter 24

dogs don't lie or cheat
brown eyes look into your soul
trust never betrayed

Rose's Haiku Diary
Rio Rancho, NM
Age 58

The first time I woke on the day of my funeral was from the recurring nightmare I'd had since my phone call to confirm the arrangements. In it, our fourth-grade teacher, Miss Maplewood, gave my eulogy. Of course, Miss Maplewood was gray and wrinkled when we were ten and must have died years ago. But there she was, taking over my nightmare.

"Agnes should not have died," she said. "She always did her homework. Always. Always treated her teachers with respect. Not like her sister Rose. Rose was a troublemaker. Rose thought she could fool me, but I knew when she copied her sister's homework."

Like some B-grade horror movie, Miss Maplewood's face started to melt as the eulogy progressed.

After saying, "And now she's copying her sister," she put her skeletal hands in front of her face. I wanted to pull my dream-hands up and cover my face, but they wouldn't budge. When Miss Maplewood lowered her hands, my mother's face was there.

"No, Rose isn't copying her sister Agnes," Mom shrieked. "Agnes is stealing her sister Rose."

I'd bolted awake, heart galloping.

It felt like hours, but I finally managed to drift in and out of fitful sleep.

The second time I woke on the day of my funeral, I ached to be back at the Marriott with the Do Not Disturb sign on the door. There, I could have shut out the world, sobbed into my pillow, pummeled it and flailed like a child having a tantrum. There, I could have pulled all of Rose's clothes from my suitcase and held them, felt close to her, tried to believe for a moment that she was not really dead. There, not even bothering to get ice, I could have poured myself a stiff bourbon, or maybe two—anything to try to numb the toxic cocktail of grief and fear with a splash of guilt I'd mixed for myself.

But I was not there. I was here, in Hank's guest bedroom, with Uncle Roger asleep on the foldout bed in the sunroom. How odd to be in this bed, when my own bed, my own cottage, were so close.

It was seven in the morning. The household would be waking soon. My heart raced. My fingers tingled, then stung as if I just yanked them from a bonfire. I hugged my knees to my chest and tried to will my heart to slow. How could I face that room of people? People who'd come here, to my little village of Sewickley, to pay their respects. Someone would know. I'd be dragged off in handcuffs.

What if Rose's friends show up, to hug and support her, as she grieves for me, her twin sister? What if Chris shows up? I don't even know what Chris looks like.

Or maybe nobody will show up. I don't have a lot of close friends. Uncle Roger, Hank and I might sit in an empty room, looking at rows of chairs. I'll be mortified. Or maybe relieved.

I slipped out of bed and crossed to the window that looked past Hank's garden toward my cottage. It seemed to almost shimmer, as a fine snow reflected the pre-dawn light. I wondered why the photosensitive light over my garage was not on.

I'm going to my own funeral today, I thought. What should I wear? My eyes returned to my cottage. I could go downstairs, slip out the back door, take the well-worn path to my garage, and get the spare key. I could stop there and grab the $500 I'd stashed in the Thermos, then walk through my mudroom, kitchen, and up the stairs. I could peruse my closet. Black? I owned enough black clothes for a pew of mourners.

The choking fear that had paced the floor with me most of the night started to recede with the light of day, although it still sulked in the corner.

The first time I was this scared, Rose and I were nine and still in our mirror-image, dress-alike, same-haircut stage. Rose dared me to shoplift something from F. W. Woolworth's.

"Why would I want to do that?" I asked. "I still have some of my allowance. And, it's wrong."

"It's fun," she said.

"You've done it?"

She nodded and produced a blue plastic coin purse. "It's not so much about what you take. It's how fast your heart beats when you've put something in your pocket and are walking toward the door."

"That sounds terrible."

"You're wondering if you're going to hear a voice tell you to stop or if some clerk is going to grab you." I looked at her as if she just told me she drowned puppies and ate them. "And then you're walking on the sidewalk and you're still waiting for that voice or hand on your shoulder. And then you turn the corner and start running as fast as you can and you think your heart will just jump out of your chest."

"I don't want anything at Woolworth's," I repeated. "Why would I steal just to steal?"

"Because I asked you to. You'll thank me, once you try it. It's better than ice cream. And it's sort of an initiation."

"A what?"

"Initiation into our secret society."

"But we already have that."

"We need secrets," she said. "Things you know about me and I know about you that nobody else knows. Like that we each shoplifted. But right now, you know I did, but I don't...well, don't you see that's not fair."

So, for the first incident in my own personal crime spree, I took two plastic, silver-colored bobby pins, each adorned with a small pink rose inside a white filigree heart that was fastened to a piece of cardboard. Rose was right. My heart pounded like the Norfolk and Southern was rumbling by our house.

We'd both sneaked into the store when the clerk's back was turned. Rose was supposed to be my lookout. I stuffed the contraband in the pocket of my winter coat and was starting to feel that anticipatory rush she told me about—I was almost at the door—when the clerk's nasally voice cried out, "Get over here, what did you put in your pocket?" I raced to the next aisle. As the clerk rushed to catch up with me, Rose stepped between us as I ducked into the next aisle, pulled the bobby pins from my pocket and stuffed them under my wool cap.

"Just my mittens," she said as she pulled them from her pocket and held them up.

I walked up behind Rose. "Mom's waiting," I managed to wheeze, sure my face was bright red. The clerk grabbed the collar of my coat and stuck her hand first in one pocket, then the other as the bobby pins burned against my scalp.

"Don't ever come back in here," she said.

Rose grabbed my hand and we ran from the store. Two blocks later, we stopped running and Rose started to laugh. "You should have seen her face," she said. "You should have seen your face."

"I hate you," I yelled and hurled the bobby pin card at her, then threw up in a trashcan.

Quite the crime spree, I thought. One shoplifting caper that caused me to avoid Woolworth's for years, not even walking by it. Then fifty years later, grand theft and insurance fraud for letting Rose pretend to be me and ripping off the insurance company. That same sick-to-my-stomach feeling that I'd had for days after shoplifting returned for an encore.

Muted sounds from downstairs told me I needed to focus on getting ready for the day. I took one last look out the window and watched Doodle race after a squirrel, chasing it to the red mulberry tree that sat on the property line between my house and Hank's. My eyes again couldn't resist making the journey from the tree to my house.

Just get through today, I told myself. The aroma of coffee and pancakes rose from the kitchen. I went into the bathroom, painted Rose on, fluffed her hair, and then donned the black wool pantsuit that I bargained from the Frau and the pearls I received as a bequest.

My finger touched her reflection in the mirror. "We were supposed to grow old together."

I started toward the bedroom door, but something nagged at me. I returned and examined the face that stared back in the mirror. The jacket. Of course. That bleak, black jacket wasn't Rose. I hung it up and pulled my peacock jacket off the hanger. That's what Rose would do, I said to myself as I put it on. Turning back to the mirror, Rose now looked back at me.

I opened the bedroom door to find Doodle, back from squirrel patrol. I sunk to the floor. She climbed into my lap and I buried my face in the top of her head. "You know me, don't you?" I whispered. "You're the only one." But is that enough?

I'm not sure how long we were there, but the next thing I heard was Uncle Roger's voice.

"Rose?"

I looked at him through bleary eyes. "Sorry," I said. "I must look silly. Guess I needed a wagging tail today."

"It's a hard day for all of us, but we'll get through it together. That's what family is for."

Uncle Roger crossed the three feet between us and held out his hand. I grabbed it and he pulled me up and put his arms around me. "You can do this. Be strong for her."

This is it, I thought. I have to tell him. Have to hope he'll understand. Not hate me. I lingered for a moment, then pulled myself out of his embrace, moving my hands to his shoulders.

"Uncle Roger, there's something..." I swallowed hard. The words stuck in my throat. All the reasons to stay Rose screamed at me. Jail. Humiliation. Scandal. Mom being ripped from Shady Oaks and sent to some hellhole.

Then Hank poked his head around the corner. "Anybody want coffee?" He looked from Uncle Roger to me. "Oh, sorry. Hope I wasn't interrupting anything. I'll be in the kitchen."

"No," I called after him, returning my arms to my sides. "Coffee sounds great."

I'll have mine with two cubes of guilt and splash of shame, please.

Chapter 25

a child died today
I did not know her well, but
wept with the village

Rose's Haiku Diary
Bandipur, Nepal
Age 21

With the pain of Rose being ripped away still razor-blade fresh, I gave an inappropriate laugh at seeing the sign above the parking spot that read *Reserved for Immediate Family*. How much more immediate can you get than having the dearly departed in the car?

The parking lot was almost full and a line of cars waited to pull in. Uncle Roger pulled me to his chest when my knees started to buckle as I got out of Hank's car.

My fears for this day, these ninety minutes, had swung from sitting among a sea of empty chairs to performing this deceit in front of every person I had ever met.

It seemed like days ago now, but the terror I felt then was returning. Was growing.

I retreated back into the car.

"Give me a minute," I told Uncle Roger, and he squeezed my hand and nodded.

Flora, my hairdresser went by, then Laarni from Shady Oaks with Gustav, Miss Nichols and four other staff members. It hadn't occurred to me that they'd come. I always figured they thought of Mom as a job and me as part of it. Then the girls from the library, other volunteers, and the staff librarians passed by, all in a knot. Olive from the Stop 'N Sip got out of a tan Rambler that must have been twenty years old.

My busybody neighbor, Clara Clarke, sashayed by. Oh God, what's she doing here? Her rat-eyes squinted toward Hank's car and I lowered my eyes. When I opened them, she was gone.

The procession of people was overwhelming. There were even people I didn't recognize. How could I not recognize people who would come to my funeral?

One woman, her back turned toward me, looked as lost as I felt as she surveyed the milling crowd. Was it her dusty pink coat that made her stand out in the sea of gray, brown and black winter coats? Like an orchid growing among rocks. I couldn't see her face, but long black hair cascaded down her back. I was mesmerized. Turn around, I thought. Her stature made me think she was someone I should recognize from the back.

When she finally turned around, my numb brain didn't make the connection right away—although even from thirty feet away, I should have recognized Rose's second-best friend, Sasha. I always envied her elegant Egyptian features, thick black hair and flawless copper skin. Sasha met Rose in the Peace Corps. She and Rose started out rivals, as they both had eyes for Derek, but ended up being lifelong friends. Although Sasha joined us on a few of our special every-five-years birthday trips, I always appreciated that she left before the big day, understanding it was just-for-us time.

Of course, Sasha would come, I thought. But did that mean that other people I didn't recognize as Rose's friends would be here, too? More people I should greet with her bear hug, more people who might expose me.

The worry of yet another person who might catch me in the trap of my own making was trumped by the need to comfort Rose's dear friend. I beckoned Uncle Roger to lean down, pointed out Sasha and whispered.

"I'll bring her over," he told me.

As I struggled to get out of the car, Hank's arm guided me as if he'd been doing it for years.

"Anything I can do to help, Rose?" he asked and it again occurred to me that I should be comforting him, too. He also lost a dear friend.

Uncle Roger arrived with Sasha on his arm, and she disentangled from him and wrapped her arms around me. "I'm sorry I got here so late," she said. "I didn't know until yesterday. I was in Rio. I tried to call you and email you to find out how Agnes was doing, but I guess you weren't...anyway, it doesn't matter. I'm so sorry." We hugged, still as statues and I wondered how often Sasha comforted Rose, giving me a twinge of guilt that I should resent her for taking my rightful role.

Hank walked ahead of us into the funeral home. I followed with Sasha on one side and Uncle Roger on the other. Just eighty-six more minutes, I told myself. Anyone can make it that long.

Inside, the four of us stood in a semi-circle, toward the front as people came up to offer condolences. I tried to be gracious, the way I knew Rose would have been, but it took most of my energy to not dissolve in the tears that lurked like some stranger in the dark.

People I hadn't seen in years approached us. The instructor at the farm where I took riding lessons. A dozen people from my old accounting firm, including Willow, the first person I mentored. She wasn't sure who to address, but chose me, I guess because I looked like the woman she'd known. "I drove here from Arkansas," she said. "I kept in touch with your sister—you can't imagine how important she was in helping me get started. I had to come. I owe her so much. I was scared when they told me my first boss would be Agnes the Ogre, but she wasn't an ogre at all."

An ogre? They called me an ogre?

"She just expected people to work as hard as she did." I murmured my thanks for her coming, feeling mostly grateful. I wondered if Rose would have laughed about the ogre comment—one of her oversized laughs—disrupting the entire mood and probably unhinging Willow.

Sasha pulled Uncle Roger to one side, leaving me stranded until Hank appeared at my side. I couldn't hear most of what she said, but caught snippets of their conversation.

"I'm so worried. She doesn't seem herself," Sasha told Uncle Roger.

"It's been so hard," he replied. "I'll take care of her."

"Thank you. I want to stay, but I have a seminar that took me two years to set up in Lagos. I'll barely make it leaving right after the funeral."

My eavesdropping was cut short when Luther arrived, guided to our circle by a young woman. Luther and I talked on the phone for an hour every Thursday after he moved in with his daughter, and sometimes I still read to him over the phone. We developed such a rapport, I sometimes forgot he was blind, which amused him no end. We'd be talking about politics or music or gardening, and I'd say something like, "Don't you see that..." and he'd laugh and remind me that no, he didn't see.

He held out his hand and shook Hank's, then mine, while explaining his friendship with Agnes.

"Thank you for coming," I said as his hand, with its gnarled fingers, cradled mine as if he was holding a wounded goldfinch.

"Your voice," he said. "Your hands. So much like hers."

"I know," I said. "We're twins. Were twins." I'm not sure why I said this, as Luther knew I had a twin sister. An aura of puzzlement still haunted Luther's face. How bizarre would that be, I thought. Having a blind man being the one to see through you.

The director asked everyone to take a seat and, as much as I hated to let go of Luther's hand, part of me was relieved not to have to continue that charade. When Hank started to play "Amazing Grace" on his bagpipes, I couldn't hold the tears back any longer and buried my head in

Uncle Roger's shoulder. I could barely hear Uncle Roger's voice as he sang along under his breath, "...saved a wretch like me, I once was lost..."

Chapter 26

keep running away
pair of dice, not paradise
always roll snake-eyes

Rose's Haiku Diary
Las Vegas, NV
Age 27

I had to get out of Sewickley. This town that held me with velvet tethers, first caring for Grandpa Luke during his six-year battle with leukemia, then renewing its grip as Mom's mind started to unravel, finally tightening the knots as a place that felt like home with its quiet small-town grace and beauty.

This town, that I loved, felt like a town of ghosts and strangers. Then it hit me that they were all strangers—almost all of the people in my life here were strangers to Rose. Even Hank.

"Come back to Arizona, stay with us," Uncle Roger said Wednesday morning as he packed his suitcase. "We'd love to have you. You need some time to think about what you're going to do next."

I actually considered it. Their cabin was secluded. Just me and those enormous pine trees, the hawks that circle and circle and that nighttime sky so filled with stars it seems to stretch into infinity. I could read, hike, and maybe figure out what I would do with my life. This life. Rose's life. I had felt at peace there the times I visited them.

"You know how much you love the Mexican frittata Gus makes," Uncle Roger added and it struck me that I'd never have that peace again. Not just because Rose loved eggs and I hated even the smell of them, but because I could never relax and just be me. Not even with Uncle Roger and Uncle Gus, these two men who were so much more than beloved uncles. They were friends, advisors, coaches, cheerleaders and even two halves of the father I never knew.

"I think I need to be closer to Mom now," I told him. "To take over for Agnes. Visit Mom, make sure she's doing all right. I need to get back to my apartment in Cleveland."

"I didn't think you'd come back with me, although I hoped you might. You always were headstrong, never listening to anybody other than your sister, and not even her when you had your Rose-i-tude on."

My eyes filled with tears. "What am I going to do without her?"

"Agnes will always be a part of you," Uncle Roger said. How was it that he always seemed to know the right thing to say, although it gave me a little shiver because his words were more true than he realized.

As I drove Uncle Roger to the airport, he kept telling me he could stay a little longer and I kept reminding him that I was fine, that I was leaving for Cleveland soon and Uncle Gus needed him.

"It's only been five weeks since his knee-replacement surgery," I said. "And I know you said he's good staying with your friends, but he needs you to help him recuperate."

Tears filled my eyes as I hugged Uncle Roger one last time before he headed inside the airport terminal. He turned after he made it through the revolving door and tipped his hat. I fought the urge to run to him and tell him everything. Then he turned away and headed to the ticket counter.

After Uncle Roger left, Sewickley changed from a place of sanctuary to one of fear. The danger of being discovered stalked me even as I drove back from the airport. I needed to get away, but I had no money or place to go. Well, almost no place. There was Rose's apartment in Cleveland. Since Rose moved there only two weeks before she showed up at my doorstep, maybe I could find some peace there and figure out what to do next with my upside-down life in a place where nobody knew Rose or me.

I packed Rose's car Beulah once more and said my goodbyes to Hank and Doodle.

"You've been so kind letting us stay in your lovely home. It's been such a comfort."

"I've loved having you here. The house has been so lonely since my wife died. It never seemed too big—even after the kids moved out—until she... It's been good taking care of someone again."

I wanted to hug him, to tell him, take care of me. Instead, I just thanked him again.

"I get to Cleveland sometimes to visit my daughter and grandson," he said as we stood in his doorway. "Maybe we could have coffee, or something." His hand brushed mine as he reached to help me put on my coat, and an unexpected tingle warmed me.

That's crazy, I thought, as I said I'd love to have coffee, gave him Rose's cell number and left.

As I backed out, melancholy notes from Hank's bagpipes bid me farewell. I tried to discern what he was playing. Was it "Both Sides Now?"

The song stayed in my head as I drove west on the PA Turnpike. It occurred to me that it was odd that I never even visited Cleveland, even though I spent most of my life in the Pittsburgh area, just a couple hours away.

Rose's directions seemed simple enough, but then Rose did tend to gloss over details. The phrase May the Force be with you was coined just for her. It was with her. Almost always. Almost never for me.

I managed to find Rose's Shaker Square apartment building, then drove around twenty minutes to find a place to park. I lugged the suitcase full of Rose's clothes and the few of mine that I bargained from the Frau to the building, all the while worrying about the boxes left in full sight in the back seat. I crossed my fingers as I tried one of the two keys in the outer door. It worked. The elevator finally dawdled its way to the first floor and I got in and punched two. Once I found 2B, I wiggled the key in the lock. It didn't respond.

"I bet you'd open for Rose," I told it, and of course, as if I'd said Open Sesame, it complied. I dragged the suitcase inside.

Alone. I was finally alone. I tried to convince myself to return to the car for the cartons, but I was just too darned tired. It was midnight. On a Monday. Shouldn't any self-respecting robber be home?

There was a note on the table that I picked up and read.

Thank you Rose for letting me stay here. You are a life saver.

Tina

Tina, I thought. Who in blue blazes was Tina? Rose never mentioned a Tina. I tried to make my brain function, but it was as useless as my body, which felt like I had run into a brick wall four or five times, the last time with my head. Trying to figure out what the note meant required more energy than I could muster. I told myself I'd just lie down for a nap on the futon that took up much of the combined living room/dining room.

I woke to the sound of knocking, looked at my watch and saw it was almost nine in the morning. Who would be knocking on my door, on Rose's door, at that hour?

"Who is it?" I peered through the peephole and saw a woman's face, probably in her early thirties.

"Rose, it's Jasmine. I hope I didn't wake you."

My bleary brain tried to digest this information. Her voice sounded nice, sounded friendly, and she knew my name. So, I opened the door. Beside Jasmine stood a girl eight or nine years old.

"Hi," I said.

"Hi," Jasmine said. She wrinkled her brow. "Is this a bad time?" She looked at the little girl, who I guessed was her daughter as they shared the same high cheekbones and deep bronze skin and eyes. "Say hi to Rose, honey."

The girl looked right through me. "You look different," she said and my stomach knotted.

"Hyacinth, where are your manners?" her mother scolded.

"You look different too, Hyacinth," I said. "Let me see, is it your hair?" She shook her head, eyes still drilling into my skull. "No, you're taller. I swear you're taller." She relaxed a little, but I still felt skepticism in her stare.

"They do grow so fast, don't they," Jasmine said. "I think she's just ornery because she doesn't want to give Elvis back." Elvis? I thought. "She's grown awfully attached to him."

"You're not wearing nail polish," Hyacinth said. Her mother gave her one of those watch-it glances and Hyacinth's gaze shifted from me to her lime-green sneakers. "Just saying is all."

"I heard you get in last night," Jasmine said. I must have looked quizzical, since she added, "you know these walls are tissue paper thin. Don't think you can have any secrets here. Anyway, I wondered if I should bring Elvis over, but thought you might be tired."

"I was. Thanks for waiting."

"We're going to miss him. But I reminded Hyacinth that you said she could come over and visit him."

"Sure," I said. "Absolutely."

"I still think you should have called him Lucky. Not every kitten has a life-and-death rescue from traffic story. If Hyacinth had done what you did, she'd have been grounded until she was thirty. Or at least for a month."

She looked at Hyacinth and stroked her head. “Let’s go get Elvis and all his stuff.” She smiled at me. “We’ll be right back.”

As I stood in the doorway, I wasn’t sure what astounded me more: that Rose, with a serious, maybe life-and-death operation pending, would adopt a kitten or that she’d ask a neighbor she’d just met to look after it.

Chapter 27

my first blog today
am I talking to myself
ego or outreach

Rose's Haiku Diary
Rio Rancho, NM
Age 56

Rose's blog. I didn't have the time or the energy to continue it. This part of her life baffled me, but maybe that was because I didn't understand blogs.

The flood of comments that came back from my two posts astonished me. But there was no way to how many of her 900 followers Rose knew—who she'd recognize if they showed up on her doorstep—and who were just people, probably nice people, who happened upon her blog and adopted her. What to Rose was her adoring public seemed more like cyber Peeping Toms to me.

Part of me just wanted to ignore her blog, but doing that felt like breaking my promise to Rose. So, I decided to do a short post—what I knew was probably my final post—saying I was going on hiatus to mourn the death of my twin sister.

"Hiatus?" I heard Rose say in my head. "They'll never believe I'd say hiatus. Tell them I'm taking a break. That I need to get my head together. Hiatus, honestly Turkle. Life is not a Scrabble game. You don't get more points for words with lots of syllables and X's and Z's."

Before I hit send, I perused the responses to my second post, offering comfort and condolences, telling me to continue to blog, that it would help me heal, telling me—telling Rose—that her posts were the highlight of their days. What a world. I wasn't the only Rose-groupie.

Besides, there were more urgent matters to take care of than blogging. I needed a job. Maybe two jobs. Although the rent was paid through April, I needed to eat, do laundry, buy kitten chow, and gas. And to pay off all that credit card debt. The three hundred dollars Hank gave me was a godsend, but my working capital when I arrived in Cleveland —money I could actually spend—was a whopping $342. Uncle Roger tried to give me money before he left, but I knew he and Uncle Gus needed it more than I did. Well, maybe not more, but at least as much. I'd checked on airfares from Phoenix and knew that his flight must have cost over $500 and he'd let it slip that Uncle Gus's knee replacement nipped their finances for $3500, despite Medicare taking care of most of the bills.

Job-hunting at age fifty-nine in a recession was daunting. My MBA, all my accounting credentials—even if I could use them—might not matter. But, of course, I couldn't use them. Poking around Rose's laptop, I found her résumé and realized that I was unqualified for any of the jobs she listed: bartender, cab driver, cosmetician, concierge, shoe salesperson, personal trainer, faux finish artist-painter, dog groomer, coffee barista, hair stylist. That last one jumped out at me. I remember when Rose, at seventeen, told Mom she was going to become a certified hair stylist to put herself through college. I'd never seen Mom so mad. She forbade Rose to do it.

"I've seen those hairstyles you do on your friends," Mom said. "And they're good. You're good. But if you start to cut and style hair, start to make what seems like good money, you'll quit college and it will seem great for a while. But in twenty years, you'll wish you'd stayed in school. Don't make the same mistake I did."

Rose promised to give up her hair styling side-business but, of course, never did. She could work magic on hair. She offered to teach me, but I refused, knowing that I had no talent for it and hated putting my hands on the hair of anyone I didn't love.

So, ironically, while I piled up debt while in college, Rose's hairdressing sideline helped her pay the bills. She would have graduated from Kent State debt-free, with a major in Art History if, three days after our Devil's Lake hike that May 1st Friday, four Kent State students hadn't been shot and killed by Ohio National Guard troops. She decided college wasn't the answer to the world's problems and quit a week later to volunteer for the Peace Corps, where she met Derek, her first real love, in Bandipur, Nepal.

Chapter 28

my life in boxes
bubble wrap my hopes and dreams
pray they don't shatter

Rose's Haiku Diary
Cleveland, OH
Age 59

There is a line that connects twins, thinner than the silk strands of a spider's web. Mine had been severed. Every day I walked through the chain of events that led me here and wondered if I should have confessed to my crime. Maybe the court would have gone easy on a sister trying to save her twin. At least in prison, I would have known the rules and when I would be released.

Instead, my prison was this apartment and the emptiness I felt living in a world without Rose. As if the world had gone from Technicolor to black and white. How was it possible to feel suffocated by something that was not there?

Rose's apartment did not feel like home. The largest window overlooked the street, some barren trees, the railroad tracks for the train to downtown and another red brick building. I closed my eyes and imagined the view from the kitchen of my Sewickley cottage. Even in the winter, life was everywhere—birds, deer, squirrels, sometimes a red fox. My birdfeeders were always as busy as a Friday night pickup bar, attracting finches, cardinals, doves and a host of sparrows, sometimes even a red-tailed hawk hoping to dine on my clientele.

I loved the season when winter started to ebb and spring to tantalize with its march of the perennials. First the crocuses and snowdrops, then the daffodils in their frilly bonnets, finally the tulips bringing up the rear. All my tulips were red, unlike Hank's, which spread a quilt of reds, pinks, oranges, yellows and whites. I wondered if my bleeding heart had started to sprout. I opened my eyes and pressed my face to the window to try to see the sky, but the cityscape blocked it. I missed my sky, missed saying goodnight to my stars every night.

The bedroom, which smelled of vanilla, had a tiny window that looked out on a red brick wall. The queen-size bed, made up in some of the silkiest sheets I'd ever felt—more expensive than anything I ever owned—took up most of the bedroom. A clock radio rested on a cardboard box next to the head of the bed. Next to it was a cherry-red plastic pair of lips about the size of an artisan loaf of nut bread that I finally figured out must be a mood light, as it bathed the room in a pale pink glow. The towels in the bathroom were equally opulent. A burnt orange color. The combination living room/dining room resembled a patio, with a futon couch, four white plastic molded chairs and matching table and one white wicker rocker with a red cushion that Elvis, the kitten, had already claimed.

Elvis made me laugh every time he climbed up on it, but its gentle rocking didn't dissuade him. "I guess you must be the young, skinny Elvis," I told him. He looked quite striking on that red pillow with his sleek, mostly white coat, accentuated with black paws, ears and tail.

I was not surprised that Rose had hung the five canvases she painted in college even though she had not completed most of her unpacking. She always put the pretty before the practical. I decided to consolidate her artwork in the living room. I left the big splashy painting of sunflowers that took up most of one wall where it was, but clustered the others—one of beach umbrellas, another of the reflection of a woman's face in a shoe store window, a third of a horse in silhouette running on a beach—on the wall behind the futon. I put my favorite in the kitchen. It was of two white butterflies, each with a delicate pattern of black wing veins. One was on a flower and the other in flight but just touching the wing of the perched butterfly. I hung the watercolor that Rose gave me of white birches in the fog in the bedroom.

Rose would have called the apartment an empty canvas waiting to be painted. Or a perfect place for a party. I called it depressing.

I wondered why most of the dozen cardboard boxes she brought were still unpacked. Was it because she only sublet the place through the summer? Did she think the wind would blow her somewhere else come September? More likely she planned to unpack while recuperating and regaining energy to charge back at life full-tilt.

One partially unpacked box, marked Next to Godliness, held cleaning supplies and more towels. Other boxes sported labels like Boring, Fun, Keep Forever, Off Limits, ZZZZZZZZ, Important and Hot Clothes. I thought hot clothes referred to the style—Rose always had style—until I found a carton labeled Cold Clothes. The one marked Gotta Eat was in a kitchen so small that I could touch the opposite walls if I stretched my arms out. A nest of red and blue plastic knives and forks, plus two dozen matching glasses and bowls were stacked in the dish-drainer. A corkscrew, a bottle opener, and a half-full fifth of tequila sat on the kitchen counter. I opened the refrigerator, expecting to find it empty, and instead found it bulging – as if some college boy's fridge had been teleported there. Five six-packs of Rolling Rock, three 2-liter boxes of white wine, a half-full bottle of Diet Coke, an almost-full bottle of margarita mix, a couple of shriveled limes and an enormous bag of the popcorn with that fluorescent-orange cheese coating on it. I wondered why the popcorn was in the refrigerator. Was it to keep it fresh or did she have a vermin problem? The cupboards held a box of corn flakes and a half dozen different jars of salsa—mild, medium, hot, peach, chipotle, and habanero. Welcome to Rose-World.

The last box I found was marked, Turkle.

Chapter 29

I just need a job
résumé is full of holes
Help Wanted: Swiss Cheese?

Rose's Haiku Diary
Searsport, ME
Age 33

It was just before eight and I was curled up on the futon reading with Elvis on my lap when the doorbell rang. "I swear," I told Elvis, "I think that doorbell has rung more in the past five days than mine did in the last five years on Compton Circle." But that was Rose—open door policy.

I peeked out the peephole and saw a fortyish couple.

"Who is it?" I called.

"Bobbie and Billy," she answered. "Are we too early for the party?"

Party? Oh, Rose, what have you done?

"No, not at all," I said and opened the door. "Well, a little. I was just going to set up the bar."

"Just like I promised, I brought my famous Cincinnati chili," the woman said, and I wondered if she was Bobbie or Billie. She marched into the kitchen and plugged in her crock-pot.

"It smells wonderful," I said. "Anything to drink?" As the she-half started to answer, the doorbell rang again. It was Jasmine and her daughter Hyacinth. Jasmine handed me the biggest bowl of chocolate chip cookies I had ever seen as Hyacinth scrutinized my fingernails momentarily. I resisted a sudden urge to hide my hands behind my back. Then she shrugged with that little head-tilt that eight-year-olds do so well and went to find Elvis.

"I love what you've done with the place," Jasmine said. "I guess you haven't had time to paint the walls yet."

"Not yet."

"Have you decided between, how did you put it, red convertible or yellow taxi?"

Red convertible? I thought. Yellow taxi? "I'm leaning toward yellow, but my decorating budget ran out, so the paint will have to wait."

"I hear you, sister. There's always too much month left at the end of the money. It's genius, your last Friday party."

The doorbell continued to ring, bringing people of all ages, shapes, sizes and colors. Everyone brought something: a vat of curry, wine, beer, brownies, veggies and dip, chips. As near as I could tell, most had met Rose, and greeted me like a long-lost friend. Some appeared to be responding to the building-wide invitation Rose asked be spread around and introduced themselves. Hyacinth and another little girl about the same age named Rayna arrived with a woman named Angela. The girls took Elvis into the bedroom to play or do whatever eight-year-olds do. I hoped they weren't as snoopy as Rose used to be at that age. The initial self-consciousness of the group faded. I pulled the clock radio from the bedroom and put on soft jazz.

"Is your bridge club coming?" Jasmine asked, suppressing a grin as she pointed at the radio.

"Would you find a good station? You know the local ones better than I do." I could almost hear Rose giggle.

She took the radio, switched channels and soon music throbbed and pulsed.

By ten, way after my bedtime, the party was rocking with over thirty people stuffed into my little place. After a while, I forgot to pretend to be Rose, and just talked to these new neighbors. People talked, laughed, some even danced.

"So, what's next, Rose?" Jasmine asked as we sipped white wine from the last of the winebox while sitting on the floor.

"Find a job," I said.

"I have a friend who works at the coffee shop on the square," she said. "I hear they're looking for a morning shift person. I could put in a good word."

"That'd be great," I told her. After all, Rose's résumé did include coffee shop barista. How hard could it be?

Chapter 30

black eye, broken heart
shortest honeymoon ever
yeah, big girls do cry

Rose's Haiku Diary
White Swan, OR
Age 42

The morning after the party, I woke up and realized I hadn't sprung awake during the night with one of the panic attacks that had been my constant nocturnal companions. I opened my eyes to see Elvis staring at me with those incredible orange eyes. My head was a bit tender; I never was in Rose's league when it came to partying. It had been fun, though. Really fun. I met so many people that I knew I could never keep them straight. And here I always thought living in an apartment building would be sterile, that you got on the elevator and pretended you didn't even recognize the other riders. Except for my college dormitory, which doesn't really count, I'd never lived in an apartment, always a house. Often a shared house, with me as the caretaker. The house I shared with Grandpa Luke while I was taking care of him. My little cottage with Mom until she went to Shady Oaks. The house in Harlow with Jack and his alcohol, pills, and pain.

When Jack got shipped back from Vietnam with a medical discharge after just two months, he left most of his right leg there along with the carefree and tender man I had loved and wanted to marry—the man I just didn't want to be forced to marry to help him avoid the draft. He came back a month before my college graduation and I scrapped my plans to take my shiny new accounting degree to some exciting big city—New York,

Chicago, San Francisco. Jack said he couldn't live with a lot of people around. Even the sound of a screen door slamming made him jump and duck.

"I need to be around the things I grew up with," he said. I thought he meant he needed to be in a place where he felt safe. So, we moved to Harlow, a dreary little manufacturing town in the Allegheny Mountains, the evil twin of Mayberry. A town of haves and have-nots, millworkers and mill owners, gossips and backbiters. We lived in a ramshackle house that his parents owned one street away from their house. No marriage. No engagement. No accounting job. No exciting new life. I told myself this would make our relationship stronger. That we would make it through this together. That I owed him this.

My mornings were spent cleaning rooms in the Pilgrim Motel, where everything from the phones to the dressers always seemed sticky no matter how hard I scrubbed. Weekday afternoons, I served hotdogs, fried chicken, and something they called pizza at the high school's cafeteria. My paychecks covered our rent, food, Jack's ever-growing bar, liquor and pot bills, and sometimes even a token payment on my college loan.

One day, I changed my route from the Pilgrim to the high school to avoid the dust from one of the houses on Granite Street being demolished. On Spruce Lane, I noticed a *For Rent* sign on a sweet little white house with sky-blue shutters. An elfish woman was watering the black-eyed Susans that surrounded the house. All that was missing was a dog sleeping on the porch and a white picket fence. The woman, Mrs. Tyler, showed me the house, which was about the same size as the one we were renting. That was the only similarity. While a mildew stench lingered in our house despite repeated attempts to eradicate it, this one smelled of peaches and sunshine. Its walls were a cheery pale yellow. I even loved the black and white tile in the kitchen, which reminded me of the Baskin Robbins in Sewickley.

I continued my walk to the high school, after begging Mrs. Tyler not to rent the house until I got back to her. It was as if the lead cloak I wore, the one that got heavier and heavier over the seven months since we moved to Harlow, had lifted. The trash in the street, the soot in the air, the stunted trees—none of it seemed to matter. This little house would be the catalyst to renew our lives, get our energy back and pull Jack out of the hole of depression he dug for himself. What was more amazing, the rent was thirty dollars a month less than we were paying his parents. I thought about calling Jack from a pay phone, but decided instead to surprise him over dinner.

I cooked one of his favorite dinners that night, spaghetti and meatballs, set the table with our best dishes and a red checkered tablecloth I bought in the Goodwill store and even picked up a bottle of Chianti. I couldn't help but grin, as the whole scene looked like I was trying to recreate Lady and the Tramp. All I needed was that candle in a bottle nested in a wicker basket.

Jack came back from the Last Chance Bar later than usual and shuffled to the kitchen table. He seemed to relax and looked almost like his old self as I poured him a glass of wine and brought our bowls of pasta to the table.

"What's all this for? It's not some bullshit anniversary, like when we met, is it?"

"No special occasion," I said, but then went on to tell him about the little house I found.

"No," he said.

"But can't you just look at it?"

"I said no."

"It's really pretty and the rent is less and I'll do all the moving."

"You think I can't help move because of this?" he said, pointing to his leg. It was a game we played almost every day since his discharge. He played the blame card. I held the guilt card close to my chest. Nobody ever won.

"No, I was just..."

"We're not moving."

"Please, just..."

Before I could finish my plea, Jack took his bowl of spaghetti and hurled it against the wall, where the noodles stuck for a moment before falling to the floor. Only a red oozing stain remained.

Our life together after that—all four months of it—wasn't so much a downward spiral as a mud sinkhole, pulling us deeper and deeper under. Rose's letters from her Peace Corps posting in Bandipur, Nepal, were one of the things that kept me going. I read them over and over. Physically, her life was harder than mine, but her letters overflowed with her love of the people and her dear friend Sasha, her pride in the school they were building, and her budding romance with Derek.

She was doing something. Something important.

I tried to tell myself that healing one life, the life I forever damaged by my selfish refusal to get married, should be just as fulfilling. Just as important. And maybe it would have been, if I succeeded. If we succeeded.

Uncle Roger called long distance every Sunday morning and came to visit me every six weeks. I told him not to, since the trip from London, where he'd landed his dream job at the Charles Dickens Museum, was long and expensive. But Uncle Roger never listened. I hated to have him see me in such a state, although I loved seeing him. We always went out for dessert, then lunch or dinner. Uncle Roger stayed in the Pilgrim Motel, telling me he didn't want to inconvenience me, but we both knew Jack became even more sullen when Uncle Roger visited.

Uncle Roger always asked how I was doing. I always told him I was fine, that we don't always choose what we want. Sometimes what we must do chooses us.

Uncle Roger and I were having dinner at Lucky's, Harlow's lone restaurant, the day Jack died. Jack refused Uncle Roger's offer to join us for dinner, his treat, and instead spent most of the day drinking and smoking dope. All that was left of our dinner of mundane meatloaf and gray green beans, the Thursday special, were splotches of catsup. The chocolate ice cream that preceded had been much tastier. We were waiting for our plates to be cleared when Sheriff Travis came in. He took off his hat and told us Jack tried to beat a railroad-crossing signal and was killed instantly when the train struck his truck.

The next morning, Jack's parents told me to move out of their house.

Chapter 31

just who would I be
if I lived in the comics
Stupefyin' Jones?

Rose's Haiku Diary
Sewickley, PA
Age 17

I justified buying the Sunday Cleveland Plain Dealer, now that I watched every penny, for the coupons and the want ads. My immediate worry was how to scrape together the money for car insurance. Too bad they didn't include coupons for that in the paper.

I poured myself a cup of cocoa and was headed to the sofa to read the comics and watch Elvis play with a scrap of paper, when my doorbell rang.

Peering through the peephole revealed Jasmine and Hyacinth. I opened the door and was rewarded with two big smiles, although I wondered if Hyacinth's might be more for Elvis than me.

"Hi," I said, figuring that since I didn't know if I should know why they were here, the less said the better. "Want to come in so the cat doesn't get out?"

Maybe it was my tone, but Jasmine looked worried for a second. "Is it still okay?" she said. I hesitated. "I can try to get Bobbie to watch Hyacinth if this isn't good for you."

I sighed. "No, it's great," I said. "It slipped my mind for a second. It'll be fun."

"Well, you two sure had fun the last time. She chattered about that day for a week."

We went over what she called the list-that-moms-always-have about bedtimes and emergency contacts, and she handed me a Tupperware container and a twenty-dollar bill.

"It's dinner for you both—just a quick reheat and there's lunch money on top." I started to protest, but she told me that it was the least she could do since I wouldn't let her pay me for babysitting. "I'll be back by midnight," she told us. "But you better be asleep, young lady," she said as she knelt and planted a noisy kiss on Hyacinth's cheek. "You've still got my key, right?" Jasmine asked, looking at me.

"I think so. So much has happened, I can't recall where I put it," I said.

Hyacinth frowned, ran to the painting of the sunflowers and felt behind it. "Still there," she said.

"Oh, right," I said and forced a smile, wondering what I was going to do with this miniature Sherlock Holmes for the next ten hours, until her eight o'clock bedtime.

"I almost forgot," Jasmine said. "I got you that interview at the coffee shop on the Square where I work a couple of nights a week. It's tomorrow at 10:30. I hope that's all right."

"That's great."

"Ask for Daniel. And don't tell him I gave you this, but here's a list of what's in the different coffee drinks. Just don't make it too obvious you got a crib sheet."

"I promise to cheat with finesse," I told her.

Jasmine hugged Hyacinth again and then me. "What did I do to get someone as special as you right next door, Rose?"

I shrugged and felt my face flush.

After Jasmine left, I put on my best Rose persona and asked Hyacinth, "So, what do you want to do today?"

She tilted her head toward the futon, which was covered with the Sunday paper.

Quick, Turkle, think. Then it dawned on me. "Read the comics?"

She gave me a thumbs up and I felt like I just passed the first of a thousand-question oral exam. "My dad used to read the comics to me. He called them the funny papers. Said that's what his dad used to call them."

"I miss my dad, too," I said, thinking, what would I give to have even one memory of him. "Remember that. It's something to treasure." I was trying to decide if I should try to get Hyacinth to talk more about her dad when I got my answer as she strode across my tiny living room and said, "You read first."

We sat on the floor and took turns reading the comics aloud. Even though I'd forgotten to give one of Rose's signature laughs, fortunately Hyacinth apparently didn't notice. Elvis climbed on her shoulder and tried to nibble a yellow bead out of one of her cornrows as she tickled his belly.

"What next?" I asked. "Want to paint our fingernails? Mine got so chipped cleaning and unpacking I had to take the polish off."

She shook her head. "Maybe later. Will you teach me more sign language?"

Rose learned sign language her freshman year at Kent State when she dated a sweet sophomore named Tommy. She tried to teach me on spring break, but the only signs I could remember were: I love you, yes, no, maybe, sister, twin and later. I used the later sign all the time that March in Fort Lauderdale as I needed to complete a couple of papers and Rose kept wanting to go to the beach, shopping or partying. So, I held up my right hand with the index finger pointing at the ceiling, like a gun, and then pointed my index finger at her.

"Later," I said and signed. I thought about asking Hyacinth what signs she remembered, but didn't, since if she got anything wrong, I wouldn't know.

Hyacinth mimicked the sign and said, "Later."

"Hey," I said. "Why don't we do things today we've never done before together?" The suggestion brought a big smile to her face.

"Cool."

"I'll pick one and you can pick one."

"Let's dress up Elvis in my old doll clothes and take videos of him. Maybe we can go viral," she said. I looked at the sleeping kitten and decided I needed to protect my roomie.

"It's a pretty day. Why don't we do something outside?"

"Let's bike to Horseshoe Lake," she said.

I shook my head. "I don't have a bike."

"You can borrow my mom's."

"But I haven't ridden in years."

"I thought you said I get to pick," she said.

What the heck, I thought. "Does your mom let you ride that far?"

She nodded. "But I have to use the bike lanes and not ride on busy streets."

Hyacinth retrieved the key to their basement storage locker and we got the bikes. At my request, we walked our bikes up Shaker Boulevard to a lovely spot Hyacinth called Southerly Park where she shouted encouragement in between peals of laughter as I attempted to ride her mom's bike.

Hyacinth relished the role of instructor. "Lean right," she yelled. Or, "Slow down, slow down, hit the brakes."

"I'm trying," I yelled back as I careened down the hill, my right foot flexing as an automatic response to the need to brake.

It took about forty minutes, but the old muscles and balance finally returned, just as that old adage said they would. We went over the traffic rules, donned our helmets and pedaled away. Hyacinth wanted to go faster, but I begged for mercy and she granted it. When we reached the bridge at Horseshoe Lake, we watched an artist in a floppy hat paint the twin views of trees and bridge—right-side up and upside down—as the calm water made a perfect reflection. We found stones and practiced skipping them, then sat under the trees picking out shapes in the clouds until Hyacinth reminded me it was lunchtime and my turn to pick something we'd never done together.

"Have you ever made s'mores in the microwave?" I asked.

She shook her head.

"That's it then. We'll get marshmallows, graham crackers and Hershey bars and give it a go."

"What about lunch?"

"As my Uncle Roger always says, eat dessert first." Her mouth opened in astonishment and I felt very Rose-like. "But it's our secret, okay?"

Chapter 32

Why aren't I cleaner
lots of soap and hot water
I'm always in it

Rose's Haiku Diary
Mud Butte, SD
Age 44

Hyacinth and I went back to her apartment after dinner and, as she took a bath, I perused the want ads. I grew to loathe the words experience required, which showed up over and over, for everything from Door & Hardware Salesperson to Drivers to Janitorial. An ad for a Fiscal Officer of a local non-profit required five plus years' experience with a Bachelor's degree, CPA preferred. Budget preparation, fund analysis and projection. I would have nailed it with my real résumé.

I sighed. The only budget preparation in my future was figuring out how to stretch my meager funds. Damn you, Rose. Why couldn't you have at least had experience at some job that I might like and could do.

Hyacinth got to bed only a little after her designated bedtime. She groused that I let her stay up later the last time.

"I don't remember," I said. "Was that a school night?" She gave me the okay-you-busted-me look.

After Hyacinth climbed into bed, I was tired enough to fall asleep too and wondered how mothers and grandmothers keep up with the unending energy of an eight-year-old?

"Want me to read you a story?" I asked, realizing the moment I said it that she was probably too old for stories. Uncle Roger told us stories at bedtime until we were ten, although he adjusted the content as we got older to be more tales of his gallivanting.

She shook her head. "How about a song? You know the best songs."

I tried to remember the songs Uncle Roger used to sing to us, opened my mental filing cabinet, reached in, pulled out one and started to sing.

"She's only a bird in a gilded cage,

A beautiful sight to see,

You may think she's happy and free from care,

She's not, though she seems to be..."

Hyacinth rolled her eyes and I knew I struck out. Failing grade on question number 272.

"'The Man I Love' is better."

"Want to do that one?" She nodded, and we belted out a version that would have made Etta James proud.

"Now it's time for you to get to sleep."

"But you promised me you'd teach me more sign language," she said and formed the word for later. "And it's..." She again formed the word.

"All right," I said, laughing. "But just one. This one you can tell your mom." I held up my hand with my index finger, pinkie finger and thumb sticking out. She held hers up in a matching image.

"What did I just say?"

"I love you. It's the letters I, L and Y all smushed together. The pinkie is the letter I. When you hold up your index finger and thumb—that's L. See, it looks like an L. And the Y is your pinkie and thumb—that looks like a Y."

"Awesome," she said.

"Now lights out." I turned off the light in her bedroom but could see Hyacinth in the faint glow of the nightlight, smiling as she fell asleep, her hand on the pillow still in the I love you sign.

I eased the door shut and gazed around Jasmine's welcoming living room, decorated in shades of hunter green and brown, before walking over to her bookcase to look for something to read while I waited. At eye level, nestled among half a dozen framed family photos, was an American flag in a triangular walnut frame with a brass plaque inscribed:

Reginald X. Jackson
June 12, 1968 – March 20, 2007
United States Army

I stared at it, resisting the urge to reach out and touch the frame, as if by doing so I could connect my grief with theirs. It's been over two years for them, I thought. The photos chronicled a life cut short. Jasmine and Reginald's wedding photo. Then pictures of the three of them. First was Hyacinth as a baby as her new dad stared down at her lovingly. Then a toddler who already had that mischievous smile followed by one of a young girl holding her dad's hand and staring up at him. Finally Hyacinth saluting her dad wearing his dress blues.

So young, I thought. He had his whole life ahead of him.

After another few minutes, I picked out a book and settled on the sofa, a melancholy tinge having seeped into the warm glow of the day, and dozed off.

The buzzer from the lobby woke me at a little after 11:00. I wondered if I should ignore it, as it seemed rather late for visitors. But then maybe Jasmine forgot her key or was giving me a friendly wake-up buzz so I wouldn't be caught napping on the job.

"Who is it?"

"You seen Rose?" a deep male voice asked, slightly slurring the words.

"Wrong apartment," I said, trying to think who this might be.

"I call her place but she didn't answer. Bitch." That last word brought back the threatening phone call I got as I left the hospital. Was it the same man? "You tell her to call Malcolm. You hear me? Tell her stay away from Tina or I break both your necks." I stood there, not able to think of a response. "You hear me?"

"Okay," I said, trying to drop my voice an octave.

Chapter 33

warmth, smell, hum, taste, jolt
either side of the counter
I love coffee shops

Rose's Haiku Diary
Kent State, OH
Age 19

My interview for the coffee shop job was equal parts bravado and confession. I went with the Rose Force-be-with-me. Somehow, it guided me to know when to be serious and when to joke. I told Daniel, the boss, how much I enjoyed the coffee shop as a patron, which was technically true, even though I was only there twice due to budget constraints. I had instantly loved the feel of the place. No cookie-cutter plastic tables and booths here. Just a garage sale assortment of tables and chairs, a sofa that had seen a lot of sitting and a smattering of stuffed chairs. One of the nicked and battered tables looked like they swiped it from the Sewickley duplex we called home until Mom couldn't afford the rent. But even more, I loved the people—solos, couples—both romantic and friends—groups of all ages drinking their coffee, cocoa, or tea and connecting. It felt like an old-time general store, or at least how I imagined one might feel.

Daniel asked me how to make a double caramel brulée latte. I had been ready to parrot the answer I memorized, but I stopped and told him, "It's coffee. We're not making a nuclear bomb. If you put in the caramel first or use two squirts instead of one, I'll learn. Every place is a little different." I got the job, although only for three mornings a week. Not enough to keep the wolf from the door. Or more accurately, the kitten food in the bowl.

Other than being on my feet for so long, this job was, dare I say, kind of fun. The endless parade of people didn't give me a chance to close in on myself too much. Being a morning person, I was happy to be there when they opened up, which made me popular with the under-30's, who mostly looked at getting to work before 7:00 AM like something between their cell phone battery dying and root canal without anesthesia.

Rose never understood my love for the solitary nature of my job as an accountant. Until now, I'd never understood Rose's love of the public.

Chapter 34

His hands could whisper,
sing a lullaby. I cried
when they said goodbye.

Rose's Haiku Diary
Kent State, OH
Age 20

I jumped when Rose's cell phone rang. Generally, it played Rambling Rose, but when Uncle Roger called, the theme from The Man from U.N.C.L.E. played. The phone numbers I programmed in rang like the old black dial phone I grew up with, as if even the cell phone knew I wasn't Rose.

The area code for the incoming phone call on the screen was 412, the same as my old Sewickley number. I knew it wasn't Shady Oaks, Mom's nursing home, but it took me a moment for my sluggish brain to register that it was Hank's phone number with its distinctive 2828 last four digits.

"Hi, Rose," his familiar voice said. "This is Hank Douglas."

I remembered his remark about calling me when he got to Cleveland to see his daughter, but assumed he'd been being polite.

"Hi. How's it going?" I kept my voice upbeat, trying to sound like Rose did in my ears.

We made small talk for a few minutes about how I was adjusting to life in Cleveland, the freakish weather and our new President's battles with Congress. I asked about his garden, then wondered if that was something Rose would have done. I always loved Hank's connection to his little plot of land. He and I would pour over garden catalogs together every spring and fall as if planning a whirlwind European vacation. At least I hadn't asked about my garden.

"The bleeding heart between our properties…I mean between my house and your sister's…is beautiful this year." I could almost picture it. The plant was scrawny for two years, then last year it tripled in size, as if it was trying out the spot where I planted it and finally decided it was home, worthy of unpacking and staying a while.

I tried to think of a Rose-like response, but only a few fumbled, disjointed words came out. Hank seemed to be fumbling, too.

Just as I got ready to tell him that I needed to get dressed for a job interview—a partial truth—he cleared his throat. "I'm not quite sure how to say this, but I have a favor to ask."

"Sure," I said, wondering what broke-little-me could possibly do. "If I can."

"My daughter Julie is getting married, well remarried, this weekend." With those words, I was certain what the next sentences would be—he'd asked me this once before—and my mind raced to decide how to answer. "Just a small wedding, family, a few of their friends. The wedding's in Twinsburg–that's south of Cleveland. Agnes was going to be my date." His voice caught when he said my name, then trailed off. He caught his breath and continued. "It's Saturday, five o'clock for the ceremony with a reception after. I was wondering if you'd go with me. I know it's short notice and you don't really know me…"

"I…I'd love to." The words came out as if someone else was saying them, but I meant them.

"I won't know anybody there except for Julie and her fiancée, and of course Chad, the teenage terror," he said. "Nothing worse than being alone at a party—unless maybe if they decide they need to fix me up."

We talked a little more and he told me he would pick me up at four.

For the next few days, I wavered between excitement at seeing Hank again and anxiety. A little voice kept telling me that going to this wedding was an incredibly stupid idea. I fussed about what to wear—finally picking a periwinkle dress that was one of Rose's favorites. I found a silvery scarf to make the neckline more modest—but could hear Rose hiss at me, You better only wear that scarf in the church. It's a wedding, not a funeral. You're allowed to show some cleavage.

There was even another emotion I couldn't quite identify until I opened my apartment door and a flutter of electricity went up my spine at seeing Hank looking quite dashing in his navy-blue suit and burgundy tie.

"You look beautiful, Rose," he said.

The words jarred me. Was it because his compliments to the old me were more sedate? You look really nice. Or, that jacket looks great on you.

"Before we head out, I brought you a book I thought you'd like," he said as he handed me a worn copy of *On the Road*, Jack Kerouac's Beat Generation autobiographical novel about his cross-country trip. "Keep it. It's an extra. Any time I see a copy at a yard sale or book store, I have to buy it."

I forced a smile and thanked him for the compliment and the book as he helped me put on my peacock jacket.

Hank handed me the directions included with the wedding invitation and asked me to navigate. Once we left the city streets behind and headed south on I-271, I searched for something to say. It felt odd, since Hank and I always talked as if we'd known each other for decades right from when we met, eight years ago.

"Your sister tells me you're a poet," Hank said. "Told me, I mean."

His comment made me search my brain—what else had I told him about Rose?

"I dabble in haiku."

"One of my favorites," he said. "I used to dabble, too, back in my very short-lived, long-haired hippie days."

"You?" I guess I put too much surprise in my voice, responding more as Agnes—how could I not know this about you—rather than Rose, who probably would have said something like, once a hippie, always a hippie.

Hank laughed. "Now you sound like Chad. I don't think he understands I was a teenager once. You should have seen his face when I told him that my buddies and I hatched a plan to hitchhike to Cleveland for the Moondog Coronation Ball when I was sixteen. Our moms caught wind of it and it never happened. I was grounded for a month." His voice was tinged with a hint of melancholy.

"I went to Woodstock in '69," I said. It was true. Rose did go. She begged me to join her, but I told her she was crazy. All those people. Where would she sleep? What would she eat?

"Wow," he said. "That's one of those legendary events. One of those, if I could turn the clock back things, that I'd do differently. I had a chance to go. A buddy of mine—actually the same crazy kid who got the idea to hitchhike to see the Moondog—Archie was his name—got tickets."

"Why didn't you go?" I asked, remembering the three days of ticket stubs for August 15, 16 and 17, 1969, I saw in the box Rose labeled Keep Forever.

They'd been embossed with Woodstock Music and Art Fair. $6.00 dollars. Good for One Admission. 10 A.M.

He sighed. "I was married. Jane was pregnant with our first. I just got my first promotion. We were more Ozzie and Harriet than John and Yoko."

"I'm sorry, I didn't mean to..."

The radio started playing, "Somebody to Love." Hank switched it off.

"No need to be sorry. That's one of the things I admire about you. Or at least the you I see in my mind based on what Agnes told me. You leap. You take chances. So, let me live vicariously. What was Woodstock like?"

I asked Rose the same question when we got together the September after Woodstock for our twentieth birthdays. Fortunately, her words stuck with me, so I parroted them.

"To this day I don't know how I got there. Nobody had a car. I don't remember hitchhiking. Four of us went."

"Did Agnes go?" Hank asked.

"No. Not Agnes. Me, my boyfriend Tommy, and another couple. Tommy was deaf, but he wanted to go. Said he felt the music. I signed him the lyrics at first, but then he told me to just enjoy the music. You should have seen the look on his face. You'd have thought for sure he could hear it."

I looked over at Hank. He was smiling. And why not? Rose's life was just that much more interesting than mine ever was or will be. "The mud. I do remember the mud. And the lines. Lines for the Porta Potties. Lines for food. It didn't matter, though. The little stuff that would drive you crazy now. It was just important to be there. The music was amazing. It flowed through you, over you, around you. Like being a rock in a river."

"There's the poet in you," Hank said, smiling again. "I'd love to read some of your poems some time."

"I have some on my blog." Again, the mouth was ahead of the brain, almost as if I was channeling Rose. What if Hank read Rose's blog and learned some small details about her that I didn't know?

Fortunately, we arrived at Exit 36 and the need to read driving instructions derailed that thread of conversation.

We found Redeemer Church, a pretty little red brick building that could have been a small office building if it hadn't sported a white steeple.

Inside, the announcement board showed the Douglas-James Wedding at 5:00 and at 6:00, Ladies Bible Study—Lord, Change My Attitude. Rose would have thrown her head back and howled.

Chapter 35

Uncle of the bride
hold my arm, walk down the aisle
small voice says, where's dad?

Rose's Haiku Diary
Las Vegas, NV
Age 29

I never cried at any wedding before, not even either time Rose tied the knot, but, for some reason, tears clouded my eyes as Julie took her vows in a brief but lovely ceremony. Was it the potent combination of pride, joy and hope usually reserved for the bride's mother on this special day? Was it Hank playing "Here Comes the Sun" on his bagpipes as the couple kissed and then held up their arms, hands clasped, in jubilation?

At the open-bar reception, I longed for Rose's talent for mingling with strangers and having them talking and laughing like lifelong friends after just minutes. After the announcement that dinner would be served in ten minutes, I excused myself and headed to the ladies' room. As I peered in the mirror, lipstick in hand, Julie came out of the stall at the end and went to the sink farthest from me to wash her hands.

"It was a beautiful ceremony," I said. I caught myself before adding, your mother would have loved it. I ached to hug Julie, but could tell by her body language that would be a mistake.

"Thanks," she said, her voice wooden, her eyes not meeting mine in the mirror.

"I'm so glad Hank invited me."

She gave her head a small shake. "I've been wondering. Why exactly did my dad invite you?" She pulled paper towels from the dispenser and seemed to be concentrating on drying her hands very thoroughly.

I struggled with the question as I'd wondered the same thing myself. "I guess he knew you would be busy with all the other guests and..."

"Don't think you can take over where your sister left off."

I stepped back, my mouth open but with no words to say.

"I don't know what you mean." I put one hand on the sink to steady myself.

"My dad loved my mother. You can't take her place."

"I never, I don't..."

I started to say I loved Jane too, but caught myself at the last minute. Julie was never prickly with me before her mother died. I had even started thinking of Julie as that old cliché, the daughter I never had. Smart. Funny. Resilient. We spent hours together at Jane's bedside. Sometimes we talked, sometimes just waited and hoped together. At times holding hands. At Jane's funeral, Julie, her son Chad, Hank and I clung together like a family.

But about six months ago, shortly after she announced her engagement, the warmth I'd always felt from her froze. It started after she walked into Hank's living room to find both of us doubled over laughing. I don't even remember what was so funny, but I think it was the first time he'd really laughed since Jane died. Julie looked at us as if she had caught us in flagrante delicto and marched out of the room. Hank's back was turned, but I'll never forget that chill in her eyes.

She put her hand to her mouth.

"I'm sorry. I don't know where that came from." She threw the crumpled paper towels towards the trash bin, but they ricocheted and landed at my feet.

I took a breath as I bent to pick them up and toss them, glad to have a moment to compose myself. I tried to think of what Rose would say. "Weddings can be stressful," I said.

Julie looked at me in the mirror from the corner of her eye.

"Especially the second time." Was that a mistake? It was something Rose would have said. "The first time is romantic, happily ever after, but the second time, you know what a lot of work a marriage is. The for better or worse part. It can be scary."

"You're right. It's different the second time. The words are the same, but somehow different. In sickness and in health." She turned to face me. "I shouldn't have snapped at you."

"It's a big day for you. It's strange how weddings can stir up a lot of emotions."

Julie seemed to relax for the first time.

"Yeah, they sure do. So weird. Thought I'd be worrying about the flowers, food, and my dress today, not my dad."

"He's special," I said.

She turned from the mirror at almost the same time I did and bit her lower lip like a little girl.

"I'm sorry about your sister. She helped me so much, helped us, when Mom was sick. I really did love her."

I wanted to cross those few feet between us that had seemed like a chasm minutes before and hug Julie, but I held back, although that's exactly what Rose would have done, even if it meant risking an awkward rebuke.

"She loved you too," I said. "She told me a lot about you. What a fine young woman you were... you are."

I walked to Julie and held out my hand. She took it and I gently squeezed. Julie's eyes started to mist. She dabbed at them, then shook off my hand.

"I didn't mean to accuse you of trying to…I guess I'm just overprotective of my dad. He's been hurt so much. First Mom, then your sister. I don't know if Agnes felt the same way, but Dad was falling in love with her. I'm sure of it."

"I, she…" I tried to digest Julie's words. I'd felt a jolt when Julie had said Hank had been falling in love with me. The months before Rose arrived, so many times I wondered if I was falling in love with him. So many times, I'd wanted to kiss him, see if he felt the way I did. So many times, I'd almost told him. That precarious moment, as if you are on a precipice, ready to jump into his arms and hoping he will catch you. I feared being rejected and ruining our friendship, but also putting my heart out and having it crushed. Maybe even a bit afraid of what would happen if we were both falling in love.

Julie took a last look in the mirror and tucked a wayward lock of hair back into her braided chignon bun. "I better get back."

"You look so beautiful," I said.

Later that night, as the cake plates were being cleared, Hank squeezed my hand and whispered, "Wish me luck. Chad mixed a special set. Julie and I have been practicing this for the last three days." Then he stood, walked to his daughter and bowed. "May I have this dance, Jellybean?"

The smile that illuminated her face made her as radiant as I'd ever seen her. Julie held out her hand. Hank took it. She stood, then curtsied and kissed him on the cheek. They walked hand in hand to the small dance floor. Hank winked at Julie and she tilted her head and winked back. Then they both nodded at Chad, who was acting as the DJ, and started to Charleston as "Ain't She Sweet" filled the air. They were a little awkward for a moment, then it looked as if Fred and Ginger were strutting their stuff. The music changed to the "Beer Barrel Polka" and they transitioned effortlessly to a polka, which melded into a swing dance to "The Way You Look Tonight." The finale was a slow dance to Nat King Cole's "Unforgettable."

I moved over and sat next to the groom and we watched Julie and Hank dance.

"She's great, isn't she?" he said.

I nodded, thinking, he's pretty great too.

Chapter 36

why be cold and poor
when you can be warm and poor
rich in sand dollars

Rose's Haiku Diary
St. Augustine FL
Age 34

I splurged and bought a box of sixteen bags of Yogi Egyptian Licorice tea. I even vowed not to dilute the extravagance by using any bag a second time. The box said the tea was warming and naturally spicy sweet. Just like Rose, I thought. Attached to the string was a tag with a little saying on it. I had bought this tea for years, yet never noticed the little sayings before. The first tag read: Your good health guide: eat right, walk right and talk to yourself right.

I stared at the little slip of paper. Easy for you to say, pal. Have you been to the grocery store lately? Do you have any idea how expensive organic apples are? Or Ethiopian free-trade coffee? And don't get me started on spices. When I saw the price, I put back a two-ounce jar of cumin and instantly wondered why I hadn't scooped up my spice rack at my grab-what-you-want session with the Frau.

"I'm arguing with a tea bag," I said. Elvis lifted his head, looked around, decided no treats were involved, and curled up again. I decided to head out for a walk, while trying to ignore the irony that I was following the doctrine the tea bag preached.

I headed for my haven, the Shaker Lakes Park—a long skinny stretch of land, home to a variety of birds, deer, squirrels, chipmunks, turtles, and fish.

My favorite spot, an old stone bridge, was about three feet across and close to the water. It faced a wider metal bridge with sides and railings and a waterfall beneath that cascaded from the lake into Doan Creek. The waterfall had its moods. Sometimes, after a heavy rain, it was rushing and frothy, like Rose. Other times it was more like me—slow and deliberate, like water overflowing a bathtub.

I reached the stone bridge, lowered myself to sit and dangled my legs over the edge, as Rose and I used to do at the Beaver Road Bridge over Big Sewickley Creek. I closed my eyes and let the sun warm my face. If I moved my hand an inch, I wondered, would it bump into hers?

I could almost smell that perfume she wore when we were sixteen. She said it smelled of moonlight and love. I thought it was more like wet grass after a rainstorm, with maybe a whiff of clover. I leaned back and let the breeze caress my face. A woodpecker's rat-a-tat drilling punctuated the water's roar, making me think of how she drummed her manicured nails, probably painted bubble-gum pink, in tune to some song she heard in her head.

Something nudged my hand. I opened my eyes. A fawn-colored greyhound, all long legs and angles with a skinny deer-like snout, stood next to me.

"Hello, pretty," I said. "Are you lost?"

The dog pushed its nose against my hand again. I examined the collar, which gave her name as Angel and a phone number. I ran my hand across Angel's head and down her back. Angel settled next to me, her warm body pressed against my thigh, her gentle breathing almost hypnotic.

An anxious shout jerked me from my trance and Angel slipped from under my hand, loped off the bridge and rushed to a woman who knelt and wrapped her arms around the dog.

She found you, Angel, I thought. Lucky you. You're going home.

As so often happens with April days, the sun disappeared and the stones of the bridge chilled my thighs, a sign for me to head home. As I waited to cross Shaker Boulevard, my cell phone rang. I used to glower at people who talked on cell phones on the street, or worse, in parks. But the nursing home called me recently and told me Mom was congested and coughing, so I joined what Mom called the face-down generation and brought mine on my walk, just in case.

"This is Lionel Bankerville, Mrs. Grimaldi," the voice said before I could even say hello. "I wanted to update you and I have a few questions."

"Okay."

"The estate sale will be a week from Saturday, and we'll be putting your sister's house on the market after we've cleaned it up and painted it."

I swallowed my anger at the implication that my house was dirty and in need of paint.

"So soon?"

"The sooner the better. Always best to get the assets liquid."

"Will I be able to buy things at the estate sale?" Every day there was something I thought of that I missed. Many times, they were just little things, like my good scissors, the dictionary from my college years, or the fuzzy red hat Rose gave me. Even that spice rack.

"Yes," he said. "The Buckinghorn Group will be managing the estate sale. It starts at ten in the morning. They'll be there by nine. You're welcome to arrive before it opens to the public."

How magnanimous, I thought.

"Thank you," I said.

"We'll need to know if you want to take over the cell phone contract that your sister set up for both of you or if we should cancel it."

"I don't know," I said. "Could you give me a couple of days to decide?" Although I thought, What's to decide? I couldn't afford the couple of hundred dollars a month I used to shell out, even though I needed a cell phone to find a job and so the nursing home could reach me.

Mr. Bankerville hesitated long enough to let me know he would have preferred an answer right there, then said, "Of course. Also let us know when you'll be in the area again. The Will stated that we should keep you apprised of the financial matters concerning the Trust. We'll be ready to go over your sister's draft tax return for last year in about a week."

Last year's tax return. Another thing to put on my list: file Rose's federal tax return. How the heck was I going to figure out how to do that? Did one of the boxes not yet unpacked have that paperwork?

Chapter 37

we are intertwined
can't sever our flaxen knot
no, never, ever

Rose's Haiku Diary
Amalfi, Italy
Age 22

Was it a curse or a blessing that I felt as if I could not mourn for Rose? Not properly. At least not the way I thought I was supposed to. My ruse, in a sense, kept Rose alive. I wondered, sometimes, if I should mourn the death of Agnes.

I still woke up most nights at least once in a panic. It was like I was having a nightmare except I never remembered any details, just the terror. Just heart pounding, brain screaming: run, hide. Elvis, the kitten, jumped off the bed when this happened, but returned when I stopped thrashing. His purring lulled me back to sleep.

As a break from scrutinizing the want ads for a second job, I went back to Rose's blog, expecting that her hundreds of fans would have dwindled to a few die-hards. Instead her readership had surged to almost 1500. The barrage of comments overwhelmed me. People, mostly strangers to Rose as near as I could tell, offered words of encouragement, comfort, and sympathy. Shame wrapped its cloak around me at fooling them. I never even thought of them after Rose died, except for those two posts I made. I assumed this was a superficial connection, like reading Ann Landers. But many readers seemed to be also in mourning, missing Rose's unconventional posts on love, life, music and whatever else got in her way. How was this possible? They didn't know her. Not like I did.

"Keep blogging. Writing will help you heal," one wrote.

Three days later, while perusing the coffee shop bulletin board in hope of a lead on another job, a flyer for a two-hour writing workshop caught my eye. It was called Helping to Heal: Learning to Grieve through Writing. I knew two hours wouldn't begin to plug the hole in my life that Rose's departure left, but it offered a hope that I could let a trickle of the pain flow from the reservoir that seemed to fill higher each day.

So, I brought my twenty-dollar fee to the church meeting room where the class was held. The instructor, Emily, was the sort of person who made you feel comfortable right away. I think if I saw a perky twenty-something, instead of Emily with her short-cropped gray hair, I might have turned tail and fled. The other workshop participants were two women and a man.

Emily asked us to introduce ourselves and, if we wanted to, tell the group about the person we lost.

"I'm Ted," said a man with unruly silver hair pulled back in a ponytail. "My wife Beth died of cancer. We were married for thirty-four years."

"I'm Mitsui," a petite Japanese woman said, and then her eyes filled up. "I can't talk about it." She turned to the woman on her right, and gave her a hand signal to speak.

"Miriam," the other woman said. She somehow reminded me of a field mouse with her too-pink skin, tiny fidgety hands and slicked down, thistle-brown hair. "My husband died eight months ago and I have a hard time just getting out of bed. I just feel so lost without him. My sister saw this workshop and signed me up for it. I'm not sure why I'm here."

"I'm Agnes," I started to say and choked, "I'm Agnes's twin sister Rose. I lost her: my sister, my best friend."

Emily thanked everyone and told us she was helped by a workshop such as this one when she lost someone special. "If you don't get anything else from today, I hope you'll leave planning to use writing to help you grieve and heal. Write about the person you've lost, even write to them. Start a journal. Just let the words out. I'll give you writing prompts, and then we'll all write. You can read what you wrote to the group, but you don't have to. Some workshops, everyone seems to want to read, sometimes nobody does."

She gave each of us one of those black-speckled notebooks I remembered from college.

"As a warm-up, draw a picture of how you feel."

Coming to this workshop was a mistake, I thought. What's next? Will she be asking me what kind of trees Rose and I would be? That would be easier. I'd be the mighty oak, always there. She'd be a palm tree, exotic, swaying with the prevailing wind. My drawing was supposed to be an oak standing straight and tall, but Rose and Mom were the artistic ones in the family, so my oak looked more like a television antenna. Maybe I should be a pine tree, I thought, but it was too late. I was committed to my oak tree. Then I drew a palm tree on its side, next to the oak and a spider web connecting them.

Well that's weird, I thought. Glad there's no psychologist to interpret what that means.

"Now write down three little things you miss about your loved one. We often focus on the big things, but the little ones are important too. Begin each sentence, I miss."

I thought of Rose. I wrote:

1. I miss her smile, then crossed out smile and wrote laughter.
2. I miss how her hair always smelled of lavender.
3. I miss how we used to sing songs when we drove somewhere together.

"Now write down one big thing you miss."

I miss the feeling of knowing that, no matter what, she was there for me, we were there for each other.

Emily asked if anyone wanted to read and nobody did.

Halfway through the workshop, Mitsui left, sobbing into her handkerchief.

The final writing prompt was one I think Rose would have liked.

"Assume you believe in reincarnation. Write about the spirit of your loved one. Some people like to write in first person."

I picked up my pen and it was as if someone else had taken over.

This is Sapphire hanging around eternity. I have to wait for my sister Turkle, so we can be reincarnated together. Did you know that twins are the most evolved form of life? Those born without a twin spend their time on earth looking for their twin. I was so lucky.

Chapter 38

loving two people
human wishbone-don't break me
one foot in each world

Rose's Haiku Diary
Amalfi, Italy
Age 22

I felt like the star in an on-acid version of *It's a Wonderful Life*. In that classic movie, George Bailey saw, with the help of his guardian angel Clarence, what the world would be like if he were never born. What I saw was a sliver of Rose's world, the world I'd secretly envied for years. Of course, I came in at what she would have called one of her valleys. A peak would have been better.

A few things kept me sane. Uncle Roger's cards and calls. The antics of my kitten Elvis. Local places I loved to go and walk or sit and think: the nearby Shaker Lakes Park, Loganberry Books, the benches that dot Shaker Square—great for people watching or reading a book. The friends in this apartment building that I inherited from Rose, especially Jasmine and Hyacinth. My job. Even the connection I felt to Hank, despite my fear of being unmasked by something I said or did that accompanied us like a clumsy chaperone.

Yet every few days I was blindsided by grief. Most nights I woke up at least once, in a panic, facing the gaping hole left behind by her. My new economic circumstance did not let me wallow for long in the abyss of my loss of Rose, the person I had felt connected to even when she was on the other side of the world.

Rose had for a brief moment considered moving permanently to the other side of the world. She met Derek in Nepal in the Peace Corps and they fell crazy in love. Her letters to me were an oasis, as her joy gushed off the pages, even though they kept reopening the wound that was my small-town prison and my efforts to make my relationship with Jack work. I was glad she never knew that her joy somehow magnified my pain. Odd that I had felt closer to Rose, seven thousand miles away, than to Jack in the next room.

It was a rainy Sunday afternoon and, after a busy six hours on my feet at the coffee shop, I was exhausted but unable to nap. I retrieved the packet labeled Letters I salvaged during my eviction by the Frau. Most of them were from Rose, although there were a dozen from Uncle Roger, one from Mom written, I think, after she imbibed too many vodka tonics, and several from my college roommate before we lost touch. Each bundle was tied with a satin ribbon. I felt a twang of sadness when Rose started emailing me her updates instead, and a stab of jealousy when her emails got shorter and ended with—see my blog for more details. Perhaps those emails said just what would have gone in one of her letters, but they felt less personal, less caring. I loved holding the envelope in my hand, feeling its texture, smelling it, knowing that her hands touched it.

My hands found the bundle from the year Rose was in the Peace Corps. Her letters were written on that thin pale blue paper we used in that era to send international correspondence to keep mailing costs down. They were brittle with age. It was always a thrill when I saw one of these envelopes in the mailbox, a lifeline from Rose, the person who was my oxygen.

Both Rose's and my letters always started the same way. I miss you. I wish you were close by, yet I still feel a connection, like I could reach out my hand and you'd be there. The letter she wrote before she came home from Italy, before she told Derek she wouldn't be going to Australia with him, was on the top of the stack for 1972. I don't know why I pulled it out and read it again.

Dear Sis-

Part of me wanted to write Derek a farewell note, like Ilsa did to Rick in Paris in Casablanca. I wasn't sure I could say goodbye if I looked into those gorgeous gray eyes of his. Wasn't sure if I could stand seeing pain there. Telling him I couldn't go with him, wouldn't marry him, was the hardest thing I've ever done.

Come to Brissie with me, he said. I'll make you happy.

I couldn't even get any words out. I just shook my head.

Part of me wanted to say, come back with me, but I knew he couldn't. Derek would not be Derek without the palm trees and mountains that seemed to shine when he spoke of them, without spending his days training horses on the ranch that had been in his family for generations, without teaching his two nephews to ride, to swim, to fish.

How could he do that in America?

Much as I loved him, I couldn't imagine being the only woman on a ranch for miles and miles. I'm a city girl. I'm a party girl. I'm a girl with places to go, people to see, things to do. I'm a girl with family – you, Uncle Gus and Uncle Roger, Grandpa Luke and yes, even Mom. I can't imagine being half a world away from all of you.

Don't you love me, he asked, even though he knew the answer. All I could do was walk away.

Do you remember how Uncle Roger used to tell us that you'll never forget your first love – but it might not be your best love. I'm sure hoping he was right.

Miss you SO much. Can't wait until we're not so many time zones apart.

Love you always-love you more,

Rose, your Sapphire sister

Chapter 39

love my flatbed Ford
new meaning to bed and board
surf's up, to the beach

Rose's Haiku Diary
St. Augustine, FL
Age 34

The day before my estate sale and scheduled visit with Mom, I committed the Trifecta of Lies: federal, state and local. I mailed an extension to file Rose's federal tax return along with a check for $202, went to the Bureau of Motor Vehicles and switched Rose's South Dakota driver's license, and used my newly minted Ohio driver's license to get a Cleveland library card. I felt the worst about lying to the library.

I had a barbwire headache by the time I got home from my illicit errands. I opened my mailbox and pulled yesterday's mail out—my car insurance bill and a card from Uncle Roger and Uncle Gus.

I opened the card in the elevator and smiled. The cover photo was a pug with an annoyed look on its face dressed in a silly hat. The printed message inside said: Hope your day is going better than mine. Underneath, Uncle Roger wrote, Always remember, you're never alone.

I waited until I'd brewed a cup of chamomile tea to open the bill. The arrival of bills had been a yawner for the past thirty years. Once I dug myself out of debt by age twenty-eight, I vowed never to go there again. Think Scarlett O'Hara silhouetted against an angry orange sky, declaring she'd never be hungry again. Except my vow to never be broke again was taken in a navy-blue Brooks Brothers pantsuit, shaking my leather briefcase at Pittsburgh's skyscrapers.

As Agnes, my monetary house was in order. But Rose and money did not get along. More precisely, Rose and saving money did not get along. And now I was Rose with no savings and no Agnes to bail me out. So, opening the car insurance bill was just one more hairpin turn in my life on Rose's careening financial ride. I gasped. How could it be $300 higher for six months?

I called Rose's agent, gave him the policy number and asked if there was some mistake.

He put me on hold and I listened to half of "Eleanor Rigby," before he returned and explained that my new urban Cleveland location was part of the reason for the increase.

"What else?"

There was a long pause, as if he was trying to decide how to phrase the answer. He finally said, "You've had two accidents in the past five years and three moving violations."

Ouch.

"The only thing not making the premiums even higher is your age."

Double ouch.

"Is there anything I can do?"

He suggested increasing the deductible and reducing the coverage.

I'd never had a claim, accident, or ticket since I got my driver's license. But that didn't matter.

"We need to get your payment within the next eight days or your coverage will be cancelled."

Eight days, I thought. The estate sale is in ten days. I got Rose's checkbook, a calculator and a yellow legal pad of paper. After almost an hour of slicing and dicing the numbers—license, registration, insurance, gas, repairs—I had to admit I could no longer afford a car.

I tried and tried to figure out a way to keep my car to get me to the sale of all my worldly goods. It seemed like such a waste of money to rent a car, but I had a circular problem. If I didn't sell Beulah before the estate sale, I'd have no money to try to retrieve a few of my treasures. If I did sell her, I'd have no car to bring them back.

It's just a car, I tried to tell myself before I threw the legal pad down and kicked it across the floor. But damn it, Beulah's not just a car. With a bit of shame, I realized this was what Mom must have felt when I took away her car keys. All I saw was the need to keep her safe. How had I not understood I was stealing her independence? Her freedom? Her dignity?

I took two aspirin with the remnants of my tea, made a list of nearby used car dealers and headed out. The dealers seemed disappointed I was selling but not buying a replacement. I was disappointed by how little they were offering.

As I drove along Coventry Road on the way to the last dealership, I noticed a garage sale being set up. I pulled onto a side street, parked and walked back to take a closer look at the purple bicycle that caught my eye.

"Ten speed Huffy," a petite woman told me as I fingered the handlebars. "My husband got it for me. We were going to ride together, but I'm just too tired chasing three kids around."

"How much?"

"Fifty-five dollars."

I must have let my poker face slip.

"It's in good condition. I hardly rode it."

I tried to imagine how much money was in my wallet.

"Maybe I'll stop back," I said. "Thanks." I started to leave.

"How about fifty dollars and I throw in the helmet?" She handed me a purple and teal helmet. I put it on and it fit.

"How's it look?" I asked

"It's definitely you," she said.

I knew I didn't want to see myself in a mirror. "It's a deal."

I paid the woman, rolled the bike to my car, and tucked it in the back seat.

An hour later, as I pedaled off from the used car dealership on Mayfield Road with a check for just over four thousand dollars, I silently thanked Hyacinth for my bike-riding lesson. I still had wheels, even if it was two and not four. And I had four thousand dollars of breathing room, a few more months before I hit dead broke.

The lone envelope I pulled from my apartment mailbox twenty minutes later was from the IRS, telling Rose she owed them eight hundred and forty-five dollars.

Chapter 40

why do I make them
plans never cooperate
like most men I know

Rose's Haiku Diary
Las Vegas, NV
Age 32

I almost fell off my chair when Mr. Bankerville told me the Buckinghorn Group would get forty percent from the estate sale, as if my life was on sale at Macy's—buy two bras, get one free.

I decided to get there an hour before the doors opened, before the hordes came to loot, sack, and pillage.

I mapped out the day with the same efficiency I previously used to juggle client meetings: 5:52 Rapid, change trains downtown, arrive at the airport eighteen minutes before my 7:00 car rental reservation, two hours to Sewickley for a nine o'clock arrival. I didn't have the luxury of going to the car rental places within biking distance, since they didn't open until 9:00 AM on Saturdays and weren't open at all on Sundays. Nothing in the budget for two extra days.

I was up at 5:25.

I reached for my jeans, but then it occurred to me I'd be running into people who expected Rose at the nursing home. Instead, I put on beige khakis, a white shirt and sweater, and the requisite make-up. I skipped a fingernail polish tune-up. My hand hovered over a pink scarf, but I closed the drawer. Enough already. I never figured out how Rose wore all these pale clothes that never seemed to get dirty or wrinkled, as if a laundry fairy watched over her.

I crinkled the cat food bag while scrutinizing my meager breakfast choices. I poured my last quarter cup of granola into one bowl and kibble into another. I could almost hear Rose chuckle and quip something like: don't get them mixed up—although I bet his tastes better. I was out of milk, so I started to munch a handful while I waited for Elvis to trot into the kitchen, tail in air.

He didn't.

"Elvis," I called. "Where are you, sweetie?" I turned off the radio. "Now's not a good time for hide and seek."

Silence. I paced my three tiny rooms like a tiger in a too-small cage as I called his name. I looked under the bed. Opened all the kitchen cabinets. Peered under the futon. I rattled the cat food bag again. Don't panic, I told myself, while a small voice screamed, I can't lose him, too.

Then a tiny meow. I sank to my knees. "Thank you, baby. Keep talking," I told him. I kept calling Elvis, Elvis, and ended up in the bathroom. Not many hiding places. The laundry hamper, my first guess, only produced a pile of dirty clothes. I opened the door of the vanity and the meow-volume increased. I shined a flashlight across the small space until the light rested on a golf-ball size hole that framed my kitten's face.

"How the heck did you get in there?" I asked. The hole wasn't big enough for my hand and Elvis had decided it wasn't big enough for him to come out. "I can't just leave you there."

I got the only tools Rose had from the kitchen drawer, a hammer and a screwdriver and used the hammer to tap the screwdriver. After a dozen taps, a couple of spider-vein cracks appeared. It took half an hour, my heart racing more with every passing minute, but finally the hole was big enough for my hand to reach in and grab Elvis.

"Don't ever do that again," I told him, pressing him to my chest.

Poor Elvis was covered in dust and grime, turning him from a mostly-white cat to a gray one. I didn't look much better, smudged and sweat-soaked. "We're quite the pair, aren't we?"

I cleaned the dust and cobwebs off him with a wet washcloth. He didn't squirm at all. Then I fed him and just watched him eat. When he chased his catnip mouse, I finally stopped holding my breath.

It was just after seven. I was an hour late already. Why today? Why today of all days? I slammed the wall with my fist and a jolt of pain traveled up my arm. Son of a bitch. That hurt. The wall seemed none the worse for my attack. That should have kicked me out of my tailspin, but it didn't. I sank to the floor and tried to breathe slowly, tried to shrink the bubble of anxiety and frustration that migrated from my stomach and now clutched my chest.

No. Oh, no, I thought. I do not have time to have a heart attack today. And I do not have medical insurance. So, go away. The absurdity of that brief introspection hit me, and my angst shrank to exasperation. Focus, I told myself. This is not hard. You're just driving to your old house to pick up a few things. Now get going.

I took off my dirty clothes, toweled down and put on jeans and a pale-blue denim shirt. After scooping the litter box, I put a carton full of books in front of the vanity and made sure that the bathroom door was firmly closed. Then I filled Elvis' water bowl again.

As I rode the Rapid to the airport, I thought about the night before, when I spent a couple of hours working up a budget. The $4000 I got for Rose's '99 Isuzu Gemini seemed like such a big chunk of money —well, compared to all the rest of my now meager resources, but the taxes and then the back-taxes Rose owed took all but about $1500 of it. When I looked at income versus outgo, the pittance I was making at the coffee shop versus my basic living expenses, I realized I'd be broke in two months, three if I were lucky. If getting a job were a baseball game, I had three strikes: being a woman pushing sixty, having an eclectic résumé that didn't match my skill set, and trying to find work in a recession. It made my frustrating job search after Jack died look like a stroll on the beach.

I once told Rose that she should make up a budget. She just rolled her eyes. "Budgets are for numbers people," she said. "They drain your soul."

I ignored the unintended implication that I had a drained soul and said no more, realizing that Rose would do what Rose always did. And make it work. And if she didn't, she had the safety net of me.

But being Rose without that safety net required me to engage in the very un-Rose-like activity of budgeting. Realistically, I shouldn't have allowed myself to use any of the money at the estate sale, but I couldn't help myself. Nostalgia triumphed over reason to the extent of $500. If that accelerated the time I'd be living in the car I no longer owned, so be it.

I got to the airport after 8:30, but thankfully, there was no line at the rental counter and traffic flowed smoothly. I didn't dare speed—no money to pay a ticket and no nerve to face another policeman.

I was five miles from Exit 28, when my view changed to a sea of red taillights. My why today mantra played in my head again as I sat boxed in by cars, all at a standstill. After five minutes I turned off the engine, ever mindful of the cost of gas. All I could do was sit and fume. The thudding beat of a Life Flight helicopter's rotor blades vibrated through the car as it swooped past me. At least that's not you up there, Rose pointed out in my head. "Shut up, Pollyanna," I muttered, even though I knew she was right.

Chapter 41

ship home steamer trunk
came with jeans, left with saris
time to backpack home

Rose's Haiku Diary
Kathmandu, Nepal
Age 22

When the traffic finally started to move, I resisted the urge to gawk at the twisted car-skeletons on the berm. Based on the acrid air, at least one had been on fire.

It was almost 11:30 when I finally got to my cottage. A half dozen cars, two pickup trucks and a van were parked out front and people were leaving with bags and boxes. I glanced at Hank's house, but his vintage Thunderbird wasn't anywhere to be seen.

The sight of my wingback chairs being loaded into a van brought me close to tears. I just sat in my rental car, staring at the people coming and going, feeling as if I was rubbernecking the accident of my life, my possessions strewn on the highway.

Let's get this done, I told myself. I pulled out the list of things I hoped my $500 would cover: the mirror that had hung in Grandpa Luke's foyer that Rose and I—well, mostly Rose—primped in front of, my favorite leather jacket, my blender, my short hiking boots, my spice rack, the watercolor of a young girl in a lilac dress running through a field of sunflowers that Hank gave me as a thank you gift after his wife Jane died. I'd figured clothing was usually pretty highly discounted, so I could probably pick up other favorites for a pittance. I added tools to my list after the fiasco with

Elvis. How did Rose get along without basic tools? "Who needs tools, when a man with tools can fix it?" she once scoffed when I offered to show her how to change the flapper in her constantly-running toilet.

Inside my house, a grandmotherly woman greeted me and identified herself as Ellen.

"It's ten dollars," she said.

"It's what?"

"Ten dollars for the early shoppers. After noon you can get in free."

"I'm her sister," I said, gesturing at the living room, which someone had rearranged. It looked out of balance to me.

"Mr. Bankerville mentioned that you'd be stopping by, although we expected you earlier."

"I got stuck in traffic." No point in telling her about the kitten fiasco.

"I guess we can forego the entrance fee. The sale is going very well," she said, not knowing that a big part of me wished it wasn't. I wondered how the real Rose would have felt. Or if she even would have been here.

"There was a mirror here," I said and gestured to the wall by the fireplace.

"Already sold," she said.

"And the watercolor of the sunflowers over the mantle?"

"Same buyer. He was here right when we opened."

Vulture, I thought. Miserable life-sucking, vile vulture.

Find out where it is, whispered Rose.

"Do you have his name? His address?"

"He paid cash, although we couldn't have told you even if he paid by check. Unless Mr. Bankerville authorized it."

I stomped my foot, startling both Ellen and me. I wanted to throw this nameless, faceless jerk against the wall and punch him. Kick him. Scream at him. How dare you steal my life?

I stood for a moment, demanding my fists unclench only to have them overrule me. I forced myself to try to slow my breathing, to ignore the pain in my jaw. Breathe, I told myself. In, out. In, out.

Ellen fiddled with the chain that held her glasses.

It was as if we were caught in amber. Me in my rage, her in her confusion. I think we both felt an odd relief when my front door opened, letting her excuse herself and turn to greet the next pillager.

"Is the clothing upstairs?" I managed to blurt before she could collect the gold doubloons price of admission from the next pirate.

"There's not a lot," she said. "People only buy lightly worn clothes. Most of it already went to Goodwill." She must have seen the distress on my face, for she added, "I'm sorry. That must have seemed insensitive. Your sister had excellent taste. I admire a woman who buys quality and hangs on to her clothes."

I grabbed a box and started for the stairs, but a force pulled me toward my kitchen, toward the picture window that framed my backyard.

I'd always loved the view of my garden from the kitchen, especially on a spring morning like this when it's dappled in sunlight and the wine-purple irises are starting to bloom. I watched the black-capped chickadees and dark-eyed juncos at my feeders and wondered who filled them. Hank? The estate sale people? In the distance, the faint sound of Hank playing Bridge Over Troubled Waters was barely audible over the buzz of muffled conversations about the pieces and parts of my life.

At least they can't sell my garden, I thought, as my possessions were laid out behind me, with price tags attached. As if you could put a price on a memory. Put a price on all these road markers of my life. For a moment I hated Rose, hated her for putting me in this predicament. I stomped up the stairs, spitting out words in my head as each footfall thudded.

Why-do-you-always-do-this-to-me? Why? Why? Why?

By the time I reached the top of the stairs, I started to feel light-headed. Get going, Turkle. I ran my fingers over the banister for the last time before I walked into my bedroom, where my eyes landed on a display of the brightly-colored silk scarves Rose gave me over the years. I was never able to convince her I wasn't a scarf person, but now I wanted them all. They were marked $6 each. I held up one that was a swirl of blues and greens, a Monet watercolor effect.

"That's my stack."

"Excuse me?" I said.

"That scarf, I set it aside."

"I don't see your name on it." It was something Rose would have said, and I felt both momentary elation and shame for my rudeness. As my busybody neighbor Clara Clarke, purveyor of unreliable and often vicious gossip, stood with her hands on her hips, the shame disappeared.

"Agnes would have wanted me to have that," Clara said.

The heck I would have. "I don't think so."

"Oh, don't think I don't know who you are. You're the trampy sister."

"How dare you," I said, managing to stop myself before saying, don't you talk about her like that.

"Don't think I don't know what you did."

"What?"

"How you let Agnes take care of your grandfather and then your mother."

"She wanted to." Why was I defending myself to this hag?

"Selfish. You don't deserve to wear her clothes."

"You old bag."

"Rude and selfish. I always wanted to tell Agnes that. But could I get a word in edgewise? She thought you walked on water." Clara snatched the scarf from my hand.

"No, I..."

"If you ask me, the wrong sister died."

My mouth was open, but no sound came out as Clara tromped out of my bedroom.

I needed to get out, grab what I could and go, before I took my cast iron skillet and whacked someone. Whacked Clara. My skillet. I forgot my skillet. I took another look around my bedroom and grabbed my three favorite scarves, my hiking boots, a pair of river-walking sandals, the fluffy red hat Rose gave me, two pairs of L. L. Bean shorts, and my navy-blue dress. I was on my way downstairs when I remembered the silly T-shirts Rose and I always gave each other on our birthdays. Most of them were nowhere in sight, but I snagged one that proclaimed 50 is the New 30 and another that said Reached Twenty a Second Time. Downstairs, my cast iron skillet was a bargain at $8, but I couldn't afford the Waterford crystal ice bucket Uncle Roger gave me. I loved it even though I'd only used it for flowers–bountiful branches of purple and lavender lilacs in the spring and lilies the rest of the summer.

My mug, I thought. Where is the princess and frog mug Rose gave me for my nineteenth birthday? I scanned the cluster of coffee mugs priced at a dollar each on the kitchen counter. I shook my head. It wasn't any of them, as my mug had a chip on the gold rim.

"This one's damaged—can I get it for a dime?" a Pillsbury Doughboy of a man said to Ellen. His pasty-white hand almost enveloped my mug.

She shook her head. "It's a dollar."

He frowned, putting it in the box with the other bits and pieces of my life he was stealing.

My mug, I thought. I've lugged it everywhere for the past forty years. It can't end up with him.

"I'll give you five dollars for it," I said.

Ellen shot me a look, but must have decided she had better things to do than get in the middle of this penny ante wrangling. Or maybe it was because I was family.

His tiny eyes went from the mug to me and back to the mug. "Ten," he said.

Think poker, Rose whispered.

"Three."

"What? You said five."

"That was before. Now I see the chip. It's three. And in thirty seconds, the deal's off the table." His jaw tightened, so I shrugged and turned to walk away.

"Okay, three," he said, muttering under his breath.

I set down my box, pulled three wrinkled singles from my pocket and held them out, waiting to release my grip until the mug was safely in my other hand, as he glowered at me once he'd grabbed the bills. I almost laughed.

"You still need to pay me the dollar, you know," Ellen said.

I grabbed a set of wrenches, a saw, my favorite gardening gloves and trowel, the champagne flutes Rose and I toasted our fiftieth birthdays with and my statue of intertwined herons. I don't know why I bought the gardening supplies, having no garden and not even a chance of one in my future. Maybe Rose's eternal optimism crept into me for a moment.

I wanted to leave but couldn't bring myself to go. It was as if I was saying goodbye to an old friend, a friend I knew I'd never see again. I sat at my beautiful cherry wood table, staring at my garden, until somebody bought the chairs and table out from under me. I wondered who snagged the stained-glass panel I called Eternal Spring, the one Rose gave me. I hoped it was someone who would love it as much as I did.

When Ellen called, "Ten minutes before the general public admission," I looked out the window and saw former friends and neighbors milling around like *Night of the Living Dead* zombies, waiting for noon and the real feeding frenzy. I knew I better skedaddle. The entire $500 I'd budgeted was gone.

I left by the back door and was loading my two boxes in the trunk of my rental car when Hank drove by and waved. He parked in his driveway and walked back.

"How's it going, Rose?" he asked.

The tsunami of emotion I kept at bay for so long unleashed itself and I started to sob.

"It's just so hard," I said, not sure if I was talking about losing Rose or my cottage and former life.

Hank's eyes were moist as he awkwardly put his arms around me. "I know. I really miss her too." I must have cried for five minutes while he held me like a porcelain doll. When my tears slowed to a trickle, I eased myself out of the comfort of his arms, only to see Clara Clarke watching us. I could almost hear her tongue clucking.

I turned my back to Clara and took the clean handkerchief Hank offered.

"Do you have time for lunch?" he asked. "I'm buying. Maybe the SpeakEasy or the Police Station?"

"The police?" My heart sped up.

"For pizza. Oh, what a dope I am. The Police Station Pizzeria is a great local joint. Agnes and I used to go there several times a month."

Chapter 42

sometimes the small things
mean so much, tell us so much
define who we are

Rose's Haiku Diary
Sturgis, SD
Age 58

"You look so much like her right now," Hank said as we were down to the last two slices of pizza. He surprised me by suggesting the cheese and roasted red pepper pizza, what I always ordered, instead of his usual double pepperoni. I forced myself to order Rose's favorite: sausage, pepperoni, banana peppers and extra cheese.

My face froze at his comment and the last piece of my pizza stopped its journey half-way to my mouth. My brain nagged that this lunch was a mistake. I hadn't bothered to put on makeup again after the Elvis rescue. And my clothes were what Agnes would wear: jeans and a shirt, even though I brought along the peacock jacket for my visit with Mom. So, the only Rose-like aspects to my appearance were my hair—still her honey blonde—and my now nicked, polished fingernails.

"I'm sorry," Hank said, reacting to my flinching. "It was a compliment. Your sister Agnes was such a beautiful person. She had this inner glow."

I did? I do?

"She was so caring. I meant every word I said at her funeral. I don't think I could have coped with the last two years of my wife's illness without her help."

I thought back to the last time I saw Hank's wife Jane. It was just a few days before she died. Hank had finally agreed to Jane's move to hospice two weeks earlier—I think she did it as much for him as for herself. I had seen the toll caregiving took on him. It was as if they were both being hollowed from the inside out. I made stews and soups a few times a week for them. He spent almost every day with Jane at hospice. That day, a Tuesday less than a week before she died, he had called to ask a favor.

"Agnes, I'm dead tired. I just need to sleep. If I get in my car, I think I'll fall asleep at the wheel and drive off an embankment."

"I'd be happy to drive," I told him.

He hesitated. "Could you just look in on her and call me later? She's sleeping a lot, but if she does wake up, I want her to see a friendly face. Tell her I'll see her soon and that I love her."

When I got to Jane's room, she looked like a child tucked among the many pillows. She held out her skeletal hand and beckoned me to sit by her.

"Hank was just exhausted," I told her. "He wanted to come, but..."

"He's been so strong," she said. "In some ways, I think it's been harder on him. I'm glad he's getting some sleep."

"I brought you black-eyed Susans from my garden," I said.

"Throw out those roses and use that vase. They're almost dead. It's funny. He always brings red roses. Valentine's Day, my birthday, our anniversary. I never had the heart to tell him I'm not that much of a rose person. Roses are lovely, but they die so quickly. Daisies last so much longer."

"It's the thought that counts," I said.

She nodded.

"He said to tell you he'll be here soon and that he loves you."

"I know. He called. I think he's afraid..." She took the pink and green scarf off her bald head. "I never thought I'd end up hating scarves, but I have."

"It's a pretty one," I said, while thinking, what a lame thing to say.

"I never thanked you for not giving me one." I must have looked puzzled. "The scarves have come to be, for me at least, a look-at-me-I've-got-cancer flag. Let's dress up for cancer."

I couldn't think of anything to say, so I busied myself tossing out the roses and putting in the black-eyed Susans.

"I'm glad you're here without Hank," Jane said. "I have a favor to ask you." I nodded. "Look after my Hank." The surprise must have shown on my face. "He's been the love of my life and I don't want him becoming a hermit after I die. This was supposed to be our time. Isn't that what they say about retirement? A chance to have those adventures you put off for years? The dreams that the kids, the house, the jobs sort of whittled down until they were just a nub."

"I guess," I said, although I always let Rose choose our adventures.

"Before we got married, we talked about taking a year off after college. Maybe even two. We were going to hitchhike through Europe. Or find jobs on a freighter and see the world. Or be ski bums for a year. The plan kept changing."

Jane closed her eyes and I wondered if she was asleep. I set the vase of flowers on a table and reached over to straighten her blanket. She put her hand over mine, her eyes still closed.

"What happened?" I asked.

She smiled. "I found out I was pregnant two months before graduation and we started talking about baby buggies instead of backpacks. Before the baby was born, Hank and I used to joke that we should name it Destiny. He was always a great dad." She squeezed my hand. "We've been married so long, I don't know how he'll do alone. Keep in touch with him. Have coffee, take walks, maybe go to a movie. Like we used to. He's a good man."

"I know he is," I had said.

Sitting across from him with the remnants of our pizza on the table between us, that thought returned. He is a good man. He'll understand. I nibbled the crust of my last slice, trying to keep my concentration as the end of a fight between two women behind me seemed to be winding up. One of them, a teen with spikey black hair and snake tattoos encircling both arms, bumped my chair as she darted past me.

"Hank," I said. "I have something to..." The word confess caught in my throat like a chicken bone.

"Hold that thought," Hank said as he raised a finger, stood, took three steps toward me, and then passed me. I turned in my seat. He was watching a gray-haired woman in a flouncy blue dress with several dollar bills clasped in her hand stomp toward the door. The younger woman, now at the restaurant's front door, turned and looked back.

Hank bit his lip as he watched the older woman join the younger one and start arguing again. Then he pulled out his wallet and placed a few dollars on the table the women had just left. His hand brushed my shoulder as he returned to his seat.

"Can you believe that?" he said. "Her mother took the tip she left for the waitress."

"That's not right," I said.

"How can she not know that? That she's stealing. It turns my stomach."

"I know," I said, and in that instant, I lost my nerve.

"I'm sorry for the interruption. You started to say something."

"I don't remember," I said.

Hank frowned, as if he didn't believe me, then stirred his coffee. "Would you like to take a walk later? There's a nice wildflower trail—the Butterfly Trail they call it—at the Fern Hollow Nature Center. The wild geraniums are blooming."

That was a sweet little trail. One that Hank and I traipsed many times. A great warm-up before tackling our vigorous jaunt up the Gas Well Path to the Woof and Hoof Spur, then the Spruce Run to the Bog Run to the Beaver Dam Path.

"I still have to visit my mother and get my rental car back." I could almost hear the dollars-clock clicking away, although, considering the day I was having, a walk among the wildflowers and pines sounded more appealing than a visit to Mom.

"I could look in on your mother when you can't make it," he said. "After all your sister did for me, it's the least I can do."

"Sure, okay. Thanks." All the words coming from my mouth sounded trite, but the words I wanted to say were gone.

Hank walked me to my car, which was decorated with a parking ticket.

"Just what I need," I said, but before I could stuff it in my purse, Hank pulled it from my hand.

"I'll take care of it," he said, and I let him.

Chapter 43

close to the painting
you only see the brush strokes
back away, see more

Rose's Haiku Diary
Paris
Age 40

My head was throbbing by the time I parked the car at Shady Oaks, put on my peacock jacket, and went to see what year Mom was living in.

"She was having a good day earlier," Laarni said as we traced the familiar corridors to the arts and crafts room. "She's better. A lot less coughing. I hope she doesn't relapse. She's still not strong."

As we approached Mom at her easel, I examined the sketch she was hunched over. The outline of a hand reached through a window, taking up the lower-left corner of the canvas. The view from the window was of a road that wound like a snake into the distance. It was winter or after the Apocalypse, as the trees lining the road were barren and shriveled. Halfway down the road, I was surprised to see not one, but two tiny figures, holding onto each other as they struggled against the wind. I couldn't tell if they were coming toward or moving away from the window.

"Look who's here," Laarni said, and Mom turned, set down her brush and examined me.

"Hi, Mom," I said, and leaned in to kiss her cheek.

"What are you doing here, Agnes?" she said. Laarni gave me that I'm-sorry look, patted my arm and left us. "I know you said to call you

Mother, but you're not my mother. Just because I married your son doesn't mean I have to call you Mother."

I decided not to correct her and ask a neutral question.

"How are you doing?"

"I can't decide what title to give this," she said, pointing at the picture.

"Do you have any ideas?"

"Richard will know," she said. I tensed, as Mom hardly ever used my father's name, usually calling him that man, short for that man who ruined my life.

"Who are the figures in the painting?"

"Can't you tell?" she said. "They're Richard and me. I was thinking of calling it Wedding Night."

"You've done a beautiful job drawing the hand," I said. "I've heard hands are hard to draw." The hand was gnarled, almost claw-like. I wondered whose hand it was supposed to be, if the two figures were the happy couple.

"Go away, Agnes. You bore me. Can't you see I'm busy?"

Without knowing which Agnes she was talking to, all I wanted to do was honor her request and leave. I told her I'd be back as soon as I could, but that I couldn't afford to visit that often any more. I tried to kiss her cheek goodbye, but she turned her head.

On the two-hour drive back to Cleveland, the events of the day fell on me like a cold, wet blanket of exhaustion. I thought of pulling over to take a nap, but kept hearing the cash register ka-ching for every minute I returned the rental car late. Instead, I stopped for overpriced coffee at one of the rest stops.

It was drizzling when I reached Cleveland and I couldn't find a parking spot close to my apartment building. I was soaked by the time I lugged the second box to my apartment. I stripped off my wet clothes, toweled my hair, put on dry clothes, and sat on the floor, again thinking all I wanted was sleep, but knowing I still had to return the rental car. Elvis trotted over and put his head under my fingers.

"I am so glad Rose found you," I told him as I picked him up and cuddled him to my chest. He purred, a purr that seemed to have magical medicinal qualities, and my headache started to wane. "You are getting a new can of something expensive when I get back," I said as I put him on the floor. "For now, let's check your dry food." I refilled his food and water bowls, cleaned his litter box, and headed back to my car. Two hours, tops, I told myself. An hour to get to the airport and turn in the car, an hour to get home, then tuna for Elvis, a hot bath, and a glass of Chardonnay for me.

The drive took fifty minutes. As I turned in my rental car, I reached for my sunglasses. I retraced my steps. I must have left them at the Police Station pizzeria in all the hubbub of the purloined tip. Walking through the airport to the Rapid train station stop, I called Hank and asked him to pick them up the next time he was in the neighborhood. He promised he would and offered to mail them to me. I told him I'd get them next time I was in Sewickley and wondered if this was how Cinderella felt when she realized she'd lost that glass slipper.

Chapter 44

I just bought something
I really hope not to use
for a long, long time

Rose's Haiku Diary
Rio Rancho, NM
Age 52

I couldn't tell you why it took me so long to find the courage to open the box Rose marked Turkle. I so often thought of that box at times when I could do nothing about it: going to Heinen's for groceries, at work at the coffee shop, in the shower, on my bicycle that I'd named Betsey,

I was drawn to it, like some Pandora's box, when I discovered it among the dozen unpacked cartons when I moved in. But for some reason, every time I remembered it and was in the apartment, with the box in my hands, I felt guilt. Like the guilt when I discovered the stash of unwrapped Christmas presents in Uncle Roger's attic. It seemed an invasion of privacy to look inside.

As I took the lid off, aromas of old paper and vanilla mingled. On top was a purple leather-bound journal. I held it to my heart, not wanting to open it, not wanting to let Rose, the essence of Rose, escape and evaporate. Would it float away, like Hope, or would I inhale it and lose yet another part of Agnes?

I placed the journal in my lap, relishing the soft leather, the weight of the book, and the little warmth it generated. I picked up each new object as tenderly as if I were an archaeologist excavating a priceless dig, not wanting to harm any of the ancient, fragile relics. And maybe I was. Excavating the King Tut tomb of Rose's belongings.

I found the letters I sent Rose when she was in the Peace Corps in Nepal and I was leading my own primitive life with Jack. They were tied with a red ribbon.

Another envelope, yellow and brittle with age, had the words I'm sorry written on it in a childish, yet definitely Rose-like, scrawl. I stared at it, ran my fingers over each letter, as apologies were not one of Rose's strengths. The envelope was lumpy and when I teased it open, out fell that card with the two plastic, silver-colored bobby pins, each adorned with a small pink rose inside a white filigree heart that I'd shoplifted from Woolworth's as Rose's partner in crime. I picked up the card and held it to my face.

"I'm sorry, too," I whispered.

I wondered if she planned to give these back to me. Or were they a reminder to herself?

I placed each item in a semi-circle around me. Half of the circle of life.

The box marked BIG 60 called to me. Inside were a dozen brochures for places Rose suggested we go to celebrate our sixty years of life together. She probably would have toasted as she always did: "Here's to the next sixty." It's like crossing a room, she told me. If each time you only go halfway, you never get there. So, you plan for the next twenty when you're twenty, the next thirty when you're thirty. You know what it's like to have lived that long, so it's not hard to imagine just doing that again.

A sealed envelope with Happy 60th written on it was taped to a small velvet box. I cradled it in both hands, as if I could absorb the molecules, the fingerprints Rose must have left on it when she signed and sealed it. I wondered why she signed it almost six months before our birthdays. Did some tiny part of her wonder if she'd be here to give it to me? I stared at it, aching to open it, but somehow feeling that doing so would be wrong. I'd never peeked at Christmas or birthday presents, even when Rose had discovered where they were hidden. It somehow felt like it would diminish her message if I read it early. That I'd regret it when it finally was our birthdays, my birthday. I decided that I needed that reward, reading her letter for the first time on my birthday, so some part of me could feel as if we were together. I set the letter down, vowing to wait until my birthday in September. But I couldn't resist finding out what was in the velvet box that looked just a little too big to hold an engagement ring. Inside was a braided silver chain with a charm shaped like a gingko leaf. The lettering on the charm read: If you live to be 100, I want to live to be 100 minus one day, so I never have to live without you.

Tears filled my eyes.

"Not fair," I said. "Not how it's supposed to be."

A manila envelope yielded an official-looking bound document and a dog-eared spiral notebook that seemed somehow out of place. Like finding a Tootsie Roll wrapper at the Tut dig. Rose labeled the columns: date, amount, total, notes. The notes column contained only one or two letters per line, most of them a capital T, although there were several UR's. The handwriting looked, at first, childish, like the I'm sorry on the envelope but then evolved into Rose's distinctive flowery scrawl. I stared at the first two pages which covered years starting in high school, trying to decipher this accounting journal. The dollar amounts started small, $7 or $4, then got progressively larger. It clicked into place when I saw the break in dates, which coincided with Rose's time in the Peace Corps. Rose had kept a record of all the money she ever borrowed, most of it from me. The T on most of the lines in the last column was, of course, Turkle. She probably figured she'd pay me back when she won the lottery. But she intended to pay me back. I was astonished. I called them loans; she called them loans, but long ago I stopped expecting repayment and thought of them as pledges of love. Something I could and wanted to do. The First National Bank of Agnes.

I turned the page and saw a new pattern of numbers emerge. There was a break that was the ten years or so when she didn't ask for my help and then, interspersed with the rows in black or blue ink, there were rows in red. For the last fifteen years, there were a couple of dozen entries with a T for Turkle in the right column where I recognized the dates and amounts I'd loaned her--$1500 one time, $2200 the next. But for each of these rows, except for the last entry, the money I sent her a few months ago for her medical tests, the next line had an entry for the same amount with a minus sign next to the amount and always a different set of initials in the last column. It took a moment for my accountant-brain to digest what I was seeing. For the past ten or so years, all those times she borrowed money from me with no explanation given—other than, trust me, it's important—and none asked from me, she was passing the money on to someone she thought needed help.

For the eighteen months she was married to her playboy husband Luis, there were no lines in black, only a spate of red lines, as she apparently went on a spree, intent on putting at least a chunk of his money to better use than jet-setting. Was that part of the reason they divorced?

The last line was a loan she made only a few months ago for $200 to a TL.

Why hadn't she told me what she was doing? But of course, in a way, she had. She'd told me so many stories about her friend Chris and how she was always helping some down-on-their-luck soul. Sonya, who needed a car so she could quit her minimum wage, fast food job and accept the hostess job at an upscale restaurant. Barbara, who needed help with her rent while she tried to fulfill her dream of becoming a painter. Bill, a singer-songwriter who played a killer guitar and had a gig lined up in Nashville if he could just get there.

"Son of a bitch," I said.

I was Chris.

I reached for the journal. I wondered why it was in the box marked Turkle, instead of the box marked Private—Keep Your Snoopy Nose Out. I turned to the first page.

"Hi, Turkle," it said. "I read about this recently, writing an ethical will, things you'd like people, special people, those you love, to know.

We share so much. I wonder what there is to tell you that you don't already know. You know I love you. That you're oxygen to me. And sunshine and rain. Things I can't live without. Did you know that I hear your voice sometimes, especially when I'm going to screw up? I know, you're thinking I must hear it a lot. Or maybe you're thinking, our voices are alike, exactly alike—how can Rose know that it's her sister Agnes's voice? How can Rose know if she's not just talking to herself. But I do know.

Unless you're snooping—that would be so unlike you, but maybe my bad influence is finally wearing off on you—I guess this may be our last communication. Just like me to want to get in the last word—even after I've died.

I'm looking at the article on what to put in this ethical will. Regrets, it says. You're probably thinking I regret not moving to Australia to marry Derek. Part of me does, I guess—the young, stupid, in-love part. But, no, I don't.

At the time, I was also afraid of losing myself, of losing the life I imagined for myself. The Peace Corps opened my eyes to some of the wonders of the world. I was only 22. Remember my high school year book goal?

swim naked, find love
see the world, never be fat
make people happy

I was still that girl. Determined to travel, see more, do more before I settled down, if I settled down. Housewife? Not me.

Do I regret my two failed marriages? No. At least I tried. Although maybe I regret that I held on too long, thought I could change Parker, get him to stop drinking and keep his pants zipped.

I regret that we never got to be little old ladies together. I can see us now, racing our wheelchairs up and down the streets of San Francisco, Paris, or Hong Kong. Or yes, even sleepy little Sewickley. I bet that would have gotten tongues wagging. Maybe we'd have even mooned that old biddy Clara. I do regret that I never got you to go skinny-dipping with me. Nothing beats the feeling of the water on your entire body. I hope you've gone skinny-dipping with somebody."

Yes, Rose, I should have joined you that night we had the beach to ourselves in Crete. Or the time in Barbados. But I was truly happy to just watch you be happy.

"What else? I have never forgiven myself for not being there when you were going through that living Hell with Jack. I would have kicked his butt. Nobody treats you that way. I would have left Nepal early if I'd known.

If regrets are part of this, shouldn't I get to tell what I did right too?"

I stopped reading and closed my eyes. I heard Rose's voice as I read, saw her face. Almost as if her ghost was with me. I thumbed through the journal. There were only four pages of writing left. I wanted to devour those last pages, like a starving woman suddenly at a banquet. Her words both eased the pain in my gut of missing her and inflamed it.

Elvis crawled in my lap and I stroked his soft fur. He purred.

Yes, Rose, I hear your voice too.

I let the room go dark, with the half-halo of the contents of the box Rose marked Turkle arranged all around me and Elvis asleep in my lap. I felt drunk on emotion. Love, loss. Then my legs started to cramp and I placed Elvis on the floor next to me. He turned his head, gave a meow protest, and then curled up to continue his nap.

I heard muffled voices from Jasmine and Hyacinth's apartment. A combination of talking and singing—what they did when they made dinner. My stomach rumbled its agreement that it was time to be fed. I began repacking the box. As I reached for the ledger with Rose's loans, I came upon one last document in a brown legal envelope. It was folded in half, and I smoothed out the pages. It took a moment for my brain to process what I saw: Rose took out a life insurance policy seven years ago and named me as beneficiary. A two-hundred-thousand-dollar life insurance policy. A wave of shame washed over me that I never thought to take out a policy just for her. Something above what I needed to set aside for Mom's care. It seemed so obvious now. And so un-Rose-like of her to do this. So un-Agnes-like of me not to.

I talked to her about life insurance once, decades ago, and she told me Parker didn't need any more reasons to get rid of her. "Besides," she said. "It's ghoulish. Betting against yourself."

"But you have car insurance, home insurance," I responded. I almost added that life insurance was a better bet, since while you might never have a car accident or have your house go up in flames, everyone dies. But she was right. That would have been a bit ghoulish.

My brain kept trying to untangle this Catch-22. The real Rose had a life insurance policy. The real Rose had died. She'd kept the promise to repay all I loaned her over the years, but of course, I couldn't collect it, because the fake Rose wasn't dead. I wasn't dead. I dug into the details of the policy and saw that another premium was due July 1st.

My cell phone buzzed and pulled my brain from the rat's maze it kept running, always stopping at a dead end. The caller ID showed it was Mr. Bankerville.

After the usual curt exchange of hellos, he got right to the point. "Shady Oaks is closing," he said. "Your mother will have to be transferred to a new facility."

I don't have time to hunt for a new nursing home, I thought. It took me six months to find this one.

"When?" I asked, although dozens of questions were jostling to go first.

"The patient relocation deadline is June 30th, but sooner would be better."

"I'm not sure when I can..."

"I'll call you when we've made the arrangements."

I almost screamed, you can't do that, but bit my hand instead, finally regaining enough composure to get out a muffled, "When?"

"When we've found a new facility and have a transfer date."

"I thought I'd be the one to choose..."

"Please, Mrs. Grimaldi. Remember that your sister left your mother's care in our hands. We have experience in these matters. Quite frankly, this was fortuitous. Shady Oaks is costing more than your sister's estate can afford. We were already planning to move your mother. This just accelerates the process."

Chapter 45

whispers, gossip, lies
I'd rather have sticks and stones
no Band-Aids for hearts

Rose's Haiku Diary
Las Vegas, NV
Age 32

Two days later, I was still stewing over my helplessness to do anything about my mother's care when I joined Hank for lunch. He seemed to have something on his mind too, since our usual easy banter was stilted and filled with long awkward pauses, as I fiddled with my newly-returned sunglasses.

After our meals arrived, he picked up his fork and pushed around his vegetarian cassoulet.

"I wasn't sure if I should say anything, but I thought you should know that there have been rumors," Hank said.

"Rumors?" I asked.

"It's that Clara Clarke."

That old biddy, I thought, but put on my best puzzled look.

"Oh, sorry. You look so much like her, sometimes I forget and think you're, you know..."

I shook my head and gazed into the restaurant's courtyard. Sparrows were landing on the flagstones, looking for crumbs.

"What kind of rumors?"

"It's stupid, really. I don't know why I brought it up. Nobody believes Clara." He placed his fork on the bread plate. "She's telling everyone, well, anyone who will listen, that..." His eyes, which were locked with mine, dropped again. "She says you're not you."

"I'm..."

"That you're Agnes."

I stabbed my salad so hard I worried the plate might crack. Hank jumped.

"I'm what?"

"I wasn't even sure if I should say anything. It is so crazy."

I stood, fighting the urge to bolt from the restaurant. My eyes darted from table to table. Was one of the diners an undercover detective, waiting for the right moment to arrest me?

Hank touched my hand. "I'm sorry. I didn't mean to upset you. You've been through so much."

I swallowed and sat, hoping my face was not the fire-engine red it felt.

"Crazy," I repeated. I wished Clara was right in front of me. I wanted to push her to the ground, kick her, shout at her: mind your own freaking business. I looked across the table at Hank's concerned eyes. "Does she say why..."

"You know her, well, no, I guess you don't."

I really do, I thought. Or maybe, I really don't. I shook my head.

"She's a conspiracy theory addict. I think she actually believes those stories in the tabloids. And gossip."

"She's a gossip?" I said, remembering to turn it into a question at the last minute.

"The worst kind. She'll repeat anything. And if there's nothing juicy going on, I swear, she makes things up."

My mind raced. What did I do to tip her off? We exchanged words at the estate sale. She looked at me—looked through me—at my funeral. Living in our cul-de-sac and always peeping out her window, of course she knew every time I stayed with Hank.

"She even started a rumor that when my wife was dying, your sister and I were..." He sighed and put his face in his hands, as if just saying the words were an effort. "That we were more than friends," he stammered and his ears and neck turned pink. "That we were sleeping together behind Jane's back."

"She did?" That malicious witch. Nobody ever told me that. I could tear her eyes out, hurting him, a man already in such pain. "Agnes never would..."

"Oh no, we never did," he said as the pink crept into his cheeks. "Never would. Never would hurt Jane like that. Either of us."

"I know."

"Anyway," he took off his glasses and polished them. "Her brother is some big muckety-muck at the Pennsylvania Department of Insurance. She's been bragging that she told him she thinks Agnes didn't die. That you, that Rose did. Her story as to why keeps changing. First it was some crime Agnes committed years ago. Embezzlement or a Ponzi scheme or some such twaddle. Imagine that?"

"Hard to imagine."

"Then it was a scheme to get some big inheritance Rose was coming into."

"That's so..." I started to say, but no words could form in my mind. What's next? Would she accuse me of murdering my twin?

"Now she's saying it was for life insurance money."

"Crazy," I said. Clara couldn't possibly know about Rose's life insurance policy. I didn't even know.

"But she henpecks her brother Clyde. He's spineless, so I'm guessing he'll have to start an investigation, a query, whatever they call it. Just to get her off his back."

"Life insurance," I repeated.

"I just didn't want you to be blindsided," he said.

I started to answer, to thank him, when our server approached. "Save room for dessert?" she asked. "We have a great bittersweet chocolate tart."

Bittersweet, I thought. Story of my life lately.

Chapter 46

I say I'm okay
how do you know I'm lying
are there x-ray ears?

Rose's Haiku Diary
Las Vegas, NV
Age 27

Laarni's words chilled me. "I'm sorry, but your mother's bronchitis has turned into pneumonia. She's been moved to the intensive care wing so we can keep a closer eye on her."

Laarni fielded my barrage of questions with her usual mixture of gentle professionalism and caring and assured me they'd taken the necessary steps. But the way she said it made me wonder.

I thought about calling Lionel Bankerville. Maybe he could get someone to check on her. The Frau, perhaps. But I could already hear the frost in his clipped response, hear him saying something like, we know how to execute our responsibilities.

I called Uncle Roger instead, setting a ten-minute timer so I wouldn't use up too many of my prepaid minutes. The sound of his voice took me to the same place I'd been, decades ago, when he'd wrapped a fleece blanket around Rose and me after we spent hours building a snowball fort. Well, I called it a fort. She called it a castle.

"How are you doing, Rose?" he asked. Not a question that should ambush a person. I wanted to say, I don't know how I'm doing. I'm confused. I'm scared. And I'm not Rose. And sometimes I'm even mad at Rose for dying, for leaving me, leaving me feeling like I'm still here, but I'm not. Like I'm the echo of a voice that's gone.

I choked back those words. Why burden Uncle Roger? "I'm okay, I guess. I'm worried about Mom. They say she's got pneumonia."

Uncle Roger sighed and I could picture him biting his thumb as he crafted his response.

"Pneumonia's never good," he said. "Well, there's a stupid statement, huh, Rosie. Is there anything I can do?"

I want you to hug me and tell me everything will be all right.

"Do you want me to come out?"

I want to turn back the clock. I want my sister back. "No, Uncle Roger, I just wanted to hear your voice. How's Uncle Gus doing?"

"The PT's going well. I know he's getting better because he's starting to criticize my cooking. When he first got home, he ate anything I made and told me how much better it was than the rehab center food. In another week, he'll toss me out of his kitchen."

For a moment, I envied their loving relationship and wished I had someone to take care of me like that. Becoming Rose opened my eyes. Since I left the corporate world, I'd insulated myself from life in my safe little house with my garden and routines. A former client, a Connecticut bank president, who'd been the ruler of his little kingdom, once told me, after a merger, how disrupted his life had become. "I used to know, every day, every week, exactly what was going to happen, exactly what I'd be doing," he'd said. "I miss that." I'd never understood his distress until I traded the meandering river of my life with its daily, weekly and seasonal chores for fording the Rose churning rapids almost every day, never knowing what was behind the next bend.

"I'm glad Uncle Gus is doing better," I said.

"How are you doing?"

"I told you, I'm okay."

The pause where neither of us spoke was so long, I wondered if we'd been disconnected.

"It's okay to say you're not okay, you know," he said.

"I never could fool you, could I?"

"No, you never could."

Chapter 47

have flu, look a mess
he brought me green tea, crackers
kissed me anyway

Rose's Haiku Diary
Bandipur, Nepal
Age 22

"Mr. Bankerville said we should defer to you about authorizing a feeding tube for your mother," Laarni told me when we talked three days later. "We can't get her to eat. She's down to eighty-five pounds."

Considering all the decisions Bankerville ripped from my hands—especially the choice of Mom's next nursing home—shifting this one to me caught me off guard. Was he actually growing a heart—or at least an ounce of compassion?

I hated such decisions. In the last months when Grandpa Luke was so sick, it felt like I was playing God, or maybe playing at being his mother, making those serious medical decisions. Mom told me she couldn't deal with it, left town, and stopped taking my calls until after he died. Uncle Roger was backpacking through Europe with Uncle Gus—off the grid—so he didn't even know Grandpa Luke was close to death.

"Whatever you decide will be the right thing," Rose told me again and again. No doubt she thought it was helpful, but it just made the boulder of those decisions on my shoulders heavier. "Do you want me to fly out?"

I wanted to say, Yes, come out here. Take over for me. Let me be you for a while. You be me. Let me have my biggest worry be which shade of blonde I should be dying my hair. Let my life not be a series of life and death decisions I have to make about somebody else's life. Somebody I love so much.

I told her I was fine.

Grandpa Luke and Mom did have one thing in common, besides their stubbornness. Both told me they never wanted to be a vegetable, as they put it. "Don't hook me up to those machines. If I can't feed and pee by myself, just shoot me," Grandpa Luke had said.

But it was not the same when the hypothetical became the reality.

"We haven't seen you for a while," Laarni's voice from the phone continued, and my cheeks flushed.

I've wanted to come, I thought. I've called on Wednesdays and Sundays, the days I used to visit. I've thought about calling every day, but didn't want to be a pest. I've been trying to figure out if I have enough money to rent a car to get there and if I can juggle my work schedule.

"I'll call you and let you know when I'm coming," I said before hanging up the phone, wondering where I'd find the money to rent a car. I was losing ground financially. I was making enough to cover kitten and people food, but not rent and my rent-free days were over. Most of the money from selling my car was already gone and the minimum payments on Rose's credit card barely budged the debt. I worried that I should be taking Elvis to the vet.

Before I could chicken out, I punched Hank's speed-dial number. I'd lied to him and told him I was working and couldn't get away the last two times he was in town to visit his daughter, son-in-law and grandson. It wasn't that I didn't want to see him, but that I did. Too much. And that I couldn't get my head around walking and talking a lie every moment I spent with him.

I told myself this call was different, that I wasn't a liar-liar-pants-on-fire for asking for his help now, that I was doing it for the right reasons, even if it felt all wrong. I was not a very convincing liar, even to myself. Part of me hoped the call would go to voicemail, but he picked up.

"Hi, Rose," he said.

He's programmed my cell number, I thought. That might seem mundane, but for me, it was still a sign of something. Recognition? Commitment? A message saying, I want to talk to this person again. I want to know when she calls.

But then again, I'd programmed his too.

"Any chance you're coming to Cleveland any time soon?" I asked. "I need to bum a ride back to Sewickley."

"I'm here now," he said. "When were you thinking of going to Sewickley?"

"I don't want to inconvenience you..."

"That's what friends are for. We are friends, I hope. Your sister..."

I couldn't bear another tribute to Saint Agnes, so I interrupted him. "When would be good for you? I'll see if I can change my work schedule."

The next morning, I dressed in Rose-clothes: sandals, a flouncy flowered skirt and a matching top. I almost grabbed my denim jacket, but could see Rose roll her eyes and threaten to turn me into the fashion police. Instead, I took her white linen jacket.

Hank's smile was welcoming. When he complimented me on my dress, a flash of annoyance jolted me, then I wondered why. Was he thinking of trying to take up with Rose? It felt like a rerun of all those boys in high school—why had it taken me so long to figure out that when they asked me out and suggested double dating, it was only so they could get closer to Rose?

As we drove the now-familiar roads, up Shaker to Richmond, Hank and I went through the usual questions of health and weather and Uncle

Roger and my job, with him doing most of the talking. It occurred to me that I was consciously playing the Rose role with him, something I had mostly shed the past couple of weeks.

After a few moments of silence, I asked, "How's your grandson doing?"

Hank smiled. "Pretty well, considering. Chad and I have a movie/pizza night now when I visit, so the newlyweds can have some private time. One of us picks the movie and we each get to pick half the pie. At first, he picked some real stinkers."

"Did he like your picks," I asked, knowing that Hank was a huge fan of classic films.

"Not at first. But we're reaching common ground. We just saw *The Bank Job* and both liked it."

"Heard it was good. Who doesn't like a good bank heist story?"

"Speaking of bank heists, did you hear about that woman they arrested for a bank robbery that happened twenty-five years ago?" he asked.

I shook my head. "Not much time to read the paper."

"She'd gone back to her brother's house and was outside washing his car when the police grabbed her."

"No wonder she got caught," I said, thinking, I guess they never stop looking for you.

"She said she just got tired of looking over her shoulder all the time."

As we got on the Ohio Turnpike, I yawned and apologized for the second time, then told Hank I worked a double shift so I could get the day off. He suggested that I take a nap and I accepted and reclined my seat, both out of exhaustion and for the break from playacting.

Hank's fingers tapping my shoulder and his voice saying, "Rose, Rose," woke me. We were at Shady Oaks. "Do you want me to come in with you or should I wait here?"

"You don't need to wait. I can call a cab, take a bus, something."

"I think your sister's ghost would haunt me if I did that."

His face fell when I winced at his attempt at humor. He started to apologize, but I cut him off.

"Yes, I guess she would," I said. "Sure, that would be nice. Why don't you come in. If Mom is in one of her moods, you can hang out in the atrium and I'll get back to you there."

We were escorted to a different part of the building and told Mom was getting closer medical supervision. She was propped up in a chair in her robe and nightgown, staring into space. I dreaded this moment every time I visited—this moment when I found out where she was and who she thought I was. A kick in the gut would have felt better.

"Your daughter is here," the aide who walked us to her room announced.

"Hi, Mom," I said. "I brought you something."

She blinked and turned her head. Her eyes went from me to Hank, back to me, then back to him.

I handed her the photo I recently found among Rose's keepsakes—the one of Rose and me at age seven in identical white sailor dresses with identical Band-Aids on our right knees, waiting for Uncle Roger to take us to the Memorial Day parade.

She stared at it. "Decoration Day," she said.

"Yes," I said. "They used to call Memorial Day that."

She put the photo on the table next to her chair, traced Rose's face with her finger, then mine, then turned it facedown and looked from Hank to me. "I know you," she said to him.

"Hi, Mrs. Blumfield," Hank said and then whispered to me, "I've been stopping out to see your mom." I turned to him, my eyes wide. "I thought I told you I would try to."

He did say that, but I assumed it was one of those things you say, like telling the dentist you're going to floss more.

"Thank you," I mouthed.

"If you two want to canoodle, why don't you get a room?" Mom said.

"Now, Mom," I said, not sure if I should laugh or blush.

"I'll leave you two alone," Hank said. "Bye, Mrs. Blumfield. I'll bring some purple iris from my garden next time."

I gave him a wave goodbye, then bent and kissed Mom's cheek.

"Laarni tells me you haven't been eating."

"Laarni should mind her own business. The food here is terrible."

"Would you like me to bring you something? Cherry pie? Chocolate amaretto cheesecake? It's your favorite. I still have your recipe."

"No. Not hungry. Why haven't you been to see me?"

"I live in Cleveland now," I told her, not sure if I was answering as Rose or Agnes. "I'm short on funds, so I can't get here as much as I'd like."

"You going to marry him?"

"Hank?" Why would she ask that? Did she even know who he was?

"You always were my favorite," she said. "I know I'm not supposed to admit that. You're supposed to tell each child that they are loved exactly the same as the other. Well, you can tell them that, but it's not true. Roger was Dad's favorite. You'd have thought he would have hated Roger for taking his wife away."

"I guess Grandpa Luke knew it wasn't Uncle Roger's fault that she died giving birth to him."

She snorted. "You can't even love twins equally. You'd think that might be the only time you could. But right from the start, you were different. As babies, I could always tell you apart. It wasn't until you made a game of trying to fool me that I sometimes had trouble. That's why I let you dress differently. Wasn't for you."

"We both loved you," I said. I wanted to add, equally, but couldn't make the words come out, unsure if it was true. And if it wasn't, not sure who loved her more. I tried to get my book stamped more often by becoming her guardian, but was that love or obligation?

"I'm not dead yet."

"You know what I meant.

"I think you should marry him."

"You do?"

"At least he visits me."

I resisted pointing out that this was, perhaps, not the leading quality for a son-in-law, but perhaps for her, it was.

"I'll try to visit more."

"That's your problem. You always try, but you never do." Was she talking to Agnes or Rose? "I had such high hopes for you. You were my golden girl. That's why I pushed you. I wanted so much more for you."

"Thanks, Mom," I said.

Her head was starting to droop. Before she closed her eyes, she said, "Have a good life Agnes."

Chapter 48

part of being young
have to make our own mistakes
wish I'd learned from mine

Rose's Haiku Diary
Mud Butte, SD
Age 44

Hank's wineglass clinked mine as we sat on the patio at Sarava, a Brazilian restaurant on Shaker Square, where even the Happy Hour prices were out of my price range. This, of course, meant Hank was buying. In my old life, I would have insisted we split the tab—knowing how his late wife Jane's medical bills decimated their retirement nest egg. I suggested finding some place less expensive—perhaps the Academy Tavern.

"Nice place," he said, "but not festive. We need festive. This is a celebration. Besides, my daughter Julie gave me a gift certificate."

"Celebration?" I asked

"Your two-month anniversary in Cleveland. We Pittsburghers have a love-hate relationship with you Clevelanders, you know. So, surviving two months in Cleveland is quite the feat. Worthy of celebration."

Rose would have given one of her belly laughs, but all I could muster was a smile. Hank was telling me about a group of three other local bagpipers he'd joined that jammed once a month when the discordant wail of a guitar blared from his cell phone.

"My grandson's calling," he said. "He programmed the ring. Sorry, thought I turned the thing off. I better take it—he never calls me."

He slipped away from the table as he opened the phone. "What's up, buddy?" I heard him ask before the din of an RTA train headed downtown blurred the rest of his conversation. I watched the other diners while I nibbled on our spicy chicken passarinho appetizer. A man and woman in their twenties glowered in silence in the midst of a fight. Five women in their eighties, a book club perhaps, talked and laughed. A group of couples seemed to be in a competition as to who could drink their mojitos the fastest.

Hank came back to the table with a worried look on his face. "I am so sorry, Rose. My grandson is in trouble. Got busted for under-age drinking. I need to go bail him out."

"Oh, no. Anything I can do to help?"

"Would you mind coming along?"

"Me?"

He nodded. "I don't have a clue how to bail somebody out," he said, "and I thought..." His ears started to turn pink. "No, that came out wrong."

"It's okay. I have a PhD in life experience, starting with Making Bail 101." This was something I heard Rose say so many times.

He gave a nervous laugh. "Thanks. Do you know where the Cleveland Heights station is? Some place called the Severance Mall?"

We stopped at an ATM on Lee Road and then drove to the police station. I filled Hank in on what I knew about posting bail from the times I got Rose sprung, starting in college.

After Hank posted bail, Chad shuffled out, staring at his enormous sneakers.

"What were you thinking?" Hank said. "And look at me when I'm talking to you."

"Sorry," Chad mumbled as he shifted his gaze up, although his eyes did not meet Hank's.

"How did you get up here?"

"Borrowed Mom's car."

"She's going to skin you alive. What did you tell her?"

"Library."

The scowl on Hank's face deepened. The last time I saw him this angry he was battling his insurance company trying to get Jane approved for a procedure they considered experimental.

"Were you planning on driving?"

Chad shrugged.

"I guess we need to get you and your mother's car home. And no, you are not driving."

"We can go together to get the car. I'll drive it and follow you," I said. "We can drop Chad and his mom's car off and come back together."

Hank smiled and mouthed a thank you.

Chad sat silent in the back seat as we drove to the parking lot next to a Marc's on Coventry Road. We all got out, which was when Hank noticed Chad texting and demanded his cell phone. For once, Chad showed some common sense and handed it over without a word.

"I'll ride with her," Chad said as he handed me the keys.

We both looked at Hank.

"If it's okay with you," he said.

I nodded and soon we were on our way. When I'd tried to talk to Chad at his mother's wedding, I got single-syllable answers. I wasn't sure where to begin this conversation, or even if I should try.

"This really sucks," Chad said.

"Yeah," I said. "Been there."

"You? For what? Like jaywalking? Like bringing back a library book late?"

"Let's see. Loitering. Drunk and disorderly. Criminal mischief. Defacing public property. Indecent exposure. My fantastic journey that started in a bar and ended behind bars."

His surly teen bravado seemed to thaw.

"No shit?" he said.

"'Fraid so. You didn't invent stupid." I took my eyes from the road for a moment and noticed that the corners of his mouth turned up ever so slightly, which I considered a victory. "My Grandpa Luke used to tell my sister and me that you only get so much luck in life, so don't waste it on stupid."

Chad stopped drumming his fingers on his ripped jeans, although he kept looking at his hands, probably aching for his cell phone.

"Think of two jars, Grandpa used to say. One is empty and one is full of marbles. You never know how many marbles you get—some people get a lot, others only a few. But every time you do something stupid or take some dumbass risk, one of those marbles goes from the luck jar to the experience jar. When your luck jar is empty..."

I waited. Rose taught me the power of silence in controlling a conversation. Chad finally turned to me—I resisted thinking, I won— "Then what?"

It was one of Rose's favorite gestures and I hoped to do her proud. I raised my right arm, finger pointed toward the roof of the car and made a whistling sound as I twirled my right hand down until it slammed into the steering wheel with a crack. "Splat," I said. "Out of luck." I considered telling Chad that you think your luck jar is bottomless when you're young, but he seemed to be mulling over what I said.

"Do me a favor, will you?" I said. "Don't tell your mom about my life of crime, please."

He smiled. "Yeah, sure." He shook his head. "You're way cooler than Grandad's old girlfriend."

Chapter 49

Halloween party
what shall I go as this year
pirate, juggler, ghost

Rose's Haiku Diary
Sewickley, PA
Age 16

I woke up thinking, what do you want to do today, Rose? It scared the hell out of me. Was I losing myself? Losing Agnes? And did I care?

When we were kids, we studied each other's idiosyncrasies to fool our friends and teachers and occasionally Mom, Uncle Roger or Grandpa Luke. By age nine, when we switched places, I felt I was Rose, not Agnes playing Rose. I loved it.

But this was different now. Then, I always went back to Agnes. That felt good, too.

Now, I sometimes felt like the juggler we saw in New York City on our 35th birthday trip. Rose and I had just finished tacos and white sangria at Tio Pepe in Greenwich Village. We walked into the September evening, wandered the crooked streets and straight avenues, looked at restaurant menus, checked out the odd little shops and engaged in New York City's best pastime, people-watching.

We ended up on 6th Avenue at a small triangle of land near the Waverly Theater.

"Want to get a drink and catch the midnight show?" Rose asked, pointing her thumb at the marquee which proclaimed, Midnight Eraserhead.

"No, let's just enjoy this night. The people. You. Us."

So, we stood on the concrete patch and watched the juggler climb onto his ten-foot unicycle. He started juggling bowling pins. He only faltered once, and only for a split second. I think it was when Rose caught his eye and winked.

After a couple of minutes, he tossed the pins, one by one, to his assistant, a small bald man. "We could double-date," Rose whispered as she nudged me and jerked her head toward the assistant. I gave her the evil eye.

When the assistant started to light torches and toss them to the juggler, Rose hunched over and proclaimed, "Look mix-master, the pillagers are blighting scorches."

"Don't worry, little Frankiesteinette, I'll protect you," I said.

The juggler added flaming baton after flaming baton to the fiery circle as the sky darkened, enhancing the spectacle. When he was juggling five, we applauded as he called to the crowd something I'll never forget. His words did seem to capture my new life as Rose: "You should see it from here."

Chapter 50

growl, zoom, vroom, screech, thud
pickup versus motorbike
it stopped, I did not

Rose's Haiku Diary
Shamrock, TX
Age 26

Hyacinth and I hung out most Saturdays, so Jasmine could spend time with her boyfriend Michael. Jasmine called it babysitting, but I called it buddy-sitting. If I'd known eight-year-olds were so much fun, I'd have made friends with one years ago. I'd given Jasmine a key to my apartment and told her Hyacinth was welcome to visit Elvis while I was out. I always felt a surge of joy when I returned to see him on her lap as she read.

"I envy you both today," Jasmine said as she dropped off Hyacinth. "Parade the Circle is a hoot. But I promised Michael we'd go to the Football Hall of Fame."

"And we always keep our promises," Hyacinth chimed in.

"You bet we do," Jasmine said, hugging her. "You two have fun and stay safe."

"I promise," I said.

After Jasmine left, Hyacinth and I discussed logistics. She wanted to bike there, but I didn't see any way to go there that didn't involve Cedar or Fairhill—both steep and scary going down and heart-straining coming back up. I talked her into taking the bus. After all, the 48/48A would take us right there.

After we got off the bus and were walking to the parade route, Hyacinth said, "Can I ask you a question?"

"Sure," I said, holding her hand as we crossed the street.

"Do you think my mom loves Michael?"

Of all the questions I was expecting and maybe even dreading, this wasn't one of them.

"I don't know."

"Does she still love my dad?"

"I'm sure she does. I see how sad she gets sometimes..."

"Yesterday was his birthday. My dad's."

"Those special days can be so hard."

"Then why is she with Michael and not us?"

"You can love and miss someone, but still need somebody else. Your dad will always be in her heart. And yours."

"I guess," Hyacinth said. She looked up at me and must have noticed me wiping a tear from beneath my sunglasses. "I'm sorry I made you sad, too."

I bent down and we hugged.

"You still want to see the parade?"

Hyacinth nodded and smiled.

We walked silently until we arrived at the grassy football-field-size oval that showcased the pre-parade festivities: musical groups playing everything from accordions to zithers, tents to make hats or save the environment or learn about sustainable farming, folk dancers and modern dancers, hula hoops, hula dancers and Frisbees. The frenzy seemed to bring Hyacinth out of her melancholy.

We both got our faces painted.

"I want a rose," Hyacinth told the artist as she grinned at me.

"Make mine a turtle," I said.

"How come?" she asked, and I just shrugged. No way I would let that Turkle out of the bag.

The warm June sun felt good on my face. We each got lemonade and a slice of Rascal House pizza. Most of the prime viewing spots were taken, but we found a stone wall by the Natural History Museum where we could sit or lean as we waited for the parade to begin. Hyacinth pointed to the arch of blue balloons that signaled the first marchers would soon arrive and for the next ninety minutes, we watched men and women on stilts in outlandish costumes of flaming reds and ocean blues, families, groups of friends, some young, some old. Some elaborate costumes, some just matching tie-dyed T-shirts.

"Let's do this next year," Hyacinth said.

"Sure, we can go next year."

"No, let's be in the parade."

"Anybody can," the man next to me said. "My family did it last year and it was a blast."

I looked at Hyacinth and saw the sparkle in her eyes. Maybe this could be my first step toward skinny-dipping, of getting what Uncle Roger called Rose-i-tude.

"Okay," I said, and Hyacinth whooped with joy. "But only if your mother says it's okay." She nodded. "And you have to help design and make our costumes." This already sounded like a bad idea, but at least it was a year away. Maybe she'd forget. Not likely, though.

Jugglers juggled. Drummers drummed. A trio of two bagpipers and a drummer played "The Rose of Kelvingrove." It was a song Hank told me about at one of the bagpipe concerts he'd persuaded me to attend. It brought a fleeting knot to my throat. The hubbub of the Parade, as participants whirled and swirled in costumes of every color, pulled me out of my brief melancholy. There was Elvis Presley and a sea of Marilyn Monroes. Trolls. Gnomes. Pixies. Living clocks. Alice in Wonderland. It seemed like the spawn that would have occurred if Lewis Carroll and Steven Spielberg went on a bender and tried to outdo each other.

When the parade was over, my knees and back complained about standing for two hours, although Hyacinth's energy seemed undiminished.

"Where do you want to go for dessert?" I asked.

"Someplace we can sit outside."

"Nighttown?" I asked. It was one of the few places I knew. Hank took me to lunch there a few weeks before and I loved its airy patio.

Hyacinth nodded.

"Where do we get the bus?" I asked.

"We don't. We walk." My eyebrows shot up. Climbing that steep hill sounded about as appealing as hiking up Mount Everest barefoot.

"We what?"

"You got to pick how we got here," she said. "Come on. They have the best Turtle Pie Sundae there."

So, our trudge began. The downside of having an eight-year-old friend was keeping up with an eight-year-old friend. The hill looked even steeper on foot than it did from the bus. At first, we chatted, but then I had no breath left for conversation. I willed my legs to keep going, one step at a time. Hyacinth took the lead.

As she skipped and I plodded single file, I thought back to my last parade, when I was seven, just a little younger than Hyacinth. Uncle Roger had taken us to the Memorial Day Parade in Coraopolis. Rose and I wore identical white sailor dresses, although Rose already knew this was a fashion faux pas, made worse by having a mirror image of herself there to remind her. But I loved the crisp white dress and its navy-blue scarf. Rose had skinned her knee when she tumbled into bushes after attempting the

60-degree incline of our favorite sledding hill next to Quaker Valley High School on roller-skates. She had a Band-Aid on. I put one on my unscraped knee in sympathy.

We watched the marchers and the bands, all playing traditional marches, regimented and formal. Uncle Roger scolded Rose after she ran up and touched one of the tubas. "I just wanted to see how it felt," she said. Trying to get him to replace his frown with a smile, she added, "It's good luck to touch one."

He laughed. "And where did you hear that?"

"I don't remember," she said, shrugging. After the parade, Uncle Roger took us to a restaurant with an outdoor café that bordered the park. He went inside to use the men's room, making us promise to wait together for him.

"Look at the puppies," Rose said, pointing across the park's smooth green expanse to a man walking two Dalmatian puppies. "C'mon, let's go see if we can pet them."

"No. We promised Uncle Roger we'd wait here."

"I had my fingers crossed. Besides, you promised we'd stay together." She slipped from her chair, ran across the street and started to cross the field. I was frozen, staring at her white dress getting smaller and smaller, like a dove flying off. Should I run after her? Or go get Uncle Roger? I was in trouble no matter what I did. I couldn't keep both promises.

A car horn jolted me from the past.

Hyacinth was twenty feet ahead of me. "Hurry up, slowpoke," she called as she turned around and started to walk backwards up the hill.

"Wait up," I called.

"La la la. I can't hear you," she said, putting her fingers in her ears.

A little red sports car raced toward the intersection ahead of us. He's going too fast, I thought. Hyacinth started moonwalking.

"Slow down," I called to Hyacinth between gasps as I started to run.

"Betcha can't catch me," she called back and picked up her pace, still walking backwards, still not watching where she was going.

He's not going to stop, I thought. He's not slowing down.

"Stop," I yelled. Both Hyacinth and the car were only a few feet from the crosswalk. I hadn't run so fast since the drugstore shoplifting caper, but I ran as if the hounds of Hades were at my heels.

"Can't hear you," she called again. The car was picking up speed as the light turned yellow, then red. Hyacinth and I reached the curb at the same time. She's too close to the curb, I thought, as she stumbled and started to fall backwards.

"No," I shouted. I grabbed her arm and swung her back to the sidewalk as if she was my square dance partner, which hurtled me into the car. Hyacinth's eyes first brimmed with mischief, then went wide with fear. Then it was as if I was seeing a series of photos of the driver, like the strip you get from a photo booth. First looking up from her cell phone. Click. A flash of anger. Click. Disbelief. Click. Horror. Click. Eyes closed.

The car did not hit me. My right side crashed into it and then I bounced off it.

I must have lost consciousness for a moment, because the next thing I remembered was being on the ground with people all around me. The first face I saw was Hyacinth's. She was kneeling next to me sobbing, with a look of panic on her face.

"Omigosh, omigosh, omigosh! Are you okay?" she asked between ragged breaths. "I'm so sorry. It was my fault. I wasn't listening. Are you okay? Mom is going to be so mad. Are you okay? Can I do anything? Do you need anything?"

"I don't know," I said. "Your mom is just going to be happy you're okay. You are okay, right?"

She nodded.

"Just a little scrape," Hyacinth said and held up her elbow which was oozing blood.

"I saw the accident," a woman said. "She started to run the light. I've called an ambulance."

Another face appeared. "I'm a nurse," she said. "My name's Judy."

I nodded. Better Nurse Judy than Judge Judy. My neck, hip, and shoulder started to throb. I'll just rest here a minute, I thought. Maybe the pain will go away.

"Don't close your eyes," Nurse Judy said, and a finger tapped my face.

I opened my eyes. The sun seemed like a giant spotlight searing my soul. Confess, it seemed to say. Confess and you can go somewhere dark and cool.

"Where are my sunglasses?" I asked.

"Got 'em," Hyacinth said, her voice still ragged between sobs.

"You sure you're okay, honey?" I asked again.

She nodded. "I'm sorry."

"You should have looked where you were going. You could have been really hurt."

"Yeah. I know. I'm really, really sorry."

The driver, a young woman in a too-tight, too-short red dress and too-tall heels held up a finger to the policeman waiting to take her statement. What can be so important for you to text right now, I wondered. Clearly, she wasn't a surgeon calling the hospital to tell them that the life-saving operation only she could perform would be delayed. Or some brilliant attorney on her way to sway a jury and save her client. Why didn't the cop tell her to stop? I wanted to shake her and yell: your little cyber friends can wait. Then she tucked the phone in her purse and shook her head like Rose used to when she was scared. It was a tiny shake. So small most people wouldn't even notice.

"My mom," she said to the officer, and a flush of shame at my mentally chiding her washed over me. Her mom. She was calling her mom.

The officer said something I couldn't hear and the girl looked over and pointed at us.

"She came out of nowhere. I didn't see her. I'm so sorry. So sorry."

You should not have been talking on your cell phone, I thought, but swallowed the words.

"Here's the ambulance," Nurse Judy said. "I'll go give a witness statement to the police while you're being examined. But first, come with me, young lady. I've got bacitracin and a Band-Aid with your name on them. Let's get that elbow cleaned up."

Hyacinth left with the woman, but not before she patted my shoulder and kissed me gently on the cheek. A man with a Fire Rescue badge on his white shirt knelt beside me and asked me questions. Some seemed reasonable, like how I felt, what hurt. Some seemed odd – why was he asking what day it was and what I'd had for breakfast? Then I realized that he was trying to make sure my brain wasn't scrambled. He was taking my blood pressure and I knew that if I didn't pass the tests, he would insist on taking me to the hospital.

"Elevated," he said, "but not surprising, considering."

The hospital. I had no insurance. None. Another thing that was once a necessity but had moved to the luxury category. With not a dime to spare, I couldn't afford to go to the hospital.

Hyacinth returned and crouched down next to us, taking in every word. She folded my hand in both of hers and that small connection breathed strength into me

So, I started to lie about how I felt. I told him the pain was a three on a scale of one to ten, when it felt more like thirty-three. That my blood pressure was always borderline high. Finally, he told me to watch his fingers and I must have done that all right—no way to cheat there—since he asked me if I wanted the ambulance to take me to the hospital. He even urged. But he didn't require.

"I'm okay," I said. "Just some bumps and bruises. I'll call my regular doctor on Monday."

And then it hit me, could I ever go to the hospital as Rose, even if I could afford it? Even if I got insurance some time in the future? Would some hospital computer look up Rose's Social Security number and pull up her diagnosis—the original one she got before she showed up at my door—and wonder how she'd been miraculously cured?

"You sure?"

"No. No hospital."

"You're going to feel worse tomorrow," he said.

You have no idea, I thought.

Chapter 51

ice cream should heal all
break your heart: Eskimo Pie
your leg: root beer float

Rose's Haiku Diary
Rio Rancho, NM
Age 57

I told Hyacinth that we could still get dessert, but this child-sage shook her head, her eyes still red from the torrent of tears that had cascaded the entire time I was being interviewed and treated. Instead, she marched over to the young woman whose car I slammed into and convinced her to give us a ride back to Shaker Square. The woman had protested that she was already late and offered to drop us off at a bus stop, but wilted under Hyacinth's stare.

Half an hour later, after picking up ice packs from CVS, we were back at my apartment.

"Paint our nails?" I asked. "Scrabble?"

She shook her head. "You need to rest."

I just nodded, glad to be relieved of my self-imposed duty to entertain this little Florence Nightingale.

Two of my last four Excedrin and the ice packs dulled the pain, but just being off my feet, curled up in my bed with the blinds closed so they shut out the daylight that persists until after nine at night in June, was wonderful. The sharp edges of pain started to soften and recede. I hoped Elvis would cuddle with me, but instead he took on the host duties and stayed with Hyacinth. The pain was swirling around in the background of half-sleep when Hyacinth jostled my arm.

"Wake up," she whispered.

"What?"

"You have a call on your cell. It kept ringing, so I finally answered it. I told them to call back later, but they said to get you. Something about your mother."

I sat up, waking every ragged nerve that my nap had dulled. Even though I was lying on the side that hadn't slammed into the girl's car, my leg hurt, my shoulder hurt, and my head hurt. Hyacinth pressed the phone in my hand.

"Yes?" I said.

"Rose, this is Laarni at Shady Oaks. I'm afraid I have some bad news."

"What is it? What's wrong?"

"Your mother. We were getting ready to move her, even though I told our director to tell that lawyer she wasn't strong enough."

"Move her? What? Where?"

"I thought that lawyer, her guardian, told you. You know that Shady Oaks is closing, right?"

"Yes, but..."

"I guess a spot opened up at Whispering Willows and he wanted her moved right away. Between you and me, I think he didn't want to be paying both here and there for the same time." The mention of Whispering Willows sent an icicle of fear up my spine. I looked at it during my search for a nursing home for Mom. I didn't like the dingy look of it. I didn't like the smell of it. I didn't like the bored eyes of the staff.

"So, they've moved her?" I'm going to kill Bankerville, I thought. I'm going to rip his eyes from their sockets and feed them to the raccoons.

"No, that's just it. When they told her she was going to move, she went crazy. She was screaming and yelling and throwing things. She smashed some of her paintings. When the orderly tried to restrain her, she fell. Just toppled over like a statue. Oh, Rose, it was awful."

"How is she? Where is she?"

"She's still here. She's in our infirmary. She broke two ribs and sprained her wrist. She's sedated, but she's still in a lot of pain. And she's very weak. Very confused."

"I'll be there as soon as I can," I said.

"Rose, don't tell anyone I called. They told me not to. Said that the attorney would. I wasn't sure if that was our attorney or your sister's. I just thought you needed to know."

"Thanks," I said. I disconnected the call, curled into a ball and started to cry. Hyacinth crawled on the bed and stroked my hair, then curled next to me spoon style. "It's gonna be all right," she chanted as I sobbed. Cried for my mother, cried for Rose, cried for me. For my helplessness. My stupidity.

Damn you, Rose. Damn you.

You should have come clean, Rose whispered. Faced the music. You still could.

Chapter 52

if you won't get mad
then I'll tell you what I did
worked when I was ten

Rose's Haiku Diary
Mud Butte, SD
Age 44

The paramedic was right. I did feel worse the next day. A lot worse. My body throbbed and a knot of pain took root in the back of my skull. I thought about calling in sick to the coffee shop, but I needed the money too much. Even the thought of inconveniencing my customers gnawed at me. I knew all the regulars and even managed to make some of the grumpiest smile. So, I limped over and put on my best good morning smile.

I knew I needed to call Uncle Roger, but I was too exhausted last night. My brain couldn't put together the words. Was my call an update or a cry for help? Crying for help seemed to be part of being Rose, a part that practical, you-can-count-on-me Agnes couldn't understand. Or abide. That adrenaline rush of living on the edge was not how I planned to live my life.

I decided to call Uncle Roger after my shift ended at 11:00—when it would be a respectable 9:00 in Arizona. Maybe the mud of my brain would have congealed enough to be coherent by then. I'd called Mr. Bankerville's office yesterday, right after my crying binge subsided. Of course, nobody was there, as it was Saturday. I left a message to call me as soon as possible. Shouldn't lawyers be like doctors and have an answering service?

No point in calling his office today.

Sundays at the coffee shop were different from weekdays, even different from Saturdays. The normal rhythm changed. Monday to Friday, there were the throngs of caffeine addicts stopping by on their way to work, then a lull, then a build-up of people just before noon. On Sunday, the usual larks showed up when we first opened, but the trade was pretty busy all day, as people staggered their arrivals and lingered over their favorite brew and the Sunday New York Times crossword.

It was my favorite day. People were more patient. They took a moment to chat. But this Sunday, I felt like I was playing a role. More accurately, playing a role within a role. Me pretending to be the pleasant—no, cheerful—purveyor of all things coffee while pretending to be Rose. The nub of pain in my head started to wrap its tentacles around the rest of my body.

"Anything wrong?" my boss Daniel asked about 9:30.

"I bounced off a car yesterday," I said and rolled up my sleeve to show the bruise.

"Why didn't you call in?"

"It's not that bad." Another lie. My specialty.

"Want to go home early?"

I tried to will myself to say no, I'll stay, but I couldn't. I nodded.

"I'll call Angie and see if she can come in early. Can you make it until 10:00?"

"Sure," I said, although I felt some nausea. Maybe from putting only coffee and my last two Excedrin in my stomach before coming to work.

I must not have been convincing, since he looked in my eyes and said, "Go home now. We'll manage. As I think you said in your interview, it's only coffee. I'll pinch-hit."

I could have kissed him, but I just smiled and thanked him.

I hit CVS for their cheapest bottle of aspirin, swallowed two, sat on a bench facing the Shaker Square Cinemas, and called Shady Oaks, hoping Laarni would be there.

The sunshine stabbed my brain like a saber. I put on my sunglasses and the floppy gardening hat I had salvaged at the estate sale. I felt like Audrey Hepburn as Holly Golightly trying to hide behind the hat and glasses but probably looked more like Norman Bates' mom. When Laarni finally came to the phone, her voice was like a tonic until her words sank in.

"Your mother's a little worse," she told me. "She's still so weak from the pneumonia and broken ribs are always so painful. She can barely move and won't talk to us, except when we ask how she's doing, she says poor. Just that one word. Except..." Laarni stopped.

"Except what?'

"Nothing."

"What Laarni? You can tell me."

"Except Gustav said she did ask for you. Once. Just once. Where is my daughter?"

"I'll be there as soon as I can," I told Laarni. "They're not transferring her now, are they?"

"It's on hold until tomorrow afternoon."

"Tomorrow? So soon? Is she well enough?"

"That's for her doctors to say. And Mr. Bankerville. Rose, I've got to go. It's crazy here since the announcement we're closing. Some staff have already left. Some are still here but I think their minds are somewhere else. It's a different place."

"Thanks," I said.

I had no energy to hobble back to my apartment and wondered where I'd find the strength and money to get to Shady Oaks tomorrow. I decided to wait to call Uncle Roger. He'd just worry. I promised myself I would call him after I confronted Bankerville and took back control of Mom's care.

I couldn't afford to rent a car, but how else could I get there? Unless... unless I called Hank. But was that taking advantage of our friendship? I stared at my cell phone, as if it could give me the answers. It obliged by ringing. The caller ID showed it was Uncle Roger. Of course it was, I thought. He always calls me on Sunday.

I answered and basked in the sound of his warm voice.

"Tell me where you are," he said, his typical greeting.

"No, you first today," I said. As he talked, his words painted a picture of him sitting on the front porch of their cabin, a cup of Earl Grey tea in his hand, watching the cool mountain mist of dawn that blurs the base of his mountains, like the ruffle on a bride's gown, waiting for the June desert heat to unravel it.

"Your turn," he said.

I planned to tell him about the pugs and poodles, the kids in strollers and the young couples, the joggers and the walkers. I even hoped I could get him to laugh by telling him that the Shaker Square Cinema marquee included two shows that seemed to be based on my life: Land of the Lost and The Hangover.

I hadn't planned to tell him. I really hadn't. Not until I took charge of the situation.

"It's Mom," I said and went through the story of Shady Oaks closing and Bankerville not telling me that he authorized Mom's transfer and her fighting with the orderlies and falling and breaking ribs. "Now they're going to...supposed to transfer her tomorrow. I don't think she's well enough to travel and I hate where he's sending her. I've got a call in to try to stop it, but I don't..."

"You don't have the authority. You're not her guardian."

Right then and there it became clear. I knew the answer to the decision that had simmered in my brain for days, probably weeks. Mom's health was at risk—her life was at risk. I needed to come clean.

"Actually, Uncle Roger, I do. I mean, I am." My throat felt like a pair of hands was choking it, but I had to keep talking or risk losing my nerve. And if I couldn't tell Uncle Roger, how could I possibly tell Bankerville? "I'm not Rose. I'm, I'm Agnes." I tried to picture his face—did he look confused? Hurt? He started to say something but I talked over him, so he fell silent. "We switched places. She needed that operation, that—it was, you know, supposed to save her life." I swallowed hard and plunged on. "She couldn't afford it. I couldn't either. But my health insurance could, I mean did. The only way. Seemed like the only way. I couldn't just let her die. I just couldn't, but she did. And then, I don't know—it all just got away from me. I was afraid I'd be sent to jail." Tears started to roll down my cheeks and I swiped them away. "And, and once I started to be Rose, I just got in deeper and deeper. Oh, you must hate me."

That terrible silence returned and I strained to hear him say something. Say anything.

"Of course, I don't hate you. I love you, Aggie-bear. Always have. Always will. I wish I was there to hug you."

I stopped holding my breath.

"I have a confession too," he said.

Silence. Was I supposed to say something?

Then I heard Uncle Roger sigh and say, "I knew."

"You what?"

"I knew it was you. I knew it was Rose who had died."

"You…how? When?"

"I didn't when I first got there for the funeral. I was numb too. Just sort of sleepwalking, how you do when somebody you love dies and it feels like you got hit with a two-by-four. But I kept seeing little things. Words you used. How you said, my sister, instead of Aggie or Agnes. Rose never did that. And remember when we used to play poker and I told you that both you and Rose had tells, things you did when you bluffed, but I wouldn't tell you what they were?"

"I remember." I thought for a moment of the three of us at Grandpa Luke's Formica kitchen table. I'd been so impressed that he had a caddy with real poker chips.

"It was that, the way you ate your pancakes, the way your lips sometimes move a little before you say something difficult. At first, I shook it off. Told myself I was nuts. Delusions brought on by grief. I'd even wondered if—this is going to sound ridiculous—but wondered if, with you two being so close, her soul decided to join yours."

"I sometimes feel like it has."

"I wasn't sure until we went for ice cream after visiting your mother in the nursing home. I wondered when you pulled out your wallet and the bills were all neatly arranged. But when you asked about your father, I knew. I told Rose a month before and was going to tell you too, but wanted to do it in person."

"Why didn't you tell me you knew?"

"I figured you'd tell me when you were ready."

I had made my first confession.

Chapter 53

strangers become friends
knit together by tears, trust
more precious than gold

Rose's Haiku Diary
Bandipur, Nepal
Age 21

When I reached my apartment building, two police cars were outside, lights flashing. They're here to arrest me, I thought. After I've decided to confess, they're going to arrest me. Take me off to jail. Son of a bitch.

Who will take care of Elvis? I'll have to call Jasmine with my one phone call to ask her to feed him. Or should I call Uncle Roger and ask him to call Jasmine?

If I go to jail, how will I take care of Mom? Would they still let me pry guardianship from Bankerville's clutches as a convicted felon? Don't you get a better deal if you confess? Should I run? How far could I get on Betsey, my bicycle?

The absurdity of the last thought caught me off guard and I started to laugh. Not a cautious Agnes-laugh, but a roaring out-loud Rose-laugh. She would have been proud.

Since the fates chose to take control of my destiny, I decided to get it over with. At least I wouldn't have to worry about how to get to Pennsylvania.

As I waited for the elevator, my leg and shoulder started to throb and my head resonated in sympathy. The bell chimed. Was it always that loud? I got on the elevator and as it rose, my nausea returned when the smell of stale French fries hit me. It hit me that I was crouched over, trying to shift my weight to ease the pain. I must look like an old crone, I thought.

I braced myself as the elevator arrived at the second floor. The door to my apartment was open and just inside it two policemen were talking to a model-thin blonde woman who looked as if some giant hand had picked her up and shaken her. A bruise covered one cheek and her arms and legs were mottled with a dozen more. Her face could have been sixteen or twenty-six, but her eyes had an almost hunted look to them that made her look a hundred.

They all turned toward the elevator and the woman's face grew decades younger when she saw me. "Rose," she called as she ran to me, threw her arms around me and began to sob. "Oh, Rose, Rose, I'm so sorry. So sorry. I didn't think this would happen. I never thought he'd find me."

"It's all right," I said, wondering who this woman was and who I was to her. "You're all right now." Her body felt like it might break into a hundred pieces as I held her and stroked her hair, something I did many a time for Rose. This was a role I knew. Caregiver. Giver of comfort.

"I told myself I wouldn't come back here. But he found me at the shelter. I didn't know where else to go."

The police kept their distance until her crying died down to a whimper and then approached us.

"This is Officer Williams. I'm Detective Mason," the older one said. "You Rose Grimaldi?" The men looked like mirror images of each other, with their taut faces, firm jaws, short-cropped hair and broad shoulders, other than the older man being black and the younger white.

For a moment, I thought of confessing, saying, "No, I'm not Rose Grimaldi. I just play her on television." Rose might have laughed at her own joke, but the kaleidoscope of images, pains and fears, kept my laughter locked far away.

I nodded. "What's going on?" Then I turned to the woman. "Are you all right?" I wished I knew her name. It seemed she needed that comfort of human connection, of hearing her name, but I couldn't give it.

"I am now," she said. "I just feel awful, like it's kinda my fault what happened to your apartment and your cat."

A stiletto of panic stabbed my gut. "My cat. Where's my cat?" Oh, Elvis, please be all right.

"The cat's with your neighbors," the detective said, jerking his head toward Jasmine's apartment. "We were just starting to take Mrs. Lister's statement. Why don't we go inside?"

The policemen exchanged glances when my sleeve folded back to reveal the bruises from my car accident. I am not a battered woman, I wanted to tell them, to shout at them.

My apartment was jumbled. Furniture overturned. The sunflowers painting was on the floor, glass cracked. Lots of broken glass, including remnants of wine glasses, coffee cups and various dishes. There was a brownish stain on the wall and the stench of beer gagged me. I was glad Elvis wasn't here, although the mayhem revved up my worry about him. The four of us sat at my plastic table, the print tablecloth that normally covered it crumpled on the floor.

"Let's go back over what you've already told us, Mrs. Lister," Officer Mason said.

"Call me Tina," she said, then bowed her head, as if she could draw strength from the hands clenched in her lap, her little-girl voice cracking.

Tina, I thought. This was the Tina that left the note I found when I moved in. I placed my hand on her shoulder, which relaxed an inch, before asking, "Anyone like some water?" She nodded but both policemen shook their heads. I picked my way through the broken glass to the kitchen. As I put ice and water in two plastic tumblers, I listened to Tina and the police.

"You said you have a restraining order against your husband, Malcolm," Officer Mason said.

"Ex-husband," she said. "Well, almost. We're separated. I filed for divorce over a year ago. My lawyer talked to him on Friday. He's refused to come to court or anything since I first filed. The judge is going to grant the divorce Monday. I think that's what set him off. Even though I didn't want his money, not any of it."

I thought of getting a broom to sweep up some of the glass, but decided it wouldn't be polite. I returned to the table and set a tumbler in front of Tina. She smiled and tentatively sipped from it, like a gazelle at a watering hole surrounded by lions.

"Go on," Detective Mason said.

Tina took my hand and I squeezed it. She went on to tell them about how we met. Actually, how she and Rose met right before Rose left for Sewickley. Rose sat next to Tina after she saw her hunched over, crying in a bus shelter near the coffee shop where I worked. Rose asked what was wrong. Tina confided that she finally got up the nerve to divorce her husband, but he told her he'd kill her sister or anybody else that gave her a place to stay. Told her no matter where she went, he would find her. She was staying at the battered women's shelter, but he found her there. She had nowhere to go and no money.

"Rose gave me two hundred dollars," she said. She turned to me, "I will pay you back, I swear I will. Then she told me I could stay here at her apartment. That he'd never find me here."

Officer Williams looked at me for confirmation. "So, you just met this woman, a stranger, and told her she could stay with you?"

I nodded, not sure if I should feel proud or foolish. Wondered if he thought me compassionate, or stupid. Probably in his line of work, the latter.

"I only stayed here a week, but it saved my life. Rose said she needed to take care of her sister, so she wouldn't be here anyway. Oh, your sister. How is your sister?" The answer must have shown on my face, as Tina's hand flew to her mouth and tears welled in her eyes and mine.

"She didn't make it," I confirmed.

Now it was Tina's turn to hug me. That hug and her tears undid what little composure I had left and we both started to sob. If the cops were impatient with our histrionics, they didn't let it show and I got myself under control and whispered to Tina to go on.

"I came here to thank Rose and give her back her keys. I'm moving to Nashville in a couple of days—after the divorce is finalized on Monday. I've got a cousin there and she said I could stay with her. I know I shouldn't have held on to them, your keys, but they made me feel safe—like I had a place to go. I should have called you, but I wasn't sure what to say. And the longer it went..."

"Mrs. Lister...Tina, could you get back to what happened here today," the young cop said.

Tina told the police she was waiting for the train when Malcolm spotted her a couple weeks after Rose left for Sewickley. He emptied Tina's purse on the platform, found the paper with Rose's phone number and address and took it.

"Thank goodness it didn't have your apartment number on it. I was there when he called you," she said, turning to me. "I felt awful. Especially knowing that you were there to take care of your sister. You shouldn't have had to worry about me, about him."

"I remember the call," I said.

"He threatened Rose," she said, turning to the police. "Told her to stay out of his business. That I was his property."

That last part must have been when I dropped the phone, I thought.

She closed her eyes, as if gathering strength.

I squeezed her hand.

"Keep going," the older cop said. "You're doing fine."

She sipped her water. "I guess he was watching this building—probably from his car. Drunk. I was at the entrance when he grabbed my arm and smashed me against the door." Her fingers went to the bruise on her cheek and she winced. I felt sick to my stomach. "He pulled the keys from my hand. I prayed you weren't here."

"I wish I had been," I said, even though I wondered if there being two of us would have made a difference.

"When we got here, he lost it. I ran into the bedroom and tried to close the door, but I wasn't fast enough. He started pulling out your clothes and ripping them with his knife." Tina put her elbows on the table and rested her head on her hands, then straightened up. "Then he dragged me to the kitchen and started breaking glasses and dishes. He pushed me to the floor and kicked me. My legs, my arms. I must have been screaming." Then her words, which had been coming out faster and louder as she relayed her story, almost as if she was trying to get it over with, stopped.

We all sat, silent.

In a hushed voice, she continued. "That's when this little girl showed up at the door."

Panic twisted my stomach. Hyacinth.

"She was trying to get the cat," Tina said. "It was in the corner all afraid. The bastard even tried to grab her, but she was too fast." Tina looked at me and I nodded to encourage her to continue, even as I tried to suppress the wave of nausea I felt for unknowingly putting Hyacinth at risk. "She even yelled, You're dead meat. I called the cops," which brought smiles to the faces of the policemen, but only magnified my fear and guilt.

The police finished taking Tina's statement and mine and asked if I needed a copy for my insurance.

I shrugged. "Don't have any."

Tina insisted on helping me clean up after the cops left. "I'll sweep the kitchen," she said.

I ventured into my bedroom where a stack of rags that were once my clothes lay in a heap. My peacock jacket was undamaged, except for a slash across the lapel. I brushed it off, hung it up, then stuffed everything else in a black garbage bag, not having the strength to figure out what could be mended, laundered and saved. When I left the bedroom, Tina was trying to scrub the stain off the living room wall. She'd opened the windows to get rid of the stench of beer and sweat.

"Want to stay here?" I asked.

Tears gathered in her eyes. "No," she said. "I'm good. My sister got a hotel room downtown. She's going to go to court with me on Monday and then take me to the airport."

Tina put her arms around me and we hugged.

"You have a good sister," I said.

Chapter 54

lost my innocence
my keys, my dog. saddest day:
I lost your friendship

Rose's Haiku Diary
St. Augustine, FL
Age 37

I stood outside of Jasmine's apartment for five minutes, or was it ten, before I worked up the nerve to knock. I don't know why I hesitated. I needed the warmth, the peace of her welcoming kitchen. Her smile. Hyacinth's laughter. The smell of her coffee brewing, the sweet but spicy taste of the ginger cookies that were Hyacinth's favorite. I needed this little piece of my upside-down world to be still intact.

I knocked and heard the peephole slide, then the clink of the chain on the door unlock. Finally, the door opened, but only about five inches.

Instead of the welcoming hug I expected, Jasmine looked at me with steel in her eyes.

"Is Hyacinth all right?"

"She's in her room. She got some cuts on her feet—she was just wearing those flip flops of hers. She won't admit she was scared, but I know she was. She keeps saying, poor Elvis."

"I'm so sorry."

"You should be. How dare you put her in danger like that."

"I didn't know. I wouldn't have. Not for the world."

"Yesterday, when she told me she almost got hit by a car, I could have smacked you."

"I'm sorry."

"But I got a grip on myself. She said it wasn't your fault. Or her fault, of course. But you were supposed to be watching her."

"I know. I..."

"Now today. She could have been hurt. Really hurt or worse. Thank God the police got here when they did. Rose, I feel like I don't know you anymore. And I definitely don't trust you.".

"I'm sorry," I said again, feeling stupid that all I could think to do was repeat that phrase.

"Wait here," Jasmine said and closed the door in my face. A minute later she reappeared. "She's fallen asleep hugging your cat. I'll bring him by later."

"Sure," I said, even though I needed the comfort of cuddling him, feeling his soft purr resonate against my chest. "He's all right, isn't he?"

"He's limping a little. One of his paws got cut."

I can't even take care of my cat, I thought. Can't even protect Elvis.

"Good bye, Rose."

"Jasmine, please forgive me. I'm so sorry."

"I want to, but I can't. You scare me, Rose. Hyacinth is my whole world. I know you didn't mean to, but you put her in danger. I can't get the image out of my mind of my dad in the street after the hit-and-run. I just keep thinking how that could have been my little girl yesterday. That could have been her today." She choked out a sob. "I was her age when he died."

She turned her back to me, balled her hands into fists and raised them to her forehead. I ached to put my arms around her, to offer comfort, but stood outside the apartment door. It was not the time. We were no longer the friends we'd been. Perhaps not even friends at all.

Jasmine dropped her arms and turned to me. "I don't want you to see Hyacinth anymore."

Her words hit like a slap in the face. I struggled to answer, my composure teetering on the edge of an abyss. It took every bit of energy I could muster to reply. It took every bit of restraint not to beg her to reconsider.

"I understand." I turned to go, but stopped as I needed Jasmine's help. I put my arm out as she was closing her door. "I need to go out of town tomorrow to see my lawyer about my mother's care." The arch in Jasmine's shoulders relaxed slightly and a hint of sympathy muted the anger on her face for a moment. "Could you take care of Elvis while I'm gone?"

"Neither of us is going near your apartment. Who knows what wacko might show up."

"I could bring over his stuff. I really need your help."

"She's too attached to him already. I don't want her upset again when you take him back and she can't see him."

"You could have him. She could. It's the least I could do. If you want him."

Jasmine studied my face. "All right. Bring his stuff over. But then stay away from her. She's my world and there's no place in it for you. She's just finally starting to get over her dad dying in Iraq. She can't take any more heartache."

Before I could reply, Jasmine said, "Just stay away from both of us, please," and slowly closed the door.

Chapter 55

full moon lights cactus
lone coyote's mournful howl
echoes in my heart

Rose's Haiku Diary
Rio Rancho, NM
Age 56

It was my day to confront Mr. Bankerville. Appointment or not, I would see him. I was determined. I'd set my alarm for six, but after a night of minutes of sleep stolen here and there, I finally fell asleep at about five and didn't wake again until just before eight. I opened my eyes, expecting to see Elvis staring at me, then remembered he was no longer mine. I was all alone.

I went in search of caffeine. My cupboard offered few choices. I was out of coffee. I brewed tea with the last two bags of Earl Grey and added a bag of my splurge licorice tea, while stashing the last two in my purse. The saying on the tag for this one was: Never utter a wrong word, think a wrong thought, or wish a wrong wish. Too late, pal, I thought. Where were you in March when this whole masquerade started? But then again, who are you to say never? Never? Really? I bet even Mother Teresa did some wrong uttering, thinking or wishing. Maybe not often, but we humans are not that good at never doing bad things.

I pulled the tiny tag off the string and shredded it. Take that, I thought. Today I admit to the world that I uttered, thought and wished wrong, wrong, wrong. Or at least I admit that to Bankerville so he can start to help me get my world back.

I had a little over three hundred dollars left, and a paycheck on Friday—enough to rent a car. I pulled out Rose's laptop—and made a three-day reservation at the Enterprise on Chagrin Boulevard. Their earliest pickup time was ten.

I wondered when I should tell Rose's blog fans she was gone. I went to her blog and was shocked that her fans had not only not dissipated, as I thought they would, but more than doubled over the past few months to almost 3000, despite my lack of posting. We can wait until you're ready, they told Rose. Please come back. We want you back.

I do too, I thought.

I packed the book Hank gave me, clothes and toiletries, walking shoes, Rose's living will and life insurance policy, and my peacock jacket – after covering up the rip with a butterfly pin. With still half an hour before I needed to leave, my laptop beckoned to me with the promise of connecting to someone, something I so needed. It was way too early to call Uncle Roger. I went to Rose's email. The backlog of messages was almost overwhelming.

I decided to start with the oldest emails and had deleted dozens without reading them before I saw the one from Sasha, Rose's lifelong second-best friend going back to her Peace Corps days, from a week after Rose's funeral. There were messages from Sasha every few days. She kept asking me, asking Rose, to call her. I considered not replying, but knew Rose would have been horrified if I did. I read previous emails Rose had sent Sasha, feeling every bit the peeping Tom. I found one that I altered slightly. After rewriting it three times, it finally read:

Sasha - Thanks for reaching out. Sorry for the radio silence. In one of my hermit phases. Still can't believe my sister is gone. Know that I love you even when I'm silent as a ghost. Friends forever, R.

I added a heart emoji after the word love and a rose emoji after Rose's initial.

My finger lingered over the send button and hit it just as my cell phone rang. I grabbed it, recognizing Bankerville's number. I was stunned when Miss Knight from his office told me she was returning my call.

The Frau, I thought, picturing her starchy blue suit and white shirt.

"I'm surprised to hear from you this early," I said.

"I'm up at 5:30 every morning and check Mr. Bankerville's messages by 6:00." she said. "You'd be surprised how many people leave messages in the middle of the night."

"I need to speak to…I need an appointment with Mr. Bankerville."

"He's booked solid this week. How about mid next week?"

"No. I need to see him today. It's important. It's about my mother and there's something else. Something I can't get into on the phone. But it has to be today."

I was almost crushing the phone as I waited for her response.

"I could give you fifteen minutes at 1:00. I'll tell him to get back from lunch early."

"Yes, I'll take it. Thank you so much."

I looked at my watch. My thirty minutes had evaporated. I called the coffee shop and told them I needed time off for a family emergency. My boss was more understanding than I would have been in my supervisor days.

I knew I didn't need to call Hank to ask if I could use his guest room. But I called anyway.

"How about a quick lunch before your appointment?" Hank asked.

I hesitated, thinking of my meager finances.

"I'm buying," he added, almost as if he read my mind.

I accepted and thought, I can tell him at lunch. Tell him before Bankerville.

I tucked my laptop into my duffel bag and surveyed the apartment I had called home for the last three months. Would I ever return to it? Or would the inside of a cell be my next home?

Chapter 56

love this city's name
stopped here just because of it
hope it will rub off

Rose's Haiku Diary
Lucknow, India
Age 22

Clara Clarke clutched a take-out container as she left the Chinese restaurant that opened in Sewickley after I left. Sweet and sour soup, I thought, heavy on the sour. A smirk flitted across her face before she turned her head, pretending not to see Hank and me. I could almost hear the gossip gears turn as she concocted a whole new set of rumors.

The new restaurant, The Complete Woks of Shakespeare, created funny Shakespearean names for each dish. As we ate—me my Midsummer's Night Dream salad and Hank's Romeo and Juliet honey walnut chicken—I tried again and again to get the words out. But again, they lodged in my throat. Was there a Heimlich maneuver for confessions?

We opened our fortune cookies. His, from The Merchant of Venice, read, To do great right, do a little wrong. I wondered if he got my fortune by mistake. Mine read, Tis one thing to be tempted, another thing to fall.

Were the fortune cookies conspiring with those little tea bag tags? Get off my case, I thought.

The speech I had rehearsed during the two-hour drive to Sewickley had vanished, replaced by second thoughts. Should I wait until we weren't in a public place? Did I have enough time before my appointment? What if Bankerville tells me to go right to the police or FBI or insurance department? Was it possible that Bankerville knew, just like Uncle Roger?

I looked around to make sure nobody was in earshot.

"I have something to confess," I said.

He tilted his head and smiled. "What?"

Again, I choked on the words, as if the sharp edges of the fortune cookie were stuck there. The waiter dropped the check on the table, but Hank's eyes held mine. I looked away, then at my watch. There was only time for a quick goodbye.

"Would it be all right if we talked after I see my attorney?"

"Sure," he said. "Why don't you come to my house after your appointment. Maybe we can go out to Fern Hollow. You've gotten my curiosity up. I don't often get beautiful women telling me they're going to confess something to me."

Chapter 57

Mom was right, damn it
eat oranges, never hitchhike
avoid scurvy men

Rose's Haiku Diary
Joplin, MO
Age 25

The sweat on my forehead, as I sat in Mr. Bankerville's waiting room, was only partly because I rushed to get there on time. I made it. He was late. I worried that would eat into my allotted fifteen minutes, but figured once he grasped the gravity of my problems, he would make more time. Maybe after his last appointment. Or tomorrow. In the movies, attorneys are always working long, crazy hours, although Bankerville looked like the type to never miss his five o'clock whisky sour. What was it that Scrooge drank to wash down his bit of undigested beef?

Bankerville arrived four minutes late, giving me a whopping eleven minutes.

"Mrs. Grimaldi," he said.

"Mr. Bankerville," I replied. "Thank you for finding time to see me." He gave one of those smiles Rose used to call cardboard smiles—so fake it wasn't even a wooden smile. "There are two matters we need to discuss. The first is moving my mother. She's not well enough to go and, even if she were, Whispering Willows is unacceptable. It's not well rated and it's too far away."

"And you would know this, how?"

"I spoke to a member of the staff at Shady Oaks."

He tilted his head. "Who?"

"I'd rather not say. The conversation was confidential." Son of a bitch. This was not going well. "And I did some research on Whispering Willows. There were thirteen complaints last year, including not keeping infections from spreading and not properly marking drugs."

"Research?"

"On the Internet..."

"Ah, the always reliable Internet."

"And I talked to..."

"As we've discussed, while I will consider your input, your sister left your mother's power of attorney in these matters with me."

So here I was on the diving board about to plunge into unknown waters. Probably more of a cliff, like those the young boys dive off for the tourists' amusement in Acapulco—where you have to jump out so far you don't hit the rocks.

"No, she didn't."

"She most certainly..."

"I mean, she did, but she's not dead. Agnes didn't die. I didn't die. Rose died. I'm Agnes. I'm Agnes Blumfield." For the first time I could remember, a look of shock—or maybe just surprise—crossed Bankerville's face. He looked at his watch and I wanted to slug him. Why did I ever trust him?

"Excuse me?" he said.

"Rose needed that operation. It was supposed to save her life. She didn't have any health insurance. I did. I know it was wrong, but I didn't have the money to pay for it and I love, I loved my sister, so I let her use my medical insurance. She wasn't supposed to die." I slammed my fist on his desk, which startled both of us. "And I just didn't know what to do. I was afraid of going to jail for fraud. So, I pretended to be Rose. But it's gone all crazy on me. I need to be in charge of my mother's care." I paused. It took all the willpower I could muster to resist telling him that he was doing a lousy job of it.

"Go on."

"I need your help. An attorney's help, in talking to the insurance company. The hospital. Maybe we can work out a deal. Maybe if I pay them back, they won't prosecute, won't send me to jail."

"And how would you pay them off? I thought you just said you... Agnes...did not have the, uh, resources to pay for the operation."

"There's what you put in trust. My investments. My pension. There will be money when my house sells. We could lower the price." He folded his hands to form a little tent. I realized that I had forgotten the biggest piece. "And Rose had a term life policy. It was for $200,000." That same brief look of surprise crossed the stone features of his face. He closed his eyes. Good, I thought. He's taking it all in. Thinking about all the legalities. Figuring how to unravel this tangled mess I've created. I let my eyes stray to the ornate antique carriage clock on his desk, which showed only one more minute of my allotted time remaining. Well, the next appointment would have to wait. Or maybe I'd come back tonight or tomorrow. Or would he need time to prepare a plan before we met again? At least he could put my mother's move on hold.

Bankerville opened his eyes and clapped his hands with the deliberation of a theater critic about to write a scathing review. Clap. Clap. Clap.

"Nice try, Mrs. Grimaldi. Quite a performance. Your sister said you'd done some acting. And how convenient. An insurance policy." His plastic smile showed a hint of a sneer before it vanished. "I must ask you to leave now. Please don't call this office again. We'll conduct any future business regarding your sister's estate by mail."

"No, I can prove it. Ask my uncle." He raised his eyebrows ever so slightly. "And maybe Rose got fingerprinted when she went in the Peace

Corps. And hospital records. Rose must have hospital records." How the heck do I prove I'm me? I was so worried about being found out. Exposed. Disgraced. What makes me Agnes?

"Enough, Mrs. Grimaldi. I am truly disappointed in you." He stood and pointed to the door. "Please leave. Now."

Chapter 58

guilt drips, honey-slow
forgot Mother's Day, again
you covered for me

Rose's Haiku Diary
St. Augustine, FL
Age 37

There were more cars than usual in the parking lot at Shady Oaks plus a couple of ambulances, which caused my heart to thump. That makes sense, I reassured myself. They would use ambulances to transport the more fragile patients, although all the patients were fragile—mentally, physically, or both.

The reception area, which was always pristine, if a bit sterile, was chaotic. Boxes were stacked in one corner, black plastic garbage bags in another. I scanned the boxes. Some of the larger ones must have held the belongings of patients being transferred. Those photos and geegaws that decorated their rooms, their pull-on sweat pants and tops, their toiletries. The last pieces left to say, I am Iris Aaronson. Or Sophia Florentine. Or Oscar Green. Or Josephine Runs-Like-the-Wind. I wondered about Josephine. Had she married a native American? Or had she been the child who ran like the wind? Louise Blumfield was not written on any of the boxes.

"Step aside, please," one of the orderlies said as he pushed a wisp of a woman in a wheelchair. I recognized his voice—Gustav—although I'd never heard it at that volume or in that tone before. It was more like the sharp cry of a crow than his usual library-soft manner. I moved aside, deciding not to disturb his concentration. A white-haired woman trailed him, calling, "It's all right, Sophia. I'm right here." I wondered if she was Sophia's sister or her daughter.

"Good luck," I said as she walked past.

She turned to me, tilted her head slightly, and gave me a brief nod and smile. "You, too."

I started to thank her, but she had caught up to the wheelchair and was scolding Gustav for going too fast.

The fogged glass window that separated the waiting room from the receptionist slid open and the face of Miss Nichols, the woman I recognized as the chief administrator, the woman I talked to for a couple of hours before choosing to bring Mom here, appeared. She strained to put a name to my face. She knew Agnes Blumfield and had offered her condolences to Rose Grimaldi, but I was sure she didn't remember that name.

"I'm here to see Louise Blumfield." I said. "I'm her daughter." I wanted to ask for Laarni, but didn't in case that would cause her trouble.

"Identification, please."

They didn't usually ask that, but I pulled out the driver's license, where the state of Ohio proclaimed me to be Rose Grimaldi, and handed it to her. She took it to the computer and tapped a few keystrokes. Her forehead grew a few lines as she scanned the screen. Why was it taking so long?

"I'm sorry. You've made the trip for nothing," she said, not meeting my eyes.

"What? Has she been moved?"

"I can't tell you that without permission from her legal guardian, a Mr. Bankerville."

"But I'm her daughter."

"You'll have to contact him. I can give you his phone number."

"No, I've got it." He must have called here right after I left. Or did his assistant call? "Is she all right?"

She just shook her head and slid the glass panel closed. I didn't know if that meant my mother wasn't all right or if Miss Nichols just couldn't tell me anything.

I went to my rental car, a fire-engine red Dodge Avenger, the kind of car Rose would have loved, but I took because it was the cheapest one. I wished the car was worthy of its name so it could grant me Emma Peel powers. She and John Steed always saved the world. Why couldn't I even save my mother? Or myself?

I got inside the car, rolled down the window and surveyed the scene. Gustav was almost done loading Sophia and her loved one in the ambulance. I called to him as he passed by. His body stiffened as he turned his head, but his shoulders relaxed when he saw me wave. He walked toward me.

I was halfway out of my car when Miss Nichols called, "Gustav, you're needed on Wing B."

Damn you, I thought.

But then my Rose shadow-brain intruded. She's losing everything too, I thought. I remembered how proud Miss Nichols was of this place. How she told me about the staff ratio, about how meticulously they screened each potential employee, and how they strived to make sure the meals were both tasty and nutritious, about all the activities, the light, even Melvin, the resident orange tabby.

"My grandmother spent her last three years in a nursing home," she had told me. "I hated going to visit her there. I mean, I loved her, but the place seemed so small and mean. It sucked the life out of her. I guess that's what made me want to be a part of something like this. A place where a granddaughter could go and know her grandma was safe and happy."

I could tell her I'm really Agnes, Mom's legal guardian, I thought. But why would she believe me? Should I call Bankerville and beg him to let me see my own mother? Even he must have a mother. But based on his parting words, I probably wouldn't even make it past his assistant.

I called Shady Oaks instead and asked for Laarni.

"Can someone else help you? Laarni no longer works here."

Chapter 59

can I get it back
trust you gave, we shared, I lost
stupid, stupid me

Rose's Haiku Diary
Paris
Age 39

The gate at the base of Fern Hollow welcomed me like an old friend. The parking lot was almost empty—only a motorcycle parked under the pines by the trailhead. I loved coming here on weekdays, often having the place to myself, especially when the weather was cold or damp.

I called Hank and asked him to join me here for a walk instead of at his house. It seemed like the right place to tell him. A place he and Agnes both shared and treasured. He asked if I brought good walking shoes. I told him I had and he said he'd arrive by 4:30.

I pulled my walking shoes, shorts and one of Rose's T-shirts from the bag I tossed in the trunk and changed in the restroom. I saturated a brown paper towel with water and scrubbed the makeup off my face.

Back at my rental Avenger, I grabbed Rose's laptop from my duffel and stowed my lawyer-meeting navy-blue suit and sensible heels. I sat at one of the picnic tables. No Wi-Fi, but I could make a list, an Agnes-list of the next steps after I told Hank.

Ask Hank about lawyers – find one that will help
(legal aid?)

How to pay?

How to prove I'm me? (was Rose fingerprinted? Hospital records?)

Who cares (financial) – hospital, medical insurance (mine), life insurance (Rose's)?

Credit cards? Driver's license.

Obstacles: Bankerville, hospital, insurance (again – both)

The list-making process calmed my raw nerves. I waved when Hank's salmon-colored vintage Thunderbird convertible, top down, pulled into the parking lot. Instead of the khakis and golf shirt he'd worn earlier, he sported his walking garb: shorts, a Bruce Springsteen E Street Band T-shirt and Nikes. He opened the passenger door and Doodle bounded out and raced to me. I reached down and scooped her up, relishing her wet kisses on my face.

"She's just what the doctor ordered," I said.

"You sounded down when you called," he said as he joined me and gave me a quick hug and a kiss on the cheek. "This dog's kept me from going off the deep end more than once. So, I'm happy to share Dr. Doodle."

"Best medicine in the world. And no adverse side effects."

"Things go all right with your lawyer?"

The words I planned to say, so clear minutes before, became garbled. I botched my confession to Bankerville. I needed to do a better job with Hank—for so many reasons.

"I don't want to talk about it right now," I said. "Okay if we walk for a while first?"

"I know a wonderful trail."

I smiled, sure of which one.

"But first, I have a surprise for you," he said.

Great, I thought. Just what I need. Another surprise. Then instantly chastised myself for my pessimism. It wasn't becoming of Rose. Or Agnes, for that matter. Maybe it was just this day. These past couple of days. Feeling like the world was really piling it on.

"What?" I asked.

He retrieved a large rectangular package wrapped in brown paper from his convertible's trunk.

"Forgive the gift-wrapping," he said as he handed it to me.

I started to loosen the tape and then remembered the Rose-rule for unwrapping and ripped off the paper. There was the ornate framed mirror from Grandpa Luke's house. The one Rose primped in front of and I stuck my tongue out at. The one I thought I'd lost forever at the estate sale. Tears gathered in my eyes as I ran my fingers over the filigree of carved birds and leaves intertwined on the frame. I knew each crease and nick. Rose and I named all the birds: Suzie, Estelle, Fabio, Bart, Jinx, and Romeo and Juliet.

"Hank, this is amazing. You don't know how I've missed this." I hugged him and he wrapped his arms around me. "Thank you, thank you, thank you." I wanted to stay safe in his embrace forever.

"You're welcome. I got to the estate sale at your sister's house early and when I saw it there, I just couldn't let some stranger buy it. Agnes told me so many stories about this mirror. About the two of you dressing up and asking it, who's the fairest of them all?"

"And it always said..."

"Rose is, but Agnes is a close second."

"She actually bored you with all those stories?" I said, trying to stall, to get my brain back into Rose-mode, since I almost blurted out Rose was, but I was a close second. Should I have said I missed the mirror? Shouldn't that have set off alarm bells? Yes, I was here to confess, but I wanted it to be my way.

"I loved her stories of the two of you."

"How about that walk," I said. "I think Miss Doodle is wondering why we're talking when we could be walking."

After pulling out the rental car keys, I rewrapped the mirror and put it in the trunk of my rental, along with my laptop and purse. I stuffed the keys in my jacket pocket and tied the jacket's arms around my waist. Although balmy now, I knew it could turn chilly this time of year by the time we got back from our hike.

"You up for this?" Hank asked. "Agnes used to say her wildlife lived in the forest and yours in the bars."

I managed not to wince. Had I really said that? No, Rose used to say that. Maybe I just mentioned it once. "I've been walking and biking a lot since I got to Cleveland," I said. "I'm good."

We took the Butterfly trail, where the foxglove and trumpet creeper nodded their heads in the breeze, then curved back to the gravel path, which connected with the Towhee Trail. Nostalgia was shoved aside by a little splat of annoyance as I realized Hank was tracing our favorite walk. Sharing it with Rose.

Hank suggested we stop to rest when we got to the Woof and Hoof Spur, as Doodle was panting, but I guessed he was worried about my stamina. He pulled out her collapsible water bowl and filled it before offering me the water bottle.

"I've decided to sell my house," he said.

"Your house? But you love that house." That was Agnes talking and I realized I better tell Hank soon.

"It's too big for just one person. And there's still too much of Jane there."

"I know," I said. I understood ghosts.

"And too much of Agnes."

"Agnes?"

"I look at her house every morning. I watch how the Blue Angel clematis she planted last year is flourishing and wish she could see it. I hear a birdcall I don't recognize and want to ask her what it is. I keep thinking I'll see her, hear her singing while she's working in her garden."

This is your opportunity, I thought. This is the time to tell him.

"Oh," I said.

"I'm going to move to Cleveland."

"What? Cleveland? I thought you said you'd get an RV and see the country when you sold your house." A puzzled look crossed his face and I realized that this was something he talked about with Agnes, but not Rose. "Why Cleveland?"

"My daughter and grandson are there." He took my hand in his and squeezed it. "And you are. I'd like to see more of you. I thought I could never fall in love again, but these past few months..."

I jerked my hand from his. He pulled his to his chest. I wasn't sure what he was going to tell me, but I wasn't ready to hear it. Not while I was still living this lie. These past couple of weeks, I'd realized I was in love with Hank, but tried to convince myself it was just because I felt safe with him. Cared for. And if he was falling in love with me—who did he love? Rose? Agnes as Rose? Maybe even Agnes?

"I'm sorry," we both said, almost simultaneously. Then there was that noisy silence. Just the wind muttering, the stream murmuring, the rhythmic sounds of Doodle's breathing as she slept.

"I've been..." Hank started to say, but I cut him off. Time to jump.

"I have to go first." He raised his head and looked into my eyes. "I can't let you finish until you know something. Something important. Something that might change..."

"Nothing could..."

"No. You have to listen. I have to talk. I have a secret." A chipmunk peeked from a log, but Doodle didn't wake.

"Do you remember when you told me you hated Jane's pot roast and made me promise to never tell a soul? That it was the first meal she cooked for you, that it was her mother's recipe and that it was horrible, but that you said it was great, so she kept making it over and over for your birthday."

"That's your secret, that Agnes told you..." Hank said, the confusion in his voice matching the puzzlement on his face.

"Or the time we argued in Robinson's about whether a Home and Family white tea rose would survive our winter. And you said it wouldn't because it was zone 7 and I said it would because it would be close to my house and protected from the wind and I bought it and planted it. And it didn't come up the next spring and you planted a cross where it should have been." He closed his eyes, as if trying to make my words stop. "Or Jane's funeral, when you played Try to Remember, her song, yours and hers, on your bagpipes and I sang solo and we both ended up crying so hard we only got through the first verse."

He shook his head. "I'm totally confused, Rose."

"I'm not Rose. I lied to you."

"You wouldn't..."

"I've been lying to everyone since March." Hank still didn't get it. He squinted at me. "I wanted to tell you before, but..."

"No, that can't be..."

"I'm Agnes. Rose needed an operation to save her life. She had no insurance. No way to get it. I couldn't let her die. I let her use my insurance. Let her pretend to be me." I couldn't tell if it was astonishment, hurt or horror on Hank's face, so I plunged on. "I didn't want to lie. To you, to everyone. But jail. Going to jail. And the publicity. The shame of lying, of cheating. So, I became Rose. I guess I was in shock from her death. It seemed that was my only choice. It seemed…this is going to sound stupid…it seemed like something she'd want me to do. She wouldn't want me in jail because of her."

I expelled my rhetoric rapid-fire, fearing I wouldn't be able to get started again if I stopped. By the time I finished, Hank was bent over, his head in his hands.

I waited for him to process what I told him, for him to jump up and hug me. Tell me how happy he was that Agnes was alive. That I was alive.

"How could you not have told me?"

"I wanted to. I tried to."

"To find out she died with a phone call, like I was her dentist."

"I'm so sorry. I knew I couldn't tell you face-to-face."

"I was starting to love her, you…"

"Sorry."

"I would have kept your secret. I would have never betrayed you. How could you betray me?"

I couldn't bear saying sorry again. How stupid to think this was a victimless crime. How stupid to have not confessed after Rose died.

He crushed the plastic dog bowl in his hand, put it in his pocket, then took out Doodle's leash, leaned over, and attached it to her collar. His foot slipped on some pebbles as he stood and he staggered. I wondered if he was having a heart attack, his face looked so gray and contorted, so pale. Doodle jumped up, tail wagging, but Hank's eyes were not on either her or me.

"I have to go," Hank said. "I just can't…I can't deal with this right now. I feel like such an idiot."

Chapter 60

one toothbrush again
no one to keep my feet warm
alone together

Rose's Haiku Diary
White Swan, OR
Age 43

Why had I thought he would open his arms, open his heart and welcome me back? Did I really not tell him to avoid burdening him? Or did part of me want to chuck Agnes and her structured life and become Rose?

I leaned back and let the warmth of the boulder where I sat seep into each finger. I tried to concentrate on the sounds of the forest, to regain the peace I so often felt here, but my brain chattered like an angry squirrel.

I need to walk, I thought. I started to climb the rock-strewn trail. The ground was muddy, making each step an effort. But that exertion helped clear my mind, as I needed to concentrate to keep my balance. I spotted a branch on the ground that looked like an overgrown baseball bat, the perfect size for a walking stick, and grabbed it.

Sweat soaked my T-shirt by the time I reached the top, but the trek energized me. At least I had control of something. The light started to take on that golden hue that comes right before sunset. I hung my jacket on a ragged tree branch and scanned the familiar view, wondering if painters ever tried to capture this vista, this feeling of being part of the fabric of the land. Being alone but not lonely.

Something nibbled at the edges of my solitude, as if something or someone was watching me.

I turned and realized there were two men, probably both in their mid-twenties, thirty feet away. One was short, burly and bearded, the other, tall, angular and clean-shaven, but with long hair tied in a red print bandana. Normally on the trails, strangers greet each other as they pass, a familiarity I've always loved. As if the trail was a small town where citizens tipped their hats to one another and extended the same courtesy to the occasional stranger.

I couldn't see eyes behind their sunglasses. Unlike most hikers, they seemed tense. I tightened the grip on my walking-stick-branch. There was no way I could outrun them and this branch was not exactly the optimal weapon.

Then I noticed they were holding hands. Maybe the caution on their faces was because they had a secret too. A secret they thought they could let out to breathe the piney air and feel the glowing sunlight, until this stranger interfered.

"Great day to be on the top of the world," I called, feeling very Rose-like. The sharp angles of their shoulders relaxed.

The shorter man took off his sunglasses. "Isn't it amazing up here?" he said. "Did you see all those the Jacks-in-the-pulpit?"

He's a hiker, I thought. They both are. I'm okay. They're hikers and friends, or boyfriends or lovers. Not axe-murderers.

"No," I said. "I was just trying to make it up here without losing my shoes in the mud." I wondered why I'd missed them, my favorite wildflower. Normally when I hike, those little details are like garnishes on a fine meal.

"We better get going," the short one said.

"You told me there was a Tiffany's up here," the tall one said, obviously an inside joke.

The short one pretended to frown, but I had to laugh. "The Tiffany's was right where you're standing. They took it down last year and planted that fifty-year old oak," I said. They rewarded me with laughter. I started to ask if I could walk down with them, but decided not to intrude any further. "You should take the Muddy Run trail some time," I said. "Believe it or not, it's not as muddy as this one."

"Thanks. We will," the tall one said. "Oh, and I'm Kevin and this is Robert." We exchanged nods.

"I'm Agnes," I said. It felt good. Like I'd somehow made another confession, but one with no ramifications. Hello world—I'm Agnes.

I watched them until they were out of sight. I envied the ease with which they bantered, how close they walked, and how they helped each other through the more treacherous spots. It reminded me of how Rose and I used to be. How Hank and I had become.

The sun was closing in on the horizon and I realized I better hurry. A fawn crossed my path, followed by its mother. Then another fawn. I held my breath as they grazed. The mother seemed a master of geometry as she kept both her offspring in sight with just tiny shifts in her position, while looking like she was concentrating on the wild hydrangea.

I recalled that Hank told me fully-grown does have twins two-thirds of the time. Lucky fawns.

I'd always felt a reverence toward deer. Even when they mistook my garden for a salad bar, they seemed like walking sculpture. "Come back," I whispered as they wandered out of my line of sight after twenty minutes.

The hike down took longer than I expected and the day was cooling. My rental car sat alone in the parking lot. Time to get going, I thought. But where? I didn't want to drive to Cleveland and then back tomorrow morning. The business I needed to resolve was here. I considered sleeping in my car, although part of my muddled brain protested that this idea was something even Rose wouldn't do. Both for comfort and for safety. I reached for my car keys and realized they were in my jacket pocket—the jacket hanging on a branch at the top of the trail.

Chapter 61

flowers in my hair
I love mud, no I hate it
dance, sing, rock and roll

Rose's Haiku Diary
Woodstock
Max Yasgur's Dairy Farm
Bethel, NY
Age 19

The rustles, crackles and thuds that sounded like a woodland symphony during the day seemed ominous at dusk as I made my way down the trail for the second time. I was almost at the parking lot, already scratched, scraped and muddy from falling once, when I lost my footing again, skidded down a steep embankment and startled a skunk just five feet away. As I tried to right myself, it hissed and stamped its feet—the warning signs, then it turned and raised its tail.

"No," I begged. "I'm sorry." I attempted to scramble away, trying to shield my eyes, but gagged on the spray as I felt it hit my left arm and leg. I coughed and retched, holding onto a tree to keep from doubling over. I instinctively tried to wipe the spray off, but only succeeded in getting the oily stench on my hands.

I crawled, then righted myself and limped to the parking lot, desperate to wash the mud and skunk-stink off in the park's restroom. But it was locked.

I opened the rental car's trunk and pulled a T-shirt and sweatshirt from my duffel. I used the T-shirt to wipe off as much skunk stench as possible before tossing it in the trash can. I covered the car's seat with the sweatshirt.

Other than Hank, I didn't have the kind of friends here where you could show up muddy and stinky and expect them to offer you bed, bath and breakfast. And sympathy. And now, I didn't even have Hank.

One of those cartoon light bulbs appeared over my head as I saw the spare key to my cottage in my mind. Was it where I left it? I could stay there overnight. It wasn't like I was breaking in—after all, it was my house. Just the idea of feeling my wood floors, touching the stones of my fireplace, and gazing at my moonlight-drenched garden hit me like a glass of wine on an empty stomach. Wine, I thought. I could really use a drink. Not practical, my Agnes-half reminded me. The money-tank is close to empty. Then Rose took over, reminding me of the $500 I had stashed in a Thermos in my garage—mad money or maybe end-of-the-world money. I felt Rose guided the car to the Stop 'n Sip. Thank goodness the parking lot was empty. The brightly lighted store looked inviting and Olive was behind the counter.

I tossed my last shred of self-respect over my shoulder and went in.

"Are you all right?" Olive asked. Then recognition sparked in her eyes. I could almost see her mind race through a maze of thoughts: Agnes Blumfield, no she died, this is her sister.

"I had a close encounter with a skunk," I said. "And Pepe Le Pew wasn't feeling amorous."

She smiled and pointed to the back of the store. "Want to clean up in the restroom?"

"Thanks. I'd really appreciate it. But are you sure? You don't want this place to smell skunked."

She shrugged. "It's smelled worse." That tiny gesture made me wonder why I never suggested we get together, that I kept our relationship at customer-clerk. But maybe I was overreacting to her small act of kindness. Clinging to any interaction that proved I was not a pariah. "Just bag the paper towels," she said as she handed me a plastic bag. "I'll toss the bag in the trash out back."

I went into the phone-booth sized restroom and scrubbed off as much mud and skunk stink as I could. I even ran my fingers through my hair, looking at a face in the mirror that seemed much older than I expected, but younger than I felt.

I picked up two bottles of Bloody Mary mix, hoping the old saw about using tomato juice to de-skunk was true and not some old wives' tale. I added a screw top bottle of chardonnay, a bag of pretzels and a can of that spray cheese, things I would never have considered buying three months ago.

"How long you in town for?" Olive asked.

"Not sure," I said. "A few days anyway. I've got some business to take care of. Maybe we can have lunch some time." I wondered why I added that, although it was something Rose would not only have suggested, but done.

"I'd like that," Olive said as she took a promotional coaster for Jim Beam and wrote on the back of it: Olive Mayfield and her phone number. I slipped it into my purse, took another and wrote my cell phone number on it. I hesitated before putting down Rose Grimaldi, fighting the urge to confess to this poor woman. I was one for three on my confessions and knew my ego-batting-average couldn't take another miff.

In the parking lot, I turned on my cell phone. I wanted to call Uncle Roger, but I knew he'd hear the stress in my voice and before I knew it, I'd be a blubbery mess and he'd be booking a flight to come here and save me. The cell phone's screen indicated one voicemail message and I retrieved it, pumping in Rose's password, TURKLE1025. As I waited for the message, I wondered why I never changed it. Maybe it was another way to try to hold onto Rose.

Laarni's familiar voice came from the phone. "Hello, Rose. This is Laarni calling." There was a quiver in her voice, something more disturbing coming from this unflappable woman than if she had been screaming. "I got laid off today. Still a shock, even though I knew it was coming. Not your problem, of course. Just wanted to let you know that your mother's not doing too well. That attorney wanted to relocate her, but our head nurse wouldn't sign off on it, insisted she go to the ICU. Not sure which hospital they took her to. Oh, and I have one of your mother's paintings. They were going to throw it out. Maybe you can pick it up the next time you're in town. Hope things go all right. For her. For both of you."

That son of a bitch Bankerville, I thought. Why didn't he tell me? Her message was sent today at around 5:00. Had they lied about Laarni being gone when I was at Shady Oaks earlier? More likely she only thought of calling me at 5:00. "The world doesn't revolve around you, Rose," I could hear Mom's voice saying.

"Well, maybe it should. Maybe it will, by the time I'm done with it," Rose always answered.

Chapter 62

T-shirt on my back
got that, open road, twelve bucks
my thumb and a smile

Rose's Haiku Diary
Wolf Point, MT
Age 41

It was a good thing I didn't need more than five percent of my brain to drive to my empty cottage. That was about all I had left. I slowed my speed when I was two blocks away and turned off my headlights as I entered the cul-de-sac, feeling every bit the criminal. I was surprised but grateful that the photosensitive light above my garage wasn't on. Hank's house was dark except for the outside porch light that came on automatically and so was Clara's—although Hank and I often speculated that she turned her lights off so she could peep out her windows undetected. My stomach lurched when I saw the Sale Pending placard dangling from the Realty For Sale sign next to my mailbox.

I eased the rental car up to my garage door, got out and punched the code in the panel. I rejoiced when the garage door started to open, then cringed at the noise made by the motor, cogs and chains. I pulled the car in, thinking that even if the spare house key was gone, the garage would provide shelter. I could feel safe here.

The spare key was where I left it. I silently thanked Rose for giving me the courage to lie to the Frau and tell her there were no other keys when she first booted me out.

I went to my garage workbench and felt underneath it, hoping nobody had discovered the Thermos which held the $500 I'd stashed. My fingers found the plastic cap and I pulled the Thermos from its hiding place. Just taking the bills from it rejuvenated me. As if I'd drawn the card that let me pass jail and collect $200.

I decided to go in through the mudroom off the kitchen, to screen myself from at least most of the prying eyes.

My penlight provided enough light to stay on the flagstone path from the garage to the mudroom. I first lugged in my duffel bag and survival kit from the Stop 'N' Sip, then went back for Grandpa Luke's mirror. It was a silly thing to do, but I needed the comfort it always gave me.

I winced again as the garage door groaned shut. I put the mirror at the entrance to the kitchen, then pulled off my socks and walking shoes.

I carried the mirror into the living room, a path my bare feet knew well, feeling my way as my eyes had not adjusted to navigating by only moonlight. I wanted to hang the mirror in the living room, its rightful place of honor, but all the hooks had been removed. So, I put it on the mantel, leaning against the rough stones.

"There you go," I said. "You're home. But don't get too comfortable. We're leaving in the morning."

My eyes adjusted to the gauzy moonlight as I returned to the mudroom. A Dandelion Moon, Hank would have called it for the puffy bits of light it bestowed. I tossed my shoes and socks in the washing machine. Then my jacket. I sniffed my T-shirt, then bent to sniff my shorts. Yup, everything needed washing. Into the washing machine went shorts, shirt, bra and panties. No soap available, of course, but I hoped the water would get rid of the remaining mud and at least some of the skunk stench. I started the washer. Anyone passing by would wonder why a middle-aged woman was standing naked in the mudroom of her house. I crouched at the thought, then straightened. It was my house, after all. Stand tall, I heard Rose say.

I reached for my duffel to get dressed, then thought better of it, not wanting to transfer the mud or skunk still on my body to fresh clothes. I need a bath, I thought.

I picked up my duffel and Stop 'N' Sip bag and padded into the kitchen. Even with the furniture gone and the walls denuded of paintings, I expected the rooms to welcome me. But my eyes and numbed brain registered something as wrong. The sunflower yellow of my kitchen, the moss-green of my dining room, and the teddy bear-brown of my living room were all gone, replaced by chalk-white walls, as if trying to obliterate the person who had lived here. I wanted to cry, or punch something. Punch someone. Instead, my knees buckled and I sank. The cold of the red brick on my naked butt as it hit the kitchen floor was like that first shock as you hit the water after a dive. I crawled to the bottle of wine, opened it and took a chug. As I tore open the bag of pretzels and squirted iridescent cheese on one, I thought of Goldilocks. Rose always defended Goldilocks, but I thought the three bears got a raw deal.

"She broke into their house," I said. "Ate their food, slept in their beds. She's a criminal. She should be locked up."

"It was only porridge," Rose replied. "And she was hungry and tired."

Rose was right. The three bears should get a life. Learn to be more forgiving. More sharing. Help a person down on her luck.

I wondered if the Bloody Mary mix would obliterate the skunk-stink better if it sat for a few minutes so it could absorb the odors. I opened the bottle and smeared it on my left side from my face to my feet, rubbing the leftover in my hair for good measure. Then I shook the Cheez Whiz can and wrote on the floor: I WANT IT BACK. Rose might have dotted the i with a heart or a flower, but I drew a lightning bolt. Take that!

I licked some cheese goop from my fingers and leaned against the dishwasher to admire my artwork, wondering if I should draw a skull-and-crossbones. Maybe I could use pretzel twists for the eyes. As I took another gulp of wine, voices pierced my musing and a flashlight's beam sliced the air. I froze, then flattened myself. A chill jolted my naked body as it hit the kitchen's brick floor. Had I locked the door to the mudroom? Should I check? I scuttled like a crab across the kitchen toward the mudroom, keeping low to the ground.

Deep voices—male voices—ricocheted off the walls. "Check the doors," one said. I was almost three feet from the doorknob and that all-important lock when two silhouettes blocked the mudroom's windows. My heart thundered in my chest as I scooted back and wedged myself into the space by the washer where the boot tray used to be. I buried my head in my arms, wishing I had grabbed my duffel bag. Stupid, stupid, stupid.

I waited for the sound of the doorknob turning to give the clack that signaled it was locked. It didn't. Then the mudroom door's latches rasped as the intruders opened the door, just a few inches based on the short duration of the creak. A flashlight's beam snaked back and forth, then a second beam joined it and they crisscrossed.

The clunk of a boot or heavy shoe reverberated.

"Should we check the house?" one asked.

"The realtor probably just forgot to lock up. Let's just make sure the other doors are secured. We'll lock this one and have the desk call them in the morning."

Cops, I thought. They're cops. Not robbers. Or rapists.

"Didn't dispatch say they saw someone by the house?"

"Probably kids. Or deer."

Yes. Deer. Definitely deer. Go away, officers.

"What's that smell? Skunk?"

"Probably died under the porch. We got any Amber Alerts for Punky Skunk?"

"Who?"

"You young rookies. Worst video game mascot ever. But my kid sister liked it. Never mind. Want to grab some coffee?"

The washer picked that moment to start a spin cycle. Chuga, chuga, chuga.

"What the Hell?" They stopped talking. I imagined the two cops looking at each other as the washing machine serenaded us. Were they drawing their guns? A newspaper headline flashed before my eyes: Naked Burglar Apprehended Doing Laundry.

"Who's there?" The voice had hardened.

"Let's call it in and check it out."

"Over here," I said, raising my right arm, while keeping the left one—the one smeared with tomato juice—across my chest, my knees clasped together and thinking, please don't shoot me.

"Let's see both hands."

I pulled my knees closer to cover my breasts and raised my right arm. "I can explain."

"Stand up slowly and keep those hands where I can see them."

"Could you get me something from my bag? It's in the kitchen."

"I said stand up," the voice barked.

"I can't stand up without pushing up with my hands." They were out of my line of sight, but their shoes thudded toward me. Their flashlight beams became brighter and soon both shone in my eyes. I squinted into them, trying not to look as guilty as I felt.

"Holy shit," the younger-sounding voice said. "Are you all right, ma'am?"

Part of me wanted to cry, but Rose wouldn't let me. You be strong, I heard her say.

I nodded. "My clothes. The bag in the kitchen. Could you bring it?"

One cop left while the other kept his flashlight and his gun on me. "You can put your arms down, but keep your hands where I can see them."

I lowered my arms and put my hands on my knees. All I could see was silhouettes and shadows. No faces. No details.

"Open bottle of wine on the floor," the cop with the older voice said as he dropped my duffel bag on the floor. "Petty vandalism. Quite the little party in there."

Some party, I thought. Leave it to me to have a party for one and still get raided by the cops.

"I'll need to look in the bag before I give it to you."

"Just hand me something from it. Anything. Please."

He pulled out my peacock jacket, checked the pockets and tossed it to me.

"I know this must look suspicious," I said.

Then Rose whispered in my brain, don't be defensive. They'll never believe you if you are.

But it was too late. I sputtered, unable to decide if I should try to convince them I was Agnes and this is my house, darn it, or her sister Rose, who was also welcome.

Without the luxury of time to ponder which might get me released, I told them I was Rose and asked them to contact Bankerville to verify it. Since I didn't have his home phone number and it wasn't listed, they told me there was nothing to be done until morning. I tried to remember his assistant's name, but it eluded me.

Maybe I should have been grateful that they let me dress before cuffing me and stuffing me in the back of their patrol car. I put on jeans and a black T-shirt Rose must have picked up at a concert, as it proclaimed THE GUESS WHO in block red letters, with AMERICAN WOMAN TOUR in smaller letters below. How appropriate, I thought. Next to the lettering was a woman's silhouette composed of alternating patterns of Old Glory's stars and stripes. The only shoes in my duffel bag were those sensible heels, that must have looked ridiculous with the jeans and T-shirt, but it beat going barefoot. I couldn't bring myself to don my navy-blue suit and white blouse. At least I had my peacock jacket to comfort me.

On the ride to the station, I realized my laundry was still in a wet lump in that Benedict Arnold of a washing machine.

Chapter 63

more interesting
people you meet in third class
share meals, ideas

Rose's Haiku Diary
Bandipur, Nepal
Age 21

The cops allowed me to use the restroom at the station, so I could attempt to scrub off most of the remaining tomato juice before my fingerprinting and mug shot. Somehow, it seemed fitting for me to wear my peacock jacket for the occasion.

My first thought was to use my one call to phone Hank, but I couldn't bring myself to cause him any more pain. Instead, I called the number on the coaster I'd gotten from Olive at the Stop 'n Sip. The call went to her voicemail, but I asked her to contact Bankerville's office in the morning so they could verify my story and get the charges dropped. I apologized at least three times for bothering her before I hung up.

Then there was nothing to do but trek to the holding cell and wait.

"I'm Stella," the woman on the other metal bench said, as I tried to sit as far from her and the woman who was pacing and mumbling as possible without looking rude. She looked like Marlon Brando's twin sister—Brando in The Godfather not Streetcar. "What you in for?"

"Cheez Whiz vandalism and breaking into my own house," I said.

She laughed. "That's a new one."

"Cops debated if any public decency laws were broken by my nudity, but dropped the idea. Maybe they were kidding."

"Cop humor," she said with a small shrug.

"How about you?"

"Murdering my no-good louse of a husband," she said, just as if we were discussing the weather or the Pittsburgh Pirates' last game. I wondered if her husband was named Stanley. She guffawed. "You should see your face. I was just pulling your leg. I just went after him with a hammer and the wuss called the cops. Don't believe everything people tell you in jail."

Good advice on either side of jail bars, I thought. I resisted the urge to tell her she was out of her league when it came to lying. She fixed her eyes on me for a moment, as if expecting a response. My mouth opened, but I could not think of anything to say, so I pressed my lips together and nodded.

"He kicked my dog. Poor Buddy," she added in a voice just above a whisper.

My prison cell got more crowded as the night wore on. Some of the women looked and smelled even worse than I did. I decided to follow Stella's lead and lean back with my eyes almost closed, although there was no sleep in my future. The pain between my eyes started to mushroom. After a couple of hours, it grew into a throbbing mass. I would have sold my soul for an Advil.

By the time the morning routine started, I wondered if my head would explode.

A woman who seemed to be carved from driftwood—she looked so weathered by time—brought something they called breakfast. The coffee smelled a bit of burnt tires and the limp roll sat in a puddle of something that might have been jelly, although the melding of red and purple colors made me wonder what fruit it once was and how long ago. I thought of my lunch-lady stint in the high school cafeteria back in Harlow when I was taking care of Jack and trying to heal him and our relationship. At least my job wasn't to dish weak coffee and limp rolls to felons.

Alleged felons, Rose reminded me. Look at you. You're not guilty. At least not of burglary and vandalism.

This is what despair sounds like, I thought. Some whimpering. Some sighing. Some sobbing. Lots of clanking and cursing. This is what despair smells like. Cabbage and feet.

"Grimaldi," a matron called. "This way." The face that went with the guttural voice looked like Liesl in The Sound of Music. Sweet, young and blonde. Sixteen going on seventeen. Shouldn't she have been working some place more fun?

I walked out of the cell, feeling the stares of the other women on my back. I turned, wondering if I should say goodbye, but only Stella's eyes were on me.

"See you in the funny pages," she said.

I smiled. "Or maybe the front page."

She returned my smile. "Give me a jury of my peers and I'll walk."

"I hope I will, too."

"Hurry it up, Grimaldi," the teenage matron said.

"What's happening?" I asked, wondering where she was taking me, as it was barely 7:30, too early for Bankerville to have verified my story, if he was going to verify it. If he was not going to press charges.

"Don't know. Just do what they tell me."

Could bail have been posted so soon? I wondered, although soon didn't actually seem like the right word. It felt like I'd spent a week in that dungeon.

We reached the desk where I inspected my possessions before they released them to me. I checked for my cell phone and wallet, rifled through my duffel bag for the laptop and tried to remember what clothes I packed.

It seemed close enough, so I signed the release form and got a bit of my dignity back. It is amazing how we can feel defined by our possessions, even when they are not ours.

"Who posted bail?" I asked. Could it have been Olive? I wondered. It made me feel even worse about calling her.

"No bail. Charges got dropped," the child-matron said. She glanced down at a clipboard. "Knight."

"Night?"

"With a K."

My knight in shining armor, I thought. About time you got here. I trudged after the matron, trying to connect Knight to a face or a name. I went through another set of locked doors, turned the corner and there, waiting in jeans and a Steelers' black and gold T-shirt, was The Frau.

Chapter 64

serendipity
thought you were my enemy
was I ever wrong

Rose's Haiku Diary
Paris
Age 39

That Dorothy Knight, the former Frau, bailed me out on her own—not as Bankerville's right hand—astonished me. When she told me I could shower at her place, it was as if I'd rubbed the magic lantern and gotten three wishes.

She drove me to my cottage to retrieve my rental car. How different from the first time we made that trip. Then I followed her PT Cruiser back to her townhouse. I decided not to mention the wet laundry or my mirror, both still inside my cottage. I hoped I could sneak back later and retrieve them, if I dared tempt another skirmish with the cops or Clara Clarke's prying eyes.

After I showered, I put on fresh clothes and my peacock jacket, despite the dank whiff of prison on it.

Dorothy offered me hot tea and cold cereal—my choice of Cheerios or granola. I opted for granola, no longer feeling like I was required to choose Cheerios, what Rose would have picked. It seemed like a banquet and I realized I was ravenous. I asked Dorothy if she had anything for a headache and she handed me a small bottle of Advil and told me to keep it. I resisted kissing both her and the bottle and took two pills, although just breathing the air of freedom already helped my headache start to fade.

Dorothy apologized for not having juice, eggs or toast. "I only get that stuff when my grandkids visit," she said, further denting my mental picture of a spinster married to her job.

Her condo didn't look like she shared it with a man, and I wondered if a Mr. Knight was still in the picture, but decided not to ask, as the probable answer was either death or divorce.

I savored the silence. It was never quiet in prison. I let the granola, tea and Advil revive my soul and my brain, grateful Dorothy didn't feel the need to chit chat. It had taken all my energy to put one foot in front of the other, then to drive. My sleep deprivation was going on its second day, fighting with the adrenaline produced by the free fall of my situation.

"You've done so much for me already," I said, "but I need to ask another favor."

She set down the Pittsburgh Post-Gazette. "I'll help if I can."

"I need to know where my mother is. I need to see her. Would you help me convince Mr. Bankerville?"

"Is it true?" I must have looked puzzled, as she added, "that you're Agnes, not Rose? Mr. Bankerville said you tried to convince him, but he was sure you were lying. That's why he cut you off from seeing her. At least that's what he told me."

I weighed how to answer her query, wondering what answer would get me the help I needed. "Would it make a difference? Shouldn't either daughter be allowed to see her mother?"

She nodded. "Three years ago, when my mother was sick...was dying...my brother had her medical power of attorney. I disagreed with almost every decision he made. We fought all the time. But at least I could visit her."

"I'm sorry." Those words felt so inadequate, but they were all I could muster.

"I'd want to see my daughter, to have my daughter visit me. Especially if my condition was as critical as your mother's." Despite the kindness intended by her words, the confirmation of my mother's failing health was like a punch to the stomach. "I argued with him, you know. Mr. Bankerville."

"You did?"

"Told him just what you said, that he had no right to keep you from seeing your mother, no matter which daughter you were." I held my breath, not wanting to say the wrong thing and derail our tenuous connection. "He reminded me that I was the paralegal and he was the attorney. And that not only did he have the right, but he had an obligation to act in what he saw as your mother's best interest. And he saw a woman trying to commit identity theft and fraud as dangerous."

"I am Agnes Blumfield."

"I don't know why, but when he told me that's what you'd said, that you were really Agnes, I believed it. At first, I didn't, maybe because of the way he told me, so sure you were lying. But after I thought about it, it didn't seem like you'd lie about being Agnes."

"Will you help me?"

She got up and stared out the kitchen window. "Give me a minute. I need to think. I'm going to change."

Her minute seemed like an hour and I pulled out my cell phone to check for emails or texts. I was confused when the screen showed a message from Jasmine, the woman who never wanted to see to me again. Then I read it and realized Hyacinth must have pinched her mom's phone.

Moms still mad @ u & Me 2. Jerk BF M dumped her. Call in 2 days. Luv- H+L-vis ^..^ miss u.

My eyes clouded up. I missed them too. All three of them. And loved them.

When Dorothy returned, she was dressed in her work uniform: a slate gray, pin-striped suit and white blouse. Her hair, which had been an auburn halo loosely framing her face, was pulled back in a knot.

"I could lose my job."

She was right. Bankerville would likely fire her for crossing him. It was wrong to ask her to jeopardize her livelihood. My life was going down the drain. How could I ask her to follow me?

"If you're lying about being Agnes and I help you, then I'm guilty too. But if you are Agnes..."

"I am. I promise."

"If you are, then you really are our client. And my obligation is to help you." She sighed. "Your mother is at Oakvale Memorial General Hospital. You know it?"

Know it, I thought. That's the hospital where Rose died. I nodded.

"I'll call from the office to put you on the approved visitors list."

"I don't know how to thank you."

Dorothy looked at her watch. "I need to get going." She picked up my cereal bowl, teacup and spoon and put them in the sink along with her cup. I tossed my duffel bag over my shoulder. "You know what you need?"

"A miracle?" I answered, producing a smile.

"You need somebody who believes you. Somebody who will fight for you."

"Fight to keep me out of jail?"

"That too." She opened her briefcase, pulled out a stack of business cards, rifled through them and handed me one. It read Ferdinand Paul III. "Ferd the Third we used to call him. He worked at the firm about ten years ago, but he and Mr. Bankerville locked horns on almost everything."

"I like him already." I regretted the words the moment they came out. I didn't mean to insult her boss. I was becoming Rose again: talk first, think later.

"Ferd's a good attorney. He can't resist a case with a lot of wrinkles and he loves an underdog."

"He may have just hit the jackpot."

Chapter 65

Got the flu. No prom.
Mom kissed and made it better.
Brought me Vogue, ice cream.

Rose's Haiku Diary
Sewickley, PA
Age 17

Maneuvering my rental car through the hospital's labyrinth parking garage brought back a tidal wave of memories and emotions. My stomach knotted. I remembered the hope I'd felt, then the fear and finally the pain at the news of Rose's death. I swore her ghost was sitting next to me. Don't take me back there, the ghost said. It's a bad place.

Of course, it wasn't. It was just a big impersonal behemoth where sometimes those laboring to save lives forget that the friends and families of the people in the beds need help too.

After I parked the car, I called Ferd Paul to schedule an appointment, but got bounced to his voicemail. I left a message saying that I urgently needed to see him and that Dorothy recommended him.

Once on the other side of the glass doors, antiseptic smells assaulted my nose. The clattering meal carts chattered down the hallways. Bland voices on the intercom called doctors, muted footsteps padded as doctors and nurses strode down the halls, elevator buttons chimed. Even the snatched whispers of loved ones—should we?... how long..., I can't...so tired—made me almost taste their tears.

I found a bench and sat, elbows on knees, head in hands, hands over face. Breathe, I told myself. In, out, in, out. Just breathe. You can do it.

A hand rested on my shoulder and I raised my head and sat up.

"Excuse me," a nurse with skin the color of burnished oak and warm brown eyes said. Her voice had that lovely sing-song lilt you hear in Jamaica. "You all right? Need help?"

"I need to see my mother. She's here, maybe in intensive care. I'm not sure where."

"Come walk with me. We will find her." She took my elbow and helped me up. "My name is Lark."

"That's lovely. I'm..." I hesitated. I hadn't asked Dorothy what name she would give the hospital. "I'm Rose," I said, since that name matched the only identification I was carrying. "My grandmother's name." That somehow made it feel like less of a lie, since Rose and I were each named after one of our grandmothers.

"My mama named me Lora, but my grandmamma called me Lark because I loved to sing in the morning."

Her hypnotic voice resonated like chiming church bells and its melody soothed my raw nerves.

"Don't you need to be somewhere?" I asked. "Be doing something?"

"No. It is my lunch break."

I protested that she shouldn't be spending her lunch hour helping me, but she would hear none of it, telling me she always took a walk to clear her head between shifts.

She finally deposited me at a nurse's station and squeezed my shoulder after telling the nurse to take good care of me.

"I'm here to see Louise Blumfield," I said. "I'm her daughter."

The nurse consulted a clipboard. "I'll need to see identification," she said.

I turned to thank Lark as I unzipped my purse to get my bogus driver's license, but she was already out of earshot.

After copying something from my driver's license, the nurse asked if I needed an update on my mother's condition and I nodded. I didn't like the tension on her face, but tried to talk myself into not reading too much into it.

"Dr. Grimsby should be by in about forty minutes. She'll brief you then." The nurse frowned at something in the chart.

"What's wrong?" I asked.

She shook her head. "I'll show you her room. This way."

The room seemed small, almost dwarfed by the machines that hummed, buzzed and clicked as they monitored Mom's vitals, their red and green lights like man-made Cyclops' eyes peering at the world. The obligatory chair waited by the bed to fulfill its role. How many mothers and daughters, husbands and wives, brothers and sisters had it cocooned?

Mom's eyes were closed and her breathing raspy. Her face, in repose, seemed so much older than the last time I saw her, only two week ago, like an apple core left in the sun to shrivel. Her white hair poked out at odd angles. I reached out, smoothed it, then sat and took her skeletal hand in mine.

We sat this way, a living sculpture, two women, a mother and a daughter, for half an hour. Her hand was limp in mine and I tried to push the images of my vigil with Rose out of my head. I had talked to Rose, but somehow could find no words to say to my mother.

Mom's eyelids fluttered and I wondered what person she would be if she opened them. Would she know where she was? Who I was? Did I know who I was?

I caressed her hand but she pulled it away. Her body contracted, shrinking back into the bed.

When she opened her eyes, they were panicked, shifting left and right and then down at her hands and white draped body.

"Let me get your glasses," I said. I didn't know if she recognized my voice or if just someone offering help soothed her. Her body relaxed although the fear remained in her eyes. "I'm your daughter," I told her as I picked her glasses up from the nightstand. I expected her to ask which one, but she didn't. I put her glasses on her and waited, not sure what to say next.

Mom stared at me. The fear wasn't gone, but confusion had joined it. She squinted at me, as if trying to put a name with a face. She opened her mouth, but no sound came out.

"Is there anything I can get you?" I asked.

She continued to stare at me, then opened her mouth, but only a wheeze came out.

"How are you feeling?" I wondered if I should push the call button. Is this how she's been? What happened?

The low rumble of someone clearing their throat intruded on my panic and I turned. A doctor, so tall she almost filled the doorway, stood there. "I'm Dr. Grimsby," she said. I felt reassured by her gray hair and weathered face, a face that said, I have experience and I don't care who knows it.

"I'm her daughter. I'm Rose Grimaldi," I said. I hated those words, that lie. I felt more unclean than when I was covered in mud, tomato juice and skunk-stink. "How is she?"

She beckoned to me and I gave Mom's hand one last squeeze, crossed the room and shook the doctor's hand. Her handshake was firm, her hand warm and dry.

"Your mother's condition has deteriorated since she arrived," the doctor said in a hushed voice. "You did know she had a stroke?" It felt like another body blow, but I just shook my head. "It's called acute aphasia. She knows what she's trying to say, but the words don't come out. For her, only one word comes out. Always the same word. Let's go somewhere where I can explain more."

I turned. "Bye, Mom. I'll be back soon."

I wasn't sure if I imagined that some of the confusion in her eyes dissipated, replaced by the steel flints I was used to seeing. She lifted her hand an inch off the bed, and said, "Agnes."

Chapter 66

need a miracle
why don't donut shops sell them
extra sprinkles please

Rose's Haiku Diary
Sturgis, SD
Age 59

My consultation with Dr. Grimsby couldn't have lasted more than five minutes, but it left me dazed, still trying to digest everything the doctor told me as I approached the nurses' station where a man who reminded me of a grizzly bear stood.

Who are you here to see? I wondered. Your wife? Your mother or father? Your child?

"There she is now," the nurse said and pointed. I had a momentary urge to run, not even knowing why.

The man turned his bulky body toward me. "Are you Rose Grimaldi?"

I nodded.

He held out a badge. "I'm Detective Wood. I need you to come to the station to answer some questions."

I wanted to ask—what questions, about what—but the nurse lingered nearby. I needed to protect the last remaining sliver of my dignity, to not let her eavesdrop on a recitation of my criminal escapades. I felt like Thelma without Louise.

"All right," I said, wondering how he had found me. Probably Bankerville, I thought. "My car's in the garage. I'll need directions and..."

"You'll need to come with me."

Just shoot me now, I thought. On TV shows, there's just one more commercial break before the suspect gets tossed in the clink. Why me, why now, I thought and Rose whispered, maybe it's a two-parter.

"Okay, just a minute, please." I didn't wait for his okay, but turned to the nurse, fumbled in my pocket, and pulled out the fortune cookie fortune and Ferd Paul's business card. I stuffed the business card in my pocket, wrote on the back of the fortune cookie slip and handed it to the nurse. "Here's my cell phone number. Please let me know if my mother's condition changes."

The detective's features softened a bit at the mention of my mother.

As I rode in the back of the detective's unmarked car, my mind was a jumble. I thought about all the interrogations I'd watched on cop shows—how I always rooted for the cops, smiled smugly as they tricked the thugs into confessing—and now I was the criminal. Would it be good cop/bad cop? They always tried to get the perp to talk before her lawyer showed up, always acted like the deal would disappear once her legal bulldog reined the hapless prisoner in and kept her from spilling her guts. But I tried to spill my guts yesterday to Bankerville and he hadn't believed me.

I expected to go through the indignity of mug shots and fingerprints again, but Detective Wood just led me to an interview room that fit the stereotype embedded in my mind: harsh light and bare white walls, hard chairs, the glass wall indicating a two-way mirror.

After he read me my Miranda rights, he asked me my name.

"I want my attorney," I told him.

The detective smiled. Good cop, I thought. "Usually we at least get that question out of the way." I shrugged my shoulders, pulled out the business card for Ferd Paul III and handed it to him.

Then I waited. And waited. And waited. I wished that I knew how to meditate. Rose learned in Nepal and extolled its virtues. I was fascinated watching her when she sat and went into that peaceful world. I decided to take my mind off of my predicament by recalling details of every place Rose and I celebrated our birthdays.

I thought about how we'd traveled across the country and the globe, rode ornery camels in Egypt and cycled the winding Annamite mountain's roads in Vietnam, swam with sea lions in the Galapagos and ran through fields of lavender in Provence, laughing like we were ten again. But on every trip the time I always loved best was when we were back at the hotel, cottage or bed and breakfast, between getting into bed and falling asleep. We would talk and talk, sometimes fighting off sleep, just like we had for the first eighteen years of our lives. How it hadn't mattered if Rose was married or had even just fallen in love again, we always took a week off together in the years we reached another five-year milestone.

A door slammed somewhere, jarring me back to the reality of my predicament. The room felt too warm and then too cold, and the hands of the clock on the wall seemed stuck, then raced, making me think of Kurt Vonnegut's *Slaughterhouse Five* when Billy Pilgrim was captured by aliens and put in a zoo where his abductors sped up and slowed down the clock to play with his mind. I wondered about calling an attorney who didn't even know me. Even with a recommendation from Dorothy, why would he make time to help me? It wasn't like he was Perry Mason, just waiting in his office for the phone to ring bringing his next juicy case.

Finally, Ferd Paul III arrived. I wasn't sure what I expected—probably some version of Jimmy Stewart, the man in the rumpled suit with tousled hair, always fighting for the underdog—not an agitated six-six Tom Selleck, complete with walnut-brown hair and eyes, handlebar mustache, jeans, denim shirt and biker jacket. No wonder he and Bankerville were oil and water.

He didn't even introduce himself, just looked at me and asked, "What have you told them?"

"Nothing," I said. He seemed to relax and I felt like the kid at the spelling bee who just spelled cataclysm correctly.

When Ferd the Third turned to the detective and said, "Please address any questions to me, not my client," I almost kissed him. I needed somebody to think for me.

"We first need to establish who your client is," the detective said.

"My client and I need to confer. If you're not charging her, we'll be leaving. You can address any inquiries to my office."

Thank you, Dorothy, I thought.

"Not going to happen," Detective Wood said. "Until proven otherwise, we are assuming you are Agnes Blumfield. You are being charged with criminal conspiracy to commit insurance fraud. You can consult with your attorney after we book you. But until you make bail, you're not going anywhere."

Chapter 67

tumbleweed sheriff
he is the outlaw, not me
let me out, damn it

Rose's Haiku Diary
Mud Butte, SD
Age 44

I wasn't surprised that they'd kept me in jail until my bail hearing, but I was shocked when Judge Lawry set my bail at $50,000. Ferd couldn't convince him to release me on my own recognizance. The judge said I was a flight risk. In truth, I wouldn't have believed I wasn't a flight risk, since I had done just that. It didn't matter that a bail bondsman would post the bond for a 10% non-refundable fee. I didn't have $5,000. Heck, about all I had was that $500 from the Thermos from my garage.

"That's old Law and Order Lawry," Ferd said. "He's always in the stratosphere on bail."

I wondered if I should have gone in by myself, confessed, and let the pieces fall where they may. That way, I at least might have known if my mailing address for the next dozen or more years would include State Prison for Women. Some of my worries were soothed just by my conversation with Ferd after I was booked. Mostly he took notes and let me talk, let me explain the pickle I created for myself. When he asked a question—like, has your sister ever been fingerprinted?—it never derailed my train of thought, but nudged it along.

Ferd looked more lawyerly the following afternoon, in his charcoal gray suit, although his gold and burgundy tie was loose around his neck.

When I commented on his change of wardrobe, he told me he'd been taking his new Harley Screamin' Eagle out when I called yesterday. He politely did not comment on my wardrobe change, although I guessed he was used to seeing jumpsuit-orange.

"If Agnes had died after surgery and you were Rose, you'd have committed no crimes, but have no money to pay for a legal defense. On the other hand, as Agnes, you've committed several serious crimes, but once you are declared no longer legally dead, you can afford representation using the money from your estate and the proceeds from your sister's life insurance."

"I really am Agnes. I'm not sure why I refused to tell the police officer. I just heard this voice telling me not to say a thing until my attorney arrived."

"Good voice," he said.

"I can't pay you anything now, but once I'm legally alive..."

"I'll take your case," he said. "My mother always used to tell me I inherited my father's love of gambling. He did it at poker, but I put my bets on people."

"Thank you," I said.

He studied his notes for several minutes before continuing. "You've created quite the tangram," he said. When I looked confused, he pulled a small box from his jacket pocket and dumped the contents—several red, blue, green and yellow wooden blocks—on the table. "Tangrams are puzzles using these seven pieces. The shapes and sizes, well, the proportions of the shapes, the five triangles, the square and the rhomboid are always the same." He moved the pieces around. "The objective is to create the required shape, such as a rabbit or a dancer." I looked at the arrangement of blocks he just created and it did look sort of like a rabbit. "Right now, though, I'm not sure if we even have all the pieces or what shape we're trying to create."

"Dorothy said you were great at sorting out complicated cases."

He smiled. "I do love a challenge. Ever play pick-up sticks? The important thing is to figure out which piece to move first. If you choose the wrong one, you're cooked. We have a lot of interested parties here. First, the Allegheny County prosecutor, then Oakvale Memorial General Hospital, and Blathmore Insurance Group. Even Awilson Life Insurance, your sister's life insurance provider. They'll have to pay up if Rose is declared legally dead."

Tell me something I don't know, I thought.

"The preliminary hearing is set for Tuesday," he continued. "The prosecutor has to come up with enough evidence to show probable cause for the charges."

My face must have shown my shock that what seemed like such a first step was almost a week away. How long would I be in this legal limbo purgatory?

"I know that seems like a long time," he said. "But that's not unusual."

I nodded as the lump in my throat grew from gumball to jawbreaker. "What happens then? Would you walk me through the process?"

"In most cases, the judge finds probable cause and binds the charges over to the grand jury. The prosecutor will take the case in within a couple of weeks."

"Will I testify before the grand jury?"

"No."

"Will you be there?"

"No."

"The grand jury, could they drop the charges?"

"Technically yes, but they almost always indict. The old saying is that most grand juries would indict a ham sandwich if the prosecutor asked them to."

Poor sandwich, I thought. What did it ever do?

Do you think the sandwich likes justice served with a little mustard, Rose whispered.

"Then comes your arraignment where you enter a formal plea. That happens a day or two later. We'll get a trial date, and then I'll file motions, start discovery and meet with the prosecutor. If we can't reach a plea agreement, if you're still in custody, we should be scheduled for trial within about 90 days."

My accountant brain began adding up the days. "So, if I can't make bail or we can't reach a plea agreement, I could be in jail for almost four months before we even go to trial?"

Ferd nodded. "I guess most people's notions about the right to a speedy trial have gotten knocked out of kilter by all those television shows where the arrest, trial and sentencing get all wrapped up in an hour including ten minutes of commercials."

I'll spend my birthday in jail, I thought.

Chapter 68

tiara of stars
why is the sky bigger here
yet I feel so small

Rose's Haiku Diary
camping near Cheyenne, WY
Age 46

June twenty-first is supposed to be the longest day of the year, but when you're in jail every day is the longest. The list of charges had grown since my initial arrest. Thirteen counts of insurance fraud and one of criminal conspiracy.

Visits from Ferd the Third provided small islands of hope in the sea of misery that had become my life. On the days when he brought good news, his eyes sparkled. But other days, I saw only a weariness that told me before his words did.

"I keep shuffling the cards," he said, "but our hand doesn't get any better. I feel like a piece to this puzzle is missing and if I could just find it..."

"I can't think what that would be."

"I can't either and it's driving me crazy." He got up and started to pace. "They've offered a plea deal."

I had hoped to hear those words every day, but the way Ferd delivered them, none of the elation I expected was there. He sat and stared into my eyes.

"We've got until the end of day on Thursday—three days—or it's off the table and we go to court. You agree that you are legally Agnes Blumfield, that you are no longer legally dead, but Rose is dead. You make restitution of $60,309 to Oakvale Memorial General Hospital and $101,403 to Blathmore Insurance Group and pay a fine of $12,000. They drop eleven of the insurance fraud charges. You plead guilty to two counts of insurance fraud and one count of criminal conspiracy, with sentences of seven years each to be served concurrently."

I gasped. That can't be right. Did he actually say that?

"Seven? Seven years?"

"I know. It's harsh."

He put his hands over mine which were trembling even though I'd clasped them in front of me.

"Parole is possible after five years," he said.

"Five."

My head sank forward until it rested on my hands as I started to sob. As my sobs turned to whimpers and then silence, outrage replaced despair. It wasn't fair, damn it. I'm a good person. I tried to do the right thing. I never even jay-walked or whispered in the theater. I was just trying to save Rose.

"I can't do that. Five years. I just can't. I've lost my sister and now I'm going to lose myself. My life. My sanity."

"You don't have to take the deal."

"It's a crappy deal. Why would I take it?"

"Concurrently is the key word. Each invoice falsely submitted to Blathmore Insurance Group could have been a separate insurance fraud charge, but some of them would have been misdemeanors, due to the amounts. The ADA, assistant district attorney, grouped them to get the thirteen felony insurance fraud counts with up to seven years in prison for each."

He paused to make sure I understood his words. I nodded.

"And?" I asked.

"Prison sentences can run consecutively or concurrently. Rumor has it that Ms. Dowden has her eye on the DA slot with her boss retiring next year. She wants her record to show she's tough on crime. They get a seven-year sentence. You get the threat of consecutive sentences—fourteen times seven years—taken off the table."

"Or?"

"Or we go to trial. If you told me you were Rose, I'd be in court in a heartbeat. But Agnes defrauded the insurance company and the hospital and is guilty of insurance fraud and criminal conspiracy. We'd have to hope for mercy, that the court, that a jury, will see you as someone pushed to the wall, someone who did the only thing she could to save her sister. A defense of necessity."

"Sometimes getting it over sounds so good. But seven more years in prison. I feel like my soul's already drained out of me, and it's only been weeks." Was it the constant din that made me unable to concentrate? The lack of a friendly face, a green space, any privacy? The food that turned my stomach? The inability to sleep, yet feeling constantly exhausted? The feeling of being swallowed alive? "Does it get easier?"

"I don't know. I guess it depends on the person. And the prison. We could make the deal contingent on your going to a minimum-security facility. But don't believe that 'country club jail' bullshit. It's a better cage, but it's a cage."

"I guess I need to think it over."

Ferd nodded.

A few hours later, as I finished picking at my lunch of brown with a side of gray-green, the guard told me my attorney was here to see me. I felt an iron band constrict my chest, since Ferd told me he would be in court for the rest of the day. Confusion replaced fear when I entered the interview room and found Lionel Bankerville standing by the gray metal table. He extended his hand and I thought of not taking it, but polite Agnes overruled spit-in-his-eyes Rose. I shook it, wishing instantly I could wash my hand.

"I'm not sure how I should address you," he said.

I shrugged and said nothing, stifling the urge to glower.

"I guess it depends on whether you're Agnes Blumfield back from the dead or Mrs. Grimaldi," he continued, with that nasty smirk usually reserved for teenage boys telling dirty stories.

I considered telling him to get to the point, but being out of my cell, even talking to a lout like Bankerville, provided a welcome break from the odd combination of fear and boredom that life behind bars entailed. I pointed to the chairs and table and we both sat.

"Why are you here?"

"Before I get to the business at hand, I want you to know that had I believed you to be Agnes Blumfield, I would not have been required to tell the police they probably would find you at Oakvale Memorial, as you would have been my client."

A sour taste filled my mouth. Was that an apology? No, probably just an explanation. Lawyers like Bankerville never admitted they were wrong. I could think of nothing to say in response.

"Due to the unusual circumstances..."

"Just get to the point," I said. Being in the same room as this cockroach made the walls feel like they were closing in. I concentrated on breathing, hoping to quell my nausea. My cell started to look inviting. An odd sanctuary.

Bankerville's face got a distressed look, as if he wasn't used to anyone not worshipping at the altar of his three-piece pinstriped Yale law degree. He was the one who meted out the penance of disdain; he didn't take it.

"It would appear that you are my client—whether again or still is yet to be determined."

"I'm what?" I asked.

"Whether you are Miss Blumfield or Mrs. Grimaldi, I am your attorney because of the death of your mother. I need to..."

"My mother..."

"I assumed you'd been..."

"When?"

"This morning."

I put my forehead on the cold metal table and pulled my arms over my head like a blanket. I was there for her for so many years, faithfully, tirelessly, and yet she died alone. I should have called Uncle Roger when I got thrown in jail. At least he might have been there for Mom.

Bankerville cleared his throat. "My condolences," he said, as if ordering a bologna sandwich. He paused for what I guess he assumed was a respectable amount of time for me to reply, but my numb brain could not formulate any response. He started to pull a sheaf of papers out of his briefcase. "Now, perhaps we can go over some details."

"Talk to my attorney."

"I'm not sure...what?"

"Talk to Ferdinand Paul III. I believe you know him."

My battered spirit was rewarded with a brief look of distaste on Bankerville's face.

"Mr. Bankerville, you're fired."

Chapter 69

the sound of your voice
tonic for my wounded soul
home, heart, help, trust, love

Rose's Haiku Diary
Searsport, ME
Age 33

"Mom died yesterday," I blurted to Uncle Roger as I squeezed the phone to my ear to blot out the jail din. My plan to walk him through the past weeks, sounding as upbeat as possible, and then go into the real reason for my call, the news about Mom, fell apart the minute I heard his voice. There was no easy way to tell him that I had screwed up my life and failed as a daughter.

"The wind started howling here yesterday," he said. "For some reason, it made me think something was wrong. Really wrong. Saying that out loud sounds pretty silly."

"There's a lot wrong," I said. "I didn't want you to worry, didn't want you to think you should come here." I started to cry. Over the next few minutes, I told him about the end of my crime spree, glossing over most details about being arrested for breaking into my own house and focusing on the charges of defrauding the hospital and insurance company.

"They've offered a deal, but I still could spend a lot of time in jail—five, maybe seven years. I just don't know if I can face that. But if we go to trial and they throw the book at me, I might be locked away ten, twenty years, maybe more."

"They're the ones who should be in jail," he said. "If you'd had any other way to get Rose the operation she needed, none of this would have happened."

I wasn't sure who they were, but his words comforted me. Part of me expected him to echo Hank's words and say, why didn't you tell me? I knew he must be thinking that.

"My poor, brave girl. You always were the one to fight battles for everyone else. Your mother was very proud of you, you know. I was…I am, too."

"I wasn't there for her."

"I think you were. I think she knew you were always there for her. Just like Rose did. I'll get a plane there as soon as I can. It's time I was there for you."

"There's nothing you can do here. Mom didn't want a service or funeral or anything. My attorney's taking care of Mom's estate, not that there's a lot to take care of. Besides, I don't want you to see me like this."

"I bailed Rose out of jail three times, besides the ones you know about. So, if you mean you don't want me to see you in an orange jumpsuit, don't worry, I can take it."

"I don't know Uncle Roger. I'm not sure there's anything you could do here."

The prison matron signaled that my call-time was up.

"I'll think of something," he said.

Chapter 70

spin life's roulette wheel
winner gets the pot of gold
odds favor the house

Rose's Haiku Diary
Las Vegas, NV
Age 28

It was the second day of the three I had to decide whether to take the plea deal or roll the dice with a jury. It seemed like a nightmare trapeze act with nobody there to catch me, so I just kept swinging from one option to the other. Back and forth, forth and back.

Ferd sent me a cardboard set of tangrams blocks and a book of puzzles, and I found that not only did I enjoy the challenge, but working them allowed part of my brain to process things. I was struggling over a tangram shaped like an old, bent-over man when the young guard who reminded me of a raccoon with his little fidgety hands and the perpetual bags under his eyes, told me I had a visitor. It seemed odd since he normally said, "Your attorney is here." Could Uncle Roger be here already?

In the visitors' area, the guard told me to go to chair eleven on the end. As I plodded across my side of the glass partition, my curiosity turned to joy and then a mixture of puzzlement and apprehension.

I must look like a wreck, I thought. It was the first time in a week I cared about my appearance. I smoothed my hair and straightened my back from its prison crouch.

"Hi," I said. Two letters. One syllable. I willed myself not to let the torrent of emotions that simmered below the surface boil over. Hank was here. But why? How many times had I ached to see him, thought of calling him? Yet, every time I stood at the pay phone, I remembered the wounded look on his face when I'd confessed. Betrayed, he'd said.

"Hi," he said. His eyes steady on my face. None of the hurt I'd so worried I would see was there. "I've missed you."

Those three words flooded me with relief. Or was it joy? It took a moment before I found my voice. "I've missed you too."

"You're a hard woman to find."

"Wasn't sure you'd want to." That sounded harsh and I regretted it the moment I said it. "I mean, thanks for coming."

"I've thought so many times about the last time we..."

"Me, too."

"I wish..."

"Me, too."

"I was so angry, so hurt..."

"I'm sorry."

"After...after you...I just drove. Didn't even go home. Just took the dog and drove." He looked down and I instinctively did the same, studying my dirt-encrusted fingernails before curling my hands into fists to hide them. I looked up but Hank's head was still bowed.

"I should have..."

"I just kept driving until, I guess, the adrenaline gave out. Crashed at an Econo-Lodge." He rubbed his temple and looked at me again. "I drove to Cleveland the next morning. Stayed with Julie. Tried to call you two days, no, three days, after we...after I...but I just got your voicemail. I figured you not calling me back told me what I needed to know."

"No cell phones here." Would I have had the courage to have called him if I'd known he'd left me a message?

"Then I saw your mother's obituary in the Herald. I felt like such a fool, so selfish to have been thinking just of me, of you and me."

"No, not selfish," I said.

"I'm sorry."

I wasn't sure if he was sorry for not finding me sooner or offering condolences about my mother.

"It was a blessing," I said. "Her mind and body just wore out."

Hank took a breath and rubbed his temple. "I saw how fast she went downhill these past couple of weeks. I visited her every day, until they moved her. They wouldn't tell me where."

"Thank you for that. I knew you were stopping by. Didn't realize it was every day." The Plexiglas that separated us felt like a yawning fissure. I ached to reach out to him. Take his hand. Touch his face. Smell the juniper and cedar of his aftershave. Feel the comfort of his arms around me.

"You didn't need to know. You were wrestling with a lot of problems."

Every day, I thought. I didn't even visit every day when I lived half an hour away. I closed my eyes and his sweet selflessness wrapped around me like a blanket.

Hank asked how my case was going and I filled him in, including the ticking clock of the decision I was facing.

"Zugzwang," I said.

Hank looked puzzled.

"Great crossword puzzle word," I continued. "In chess, it's when you have to make a move, but every choice makes your position worse. Arthur Bisguier—he was a chess champion in the 50's—said, 'Zugzwang is like getting trapped on a safety island in the middle of a highway when a thunderstorm starts. You don't want to move but you have to.' So, I have to choose, but..."

"Whatever you choose, I'll be there for you," he said.

He lifted his hand and pressed his fingers to the glass. I reached up and did the same, while thinking, but where will I be?

Chapter 71

we stand, sing, shout, cry
you can't ignore all of us
resolve in our hearts

Rose's Haiku Diary
Washington, DC
Age 19

I've heard that an avalanche can start with a single pebble. I didn't know that pebble was going to be Hank, standing outside the Allegheny County Jail with a placard held above his head that read FREE AGNES BLUMFIELD on one side and SHE'S ONLY GUILTY OF LOVING HER TWIN SISTER on the other.

"You won't believe what's happened," Ferd said. "Why didn't I think of this?"

"What?" I asked.

"The searchlight of public opinion. Until yesterday, it was just me negotiating. But today, there were a hundred and eighty-five people with me. And it's growing exponentially."

I shook my head. "I don't understand."

Ferd handed me a copy of the Pittsburgh Post-Gazette, where a page-one story showed Hank with his picket sign. I gulped. "His interview with the paper was great. If there's something big corporations hate worse than paying out money, it's bad publicity."

"I don't know what to say."

"He's taking a second mortgage on his house to help post your bail."

"He's doing what?"

"It's all right here." Ferd pointed to the newspaper. "Once he posted your story on Rose's blog, they started sending in money for your bail, too. Then there are what the press is calling the woodwork people."

"Woodwork people?"

"People out there that Rose helped at some time. It's amazing. I guess they wanted to pay her back, but couldn't find her before."

I scanned the newspaper story on the woodwork people: Wild Bill from Sturgis sent $400 with a note, "You helped me save my bar." Henri from Paris sent $229 and Tina in Nashville $300, and the list went on.

"Oh publicity, sweet publicity," Ferd said. "We should have you out on bail soon. Maybe even tomorrow."

"Really?" Out, I thought. I had doubted I would ever get out, and now it seemed feasible. I could count the hours on my fingers and toes. I pushed back the thought that it could make it even more painful if I had to return.

"Oh, and Rose's blog followers—she has over ten thousand now—are emailing Oakvale Memorial General, Blathmore Insurance Group, the assistant district attorney, their senators and representatives. Groups are picketing in Cleveland, Washington, Arizona and South Dakota. A big rally of your supporters is scheduled for Friday here. You're becoming the poster child for healthcare reform."

I turned the newspaper to the continuation of the story on page eight, only to see a photo of the Cleveland protest. It showed a crowd by the Old Stone Church downtown, the camera zoomed in on Hyacinth and Jasmine. Their arms were raised and their hands formed, in sign language, the sentence I taught Hyacinth: I love you.

Chapter 72

no compass, no map
still have the stars to guide me
where will they take me?

Rose's Haiku Diary
Yosemite National Park, CA
Age 58

I hated waiting in the Starbucks for him to return. It was a week later, our first meeting after my release on bail, and Ferd assured me that the client was never present when he met with the assistant district attorney and, really, it was for my own good. Shouldn't I have been allowed to be there as they negotiated my future? Was he worried I would blurt something stupid? I tried to convince him that my corporate experience would be an asset, but he just shook his head and reiterated that it didn't work that way in the legal world.

The corporate world had been my ocean. While I wasn't a great white shark, by the time Rose and I celebrated our 40th birthdays, I felt invincible in the boardroom. Not a shark, but perhaps an orca that knows it is bigger than every other denizen of the deep. Of course, the whale doesn't know that something as tiny as a bit of toxic sludge, polluted plankton, or even a puny man with a harpoon could cause its demise.

My career as an accountant progressed from simple audits that took days or weeks to complex ones that took months to special projects.

Rose thought I'd sentenced myself to a life of boredom. She once asked me, "Could you have found anything more tedious?" It was one of the few things that generated arguments between us. Each of us thought the other was wasting her life. I looked at beautiful, talented Rose and pleaded with her to do something meaningful with her life—not drift from one series of bad relationships and dead-end jobs to the next.

"And by meaningful," she said, "you mean bringing in the big bucks."

I wasn't sure how to respond. After all, there was nothing wrong with earning a good salary, getting a handsome bonus for your efforts, a bonus that financed our 5-year birthday galas.

My rejoinder was weak, but it did fit my situation. "As Harvey MacKay said, find something you love to do, and you'll never work a day in your life."

"Something you love to do?" Rose repeated.

I nodded.

She gazed at the clouds before replying. We were lying on a blanket at the War Memorial park in Sewickley on her visit home for our 49th birthdays, taking turns finding images in the cumulus clouds.

"I do honest work," she said. "I make people feel better. Feel happy. I make them a cosmopolitan or draw them a Bud and tell a joke and it helps them forget that they're broke or their girlfriend dumped them or their boss is always riding them. I give a woman a new hairstyle or makeover and watch her face light up. Sometimes I give them their grocery receipt with a big smile, and they feel just a little happier. What did you ever do as an accountant that made somebody happy?"

I squirmed, focusing on a cloud that looked like a piggy bank or perhaps a hippo. "Maybe you need to make people happy for the both of us," I told her.

"Maybe I will," she said as she sat up and started to tie the clover she'd picked into a chain. "For both of us." She picked up my hand and put the clover bracelet on my wrist. "I don't try to make you into me. Why don't you stop trying to make me into you?"

I spluttered and part of me knew she was right, but I also knew Rose could never understand my love of numbers. Each audit or project I did honed my skills so, on the next one, I could dig a little deeper. I loved my last ten years in the field when I was part of an elite team that worked with companies that bought other companies—sometimes just certain divisions or factories, sometimes the whole corporation. My role sounded trivial—technical audit support for the negotiators of either the buyer or the seller—but my research and recommendations could make or break a deal. My delicious job was to excavate the walls of boxes that held the books, annual reports, memos, documents, and spreadsheets that were supplied as part of due diligence. I loved being the expert-from-afar and strategizing with the real sharks who swam around each other, each focused only on how to make the killer deal. I could think on my feet and find the secrets buried in the the rattlesnake nests of numbers I had to examine. I even did some number sleuthing as a hobby on my own time, trying to figure out what made Enron tick. It frustrated me, since I came to the same conclusion over and over—that the company's strategic plan shouldn't work. That frustration poked holes in my superhero cape of accounting confidence until news of Enron's massive deceit broke. My cape not only mended, but it also became Kryptonite-proof.

In this coffee shop, my cloak of confidence was again in tatters. I kept rubbing the heart-shaped piece of rose quartz Hyacinth had sent me for luck between my fingers as I waited for Ferd to return. The blueberry scone and coffee I ordered sat untouched. Just looking at them made me queasy.

Before Ferd left, he told me the tidal wave of publicity was working in our favor. They wanted to make it, and me, go away. I tried to cling to that.

I looked at my watch again, astounded that it had been only twenty-five minutes. I thought of calling Hank, just to hear his voice, then realized he'd expect news.

As I watched an argument between a man and a woman across the street, both dressed in identical navy-blue suits, trying to decide if they were adversaries or lovers, Ferd slipped into the chair across from mine. I jumped. It only took one look in his eyes to know that he wasn't bringing the rainbows and puppies plea deal I'd stupidly allowed myself to hope for.

"Bottom line," I said. "Quick."

He nodded. "Bottom line: they offered a nonbinding agreement where they drop all charges except one count of insurance fraud and one count of criminal conspiracy. You plead guilty to those, serve three years and pay restitution acceptable to the insurance company and hospital. If things go well, you might be out on parole in eighteen months."

Eighteen months, I thought. I'll spend my next two birthdays in jail. Maybe more. The two weeks I spent there already were soul-killing. Always tired but never able to sleep. Always hungry but nauseated by the smell and sight of the food they served. Too hot, then too cold, then too hot again. Never able to concentrate. Never even able to lose myself in a book or a song.

"What does nonbinding mean?"

"It means the judge is not required to agree to the terms. He or she can modify the sentence."

"So, the judge could reduce the jail time?"

"The judge could, I guess. But they almost never do. Usually they increase it. Offer expires Friday."

Who would I be after I spent eighteen months in jail? Or eighteen years if we went to trial and things went sour?

I waited for that familiar voice, for Rose to tell me what to do, but there was only silence.

Chapter 73

Never play chicken
not with cars, not with your heart
Both easily break

Rose's Haiku Diary
Rio Rancho, NM
Age 57

"I have some good news," Ferd said as we sat on the granite bench in Hank's garden staring at the mounds of lilies at the back of his property.

My heart sped up. Had the ADA reconsidered after I'd turned down their plea deal yesterday?

"What is it? I could use some good news."

"The insurance company and hospital have accepted your offer of full restitution in exchange for their agreement to not file a civil suit."

"That's great," I said and hugged him. "It was never about the money. I would have paid them if I could have."

"I know," he said.

"What better way to spend the money from Rose's life insurance policy?"

"Besides my legal fees?" Ferd said with a grin.

"Besides them, yes. Worth every nickel."

Hank was filling the birdfeeders by the birches and we called him over to witness my signature on the agreement. Then Ferd packed his battered leather briefcase and headed to his car, whistling.

Hank and I returned to the granite bench.

"What was that song?" I asked. "It sounds so familiar."

"I'm hoping Ferd was sending us both a message."

I shook my head. "The song?"

"Don't Worry, Be Happy."

I snapped my fingers and smiled. "Yes, that's it. At least it wasn't the theme from *The Good, the Bad and the Ugly.*"

"Or 'Bridge over Troubled Waters.'"

We bantered song titles back and forth—"Bad Moon Rising," "A Hard Day's Night," "Nowhere to Run," "Jailhouse Rock"—until we were laughing so hard we couldn't speak. As our laughter subsided, he put his arm around me just as the light reached that point photographers call the magic hour, when colors seem deeper, almost magically golden. Our shadows merged. Our hands just touched as we stared at the tall pure-white Casablanca lilies, now the color of ivory vellum.

Hank ran two fingers down the side of my face, then picked up my hand and kissed it. I turned my gaze toward him.

"I know this seems a crazy time to ask this," he said. "But it seems that crazy times are all we've got right now. I love you, Agnes. Will you marry me?"

I wanted to say, I love you, too, but the upcoming trial strangled the words in my throat.

As if he could read my mind, Hank continued. "I'll wait for you if I have to," he said. "I'll work with Ferd if we have to appeal. I'll be there for you." He leaned forward as if to hear my response better.

The only decent thing was to tell him no.

"Okay if I think about it?" I asked, almost choking on the words.

As if some unseen hand had stricken him, Hank leaned forward, elbows on knees and brought both hands up, covering his face.

Did he know I'd have said, "Yes, oh yes please, yes can we do it right now," if I was in a place to commit? But how could I make that promise, not knowing if I could keep it? When the for worse might devour a dozen or more years before the for better part started?

Would he be grateful at some time in the future that I didn't saddle him with the burden of a wife rotting in jail? Rotting—an interesting metaphor. That's what you always hear: rot in jail. No, you don't rot. You shrivel. You melt. Disintegrate.

Chapter 74

extending your hand
invites others to reach out
dare to touch, love, care

Rose's Haiku Diary
Lucknow, India
Age 22

It never occurred to me that the readers of Rose's blog would want to come to her funeral. I was startled when the first blog reader said she was driving from Port Clinton, Ohio, to attend and, in doing so, lit the match to the dry tinder of the grief of Rose's blog readers. Then a man posted that he and his sixteen-year-old daughter planned to make the trip from Fincastle, Virginia. Post after post bounced around like a silver pinball from people who said they were coming: Badger Falls, Idaho; Jupiter, Florida; Mayflower, Arkansas; Rio Rancho, New Mexico; Sturgis, South Dakota; Richmond, Texas; Madison, Wisconsin and more.

At first, I thought it was one of those things said in the heat of the moment that, the next day, seemed so foolish or impetuous that you insisted you were never serious about it. But part of you was serious. Part of you really did want to do that impulsive thing—take that trip to the Seychelles Islands, buy that lime green dress with the plunging neckline or that vintage pinball machine, jump in that fountain with all your clothes on—that thing that would cause your friends to say, you did what?

Maybe that was the most fitting tribute to Rose, after all. I was always saying to her, you did what?

I was sure Rose's blog-readers wouldn't actually show up until her Peace Corps friend Sasha—Sasha who came to my funeral—called me to say that the Marriott where she stayed before was booked, and so were all the other nearby hotels and motels.

Of course, Hank insisted she stay at his house, along with me, Uncle Roger and Uncle Gus, and Hyacinth and Jasmine. I alternated between anticipation of the joy of welcoming those I loved and holding them close to me and anxiety about the funeral and my upcoming trial. It made me wonder if my impersonation of Rose was a form of denial, as if pretending to be her kept her alive in my head.

Even in the cocooning comfort of Hank's guestroom, worry woke me at five in the morning. I slipped out of bed, walked to the painting of the fawns in the woods and stared at it in the dim light. I still wasn't sure if the eyes in the thicket that watched them belonged to their mother or a predator. Then I put on my sandals and robe and tiptoed into Hank's garden. I sat on the bench he carved from a piece of granite, ran my fingers across its cool smoothness, and studied the bay window of my cottage. Clara Clarke's curtains were drawn, but I bet myself she was watching—that woman could peep through an opening so narrow you couldn't fit a dime through it sideways.

Then my garden beckoned me and I walked to it and sat on the swing Rose bought me—the one she said reminded her of the swing at Grandpa Luke and Uncle Roger's house. It was where, as kids, we laughed, sang, told stories, and traded secrets—hers always better than mine.

I thought about the last words Rose said at the hospital when she told me she would give me a new secret name for the next fifty years when we celebrated our birthdays in September. Had she already picked it out? I wondered.

"I'm sorry, Rose," I said. "I wanted to keep my promise that we'd always take care of each other. But I failed. I'm so sorry. Sometimes things just get too big. Bigger than you, bigger than me, bigger than both of us."

Clouds hid and revealed a crescent moon. Even though it was just before the first light of dawn, a mourning dove started to warble—woo-OO-oo-oo-oo.

Chapter 75

gunmetal gray clouds
will the deluge never end
where are my rainbows

Rose's Haiku Diary
White Swan, OR
Age 42

Watching Ferd on the courtroom floor was like seeing Baryshnikov dance: part of me just wanted to sit back in awe of his skill as he questioned witnesses and engaged with the jury, while the other part wanted to analyze each word, phrase, arched eyebrow, and cough. I clasped the lucky rose quartz Hyacinth sent me, hoping it would work its magic.

Ms. Dowden, the assistant district attorney, looked very Brooks Brothers in her white blouse and black skirt and jacket. With it being the last day of my trial, I wondered if I should have worn my navy-blue suit, the suit of armor from my accounting days. I had reached for it as I got dressed, but Rose hissed at me, You're not that person anymore.

So, I put on the turquoise dress I gave her three years ago and my peacock jacket, and painted my fingernails and face.

To my eyes, Ms. Dowden, projected an air of confidence. I wondered if, in my previous life, my counterpart on the opposite side of the negotiating table put me in that category. The tough broad with a heart of stone. Human calculator. I thought it a compliment at the time. Back then, I told myself that our negotiations were only about money, but as I sat in the courtroom, I realized it was much more. The deals I helped close changed people's jobs, their lives. And not always for the better.

Dorothy had told me Ferd excelled at juror selection, an art he claimed he perfected driving cabs and selling women's shoes. Despite that, those twelve citizens terrified me.

But it was more than that, more than even knowing that their decision could make or break my life. It was the helplessness. I wasn't in charge. I always preferred chess to poker. With chess, you know exactly what your opponent knows and it is your skill, knowledge and strategy that will prevail. Now I was a pawn, hoping that a sympathetic jury would give me back my life.

It was time for closing arguments. Unable to help myself, I constructed an accounting ledger, with our arguments on one side and theirs on the other. If this was a movie Rose and I were watching, she would have been rooting for the heroine—me—and I would have looked at the cold hard facts. Criminal conspiracy. Insurance fraud. No mercy—toss her in jail, I would have said.

Rose would have been with Ferd.

"This woman, Agnes, is not a criminal. She didn't want to do this—but she had to, so she could protect someone she loved. Someone so close that when she looked in the mirror every day, she saw not only herself, but also the woman she tried to save, her twin. Agnes suffered post-traumatic stress syndrome when her sister died, leaving her in a mental state where she no longer could think clearly, a state where continuing to impersonate her sister seemed to be her only option. We all know there is no such thing as one lie. Once you tell one, you need another and another."

Is that all you've got? I would have rebutted in my imaginary argument with Rose.

"Don't forget," Ferd continued, "that as Agnes Blumfield started to emerge from the shock of her sister's death, she realized she needed to make things right. To end the life of lies she had constructed. She consulted with Lionel Bankerville—the attorney to whom she had entrusted her own estate, including her elderly mother's care, a man who was supposed to be her advocate—and confessed. What did she get in return? Disbelief."

And betrayal, I thought.

"Ladies and gentlemen of the jury, I ask you to recall the testimony of legal scholar Hillary McGraw when she explained the concept of the necessity defense—which asserts that there are circumstances when a defendant has no choice but to break the law, and that such an action is, indeed, more advantageous to society. Think of the three elements required for a necessity defense.

First, that the defendant acted to avoid a significant risk of harm. Agnes was trying to prevent her sister's death, by anyone's definition a significant risk of harm.

Second, that there was no adequate lawful means to escape the harm. Agnes did not have the money to pay for Rose's operation. Rose could not get insurance because of her preexisting condition. Rose was not eligible for Medicaid. And Rose needed the operation fast—in less than a month—if she was going to survive. Certainly, Agnes felt that there was no lawful means to escape the harm quickly enough to save her sister.

Third, the harm avoided was greater than that caused by breaking the law. The harm, Rose's death if she did not get the operation she needed, was imminent. By letting Rose use her health insurance, Agnes took an action that was reasonably expected to avoid the imminent danger. The harm could be measured in dollars and cents. Can any of us put a price tag on the life of a loved one?"

Did the members of the jury feel the same ache that I did at Ferd's last words? Did Hank?

Chapter 76

watched Berlin Wall fall
anguish of apart crumble
two halves united

Rose's Haiku Diary
Paris
Age 40

The second time I woke on the day of Rose's funeral—Rose's real funeral—I reached my arm out for Hank, but felt fur instead. As I blinked myself awake, instead of Hank's hazel eyes, Doodle waited for me to show signs of life.

Uncle Gus and Uncle Roger were already at breakfast savoring Hank's famous lemon-blueberry pancakes when I arrived. A red, white and pink bouquet of Cosmos, one of my favorite flowers, rested in a cobalt-blue ceramic vase in the center of the table. Freshly-squeezed orange juice waited in crystal goblets, while coffee steamed in oversized handcrafted mugs. The beverages made me smile, as Hank wasn't a fan of coffee or orange food.

"The table is lovely," I said, and Hank smiled, walked to my side and put his arm around my waist.

"Rose would approve," Uncle Roger concurred. "She always loved pretty things."

"Where's Hyacinth?" I asked, hugging Jasmine.

"Probably texting her friends. You know girls that age."

"Hard for me to be critical of her practicing her networking skills," I said.

"I can't believe that lawyer of yours thought I started the cyber-revolt protesting your being in jail," Hank said. "I'm still at the rub two sticks together for smoke signals stage."

"She can be one determined little girl," Jasmine said. "I sometimes think kids these days are going to wear out their thumbs."

"You did do the first post," I reminded Hank.

"With my grandson's help," he replied. "But the words were mine."

I remembered the thrill of reading his words, posted on Rose's blog.

I know many of you found in Rose something special,
magical. You felt her love, her spirit, her sense of adventure.
Her sister Agnes, her twin, was her first fan, her biggest fan.
If you loved Rose, help get Agnes out of jail.

Hyacinth and Sasha joined us. Conversation and laughter catapulted around the room like kids in a bouncy house. I could almost feel the glow of Rose's spirit. She blogged about this day a week before she died.

"I want a party, not a funeral," she wrote. "When I die, get together to celebrate my life. Dance. Drink. Eat. Party! After all, I am half Irish. And black is not an option, unless it has a killer neckline."

I hated to excuse myself when I finished eating, but I needed to get ready. Hyacinth joined me and helped paint my nails a shade called pink lingerie. After applying makeup, I put on my pearls, Rose's favorite dress—the turquoise one—and my peacock jacket.

"I thought people were supposed to wear black to funerals," Hyacinth said.

"It depends on the person."

"Which one? The one who died or the one getting dressed?"

"Both. Rose loved everything to be bright and beautiful, so she wouldn't want people in drab colors at her memorial celebration."

"Can I wear my pink jacket?"

I started to say, of course, but stopped myself. "If your mother says it's okay. And tell her I said Rose would want you to."

"Okay."

As Hyacinth opened the bedroom door, I called after her, "Thanks for starting the blog-revolution." She beamed. "And for this." I held up the heart-shaped piece of rose quartz good luck charm she'd sent.

"Don't forget, no matter what, you promised we'd march in Parade the Circle together next year," Hyacinth said as she closed the door.

I'll be there, I thought, unless I'm in prison. Then I pushed the thought away. I will not let that specter lurk today, I vowed.

Our group assembled twenty minutes later, looking like we were going to a spring tea, with Hyacinth in her pink dress and jacket and red shoes, Sasha in a tulip-yellow dress and Jasmine in a moss green dress and matching jacket topped by a scarf decorated with swirling Monarch butterflies.

"We look like a rainbow," Hyacinth said. "No, a rose-bow." We all laughed.

Uncle Roger put his arm around my shoulder. "How you doing, Aggie-bear?"

I hugged him back. "Better than last time," I said. The edges of his mouth crinkled at my attempt at humor as I buried my face in his shoulder for a moment.

"That's my girl," he said.

As the others walked to the two cars we were taking, I lingered by the door with Hank. Rose's wishes nixed limousines. "Had those for my two marriages—you see how well that worked out. Besides, they're dreary. And expensive. Spend that money on my party."

Hank slid one arm around my waist and handed me a small square black velvet box with the other. My heart started to race.

"Do I get three guesses?" I asked.

"Of course," he said.

"A watermelon?"

He shook his head.

"A parachute?" My tactic of stalling to slow my heart rate seemed to have the opposite effect.

"Nope. Getting colder."

I sniffed it. "Pecan pie."

He shook his head again. "Guess you'll just have to open it." He let go of my waist and handed me the box as he stepped in front of me.

"Boy, I was sure it was a pecan pie," I said as I lifted the lid to reveal an ivory cameo pin.

"Would you like to wear it?" he asked. "It's the one you found six months ago when we were antiquing. You kept going back to look at it. I was saving it for your birthday, but today seemed more fitting."

I kissed him on the cheek and stared at the pin. I remembered the little antique shop and that pin catching my eye. We wandered around the store, a treasure trove of eras long gone. Hank found a pipe like the one his grandfather used to smoke. I discovered this pin. The store's owner put it in my hand and I caressed the tiny piece of sculpture, intrigued by the resemblance to Rose's face. I contemplated buying it for Rose for her birthday, but changed my mind when I learned the price.

I held it in my hand for a moment longer before pinning it to my jacket.

The venue for Rose's service was a rustic ten-acre farm complete with weathered barn, tree swing, meadows and sheep, a place normally used to host weddings and corporate retreats.

It's perfect, I thought. Rose would have loved it. A Latin-lover of a guitar player stood on the porch playing "Moon River." I silently thanked Hank, wondering how he found this tranquil farm, how he got the details just right.

Laarni rushed up as soon as I got out of the car and handed me a small shopping bag. "It's the last painting your mother did," she said. "They'd thrown it in the trash, maybe because it wasn't totally finished, but I rescued it. I thought you'd want it."

"Thank you," I said as I hugged her. Then I pulled the painting from the tissue paper and stared at it. I expected one of the vivid but often grotesque images that were Mom's specialty. Instead, it was as if a different painter created this canvas. She had meticulously copied the photo I gave her a few months ago of Rose and me in our sailor dresses as we sat on the back steps waiting for Uncle Roger to take us to the parade when we were seven.

"I don't think I ever saw her happier," Laarni said. "She always smiled when she worked on this. Can you believe she drew each hair and eyelash with a brush with a single bristle? Sometimes she just stared at it—the way a mom watches her kids when they're sleeping."

"That's beautiful," Hank said as he put his arm around me. "Do you want to put it in the trunk?"

"No," I said. "Let's put it next to the photographs inside. It kind of makes me feel like Mom is here."

As I carried the painting to the hall, it was evident that most people there had read Rose's blog and heeded her request for colorful attire. From a distance, it looked like a Jackson Pollock painting, with people wearing a panoply of colors interspersed with streaks of brown, gray or black.

I put Mom's painting on a table that overflowed with photos of Rose at all ages of her too-short life, many posed with me, many with others she loved and who loved her.

Ferd came by and gave me a quick pat on the shoulder. Olive squeezed my hand. Julie hugged me, and even her son Chad shuffled over and extended his hand for a fist bump.

I shouldn't have been surprised when Luther walked up and put his arm around my shoulders. How he managed that so gracefully without the benefit of sight amazed me. "Good to have you back," he whispered in my ear. He took my hand in his, raised it and kissed my pinkie finger.

My library cronies, Gustav and Miss Nichols from Shady Oaks, my former accounting firm colleagues and clients, even my hairdresser surrounded me like a celebrity. Or maybe like a friend who died and had been resurrected. There was none of the scorn I expected and feared from my charade and crime spree.

I stared in disbelief, my mouth open as if ready to say something, at seeing over half of the people from the Friday night party Rose started in the Cleveland apartment I inherited. Even a few of my coffee shop regulars had made the two-hour trip. Rose's friends from around the country and around the world mingled with her blog followers. I caught bits of conversations as they exchanged Rose stories. Pockets of laughter bubbled to the surface.

Hank, Uncle Roger, Uncle Gus, Hyacinth and Jasmine, Sasha, and I settled in the first row.

Figuring out the logistics of Rose's funeral had kept my mind off my upcoming verdicts. Uncle Gus suggested that we start a Plant-A-Rose foundation to honor Rose and request donations to it in lieu of flowers.

Some people sent flowers anyway, all of them roses. I wondered who sent the miniature rosebush in a copper pot, but the only card I could find proclaimed it to be a Summer of Love Hybrid Tea Rose. Each rose had white petals edged in pinkish coral fading to yellow and an almost orange center. I wished for a garden where I could plant it.

Many small vases contained a single rose. Yes, I thought, you are… you were, one of a kind.

"Let's give everyone a rose as they leave," Uncle Roger whispered, and I nodded.

One of Rose's blog-followers caught my hand. "I'm Bea, president of Rose's fan club," she said. "We've booked the Stone Mansion for after the funeral. We're holding a Day of Wine and Rose party. We've got over a hundred people coming."

How a hundred-plus people from around the country, who didn't know one another, managed that trick amazed me. I resisted the urge to tell Bea that, actually, I was the president of Rose's fan club.

"That's amazing," I said.

"We'd love it if you could stop by," Bea said, "but, of course, would understand if you have other plans."

"Maybe just for a couple of minutes," I said, knowing that Hank had booked lunch in one of the Sewickley SpeakEasy's private rooms for family and close friends.

After I thanked Bea for her support, Dorothy, the former Frau, approached me, took both my hands in hers, and murmured her condolences. "I just wanted you to know that I've decided to go back to law school."

"That's great," I said. "How brave." The unsaid at your age hung in the air for a moment.

"I turned in my resignation yesterday. I hadn't been happy there for a long time, but needed a push to get me going. You were that push."

"You're going to be a great lawyer."

"I'll work part-time as Ferd's paralegal until I get through law school."

I squeezed her hand and she excused herself and went to find a seat.

Uncle Roger and I wrestled over the program for Rose's service, but in the end the postscript to Rose's ethical will provided the answer. Keep it short and sweet, like me, she told us.

Sasha's soprano voice carried through the hall as she started the service by singing, "When Irish Eyes are Smiling," one of Rose's favorites.

As she sang the line "the love in your heart makes the sunshine more bright," I realized that Rose had been my sunshine. I lost her for a while, but this group gathered together to celebrate her life gave her back. Or maybe when I shed my cloak of deceit and let Rose go, I absorbed all the best parts of her.

Everyone was standing by the time Sasha reached the final refrain.

Then it was time for me to speak. I looked at the speech I had written, then tucked it back into my pocket.

"Rose and I were nineteen and home from college for the summer on the night we watched the first steps of a man on the moon. Rose turned to me and said, I want to go there someday.

I'll go with you, I told her. I wish I could tell you that this was where we hugged, as we so often did, and said together forever. Instead, Rose said, you can't go there—you're afraid of heights."

Scattered laughter met my ears.

"It was true. I dreaded the tops of lighthouses and observation decks Rose dragged me to in every city we visited. All places Rose loved. She used to say, I think I was a bird in a former life.

My stomach twisted at the thought of Rose being so far away, up there on the moon and me down here. I grabbed her hand and told Rose, If you go there, I'll figure out a way to be there with you. I still feel like Rose is with me and will be every day of my life."

Chapter 77

why is it so hard
waiting, watching the clock's hands
minutes drip, hours ooze

Rose's Haiku Diary
Rio Rancho, NM
Age 55

The day we would hear the verdicts, the day I had dreaded since I started my one-woman crime wave, had the nerve to be sunny and cool, more like June than early August. As we drove to the courthouse, there should have been butterflies in my stomach. Or more likely hornets. Instead I felt oddly calm, like being in the eye of the hurricane, in that small moment of repose before chaos strikes.

When we arrived at the courthouse, dozens of protestors occupied the plaza. LOVE IS NOT A CRIME, one placard proclaimed. FREE AGNES, another said. On the local morning news over breakfast, I learned that most of them stayed all night. The caring of these strangers filled me with hope.

"How does it feel to be a rock star?" Ferd whispered to me as we entered the packed courtroom and took our assigned spots: Ferd by my side, Uncle Roger, Uncle Gus and Hank behind us. If this was what being a rock star felt like, no wonder so many of them try to escape with drugs or booze.

I shrugged and tried to force a smile as I studied the jurors. Was the young Latina dancer on my side? Or did she think, well, she's so old, what does it matter? Did the truck driver see his wife and think of her stroke and their mounting medical bills? Did that make him want to go easy on me or hate me for trying to game the system?

Then we all rose as the judge entered the courtroom and sat when told to do so. Ferd slipped his hand just under my elbow to steady me when the judge told us to stand.

"Have you reached a verdict, mister foreman?" the judge asked.

"We have, your honor."

The judge nodded.

As the jury foreman started to read the verdict for the first insurance fraud charge, I held my breath and crushed the rose quartz heart in my hand.

"We find the defendant, Agnes Blumfield, not guilty, your honor," he said. A bolt of elation jolted me.

Again and again, for twelve more counts of insurance fraud, those two beautiful words rang out: not guilty.

Would I be walking out the door a free woman? I could almost feel the sunshine on my face.

Then the jury foreman started to cough before he could read the last verdict, the one for the charge of criminal conspiracy.

His throat couldn't be as parched as mine, I thought. Could he not speak because he had to say the word guilty?

We waited.

He looked at the judge.

We looked at the judge.

She started to motion to the bailiff when he croaked, "I can do it." He straightened his shoulders and looked right at me. "In the case of the People v. Agnes Blumfield, on the charge of criminal conspiracy, we find the defendant not guilty."

It took a moment for the verdict to register in the brains of the courtroom spectators also, because it wasn't until the judge said, "Ms. Blumfield, you are free to go," that a cheer erupted, with Hank's voice the loudest. The judge banged her gavel, calling for quiet and decorum. Someone in the courtroom must have texted the crowd outside, as muffled voices shouting from the plaza penetrated the courtroom.

The bailiff said, "All rise," but we were already on our feet.

I hugged Ferd, then turned and held out my arms. Uncle Roger, Uncle Gus and Hank's arms encircled me and I held them close, giddy with the freedom given back to me.

Ferd shook Ms. Dowden's hand and she whispered something in his ear. I expected to see disappointment on her face, maybe anger. But instead, it looked like relief.

Hank and I started to walk, then almost ran, hand in hand, through the ornate arches, down the marble corridor. Ferd, Uncle Roger and Uncle Gus trailed us. We reached the top of the grand staircase with its steps leading to the rest of my life.

I turned to Hank. "Ask me again."

He looked puzzled for a moment, then he got down on one knee and took my hand in his "Agnes, will you..."

"Yes, yes, and yes," I said before I pulled him to his feet and kissed him.

Chapter 78

carry you always
in my heart, life – you are
the music of my soul

Agnes' Haiku Diary
Devil's Lake, Baraboo, WI
Age 60

A month after our wedding, Doodle snoozed in my lap as Hank eased the Rose-bus into RV parking spot Quartzite 62 in Devil's Lake State Park, the second stop on our Plant-A-Rose Tour, as we called it. Our new home until next June, when we'd be back in Cleveland to join Hyacinth to march in Parade the Circle, was a former inter-city bus Hank saved from the scrap-yard. All thirty-five feet of it. We repainted the original turquoise trim and the torpedo lights hot pink and its silver panels white, a canvas to be filled as we drove a variation on the route Jack Kerouac took in his *On the Road* odyssey.

In the flurry of marriage plans, Hank asked where we should live and I remembered his dream of seeing the United States in an RV.

When Hank posed the question, *On the Road* was open on my lap and I realized the answer was right in front of me. What we needed was a crazy adventure, open road and endless skies.

"Let's get a bus and take off. See the country."

"A bus?" He said the word as if he had never heard of one. Then his eyes followed mine to the book and he gave me a smile the size of the Grand Canyon. "A bus," he said. "Yes, of course, a bus." He jumped to his feet, pulled me from my chair and we hugged.

"A big old, hippie..."

"... rock-band bus."

We found a wonderful company that specialized in converting old buses and they spent a month gutting the bus and turning it into our personal paradise on wheels. I loved the two super-comfortable chairs that locked while driving, but then swiveled around to face the living area whenever the bus was parked. The bathroom and kitchen were tiny, but we decided on a real queen-size bed. The dining, card-playing, bill-paying, tangram-playing and crossword-puzzling table with four chairs was a slide-out. The area where passengers used to stow their suitcases was crammed with our clothes for various seasons, our pantry, lawn chairs, bicycles and, of course, the paint and brushes for the bus.

The mirror from my cottage that used to be in Grandpa Luke's house and two framed black and white photographs hung on the wall that separated the living area from the bedroom. One photograph was of Hank's parents on their wedding day. The other was of Mom and Dad—a photo I never knew existed—that Uncle Roger kept and gave us as a wedding present. Next to it was Mom's last painting, the one of Rose and me at age seven in identical white sailor dresses, the one Laarni saved for me. The sunflowers watercolor Hank bought back at my estate sale for me graced the bedroom side of the wall beside the watercolor of birches in fog that Rose gave me. We insisted on a special glass-front case for Hank's bagpipes. In the back was what Hank called my portable garden: that lovely miniature rosebush in the copper pot from Rose's memorial celebration that I learned was sent by Sasha and an enormous hanging planter with basil, oregano, sage, thyme, and rosemary. Rosemary for remembrance.

On the back wall of the bedroom was a three-foot wide map of the United States with our planned route, snaking from Sewickley to Chicago, Wisconsin, Salt Lake City, Reno and San Francisco and back via Albuquerque and St. Louis. The route Kerouac and his cronies took was in purple, our detours in blue. Little green pushpins marked the half a dozen spots where Hank found bagpipe concerts to attend or where he could jam with other players. The red pins were stops where we would give grants to the first Plant-A-Rose Foundation recipients. Gifts from friends and strangers touched by my plight, by Rose's plight, funded the foundation generously. We used $173,712 from the life insurance policy Rose took out to pay the hospital, insurance company, and fine and put the remaining $26,288 plus over $25,000 contributions from Rose's fans in the foundation.

While the foundation fund's name came quickly, the idea of how to use the money was harder. Then, the plan came to life over glasses of sangria and a medley of various flavors of guacamole.

"Rose would want to help people..."

"...those down on their luck..."

"through no fault of their own..."

"...like the guy on the news yesterday who had his food truck stolen..."

"...and that young mother who lost everything in that fire..."

"...but especially those who are sick and can't afford the medical care they need."

There were already three red pins and I planned to continue deciphering the ledger Rose left with debts she planned to repay.

We'll find those people, too, I thought. Maybe they'll find us.

The yellow pins were stops to meet groups of Rose-fans who couldn't make it to her funeral. Those were the people who would paint the rest of the bus, if they wanted to. Hank sectioned off the sides of the bus into three-by-three-foot squares, one for each stop.

After the wedding, our friends and family painted the mural on the driver-side door. Hyacinth painted a picture of Elvis, Jasmine a waterfall, Uncle Roger a sun that Uncle Gus adorned with curlicues radiating from it. Sasha painted a rainbow. Olive, a martini glass with a rose instead of an olive. Ferd drew two tangrams—one of a man and one of a woman, both running or maybe skipping or dancing. The back of the bus was where each person could draw a rose, until it bloomed like a garden.

There was already one blue pin, at Pewit's Nest Gorge. It marked the skinny-dipping spot Hank and I had initiated the morning before we arrived at Devil's Lake, just before the sun rose, before any of the other campers were awake. Even Doodle joined us in the water. I remember looking at the sky as it started to slip from black to misty gray. I put my finger to my lips and mouthed, Thank you, Rose. Then Hank splashed me and we heard signs of life from other campers and ran for our towels.

After Hank logged the day's mileage in our journal, I put Doodle on the floor and we stood and hugged, then kissed as if trying to outdo Rick and Ilsa in Casablanca. A long, luxurious kiss was our ritual before driving and after we'd stopped, for our first-thing-in-the-morning and our last-thing-at-night.

After our embrace ended, we bicycled to the south shore's beach to watch the sun set over the water and into the nook between the south and west bluffs.

"She lives on in you," Hank said.

I looked at him, puzzled.

"Rose," he said. "I think if you hadn't spent those months pretending to be her, no, actually being her, her legacy might have faded over time. Like how we're sure we'll remember forever what our mother's voice sounded like or the title of that poem we memorized in third grade or the name of the person who gave us our first kiss. But one day, that memory is no longer there. Sometimes that's good, but sometimes you wonder where it went and want it back. But you—Rose is in you now, is part of you. "

He picked up my hand and kissed it…kissed it as if it were a delicate flower. I closed my eyes and let the warmth of that kiss radiate throughout my entire body.

I am different, I thought. I see a different person in the mirror. And it's not just my hair and clothes—although I've traded most of my pen and ink wardrobe for a Technicolor palette. I think about life differently. I'm not afraid to take chances. I don't think, what's the worst that could happen, but what's the best? I was so afraid to be burned again, I forgot that the flame also gives light and warmth.

"I hadn't thought about it like that," I said. "You know sometimes I was scared I was losing myself—that Agnes might cease to exist. But it's like I've absorbed Rose's life—at least some of it—and her energy flows through me."

"Lucky me," he said. "Getting to know you both."

I picked up my coffee mug—the one Rose gave me forty-one years ago that declared, *Don't waste your time kissing frogs, there are very few enchanted princes left*—and smiled.

It was the day before my 60th birthday and tomorrow I'd finish reading the card Rose left for me. I had planned to wait to open it, but I peeked. These were her first words.

Hey, Turkle-

I know now your secret name should have been Chrysalis.
You've been waiting a long time to turn into a butterfly.
You've always been one to me. It's time to spread your wings.

About the Author

Melissa Hintz is a novelist and poet who left the corporate world to pursue her passion for writing. With her left brain exhausted from years as a number-crunching actuary, Melissa's right brain was eager to let her imagination run wild again. She loves creating complex characters and plot twists in her novels, as well as the challenge of condensing a story or emotion into just a few words in her poetry.

Her first book, "On Chagrin Boulevard: A Collection of Fluff, Fables, Fabrications, Flapdoodle, Free Verse and Flash Fiction," uses flash fiction and poetry to explore universal themes of love, desire, loss, and joy.

When she's not writing, Melissa enjoys traveling, exploring nature, indulging in good conversation, and discovering new books, music, and restaurants. She treasures her friends and family, as well as her four writing groups: The Lliterary Llamas, WOW, the Thursday Poets, and the Occasional Poets.

Originally from Madison, Wisconsin, Melissa lived and worked in New York for twenty years before returning to the Midwest, where she currently resides with her husband Jim in Cleveland. She cherishes Cleveland's rich literary environment, with its libraries, bookstores, avid readers, and talented writers. The only thing she wishes she could change? The winters.

About the Author

Book Club Discussion Questions

1. What surprised you most about the book?
2. If you were making a movie of this book, who would you cast?
3. What scene has stuck with you?
4. If you had to trade places with one character, who would it be?
5. Which character in the book would you most like to meet/know? Least like to meet/know?
6. How do you view Agnes? Is she a victim? A savior? Something else?
7. How do you view Rose? Is she a victim? A manipulator? Something else?
8. Would you want to be friends with Agnes? With Rose? Neither? Both? Why or why not?
9. Do you think Agnes was justified in breaking the law to try to save her sister? Why or why not? What would you have done if you faced the same choices?
10. If you were on the jury, how would you have voted?
11. What insights did you gain from the haikus at the beginning of each chapter?
12. Are there lingering questions from the book you're still thinking about?
13. What do you think happens to Agnes and Hank after the ending?
14. If you got the chance to ask the author of this book one question, what would it be?